Despair Not

Murad Karim

iUniverse, Inc.
Bloomington

DESPAIR NOT

iUniverse books may be ordered through booksellers or by contacting:

iUniverse
1663 Liberty Drive
Bloomington, IN 47403
www.iuniverse.com
1-800-Authors (1-800-288-4677)

Because of the dynamic nature of the Internet, any web addresses or links contained in this book may have changed since publication and may no longer be valid. The views expressed in this work are solely those of the author and do not necessarily reflect the views of the publisher, and the publisher hereby disclaims any responsibility for them.

Any people depicted in stock imagery provided by Thinkstock are models, and such images are being used for illustrative purposes only.

Certain stock imagery © Thinkstock.

ISBN: 978-1-4759-9514-5 (sc)
ISBN: 978-1-4759-9516-9 (hc)
ISBN: 978-1-4759-9515-2 (e)

Library of Congress Control Number: 2013910812

Printed in the United States of America.

iUniverse rev. date: 6/17/2013

Dedication

THIS BOOK IS DEDICATED TO NASREEN,
My beloved wife and lifelong companion,
And without whom I would not have been able to write this book.

Thank you for being patient, loving and caring:
You encouraged me whenever I felt low;
You pushed me when I wanted to quit;
You have always been supportive and positive in helping me achieve my dreams.

Thank you my darling, the one and only.

A Better Tomorrow

I never knew there would be a better tomorrow
But you've come into my life and taken away all my sorrow
My days of sadness are a thing of the past
Because I have found true love at last
My days of emptiness are gone for good
Because you fill a void in my heart that you should
You've opened a window
You've shown me the light
And my love for you will continue to burn bright......

Web source:
Thoughts to Ponder, http://pinaymeh.blogspot.com/
(accessed April 25, 2013).

Chapter One

"**Y**OU HAVE CANCER." THE DOCTOR said to me. At that moment my world fell apart; it was the end of the world for me and the first thing to come in my mind was about my poor mom and how would she take the news. I felt like the hospital room was spinning...or was it all in my head?

"Oh my God, it can't be," I cried. "Are you fucking crazy?" I screamed at the doctor. "Shit, I cannot have cancer; I am barely twenty six, man." I was hysterical. The doctor was about six feet in height and wearing glasses, he had a white hospital overcoat on a grey suit and he looked to be about sixty five years old or so, with a receding silver hairline.

He waited for me to calm down and he looked at the nurse who was also in the room. The nurse was of medium height, maybe five feet six inches tall with dark hair, black eyes, and smart in her white hospital uniform of a long blouse and trousers; she was maybe in her fifties. Neither could look me in the eyes; I was mad, in shock and horrified.

"Do you have anyone?" The nurse asked me. "Did anyone come with you?"

"I came alone." I replied in anger and then asked, "What has that got to do with this?" In my head I thought there might be a mistake. I cannot have cancer. I am healthy and I am just twenty six. Also as far as I knew, this disease affects only old people. These people are just mistaken. "Look doctor," I told the doctor after a while and pointing at my thigh. "I fell down from me motorbike and hurt me leg, here on me thigh and got a bruise, but now you're telling me I have this fucking disease. Doctor you see, maybe you have some old man's report or something. It doesn't make sense. There is no other way, man. You know what I'm saying?"

"I know what you're trying to say Mathew," the doctor was calm, and it seemed like he was experienced in these kinds of reactions from patients. "But it is true. Let me just remind you of the recent events, Mathew. You came in the hospital about 3 weeks ago and you were attended to at the 'A & E'. You were seen by a doctor on duty and, after looking at your leg, the doctor noticed a swelling on your thigh and therefore she ordered for you to have an x-ray taken of your thigh. Then once again the doctor who saw you looked at the x-ray report and she then decided for you to have an ultrasound. Mathew, are you with me so far?" The doctor asked me.

I just looked at him blankly as he continued speaking. "From what the doctor on duty saw from both the x-ray and ultrasound reports, she then went further and consulted with the Consultant on duty at the 'A&E' department. Then they took a decision to send you for an MRI scan, are you still with me Mathew?" The doctor asked.

"Shit." I mumbled, nodding my head but still not accepting his explanation. I didn't understand what he was talking about, especially about the names he was mentioning, but still I nodded my head for him to continue.

"You were called by phone the next day and given an appointment for an MRI scan," the doctor continued talking and seemed to be buying time for me to cool down. "And you attended the hospital and MRI was done, right?"

I just kept on nodding; there was nothing for me to say.

"When the doctors saw the results of all your tests, they got worried, but they did not want to alarm you. Your file was then sent to me because I am the Oncology Consultant, and I arranged for you to have a needle biopsy before seeing you myself; I wanted to have all your reports and results in my hands first." The doctor paused for effect and then he went on. "Now the biopsy results have come came back and results show that you have...........do you understand, Mathew?" He stopped, unable to continue.

"The results are yours, Mathew. It is positive." The nurse said as she put her hand on my shoulder. "What you have is " But then the doctor took over from her.

"A malignant tumour in your leg, in other words you have CANCER, Mathew." He said and went on, "I'm so sorry young man."

I couldn't remember anything else after that. The doctor and the nurse had given me their names, but nothing registered in my head. The Royal Hospital was in Cabra but I walked and just kept walking to nowhere in particular. I was like a zombie walking the streets of Dublin.

At the hospital, the nurse gave me some painkillers and she gave me a note the doctor had written, a prescription for me to get from the pharmacy. The doctor had told me that they will contact me once they got a bed for me and will schedule some sort of an operation to remove the 'malignant tumour', or *the lump* as I understood it.

Accepting this terrible news was disheartening and I didn't know how I was going to tell me ma. She was already depressed for the last many years; she's been receiving bad news of one sort after the other, and besides she wasn't keeping well.

I decided to go see my cousin Kevin, who lived down the road in a different housing estate in Dublin, but not far from where I lived with me ma. Kevin was older than I was; he was a friend of my late older brother Donald. They were about the same age and he was with him in the car at the time when Donald was shot dead. Kevin was the closest person I had and could trust. I then walked to Milton Street where Kevin lived. I called Kevin on the mobile phone while I was still out but it was busy. So I just went to his house where he lives with his family; he had a wife named Mary and two small kids, a girl Kelly and a boy Sean.

Mary was about twenty four years old and about five feet four inches and a bit plump. She was also from the locality; she and Kevin had met in school. Kelly was six and she was a sweet girl, while Sean was just four. When the kids saw me they came running to me, but I was in no mood to fool around so I just chose to ignore them. Mary was there just sitting on the sofa texting on her mobile.

"Is Kevin in?" I asked aloud.

"I don't fucking know where he is but he's not here, did you try the 'Joy'?" Mary said while turning to look at me. "Or call him on his …………." then she noticed my face. "What's wrong, you don't fucking look too well Mathew, is everything okay?" I did not respond and I just went out the door and into the street.

The Joy Carvery pub was about three hundred meters away, so I walked. My leg was hurting and I was trying not to limp, but it hurt like hell. I didn't want to attract attention to myself, otherwise people who knew me will start asking 'What's wrong?' and so on so I pulled my hoodie up on top of my cap, hiding my face.

The pub was situated on a corner, a two story-building that was painted terracotta on the outside walls while the doors and windows were painted black. A big sign in black with 'The Joy Carvery, Traditional Irish pub' beautifully written, was hanging from the top of the door and both sides of the building were also sign-painted with 'Food served all day' and 'Traditional Irish Dancing'.

I walked into the pub looking for Kevin. When I could not see him, I think my mind was not straight. The owner of the pub was Finbar, a fella of about fifty-five; short, maybe about five feet two inches but real heavy with a big stomach hanging out of his jeans; he had earrings on both ears and tattoos on his arms. He saw me.

"Hey kid," Finbar shouted, "you got lost or something?" He was always jolly and full of life. He knew me alright but maybe from my looks seemed like I was lost.

"Hi Finbar," I said faintly, "have you seen Kevin?"

"He's in his usual corner over there." Finbar replied while pointing and added. "Mathew you look like shit," He paused and added,

"Somebody gave you a beating or what?" He was laughing and shaking his head as he continued his rounds. He was a happy man, he did not like to stay behind the counter and his money machine; he enjoyed walking around and talking to his customers instead.

I searched for Kevin and then I saw him at our usual corner. He was there with the other fellas. Kevin was tall, about six feet and hefty and a tough looking guy. His head was shaved as always, maybe to hide his balding. He had a lot of tattoos on his arms and neck. He was wearing a blue Adidas jumper, grey Adidas jog pants, and white Adidas runners, which is how he usually dressed and had earrings on both ears. He was a loud talking fella and boasty with a loud voice, always boasting about his feats and fights and women.

But I knew him a long time, and half of his talk was not true, but nobody could tell him to his face since he was quick with his fists and short tempered too. Kevin was a mean looking fella, and his looks said it all, like 'Don't mess with me' but I knew him as a kind and helpful guy and he was okay with me. He was looking out for me since after my brothers got killed.

Meself, I was five feet seven inches tall and medium built from weightlifting. I had some tattoos on me shoulders and arms, an earring in one ear with short ginger hair and wearing a cap, jumper, jog pants and trainers. Me favourite brand was Nike. I tried to give the impression to any stranger that I was a tough, dangerous, and mean and not to be messed with. My walk was the 'cool' or bouncing as it was really.

I knew myself as a low life criminal who has served two sentences at Mountjoy Prison in the city for some things I had done and was stupid enough to leave evidence and get caught. When I saw Kevin in the usual corner I shouted at him so he could hear me 'cause of the loud music in the pub.

"Hey Kevin, I need to talk with ya." He gestured by his hand for me to come over, so I went and whispered in his ear. "Can we talk outside?" He offered me a pint but I refused and when he saw the look on my face, he took his pint and followed me outside. "I'm coming from the doctors." I was trembling and he looked at me.

"Which doctors, why?" Kevin quickly said, "Who's not well?" My eyes were red and teary. I asked for a cigarette from Kevin, he removed his packet and he gave me one Benson & Hedges and he took one; he lighted for me, then for himself while he was looking at me and trying to read my face. I explained to Kevin what I was told by the doctor and Kevin looked at me with confusion.

"Oh man, this is fucking serious...what the hell is wrong with you man, oh shit, it cannot be." I did not finish my smoke and threw it on the ground and stamped it with my shoe. Kevin flipped his away and blew the smoke upwards while shaking his head. I told Kevin we have to go home to tell ma.

"I cannot tell me ma on me own, you know what I'm saying Kevin?" I said while shaking my head. "You've to come with me man, I….I…." I couldn't finish the sentence.

"Aah, it cannot be man, it cannot fucking be," Kevin went on shaking his head and taking a sip from his pint every now and then while licking his lips from the froth of the beer. "Tell me what happened …………." He was speaking when I cut him off.

"Kevin, I'm dying, man, I'm fucking dead ……………don't you understand?"

"But it can't be Mathew, you are just …………just a fucking baby and we have big plan. I have big plans for you man; you know the fucking job we're planning, it's going to happen soon, man." Kevin was walking around slowly.

"I'm telling you man, it's shit man, that's what the fucking doctor told me." I pleaded. "I don't know what to do and how I'm going tell me Ma? I am dying, oh shit." After what seemed a long pause and thought, Kevin looked at me.

"Let's first get fucking drunk, man," Kevin said. "My head's not working right now and then we'll go to your ma...oh no man it cannot be…are you so damned sure about this now?"

I didn't reply. There was no use replying, it was unbelievable. I wiped my eyes and we went inside. He ordered a pint for me and we drank. Then he ordered some more. I tried to refuse but it was better this way than facing me ma and so we drank some more. The music was loud and it was good in my head. It was at one in the morning when we heard someone shouting.

"Lads, it's time to go home," the pub owner Finbar shouted at us.

"Need to close down now lads, sorry lads." We went walking back to Kevin's house to sleep, drunk as hell. Mary was used to me sleeping in her house, as I often did, but only if Kevin was around. I just threw myself down like a log and slept like a dead dog. Mary came to wake me up the next morning.

"Hey Mathew," she said while smiling. "It's eleven in the morning, any plans to wake up?" I woke up and got my packet of cigarettes from my pocket and lit one up and smoked. After a few puffs I stood up and went in the toilet and washed my face. While coming out of the room I saw Mary. "Here Mathew," and she gave me a mug of hot coffee. "Are you better, now?"

"Yeah, thanks Mary" I replied, "I am good, I feel better now." Then Kevin and I went out; he wanted us to go with his car, a white Mitsubishi Gallant with a spoiler and wide tyres, darkened windows and all that shit, but I told him. "Let's take a walk man, we can clear our heads and……… "

"What for man?" Kevin cut in. "Let's go with my car and we'll talk along the way."

"Okay man, whatever." I replied not wanting to anger him. Trying to do anything to delay facing me Ma, I told Kevin. "Let's pass at the pharmacy I need to take the painkillers, you know?" So he drove and we parked near the Joy Carvery pub, we got out and walked to the pharmacy. The City Pharmacy was a few shops besides the pub. We walked in and gave the prescription note from the doctor to the lady.

She asked me, "Are you paying cash?" When I didn't reply she asked again, "Where's your medical card?"

"Yeah got it somewhere in my pocket," I replied while searching my pockets. Got my wallet out and removed the medical card and handed it over to her. She took the card and after a while brought me the Solpadine painkillers and my card. "Let's get something to drink." I told Kevin while coming out of the pharmacy. We entered the grocery shop next door to the pharmacy and got two cans of Coke. Kevin paid and we went back to the car.

"What are we going to do Kevin?" I was talking absent-minded, "When's the big job to happen?" Kevin just looked ahead, he didn't hear me.

"Soon, but you cannot even walk or run properly now. This job I'm planning is big; it involves a lot of money. If I pull this job, every fucking bastard will know me, you know Mathew, we'll be big and we get respect." Kevin proudly said all this and then turned to look at me. "Mathew, maybe you'll be in the team and there'll be your share you know, so don't worry man, I'll take care of you, you're my bro." He put his hand on my shoulder. "I'll soon tell you all about the plan but you promise me you're fucking not going to die on me, man."

Chapter Two

WHEN WE REACHED HOME, KEVIN parked outside the house on the pavement and we went inside. The door was open and Ma was smoking a cigarette. Her favourite was Benson & Hedges but, like me, she would smoke any brand if she can't get the Bensons. She was sitting there with a mug of coffee on the stool and watching the telly, some RTE programme or whatever.

"Hey Maggie, how's it going?" Kevin said to me ma. Even though she was his auntie, she was the younger sister of Kevin's ma, but he was used to calling her by name.

"Hey Kevin," Ma said to Kevin and then to me, "Hey Mathew." She then asked aloud, "you lads want some coffee?"

"How's it going Maggie?" Kevin asked again. "What's on the telly?"

"Aah the usual stuff and how's your ma, is she coming over?" Ma asked Kevin, "Not seen her in a while now."

"Ma is grand, yeah she might come over to visit, you know?" replied Kevin, "Spoke to her the day before ...she's doing alright."

"How are you feeling Ma?" I said feeling left out. "Did you see the doctor about your chest pains?" I was thinking on how to start telling her about my visit to the hospital while she herself wasn't doing well. She was always complaining about the pain in her heart and I was worried about her. "Ma, you should see the doctor about your chest pain, you know?" I said. "Let them doctors do some tests, they have these new machines and computers and ...."

"What do they know, these doctors," Ma cut in. "Every time I go after, they just give me paracetomol and they say I'm just tired, that I should get some rest."

"Yeah Ma, but you know they have these new yokes - CAT machines and MRI or something - they put your whole body in and they tell you if something is wrong, you know." I said that with confidence, thinking myself as being more of an expert now.

"Where do you get these machines Mathew? Every time I go see the doctors, I don't see any machines." Ma replied while shaking her head.

"Maggie, you go after the GP," Kevin said, then added. "But Mathew is talking about the big hospital, Royal Hospital in Cabra, you know?" Feeling left out I then took over and added.

"That's where these big doctors and their machines and computers are, and they test you well, you know?" I paused to gain more strength, "They can tell when something is wrong with ya, you know." I added, "Ma, I shall bring you meself to the GP," I said, and went on, "I shall tell the doctor, give me ma letter to go to the Royal Hospital, he will give you letter, yeah Ma, meself will bring you."

"Mathew. How do you know all this?" Ma said while smiling, "You after studying becoming a doctor now or what?" She laughed aloud. She had no clue of the news I brought her. I thought this is it now, Ma gave me an opening and I'd better get over with this.

"Ma, I been after seeing the doctor at the Royal Hospital in Cabra," I started, and added. "You know that big hospital you been before?" Ma started to say something but I continued quickly. "You remember when

I fell off my motorbike last month and I went at the A&E? You see Ma; they checked me with all those new machines I'm telling you about."

"So why are you telling me this?" Ma started to wonder, and then turned to Kevin. "What's wrong? Kevin is your ma OK?" She then added, "How's me sister ...." Ma asked, but I cut her off.

"Ma, it's me is all about. The doctors tell me I have this terrible disease ...." I got stuck; it was difficult telling me ma. "What they call.........."

"Maggie," Kevin said. "You see Mathew here you know, he has cancer."

"What?" Ma screamed and said, "Can you repeat what you just said?" I shook my head at Kevin who slowly repeated.

"The doctors say Mathew here, has cancer Maggie ...." Ma started crying and wailing.

"Oh me Mathew, me son..." more crying. "Oh...haa.... Oh Jaysus.....Oh my God it can't be aaaa me son is dying "

"Maggie stop, don't do that." Kevin said amidst the crying. I went to hug me ma.

"Ma, Ma," my eyes started to water, tears coming out but trying to control myself. "Ma, don't cry please Ma." I whispered to me Ma.

Kevin tried to control the situation. "Maggie, please listen to me." but Ma was wailing more loudly.

"No, no, not my son," Ma continued, "not my baby, not true "

"It's true," said Kevin, "that's what the doctors tell him, you know." The neighbours heard the commotion and started to peek from the front door and then some of them entered. Ma hugged me more tightly and kissing me on my cheeks, on my head and holding my hands.

"Mathew me baby, it can't fuck be," she was wailing. "The fucking doctors know nothing, I tell ya," she couldn't stop, "they know nothing...Aah ha ha ...No..." Me ma is not a person who uses the 'F' words but today is different. She kept on crying and holding me tight and not letting me go. "Please help me," she wailed. "Oh Jaysus, help my poor baby."

A few lady neighbours came over and heard bits and pieces, and though nobody was crying or wailing, there were a few teary eyes around. They tried to comfort me ma, but it was hard, as me ma was still holding me. Slowly I tried to get her to sit on the chair.

"Oh Jaysus, me baby, me baby." She kept on crying and holding her heart. This was what I was afraid of, my poor ma, how can she take more bad news after bad news about the people she loved? She's had a hard life, poor her. After a while, which for me it seemed ages, Kevin asked one of the neighbours to find some paracetomol in the kitchen and a glass of water; the lady did not find any painkillers in the house but another lady said she'll get from her house. She went and brought two tablets of panadol.

"Maggie," said Kevin, "take these tablets and you'll feel better." Kevin gave her the tablets and the glass of water. She took the tablets without a problem, but her eyes while looking at me, asking the questions she had no answers to.

"Ma, I think you should go lie down now," I said, "you'll feel better in a while." Kevin then addressed the neighbours.

"Thanks everybody, can we leave Maggie now. She needs to rest, you know?"

"Oh yeah," one lady said. "Let's leave Maggie now."

"Alright," another said. "She needs to rest, you know."

"Poor Maggie." said another lady, and they went out of the house, one by one.

"Oh poor Mathew, he has cancer you know, he's gonna die." I overheard one neighbour saying to the other. Kevin and me self, we took ma, one on each side of her and holding her hands to the room as I spoke softly to her.

"Ma, please lie down and rest, okay Ma?" She was sobbing and she just nodded. She lay down; I covered her with a duvet.

"I have to go somewhere, Mathew." Kevin said while whispering, "Are you alright on your own?"

"Yeah, am alright," I replied. "Thanks Kevin, you take care, man."

"I'll be back, Mathew," said Kevin, "if you need anything give me a buzz." Putting his hand on his ear, a sign of the phone I heard and understood. I pulled a stool and sat near me ma on the side of her head. I started stroking her hair and feeling love for her. She took the news about my cancer more strongly than I thought. I was her baby, but right now I felt like she was my baby. She was sobbing.

"Mathew me baby, are you there?"

"I am here Ma." I said, with tears strolling down my cheeks but I was trying to be brave for her, "I am here with you, Ma."

"Don't leave me, me baby," she was holding my hand, "don't leave me like Pa, like Donald, like Daniel." She continued sobbing. "You're all I'm left with, Mathew." She continued, "Please don't leave me, please Lord don't take me son away." She was speaking between sobs and wailing, "I'll die of sorrow, Mathew if you ."

"Ma, I love you Ma and I am not leaving you," I told her, "now please rest and stop thinking. Nothing will happen to me, Ma."

Me Ma was only sixteen years old when she met Da. Da was twenty-one; he was working in Manchester, England. But about every three months he was coming back to Ireland. His parents were in Waterford and that's where he went whenever he came from Manchester. He usually was staying a few weeks and off he went again. He was a strong and tough man, worked hard in the ship yard in Manchester. Me Da was about five feet ten inches tall, thinly built. And although he was young in age, but he was tough and focused in life. Me Ma was a sixteen year old, sweet and innocent; she was five feet four inches tall, but she looked more mature.

She was also intelligent, and she was working part-time in the local pub 'The Village Inn'. She was hearing a lot of stories of different cities and life in the world, but Ma had not even been to Dublin, but she already heard and learnt a lot about Dublin. Also her older sister was married and living in Dublin. On one particular day it was raining, and as Ma was waiting at the bus stop while going to work and hiding from the rain, she was becoming restless as she was already late. Then a car stopped, and inside was a handsome young lad.

"You want a lift?" The guy shouted from the car, "I am going the same way."

How does he know where I am going? Ma thought.

"You talk to me?" She shouted back at him.

"Yes, come on in I won't kidnap you," he shouted back, "I am going to the same pub you're working at, 'The Village Inn' come on now."

She took a chance, as she was already late, and got in the car. "Hi, I am Brian, Brian Kavanagh." He introduced himself like a true gentleman. "I live not far from where you live." He said.

"I am Margaret, and you already know where I live and also where I work, right?" Me ma said in reply.

"Oh yeah, sorry about that, I work in a shipyard in Manchester. I come back home every two to three months," he said and turned to look at ma, "and by the way, this is not my car I just borrowed it." He smiled.

"So it's my lucky day." Ma said. Starting to notice the young man and his manners, she thought he was polite and was soft spoken.

"No, it's my lucky day," Da had said, "I've been looking at you a while now, from far of course," and he smiled again, "admiring you, you might say."

And that is how they hit it off, and whenever they got a chance they would meet and talk. When he went back, she would write to him and he would do the same. Two years later, they got married in Waterford, with the blessing of both families. Da was twenty-three and Ma was eighteen years old. It was okay then for people to marry young.

Da continued to go to work in Manchester, coming back during his leave, and Ma continued to work in 'The Village Inn'. After two and a half years Da was let go from his job in Manchester and moved back to Ireland. Six months later he got a job in Dublin port so they moved to Dublin City. There they got themselves a house in the inner city, where me Ma's older sister lived, in the same corporation estate. Ma got pregnant, and soon after Donald was born when Ma was twenty-one, and then when Ma was twenty-three, Daniel was born. There was a big gap till my birth, Ma was twenty-nine then, and Da was thirty-four. I don't know much of my childhood, but I came to learn later, like I learnt about Ma and Da, from me ma, that I was sort of loved by everybody in the family and I was sort of spoiled and I was bold.

"Hi Kevin, it's me, man." I spoke on my mobile, "Where are you?" It was eleven in the morning on Saturday the second, this cold November, and winter was here, and it was getting cold and colder.

"Hi Mathew, I'm somewhere far at the moment," said Kevin on the mobile. "A bit busy right now you know?" He said and went on, "I'll call you later, is that okay with you?"

"Yeah, yeah man, bye now…." I said, and he went off the phone.

"Bye now, bye…."

"Bye, bye now." I said and disconnected. It was after eight at night that finally he came looking for me. I was at the Joy Carvery having my third pint when Kevin approached and sat by me and ordered his pint.

"What's up Mathew," he said, "is Maggie alright?"

"Yeah, Ma is doing great." I said, "The hospital called me today, you know?"

"What they want?" Kevin said, "Did they finally realise that you are okay or something?" I remained quiet for a while, thinking wouldn't that be the greatest news? But it was not to be.

"The lady at the hospital called me." I said, "They finally got a bed for me, you know?"

"What bed?" Kevin said, "You don't have a fucking bed? You should've asked me for one," continued Kevin, "I would've got you one, you know? Why will the damn hospital want to give you a bed?" He was serious. I had to laugh aloud. "What's wrong now," Kevin was pissed off, "why you laughing now? Believe me man; I would get you a bed if you needed one."

I continued laughing; it was funny, if you come to think of it but Kevin did not see where the joke lies so far. "Listen Mathew," Kevin looked annoyed as he said, "I don't know why you think it's fucking funny." He became red with anger and ready to blow off. I continued laughing till tears were coming from my eyes; I was in stitches bending down and all. All around me people were wondering if I was drunk, crazy or both.

"Let me laugh, man," I said to Kevin as I continued, "I haven't laughed for a long time." After a while, I stopped laughing, I looked at Kevin who was a bit agitated now, not understanding what's going on. "You see Kevin, the Royal Hospital in Cabra." I said to Kevin, "Some lady, from maybe reception or something called me this morning telling me they've now got an empty bed for me to go in there for some tests and other stuff."

"Okay," said Kevin, "go on."

"Now they told me to go there tomorrow at five in the afternoon," I said, "for admission, you know?" And I continued, "She told me to bring some pyjamas and toothbrush and things like that, you know what I mean?"

"But tomorrow's Sunday," Kevin said, "isn't the hospital closed, know what I mean?"

"Now, now I don't know," I said, "this what she said and I didn't ask more, you know?"

"So what then," Kevin said, "after admission I mean," he continued, "they give you a bed, right?"

"Oh, she said........." I said, trying to think. "Aaah, she said, Monday the big doctor, the consultant, you know, will do the fucking operation on my leg." Kevin looked worried, unsure. "Kevin, you got to bring me to the hospital," I said to Kevin "I don't fucking know where it is, this new hospital."

"What do you mean; you don't know where it is?" Kevin said, "You been there before, right?" he paused then asked again, "Same hospital, isn't that right?" Kevin continued, "Royal Hospital, right?"

"No, she mentioned" I was trying to remember what the name of the hospital was, "University.......... Hospital....Royal....Dublin.... something like that, you know. I mean?"

"You know, Mathew." Kevin said, "They're too many fucking hospitals in Dublin. So"

"Wait, wait, Kevin," I said, while remembering something and holding my head, "she said the hospital is near the sea, you know?"

"So what, that'll help us?" Kevin said, "We go around Dublin, and we go around the sea looking for hospitals?"

"Ha ha ha, Now you're making me laugh," continued Kevin, "I think only hotels are near the sea, you know what I mean, the beaches, Malahide, Portmanock, Clontarf, Killeney, eh come on man, let's dance, oh la la la." And he was dancing and fooling around, "Maybe they want you in the hotel, man, to have a good time, you know what I mean?" While holding my hands and pulling me to dance around, already the music was loud. It was Kevin's turn now to laugh. "You know what, Mathew?" Kevin said amid the laughter.

"Yeah, what is it?" I asked him.

"I think this all is just craic, you know?" said Kevin, "First they get you a bed, and then they want you to go in hospital near the beach you said? Or sea?" He burst out laughing. I thought what the hell? Why be serious? It was funny anyway; the whole situation was confusing and funny. I have only a day till admission and you never know what then, maybe they'll cut my leg off, maybe I will die in the hospital. What the hell?

So I decided to join in and laugh with him, and the other lads in the group joined in the mood. We laughed and drank, forgetting everything else for the moment. The pub owner, Finbar came over.

"What's the craic now lads?" he said, "You guys are having fun?"

"Mathew here, you know?" Kevin said, "The fucking hospital is gonna give him a bed in a hotel by the beach, you know what I mean ?" he burst out laughing and so was everybody but Finbar, he seemed somewhat confused.

"You guys are drunk." He said. "…..Enjoy." Finbar could not get the joke, and he just shook his head, thinking to himself, I have seen this every day, some people get drunk and are happy, and some get drunk and start to fight. So it's better when the lads are just having a craic and jolly, that's alright.

Chapter Three

$\int$UNDAY I WOKE UP AT eleven, had a cup of coffee and toast. I looked around for Ma. She was not there, but then I remembered she had gone to church, she always goes to church on Sundays and on other occasions as well. I had also heard my Da used to be the same, never missed Sunday Mass.

But me and my brothers, when they were alive, we never used to go to church. I still don't. Ma always talks to me about God, Jaysus and things. She talks about going to church, about praying; about visiting the graves of my Da, Donald and Daniel...they are all buried in the family plot at the Glasnevin Cemetery in Dublin.

No, not me, I don't believe in Heaven or Hell, I say once you die that is it, the story is over. The priests are just lying to us, and they want us to go to church and pray. Or they just need donations, you know what I mean?

At about half three in the afternoon, after I had my lunch, Kevin came over to me house. And at four, we decided as we didn't know the hospital's location, so we would go early to look and ask around. So it was time to leave for the hospital.

"Ma," I said, "I've got to go now."

"Now," Ma asked in surprise, "now you've to go to the hospital?"

"Yeah Ma, now I've to go." I replied as I added, "Today the hospital will let me get a bed, you know?" Then I remember the joke we had with Kevin and looked at him, and he shook his head and I chuckled. "Ma, Kevin will let ya know," I said, "when they'll do the operation, and things. Kevin will bring ya to the hospital to see me, alright?"

"Okay ...." she said, while her eyes started to be teary, "Mathew, me son, you'll be alright, yeah?"

"I'll see ya Ma," I told her, "Kevin will bring ya to see me, okay Ma?" I bent down and kissed her forehead. I wanted to tell her I love her, but you know, I couldn't, you know what I mean? I took my small holdall, stuffed with a toothbrush and a few things and went out, got in the car. Kevin was already sitting in the driver's seat and he drove us away. In the car, I asked Kevin. "Can we pass by Phoenix Park?"

"What for you need to pass there?" Kevin said. "It is way fucking out of the hospital's direction, you know what I mean?"

"I know, but we've the time, and ...." I said, "I just want to pass and see for last time maybe."

"What do you mean?" Kevin said as he was getting irritated, "Last time You're not going to die, you know what I mean?"

"It's okay, man." I pleaded, "Let's just pass, man, we have the time." I opened the glove compartment, looked around for a nice music CD. I got one by Kenny Rogers and I felt like listening to country music, so I put it in and relaxed back in the seat, enjoying the music. Kevin glanced at me, wanted to say something but he just mumbled and shook his head in amazement.

So Kevin drove to Phoenix Park. We entered the gate from Conyngham Road, and we drove onto Chesterfield Avenue. I told Kevin to stop at the Wellington Monument; I got out of the car.

"Come on out, Kevin." I said to Kevin, whose looks said he was not sure what's happening with me. Kevin came out of the car but did not follow me; he took his cigarette and lighted it and just smoked. I walked and ran around with my arms stretched outwards as if I was flying, and saying. "Ooooh, Ooooooh" I just enjoyed myself for maybe about ten minutes. I came back in the car, I was laughing, "That feels good," I told Kevin, "now we can go." And we drove on.

"Where to....?" Kevin asked me.

"Now to...," I started, "to…….." I said after a pause, "the Papal Cross." Kevin's face said like you what? Oh, Since when? Anyway he drove silently, and parked at the Papal Cross.

The Cross was built in 1979 for the Pope's visit to Ireland; the Pope then was John Paul II. I remember me ma telling this story. Me ma was here in Phoenix Park and attended the Mass and she saw Pope John Paul II. I got down, walked all the way up to the base of the cross, I just stood there for a while and when I did not see any one around. I was trying to find words to pray for the first time. I did not know how to say prayers, but I just spoke.

"God, if you're up there, you know that I know I'm going to die, so please dear God, take care of me Ma. That's all I'm asking of you today God." Tears slowly flowing down my face, I myself couldn't believe that I was praying. "Amen." I said faintly. I then walked slowly down the hill, looking at all the deer, far away; they were feeding with no worries in the world.

I went back to the car, Kevin was looking at his watch and I understood and said. "Now we can go to the hospital." And happily I continued, "Let's go and find that damned hospital." I said, and then added, "In the sea or near the beach, whatever, but I've just remembered the name, it is Dublin University Hospital, right Kevin."

It was six in the evening. We drove around and after passing a few places and getting lost, asking people, we finally arrived at Dublin University Hospital, and we had to find parking. We found a parking lot and parked. Then we walked together, it was seven at night, this Sunday, the third of chilly November. We crossed the road, from the parking building to the hospital building.

The hospital building was impressive and about six or seven stories high and it had large and wide windows. We entered the hospital, and in the foyer, there was a reception desk, and there was an elderly man sitting there reading the newspaper and a few people walking about, doctors, nurses, staff, and patients. Maybe at this time it wasn't as busy as in the mornings.

I asked and explained to the old man at this desk why I was there, and the old man called a few numbers, and he said while looking at us.

"Take the lift, to third floor, walk straight to your left for maybe twenty meters, then take a left, after another ten meters, the first door on your right, they are expecting you, Good luck." And he went back to his newspaper.

"Grand." I said and we took the lift. We got lost maybe two times, but then we reached the right place. On entering and walking in a long corridor, there was a reception desk.

"Name?" asked a nurse, appearing from one of the rooms or office, holding a file.

"Mathew." I replied.

"Surname?" she asked again.

"Kavanagh" I replied again. She then checked her papers.

"Follow me." she commanded. She was serious and businesslike. We followed her to a room, where there were three beds on one side, and the opposite side on the wall there was a big flat screen television. Behind the door there was a wash basin, straight opposite the door there was a wall of about three feet in height and big wide windows from wall to wall. Two beds were occupied already, and the third one near the entrance to the room was empty. "This is your bed," she said, "change into your pyjamas and relax, someone will come to take your details, okay?" and off she went.

"Okay Kevin," I said loudly, "here I am."

"Yeah," said Kevin, "and your bed we spoke about, is here." And we started laughing, remembering the joke. I was still nervous and in awe, being admitted in the hospital for the first time, not knowing what to expect, what tomorrow holds, the people, the doctors, nurses, are they going to be nice? Or they are going to be rude? I felt like I should just take my holdall and leave, now. The feeling is like a small boy in a new school, lost and nervous. We sat there, maybe for an hour, and then Kevin said.

"I think I'd better go now."

"Yeah, yeah, sure," I said. "I'll see you tomorrow, anyway." But in my heart I was crying, 'Please don't leave me alone here in a strange place with strange people, oh my God.'

"Yeah, if there's anything, just give me a buzz." Kevin said as he put his hand to his ear, signalling a phone. Yeah, when the doctors come to cut my leg tonight, I'll call you to come help me with the escape, I thought silently.

I waited, and then I put on my new pyjamas. Not being used to this life, I never used and I never wore pyjamas in my whole adult life, but I had to buy them, just because it was sort of a rule in the hospital, as they had informed me. At eight fifteen another nurse came, maybe she was from the Philippines, with a file. She started asking me questions, and me answering the best I could, she took my weight, sixty five kilos. My height, five feet, seven inches, my blood pressure, one hundred forty over ninety five, my blood glucose, seven and a half, and a few more questions.

"What's your address?" The nurse asked me.

"Forty five at the Castle Grange Gardens, Dublin"

"Do you smoke?"

"Yes" I replied, but silently I thought yes, everything, cigarettes, marijuana, hash, etc.

"Do you drink?"

"Yes" I said, but again in my thoughts, I replied silently, everything, beer, brandy, coffee, Tea, and Coke. When she finished, she closed the file.

"Okay you can rest now, the doctor will come later to see you, okay?" She said. I wanted to tell her, what about my bank account number? Also what about my password, and my pin number? You don't need these?

"All those measurements you took, what do they mean?" I asked her.

"The doctor will talk to you and answer all your questions." The nurse responded. Oh, I'm supposed to ask questions to the doctor? I didn't know that, so what shall I ask? I haven't a clue. Hello doctor, I said to myself, your name, surname, weight, and height. And I laughed at myself. At nine, a doctor came.

"Hello, Mathew," he said, "may I call you Mathew?" he was very polite. I could not speak, I just nodded.

"My name is Dr. Browne," he introduced himself and asked me. "I want to ask you a few questions, is that alright?" He was youngish, maybe in his late thirties or early forties, tall, maybe six two, thin, wearing glasses, and very soft spoken. He had a green file with him; I think that is the same file that the nurse had written on earlier. I nodded again, still not trusting myself to open my mouth. "Okay, your name is Mathew," he started, "and your surname is Kavanagh." This was not exactly asking but mentioning. After he checked if my address was correct and other questions, I just nodded to everything as it was correct. He then asked me. "Who is your next of kin, Mathew?"

"Me Ma" I replied.

"Oh, you can talk?" he smiled, "Are you nervous, Mathew?"

"Yeah doctor," I said "This is me first time in a fucking hospital, you know what I mean?"

"Okay, Mathew, I appreciate that." Dr Browne said. "But one thing I have to tell you early on, okay?" I just nodded my head. "In every place they have rules," he said, "and so also hospitals have rules, and here in Dublin University Hospital there is no difference, okay?" I nodded again. "Rule number one," he said as he winked. "They don't like bad language, do you understand me?" He paused, looked at my reaction and went on, "The 'F' word shall not be used here; otherwise, all the nurses and staff will mark you as a bad one." He continued, and asked me, "We don't want that, now, do we, Mathew?" I shook my head; first time anybody telling me not to use the 'F' word.

"Okay Mathew," he said, "you can now ask me any questions, which you may have," he went on, "you must have some unanswered questions, right, Mathew?" I nodded yet again. I thought to myself, what the hell, let me talk, even just a bit, it might help to regain my confidence.

"Okay, first question," I started, "what's wrong with me and why did it have to happen to me, Doctor?"

"What you have is called a soft tissue cancer. In scientific language we call it sarcoma, and it is a type of cancer which attacks soft tissue or muscle in the body. And your type of cancer is a subtype of sarcoma called

Leiomyosarcoma or LMS for short." The doctor paused and thought for a while. "Why you?" he continued. "Yes you are an energetic young man of twenty six years, that's correct, but this terrible disease attacks people of all ages, from the very young to the very old. Some types of cancers are prevalent to a particular group of people, which can be age group, or gender group, skin colour, or area or location and other factors as well."

"What causes my type of cancer?" I then asked, "The soft tissue thingy?"

"The causes are still unknown," Dr Browne answered, "the sarcoma is one of many of those rare cancers, so not much is spent on research, either to the causes or to the prevention." He paused, then added, "Which if research is done to know the causes it might eventually lead to the cure, but unfortunately it is not so." He went on, "Also some cancers are genetically inherited, or if someone from the line of parents had a particular cancer, then there is higher chances of the offspring getting it, or it can even jump a generation."

"Are you going to do the operation?" I eventually gathered my courage. "What'll happen to my leg?" I asked.

"No sir, I am not going to perform your surgical procedure, I am only a Registrar. The Oncology Consultant Dr Livingstone is your doctor and I believe you have already met him at the 'Royal Hospital'. He will lead a team of doctors and I will be with the team in the operating theatre." Dr Browne spoke with a smile, looking at me, "Your leg, now let me see." he looked up as he was thinking, index finger on his cheek. "As for the tumour, that is the malignant lump, which is on the lateral side of your right thigh, will be surgically removed and you shall then be bandaged. The tumour will be sent to the lab for further tests to see how much we got out and the margins, also and it will tell us a lot about your cancer." He continued, "Your thigh, once the lump is removed, will have a hole, if you may. It will be fitted with a black sponge which is medicated, and a tube, and the wound will then be bandaged." he continued, "The tube then will lead to the vacuum pump which sucks out air and fluid, which is then drained out into a plastic packet to be disposed."

"So you mean my leg will not be cut?" I asked the question which I was scared of the answer.

"The first surgery, which will be tomorrow, and your leg will not be amputated."

"What do you mean the first surgery?" I started to look worried, "How many do you plan to do?"

"Well it all depends on the results of the biopsy, which the lab will do to the tumour after it is removed from your leg." Dr Browne said to reassure me. "But having said that, you still have to have a few surgeries, after everything is clear, and then the plastic surgeons will have to perform a skin graft, which is to remove skin from one part of your body to try to cover the place where the tumour was removed."

"How long will I stay at the hospital?" I said "Or after the operation, I can go home?"

"Now, that all depends on the answers I gave you just now." Dr Browne said. "The minimum you will have to stay in the hospital, if and when everything goes okay, will be about two to three weeks, but you can be here for a while longer."

"You can let me go home after the operation, you know?" I said as I thought Is this me negotiating a business deal? "I can come back if you need me, just give me a buzz, you know what I mean?"

"Very smart try Mathew," Dr. Browne laughed aloud, "you cannot run away even if you want to, the nurses will not let you out of their sight and the front reception people will not let you go. You are ours Mathew, until we say so and after we discharge you." He also explained to me the procedures of the intended surgery...the pros & cons, about the vessels, veins, injuries, muscles, damages, infection, vascular, recurrence, everything. "If you have understood everything, and you don't have more questions," Dr. Browne said, "can you now please sign this consent form?" He asked me while giving me the green folder, and pointing to the bottom of the page.

Okay, another prison stay, now I am at the 'Joy' or what? I started to think in my head. What have I got myself into? Many of the words he used I didn't understand, but I cannot ask now. I signed the consent form. I could not ask any more questions, all the strength in my body was drained. I could not even remember when Dr. Browne left, or if he said anything else. Of course, I didn't understand a lot; my head was in confusion and denial, things were going very fast, I couldn't digest all the information, but what I can say? Leave it. I fell asleep, but it was not to be.

Chapter Four

*A*ROUND ELEVEN AT NIGHT, I was awakened by the nurse. "Have you had a chest x-ray?" she asked, while I was still in la-la land.

"I don't know." was my reply. I thought. You've the green file in your hands, why don't you check to see if I had a chest x-ray or not instead of waking me up? "Okay he did not have a chest x-ray." I heard the nurse saying. "You can take him now." Take who? Take whom and where? Whom should I take?

"Okay lad, are you able to sit in the wheelchair?" someone said, and I presumed it was to me, "I have to bring you for an x-ray," he said to me. I opened my eyes. Yes, the night porter or security guard or somebody, wearing a uniform and tall, with a sharp shrill commanding voice was talking to me; I checked to see...did he have a gun? Or did he have a truncheon, or maybe a stick? Before he gave me one on the head, I quickly jumped from the bed and sat on the wheelchair, ready. I am being taken to the execution chamber, and I dare not ask.

The attendant or porter, actually 'drove' me along the corridors, left, right, vroom .... Vroom, It was like a Ferrari speeding somewhere in a Formula One race. I could have put a safety belt on, if there was one. Then in the lift, I didn't have the faintest idea if he took me up or down, left or right, but we reached the floor he wanted. And then again some corridors, and finally we arrived at some sort of a destination, because he put the handbrakes on, and he commanded me.

"Wait here, lad, and when you're done, you'll also wait here, you know what I mean?" As if was I planning to run away, I didn't know where I was, so how can I run away? Also run away in my pyjamas? If the fellas at the Joy Carvery would see me now, I am sure they will not believe what they see. Me, Mathew, the tough talking guy, and no cap on me head? Also, I was in a pair of pyjamas? Ha Ha Ha. After a while, a lady nurse came out, and called my name.

"Can you walk?" she asked me. Yeah, I'd like to walk away, but I just nodded. She took me inside the x-ray theatre. "Okay now remove your shirt." She told me. I removed my shirt and was left with my skinny chest and false six pack muscles. "Stand there." And she went on, "Breathe in, breathe out, okay, hold it there." After a few of these orders I heard, "Okay you're done. Put your shirt on and you can go now," the nurse said. I quickly put my shirt back on.

"Really, I can go now?" I was delighted. "Go home?" I thought maybe I don't have to call Kevin; I saw taxis outside the hospital, when we came in earlier on, and I shall just take one home, now.

"No, no, no," she said quickly. "You came with the porter, right? Wait outside, he will come to collect you." and she smiled, but my heart fell. She meant the 'commando' will come to collect me, his prisoner.

"You are going back to your ward; you have surgery tomorrow, right?" the x-ray nurse asked me. I could not answer, I nodded my head. I waited outside, shivering on this cold November night; I should have taken my duvet or some covering. The 'commando' did not tell me it was going to be cold. Maybe we were in the basement, which is where they torture prisoners, right? That's it, I am sure now.

I was dozing away nicely when the commando came to get me and without a word he started his Monte Carlo Formula One racing. I think he was trying to break his previous record time because we came very fast back at my prison room, at 'Dolphin Ward' bed number seventy seven. They should have named it 'zero zero seven' 007, it would have been better, but anyway before he pushed me from his wheelchair, I jumped out and on to my bed, which was my safe place now from the commando. He did not even say goodnight... as if I cared.

I was glad I came back safely from the torture chamber in the basement and now for a beautiful sleep. 'Night Duty' nurse came and fitted me with a name tag on my wrist and left leg; she also put a stocking on one leg, the left, and she said "Just to prevent blood from clotting in your leg." As I dozed off, I then heard.

"Mathew, Mathew." Someone was calling my name, or was there another Mathew? I opened my eyes; it was one or two in the morning, or night, whatever. The night duty nurse, she was, yes 'night duty', her duty was not to let me sleep on my last day in this world. "You were supposed to be fasting, from midnight," she said aloud, "for your surgery tomorrow." I thought what now? Fasting from what? I wasn't a Muslim; I heard that Muslims fast in the month of Ramadan, so I didn't need to fast, and also surgery is tomorrow and you are waking me up today, why? Did somebody pay these people or what, why are they all after me?

Since I came last evening at seven, you did not give me anything to eat, now at one in the morning you are asking me if I am fasting. Are you for real, lady 'night duty'?

"I have to check your blood pressure and blood glucose." She then poked her needles and whatever else she was doing. Once it was over I felt that now I was going to rest. 'Mhhh mmmhh ..... mmmmmhh...' I managed to mumble and went back to sleep.

"Mathew, Mathew." again somebody was calling Mathew. Oh no, it's four in the morning, for God's sake, leave Mathew alone. I think Mathew is dead, now go away. It was 'night duty' again. "I have to check your blood pressure and blood glucose."

"Go ahead," I said in my sleep to the 'torturer'. "Do whatever you need to do." She poked her needles and whatever she had to do.

"Wake up, Wake up." I heard a voice, I think I know this voice, I heard it somewhere. "Wake up." Oh no, not again, the 'night duty' is waking me up, it's six in the morning. I wanted to shout and tell her, I don't usually wake up at this time, my time is from nine in the morning, so stop bothering me, lady, and nobody wakes me up. I opened my eyes, yes she was the one. "Go wash up thoroughly, and brush your teeth," she said, "and put this on." She handed me a piece of cloth, "You have to prepare for your operation." And she was gone.

Why should I go to wash up, do I smell bad? Why did she tell me to brush my teeth? I got up from the bed but in my heart I started to be scared. I took the folded cloth and looked around, then took my holdall, and went out of the room, and then I saw the night duty nurse outside in the nurses' station.

"Where are the toilets?" I asked her as she was looking at me like I was going to run away.

"Walk that way, on your right." she replied as she pointed with no smile on her face, whatsoever. After I washed up, brushed my teeth, I opened the folded cloth and was shocked: it was a hospital gown, and it was half open with strings only. Anyway after I put on my pyjamas, I put on the gown on top of my pyjamas, and I walked, limping back to my room. I jumped back on my bed and waited for my destiny.

Night duty nurse came in the room; she said, "I have to check you again your blood pressure and blood glucose." She poked her needles and did whatever she had to do. I managed to read a tag on her uniform; oh her name was 'Imelda', now I knew the name of my night duty my torturer.

She was about five feet two inches, short and plump and wearing thin glasses, black hair and she was about fifty or so with a shrill voice.

"Oh...what ....you didn't remove your pyjamas?" she noticed now. "You only have to be in the hospital gown." she said with commanding voice. "Now remove your watch, your chain, bracelet, your earring, all your metals, and everything else, except your hospital gown." Now I felt, there's going to be a fight on, what the fuck she's thinking? Who's she to tell me to remove everything?

"You want me to be naked?" I shouted, angrily, "Are you fucking crazy?" I shouted again, thinking of the night's 'torture' I had endured. "The whole night, you don't let me sleep; now you want me to remove my clothes, and stay naked?" I wasn't going to take this shit from her, "No way, man I'm not gonna be naked."

Another nurse came in; maybe she was a senior nurse. She tried to talk to me but I was mad and angry, the commotion woke the other two people in the room. I was mad as I said loudly to no one in particular.

"I can remove the watches and everything but to stay naked and be covered by a piece of cloth? No way man, this is not going to be." I screamed at them. They then had to call the doctor on duty or my doctor. They got Dr. Browne, who after talking to the nurses, who were furious at me, came in smiling, and he said politely to me.

"Mathew, what seems to be the problem?" I just sat there fuming and looked at him while I shook my head. He gave a sign for the nurses to go out and leave us alone. He waited patiently, and after a while he touched my shoulder, "Tell me Mathew." He said, "We can discuss this." I could not shout or talk loudly with this gentle man; he was a nice man.

"She's telling me to stay naked," I started saying and continued. "How can I stay with only one half a piece of cloth?" No way. Shaking my head and showing him the piece of cloth while I was turning it over and around.

"You see Mathew," Dr. Browne gently said, "you are going to be taken in the operation theatre and the doctors need to put a few things on your body, for monitoring, for checking your breath and so on and also your leg has to be reachable from every part without disruption." he continued. "I understand your concern but it is also for your own safety. And then after that you will be on the bed most of the time and covered, okay?" he said.

"So this is only for the operation? I asked while looking at him in the eye, "Then afterwards, I can put my pyjamas on?" Only yesterday I had detested wearing pyjamas and yet today here I was eager to put them on.

"Yes Mathew," Dr. Browne smiled, knowing he had won. "You can do that." I then removed the pyjamas and the rings and watch and all and I put back on the hospital gown. And so I was left with only the hospital gown. It was covering only the front while the back was a free movie for all and it was up to the knees in length. Dr. Browne was satisfied, the night duty nurse was satisfied, and I was satisfied.

At seven this morning, Monday the fourth of November, a team of doctors passed and were stopping at each patient and either whispering among themselves or talking to the patients. Among them were Dr. Browne and one of the doctors told me "Your operation is scheduled for today."

"Around, what time?" I asked.

"That is up to the consultant oncologist, Dr Livingstone, and his busy schedule." But at eight in the morning Dr. Livingstone came to see me.

"Hi Mathew," he said. "How are you feeling today?"

"Very nervous, Doctor," I replied.

"That is understandable, but don't be," he said with a smile, "you will be alright and you are in good hands, okay?" As if that is the magic assurance to my life. I just shrugged.

At nine in the morning a nurse came in the room. "Hi, my name is Janet; I am the nurse for the day." She seemed nice and polite; she introduced herself, so that's a good sign. "I need to ask you a few questions. Is that alright?" she had the green file and I nodded. "What's your name?" it was all over again, same questions, same answers. She then checked my blood pressure. She was blond and had a small scar under her left eye. I wanted to reach and touch the scar and ask her about the history behind the scar...you see I am fascinated by scars. But I couldn't.

They came for me at half past nine in the morning; they did not even talk to me, there were two porters or attendants and they asked Janet the day nurse, "Is this the patient?" one of them said, and the other one. "Bed Seventy Seven?" No, I wanted to say, Zero, zero seven, James Bond, licensed to kill.

"Yes." Janet replied and brought the green file. They started to push me with my bed and Janet 'the scar' came with me, "To give you some moral support," She told me. I thought that was nice of her. We moved along the corridors and lift but this time they took me slowly, not like the 'commando' of the wheelchair. We arrived at a place which looked like a parking lot for hospital beds. Janet handed over the green file to another nurse and she wished me good luck. Of course I need all the luck in the world. I was tense, I was nervous too and I was looking around for anybody to help me in escaping this place, but of course there was nobody.

They came again with the green file, asked me the same questions over again and checked my two name tags. Then it was my turn to be taken in another room with my bed trolley. A female doctor this time, she introduced herself and she said she was going to give me a 'full general anaesthetic' whatever that means. She injected her anaesthetic to the already, connected injection in my arm. She smiled at me, I smiled back at her and I don't remember anything after that; I was gone maybe forever.

Chapter Five

I CAME TO, SLOWLY, MAYBE ABOUT four in the afternoon, my mouth dry and I tried to tell someone that I needed water to drink, but I couldn't talk. I could see things and people, but I could not recognise anyone. At six, being hungry and having been 'fasting' a long time, I asked Janet, 'the scar', if I could have something to eat. She got me a sandwich and a cup of tea. I took it slowly, was about halfway through it, and I vomited everything. Then she decided to give me sips of water and a tablet.

"To stop you getting sick." she said. The good news was that the night nurse was a different one than before, but I was not sure how she would be. She gave me some tablets at about eight o'clock, and an hour later I had to pee.

"I need to pee but I can't go to the toilet." I told the nurse and she brought me a special container.

"You can do it in here." she said.

"But…but…" I began to argue. I thought she was only messing.

"No problem, go ahead, you can do it in there," the nurse said. She then closed the curtain, left me to do my business alone. First it was difficult and not being used to but I managed to do in the bottle or can or whatever, and I felt so good and relieved. I did not ask for and was not given anything to eat after that, but I could not get sleep and I kept peeing every forty five to sixty minutes, the whole night in my special can, I just had to reach below the bed and do my business with difficulty and clean myself with bog roll, and then put the can down again.

The next day Tuesday, at six in the morning, the night nurse did not need to wake me up, as I was wide eyed. She took a blood glucose test and blood pressure again. Later on in the morning one of the assistant nurses or helper came to remove the can of urine, I felt embarrassed for someone else to remove my pee, but I couldn't help it. I felt I should apologise, and said faintly "Sorry for being a bother" but mostly I said it to myself.

At seven in the morning Dr. Browne and the team passed through on their rounds. He said a few words to me and nodded as they left. After that I was given breakfast, and I felt good for the first time in my life: 'breakfast in bed', ha ha ha, but I did not have a clue what lay ahead.

Later I was given an injection in my stomach by a male nurse; they called it 'the bee sting', or something and it sure was stinging. True it was a bee sting; he told me I would be having the injection every day while I was in the hospital.

That night, one of the junior doctors passed through and told me to stop eating at midnight, and to fast for tomorrow, Wednesday. I was going to be brought to the operating theatre again, and they wanted to see my wound and dress it. I thought here goes, I was starting to enjoy my stay, but anyway let's hope for the best. I woke in the middle of night, shouting for help, as the pain that I was experiencing was severe. The night nurse quickly came and she injected some sort of painkillers in a drip and after a while I felt relief.

Wednesday morning at six the nurse brought me a basin filled with warm water and a towel. "Take a minimal wash," she told me, "and be ready for the theatre." I did take the 'minimal wash' and wiped myself, and was ready with a fresh gown, as my gown was full of blood. The bed sheets were wet with blood as well. Dr Browne passed at nine in the morning and he explained to me what the day's planned procedure would be, and the risks involved, and he asked me to sign the consent form, which I did.

"Dr. Livingstone will lead the team and also a doctor from the plastic surgeons team will be in the operating theatre, to observe." Dr. Browne said to me. I thought observe, observe what? Are they the United Nations? They want to observe if crimes against humanity are being committed? Ha ha ha. At ten in the morning, the porters came for me and I was again 'driven' to the operating theatre.

And so it went like it did on Monday: I came to my senses late in the evening, when the nurse gave me something to eat, I vomited and it went on. At night I noticed one of my 'room mates' had been discharged and the middle bed was empty. The last bed, which was near the window, still had someone there, but so far no contact had been made. I thought we might need to make contact, as he was near the window, because then we could plan our escape together from this 'prison'. At night again the pain was severe, and again I got the drip with morphine. The sleep wasn't good, but I still had to enjoy my hotel stay.

On Thursday morning, the fifth day since my arrival on Sunday, I wasn't expecting anything eventful. I started to remember people and things I missed during the past few days. I hadn't seen Kevin since he left on Sunday, and I didn't bring my mobile phone, so I didn't know how's me Ma. Why didn't Kevin bring me Ma to see me? Why didn't even Kevin himself come to see me? I didn't know the answers.

Anyway I was at least looking forward to getting rid of the hospital gown and put on my 'beloved' pyjamas. I tried to get out of the bed, so I could go to the toilet myself and do the stuff in the toilet and change into my pyjamas. But as much as I tried, I just wasn't able to bend or move my leg, it was too painful. It was just pain. "Aaaah, ooooh"

I could not go to the toilet, so I thought okay, I will take my 'minimal wash' on the bed, then change into pyjamas. I asked and the assistant nurse brought me warm water in the wash basin. Okay, I washed myself at all the relevant places and brushed my teeth, washed my face, and once done, now to change clothes, from the one piece to the pyjamas, ha ha ha, I was happy.

No way could I lift my leg, it was not possible at all. I turned and I turned like an acrobat, but I just could not, and the pain I was inflicting on myself, pain, and blood was oozing from my leg. The gown was all wet with blood, and the bed sheets turned a bright red colour. After a struggle that seemed an eternity, I stopped, I had to.

Now, I decided, I can remain half naked, or whatever, not with this pain. Let any nurse, let alone doctor, come to tell me, "Remove all your clothes plus you gown and remain as you are, like the day you were born." I truly would not object or hesitate, not with this pain. "No way, man," I said to myself half aloud.

The guy near the window bed got discharged and two other guys were brought in. The news was on the telly, I came to know that it had started snowing around Ireland and in Dublin, that out there it was really becoming cold. One of the nurses told us.

"You lads are lucky, you are inside here and it is warm and comfy," she said. "But outside there? It is freezing." I thought are we really lucky? We are in prison here; you guys can go out and come in as you wish, free movement and all that, you know. At one time, while the nurses were talking among themselves. I overheard one saying.

"Many patients are being brought in because of falls and slipping in the snow, especially older folks, breaking their bones, legs, hips, and hands." And that if the snow continues, they are going to be very busy in the coming days as the wards will be all full. I thought it was a good time, now, if I was out there, to go rob a few houses. I was not sure what Kevin and the lads were up to, robbing banks or post offices or what? I am not even sure will I get my cut? Ah, I am inside here missing the fun outside there, and the booze and girls, ooh la la, what a waste.

I noticed our day nurse was different today, she had blond hair, was tall, thin, and grumpy, plus she had no smile. Okay, we shall see, I thought. I sat there on the bed and dreaming and thinking, how long has it been since I had my last pint? Or smoked? When will Kevin bring Ma over to see me? I have a lot to talk to Kevin about to update him of the events since we last met, when was it? Five days ago? That long, eh? Okay I am looking forward for their visits soon. Nowadays they were giving me a strong dosage of painkillers all the time, and even that is not enough at times, they have to give me the 'drip' with their secret formula of relaxation, which I came to know later that it was morphine.

Since earlier on I was given 'Lyrica' tablets, 50mg twice daily, and now it was increased to 100mg twice daily, and the nurse told me depending on how I will react, they will be increasing by 50mg at weekly increments, up to 200mg or 250mg. Some other tablets as well, which I didn't know the names of yet, they just give me, and I just put them in my mouth, wash them down with water. I trust them; they love me too much to give me poison, right? Right oh man, right.

It was at twelve thirty when I could hear the trolley wheels and, aha, the aroma. Food was coming, and when the guy with the food trolley arrived, he read from his paper and looked at my bed number; I nodded at him, as to say come on now, it is me, okay, give me my lunch. I read from his name tag, 'Elvis', okay I thought, he is my guy; he looked as if he was from the Philippines. This guy is important for my survival, so I must try to make friends with him earlier on. He gave me my tray; it was sandwiches and some green salad, and ice cream.

"Good man." I said to him, with a smile and a wink. I started eating right away, I was hungry, man, the food tasted really nice, I thought, where is Kevin and the lads now? If only they could see me now. I am in the hotel, ha ha ha. Once I finished my lunch, had a glass of water, I was okay now, I felt good, I can survive this 'prison'.

I noticed the guy in the middle bed, and he nodded at me, and he asked me, "Hi, what are you here for?" I chose to ignore him as I was not in the mood to talk; I was not here to make friends. Then he turned and spoke to the guy near the window.

"Hi, what are you here for?"

"Ah, I fell in snow." he answered, "And what about you?"

"Same boat it seems, the snow, you know," Middle Guy said, "I was getting down off my truck and slipped, dislocated my collar bone." I was listening without looking at them.

"I was doing my garden and slipped in the snow," said the window man, "They said I broke my ankle." Later on, one by one, they were taken with their trolleys, and I was glad to be alone. After a few hours they were brought back separately, with plaster casings, one in the leg and the other one with bandages around the shoulder and arm.

I came to understand later that people are brought first to the emergency A&E department downstairs, where they will be seen by the triage nurse, and then by the doctors. Depending on the seriousness of their problem, after a while or a few hours, they will get x-rayed, like if they have broken bones or something serious, they will be admitted in the wards, as they are now, in 'my room', and if they are ok, they are discharged and sent home.

So the night passed, and the next day they were both discharged and just as soon, others occupied their beds. I was starting to have a feeling that now I am a veteran in this room, the war hero, as I am going nowhere, and I have no news of outside except to do with the severe weather. This time, the middle bed was occupied by a patient who was just moaning, poor him, he was very old, I understood he also fell in the snow and broke his hip bone, and that after he got 'repaired' he would be sent to a respite home to rest for a few days, before being sent home completely since they need beds here.

At the window bed, a guy came who was loud and talking nonstop to the staff, and the staff were getting annoyed by him, and I was better off in my far corner from, whenever he looked at my side, maybe he wanted to talk, I pretended to be asleep, and closed my eyes. I said to myself, sorry man you cannot get me; I am too smart for you. The hospital's physiotherapists came.

"Hi Mathew, my name is Lucy and this is Mona," the older one of the two ladies said. "Can we take you for a walk?" Yeah, I thought, take me for a walk outside the main entrance, put me in a taxi and I'll go home, how sweet of you ladies.

"Okay" I managed to say. They gave me a walker, where the patient will hold the bar in front, and it had four small wheels. They held me from both sides, and we started walking.

"Right leg forward, left leg forward." The older one was saying, "Slowly, take your time." Oh, I didn't imagine it was going to be this difficult. "Right leg forward, left leg forward," the older one again. "Yes, you are doing great." I never thought in my life that I was going to have to learn to walk all over again, like a baby, like a toddler. We continued.

"Right leg forward, left leg forward. Slowly now, don't rush."

Maybe we went twenty meters and then we turned and went back. "That's very good," the older one said. "You did very well." I was being praised for walking twenty meters with two people holding me and a walker... man; this world is full of surprises. "We shall try again tomorrow," said the older one. "Okay?" I nodded my head. Yeah sure, why not, I thought, but it was painful. Because of my severe pain now, and lack of sleep, they put me on a permanent drip, so it was easier just for them to inject fluid or something, which I came to understand later was morphine as the pain killer.

They continued to give me the bee sting injections every day, and I couldn't hide or run away from them. I stopped counting how many days I was in the hospital, but was just counting and listening to the ever changing occupants of middle and window bed. And I was always nervous whenever a new nurse came on duty; I also came to understand that they change their shifts between seven and eight in the morning and at night.

I was always apprehensive to see the doctors going their rounds, as I was not sure if they were going to cut my leg or leave it as it is or what. I was scared, scared of this terrible disease, cancer. Oh my God, I never thought in a million years I would get cancer.

I kept remembering about Ma, about Kevin, and the fellas, what they were up to, what were they doing at this particular time, what were they talking about. I kept remembering, about the booze, the smoke, and the girls. I kept remembering the Joy Carvery and the music, the Irish dancing, life in the streets of Dublin.

Chapter Six

O<small>N THE SEVENTH DAY AT</small> the hospital, this Saturday in cold November, Dr. Browne came to see me. He pulled a chair and sat down; I sensed here it comes, the bad news.

"Hi Mathew." he said, "How have you been coping? I hope you're improving and getting well." I did not answer; I just looked at him, waiting for the bombshell. "I understand the physiotherapists are taking you for short walks, right?" he asked me again, "How do you feel now?"

"Yeah, the ladies are taking me for short walks, it is painful, but we are doing fine, bit by bit. They also tried to get me to do some other exercises but it's too painful." I said, and added. "But the walking is slowly improving, you know what I mean?" I thought he knew about all this, and that he was just softening me for the hard blow.

"Okay, the histopathology report is... ...." he started to say.

"The histo..... What doctor?" I interrupted him as I had no clue of this 'histo' thing.

"Histopathology is the lab test on the tissue, or let us say the lump we removed from your leg." he said. "You know that we sent it to the lab, right?" He continued, "To be checked, and it will tell us, the doctors, more about your sarcoma."

"Okay, go ahead, doctor." I said so as to let him get to the point.

"As I was saying the histopathology report is not yet ready," he said. "There are some complications." He paused, maybe unsure how to continue. "But we shall get the report within the week. Meanwhile; you will remain here at the hospital, alright?"

"What does it mean for me?" I asked. "I mean, besides staying in the hospital, you know what I mean?"

"It means, we just wait and see," he said, "and you keep on praying," and went on, "we keep our fingers crossed, I suppose?" What? I thought, he is telling me now to pray, to pray to whom? 'To cross our fingers', that's what he said. Now it has come to this? I don't fucking understand this. And the doctor went away; I didn't know or hear, what he said after that. I was angry. I know they're planning to cut off my leg...what did he mention before? To ampu-something my leg, what was happening now, I couldn't understand.

That night I did not get much sleep, then I remembered me ma, I started to think about her, why she has not come to see me till now? I missed her, I love me ma. If Kevin cannot bring her, then she could have taken a taxi and come see me, right? I knew she didn't like Kevin much. She was always saying Kevin was bad company to be around with; Kevin was a bad influence on us, her boys. She was always blaming Kevin, for my brother Donald's death, my brother Daniel's and even for my father's death; she claimed he was somehow involved.

"I tell ya, now, Mathew." she always used to say, "Your man's into drugs, and gangs since he was a young fella, you know?"

"Ma, come on, Ma," I would say, "Kevin's your nephew."

"I know, I know, but I tell ya, he is up to no good." she said. "He already been in prison, too many times, you know?" I couldn't argue with that. But me Ma knew more than she said; only once in a while, when she is really pissed off, she would say something, and I would pick up bits and pieces. "If not for your man, me beloved Brian, would still be alive today, and me two sons." she said to me once. "I tell you this Mathew, be careful, my son, I fear I would lose you also."

"But Ma," I protested. "When Da was killed, Kevin was only a twelve years old boy." I then continued. "Even the Gardai` said Da was shot accidentally and by unknown people, Ma."

"I tell ya, Mathew, Kevin was into gangs and drugs since he was a small boy," Ma would argue. "Kevin's dangerous, and he's a killer. I tell ya. Okay, was accidental shot that killed me Brian, that was, but gangs shooting after each other, and where was Kevin? Outside my window, this very window, I tell ya. After that he ran away, you know? Why he ran away, I ask you now, Mathew." And she would start to cry, it was too painful for her.

Me Ma, she was once a happy and jolly lady, she was friendly to everyone in the estate, and she would take care of old ladies, she would always help around, sometimes she would just baby sit for the neighbours. And she was always proud of her three boys. But when after me Da was shot, that was the start of me ma's decline in health as well as emotionally.

But still she was a strong lady, she would not give up easily, she had her three boys to take care of and bring them up, and to educate them. So she continued going to work at the local supermarket. Life was hard; she tried to shield her boys from the likes of the Kevin's, and away from the streets. If something happened to one of her boys, and she could not manage, she would say:

"If only your Da was here, nobody would do something like this to his children, he was a man not to be messed." she said. "Everybody in the estate knew Brian, and they liked and respected him, he was a polite man to those who respected him, but no nonsense man to those who tried to mess with him or his beloved family."

I finally managed to get to sleep at four in the morning, wondering about tomorrow, which is actually today. Was it going to be the usual normal day, or was it something new? Later after lunch, about three in the afternoon, I heard a voice.

"Nurse, Nurse."

I looked at the next bed, the middle one. The patient there was an old fellow, he was calling the nurse. I looked at him, he turned and looked at me and he seemed not really that old, but in some sort of pain. He had all white hair, and blue eyes with big reading glasses. It seemed like he was pleading to me for help. He spoke with an English accent. I called out loudly without another thought in my mind.

"Nurse, NURSE!" I called loudly again and the 'grumpy' nurse appeared, she looked pissed off.

"Who is calling and shouting for the nurse?" she shouted, and I was pissed as I told her.

"Your man needs some help." I nodded towards the middle bed; she looked annoyed, and asked the old man in a loud voice.

"What is it? What do you need?"

The old man answered something I didn't hear, and the nurse called somebody, maybe an assistant nurse or whatever, with a blue uniform, and they closed the curtains around the old man, and were helping with whatever he needed. Once they were done, the nurse shouted at the old man.

"Next time don't shout calling for a nurse, ring the bell." I thought oh my God, this 'grumpy' nurse is rude also.

"Listen nurse, don't shout at the poor man, he needed help and you have to help him, you know what I mean?" I spoke with anger in my voice. She looked at me in such a bad way.

"No you listen." she said loudly enough for everyone in the room to hear. "If anyone needs help, ring the bell beside your bed, and don't shout at me." Oh, I thought, now you want a fight with me, which is my game by the way and I am used to brawls.

"Nurse, you fucking don't shout at us patients." I said threatening. "You'd better have manners; you know what I fucking mean?" With me finger pointing at her. She turned red in the face as she didn't expect this; I knew then, that I've just made an enemy. She turned angrily and stormed out of the room. Later in the evening, when the old man woke up, he turned to me.

"Thank you. You stood up for me." He said politely.

I nodded and said. "No bother." The guy in the last bed stood up.

"Yeah, the nurse was rude." he said. He was young, tall and well built. I noticed he didn't have the silly gown on, but he was wearing a track suit bottom and a polo shirt, muscles bulging. He looked at me, and then the old man, and he said, "I am John."

Then the old man replied, "I am James." And he further said, "She need not have shouted at us. I feel embarrassed by this situation."

"I don't know, I just lost my fucking head, you know what I mean?" I said shaking my head. "She was fucking rude, man."

"It was all my fault." the old man James said, and added, "But thank you, young man." He then asked me, "What is your name, sir?" Oh, I thought, he is calling me sir? He is being polite; I think today I am with two gentlemen in the room, not my type of company; I have never been called 'sir' in my life.

"I'm Mathew." I said, "I'm sorry to use the 'F' word, you know what I mean?" Then I pointed to the young man, John. "You don't have the hospital dress on."

"Yeah, I came in yesterday," he said, "I was down at the 'A&E'. They took an X-ray of my shoulder and the doctor said it's OK, it's only a bruise. So I am just waiting for the doctor to discharge me."

"How did you get hurt?" James, the old man with white hair said. "Did you fall in the snow?"

"Ah, no, I was playing rugby, and someone rammed into me." John replied. "I thought maybe I broke some bones, but it's just a bruise, I am lucky, I will be fine." I thought lucky guy, the rugby man, then I became bolder.

"What about you James?" I said, "You didn't play rugby, now, right?" with a smile.

"Oh no, not at my age," James said, smiling back. "I was coming back from the office, and I slipped in the snow," he laughed. "Just outside my house, would you believe it?" They both didn't ask about me, but I thought, that is good, as already they saw the blood on my hospital one piece and the bed sheets, both being changed every day in the morning. Life will be fun, I thought.

Later on, John the rugby player was discharged, and his bed was quickly occupied by another patient. Elvis brought us our dinner, and so it was eaten quickly since we were hungry. At seven the doctors did their rounds and they avoided me. I thought, maybe they had heard about the incident with 'grumpy'. Or maybe they just didn't know what to actually say to me.

The night nurse was Imelda 'the scar'. She was okay, and even though she is shrill, she is better than 'grumpy' anytime. But I will survive, as she has also been giving me the drip and pain killers at night. In the next morning before breakfast I then heard someone.

"Good morning, Mathew." I thought who is it now, for me Mathew, to be asked 'good morning'? I looked around then remembered where I was and yesterday's brawl with the nurse. "Are you awake, Mathew?" Okay this must be the old man, middle bed, what's his name again? Yeah, it was John.

"Morning John," I said with confidence that I remembered his name.

"No. Not John. John was discharged yesterday, this is James." he said. "Do you remember?"

"Hi James, sorry, I was far away, you know what I mean?" I shrugged. After Elvis brought us our breakfast, the old man looked at me.

"Young man, you don't talk much, now, do you?" James asked me. I thought, Okay now I am supposed to be talking. I was avoiding this situation, but just because I helped him yesterday does not mean we have to be mates now, you know what I mean? I don't need friends, I have my friends, I have Kevin and the lads, and that's enough. "Hello Mathew" James said, "Are you there?"

"Yeah, I'm here." Where could I go now? I am here to stay and I will die here, mister middle bed, old man.

"Have you seen outside, it is snowing heavily," James said, and went on, "and it seems it's very cold." How can I see outside, old man? I am far away from the window, and I don't care if it is cold or not outside, as long as inside here I am warm.

"Yeah, I know," I said.

"Today, the doctors are going to mend my broken hip bone." he said. "I am nervous, you know? I hope they do not tell me something else is wrong." he confided and continued. "What about you Mathew, what is wrong with you?" I thought here goes, I don't want to hear your story and I don't want to give you my story. He should do his operation and be discharged today, I hope.

"Ah James, you're going to be alright, you know what I mean?" I said. "Stop worrying." and I stopped there, no more conversation.

"I received a call from my wife and daughter just now." James said. "They said they cannot get to the hospital, all roads are blocked with the snowing, and it is dangerous driving conditions." I thought tar..ra ra….here comes, the unwanted life story of the middle bed, old man, about his beautiful wife and a gorgeous daughter.

"I have a son and a daughter." James said. Feeling sad, I thought, because his family can't come to see him. Just one day and he already misses his family, man, what about me? How many days now, I lost count, and nobody cares to comes to see me. "But my son is not here in Ireland; he is living and working in the United States, in the state of Michigan." Middle bed continued. "He has a wife and one handsome son."

I thought okay go on, when you finish, can you go to sleep. I turned my face from his side, as I couldn't turn my body because of my leg; every movement for me was hard work. 'Middle bed' got the hint I think, because he then kept quiet. I was saved by the physiotherapist who took me for my normal 'baby' walk, and after that I went to sit in the telly room, and watched the snow from the window. When I got back to my room, I did not see the bed in the middle and the old man. I looked around searching, and then the 'window man' noticed me.

"They took him down for his operation, you know."

"Okay," I said, "will he be long?" I asked just for the sake of talking only. Hoping he'll never come back.

"Ah, no idea." window man said, "Meself, today I'm going home." Okay, I thought, that is more than enough said already, so I turned and went back in my bed. Time passed, and lunch came, and late in the evening, James was brought back with his bed but he was unconscious, and that was good for me, no talking. At night when I couldn't get sleep, I started to remember my Da. When he died, he was still young, he was just thirty eight, and he was still working in Dublin Port. He used to say to us, his children.

"A man has to work hard," and added, "Work hard and let it be legal work, he has to take care of his family." Once when I was four, I think and I still remember, as I was on his lap while he was reading the paper. "You Mathew," he said as he tickled me. "What you'll be when you grow up, Eh?"

"Oh, Da, I want to be like you Da," I said, "Working in the port." and quickly I added "Da, Da, but I want to work in the bank, and I'll have a lot of money to give you, and Ma." I added quickly, "I can then buy you a nice car."

"Good boy. And you already noticed your Pa drives a wreck?" Da said, "What about you Daniel?" Daniel was the shy one, he was older than me by six years, and he wouldn't talk much. "Da, I want to go to college." Daniel said. "I want to be a doctor, and help sick people." Da nodded his head in approval as he smiled.

"Good boy, what about you Donald, my boy?" Donald was the oldest, he was one year older than Daniel, and he was quick tempered.

"Da, I want to be a boxer." he said in a confident voice. "I want to fight in the Olympics, you know?" Da stopped smiling and was silent for some time.

"But Donald you need an education first, you know?" he said, bringing Donald near him. Then he held us all three together in a hug. "You know what, my boys?" he said, "I want you all first to get good education, then you can work in whatever you like, and be good citizens of your country."

"But Da," Donald protested, "but I don't like school, my teacher is mean and I don't like her one bit."

I jumped in not to be outdone. "Yeah, yeah Da, first I go to school," I said. "Can you tell Ma to take me to school, Da?" I pleaded as I pulled his coat. As the youngest I could get away with a lot especially with my Da. I know he used to love me the most.

"Okay, Mathew." Da said, "Next year you will be five and Ma will take you to school, okay boy?" I chuckled and was happy.

Okay Da." I said. "Ma, Ma, you hear Da said next year, you've to take me to school?" I shouted to Ma. Ma was in the kitchen and she came over.

"What is it boys?" she asked while smiling. "Why are you boys are after your Da?"

My Da frowned. "Leave them my boys," he said. "They are intelligent and good boys," he said proudly, while holding us. "One day, they're going to be big lads," he said. "They will have good jobs and they will take care of their old man and Ma." He smiled and he was very happy and proud. "Right me boys?"

Chapter Seven

I DON'T REMEMBER WHAT TIME I fell asleep, but was woken up at about three in the night, when James was groaning in pain, and he was saying something, but I couldn't understand...then I heard him.

"Nurse, Nurse." James was calling the nurse. I thought only a few days ago or was it yesterday you got us all in trouble for calling the nurse, and today you're doing again? You haven't learned? I used the bell near my head and rang for the nurse. The night duty nurse came.

"Yes, who rang the bell?" she asked.

"I rang the bell," I said, "The old man needs some help, I think." She went to old James, and I went back to sleep. Six in the morning, as usual, I got poked by the nurse for the blood pressure and blood glucose check. I have to open my eyes. Another day and I don't know what is in store for me. We shall wait and see. After breakfast, 'window man' was discharged.

"Thank you young man, Mathew." old man James said to me. "You have saved me once again." I thought okay I have to say something.

"Oh, no bother at all." I said smiling, "Anytime you need my help, just shout." Aha the thug in me is talking now. "How was your operation?" I said, "Are they releasing you today?"

"I don't know, the doctor will come later to talk with me," he replied, "but I hope they discharge me today." I too hoped to be discharged today, I thought, feeling good. Later someone was brought in on a trolley with his leg in the air; he was taken to the window side. So he became 'window man' or leg up', I thought. He was unconscious for some time, and when he came to, he looked around and he burst out laughing. I thought that was funny, how he can just start laughing?

"Hello. I am James, and this is Mathew." James did the introduction for both of us, even though, I hadn't chosen for him to be my spokesperson. Leg up window man said.

"I am Spiderman, ha ha ha." he was laughing loudly again. I looked at him; he was about forty, plump, thick, black moustache and black hair, big glasses. "That was a joke, you know what I mean? Ha ha ha, I'm Patrick." he said.

"What happened to your leg?" James said, "You slipped on the snow?"

"Coming from the pub, you know, drunk, fully loaded and I slipped in the fucking snow, you know what I mean?" he said, "Broke, me leg and me arm." He raised his left hand and it was in a cast as well, and he started laughing again. I thought this is going to be fun. Later on James's doctor passed to see him, and the nurse went in as well. The curtain was closed and they spent some time there. After they were gone, James was quiet for a long while.

"I am not being discharged today." he said at last, not sounding good. "They found some complication while doing my hip." Oh, I thought, here goes my freedom. "So I have to stay a few more days, they will do some more tests," James said, "to confirm what they suspect, is or is not." he sighed.

"What do they suspect?" leg up man asked, "Is it something serious?"

"They found there is a growth in my stomach." James said. "So they want to know, before they fix the hip bone."

"I hope nothing serious." Okay, now I felt sorry for him...why doesn't his family come and give him some company? He will be fine and he can be released, I am sure. I myself started to be scared: what will the doctors tell me about my leg? I started to think, if I am going to die, at twenty six years young. What have I got to lose? I don't usually like girl commitments, so I am not tied to anyone and therefore I am free, number one. And two, I have no children to worry about either.

And number three, I have no properties or any type of asset which I can call my own, even a pet. Ha ha. On the other side, there is only one living relative I can call my own, which is me Ma. Now, she will be fine, her sister will take care of her, but will she go to her sister's? She has been living on her own since she was married thirty seven years ago, for this I'd better be alive to take care of her. I thought, I don't listen to me Ma, I don't help her much, and I'm not the good son, she dreamed of, but that has to change. After I come out of the hospital alive, maybe I can try to change. Look, I am one week in the hospital now, no drinking, no smoking, and no any *'thingy majingy'* of any sort. So what will stop me after? Yeah, I can change and become a better man, I hope so.

Later on in the day, at about eleven in the morning, suddenly there appeared a girl from nowhere, and she peeked in the room, looking for someone, but I thought she might be lost, not only in the room, but to come in the hospital. She had very beautiful penetrating brown eyes, long brown hair with a golden touch, up to her shoulders, with a red hair band, small fashionable glasses, and red lipstick. She wore a red overcoat, and she wore red shoes.

She was thin and was about five feet six. She looked eighteen, and she was like a movie actress. She was beautiful to say the least, and I was lost for words. Behind her was another elegant lady of about sixty, and she wore a brown coat and brown shoes and brown hat, and she was about five feet four inches. I think she was an assistant to the movie star or her personal secretary. Then the girl noticed James, the old man in the middle bed, who was annoying me with nonstop chatter, and she went to him.

"Daddy, Oh daddy." she was singing, "Mommy look at my poor daddy." as she hugged him closely. The 'assistant', who was really her mommy, came and gave a peck on each cheek to James. Oh my God, if this is the daughter and wife, he has a beautiful daughter. She removed her overcoat, and inside she wore a skirt and blouse with a jacket, and she was very elegant. When she smiled, it was a very radiant smile, and I noticed her perfect white teeth. James was delighted and tears flowed down his cheeks, and the movie star was wiping his tears. And she closed the curtains, end of the movie for me. After a long while of talking among the three of them, I think then he remembered me, and 'hanging leg' near the window. He introduced us.

"This is Patrick, broke a few bones." They said hello to him and quickly he said in a funny way.

"Hi there, I'm Spiderman," and they chuckled. Then James turned towards me.

"And this is Mathew, my hero, the one I told you about." James as 'mummy' turned to look at me.

"Hello." Movie star coldly said as if she was forced.

"Hi" and I was frozen. I could not utter a word. Movie star had spoken to me, even though as I thought, they should have said more. After the acknowledgement, they quickly turned back to their patient, closed the curtains and continued in their little reunion. What about me, the real hero, already forgotten, ages ago.

But she had spoken to me, that's great, man, I feel good, ooh la la. I instantly felt I was in love, I have never felt this way before with any girl I was with, but she was young, she looked maybe she was eighteen. Oh, I thought, I can't wait for her to grow up. What, for my movie star? I can wait, she was the one, I am already a hero in her eyes, I saved and fought for her poor old man, in this wild and dangerous place, I am the thug and hero. Mother and daughter sat there talking with James for a while, and I overheard some sobbing and also some laughter.

Later on they left, and I was expecting my movie star would say something to me, but my expectation was in vain, she didn't even look at me, let alone say 'bye'. Both daughter and mother just walked out as if they wanted to get as far away as possible from this place. They were used to Hollywood red carpets and other places, not hospitals full of sick people wearing one piece hospital gowns.

After lunch, I fell asleep in this mid afternoon siesta, dreaming of the movie star, daughter of my 'friend' James. Now I am going to talk with him all he wants, and even if he wants to talk the whole night, I shall give up my sleep, no problem for my 'dear friend'. My God, I didn't think God made such beautiful creatures anymore. Oh I was so in love, or so I thought. I have to talk with Kevin and Ma; I have to tell them about the movie star, though I don't even know her name yet. I knew she was the one.

Oh, I thought Kevin and Ma and the rest, where are they? Ma always was asking me about marriage, she said she wanted a grandson or granddaughter, and now I'm going to give her one. I opened my eyes and looked over at my 'friend' James, not anymore as 'old man', but my as my 'dear friend, James'. He was awake, and I quickly smiled at him, checking if the friendliness is still there. He smiled back, that was good sign.

"James." I said after gathering my courage, "That's your wife and daughter?"

"Yes, sir," James said. "That is my lovely wife Clara and my beautiful daughter."

"It's good they came to see you," I said, "with all the snow, you know."

"Yes, my wife said it was dangerous driving." James said. "They nearly got into an accident; the car was slipping so often."

"They both looked cool, you know what I mean?" I said and quickly added, "Coming to see you in this snow and all, you know?" A long pause, I was trying to find words so I can connect to the father of the golden girl. "I say James," I said after a while, "you said you have a son and a daughter?"

"Yes, my son Bernard lives in the States with his wife and son, they live in Michigan." James replied, "And my daughter Iris, whom you have already met." Iris, that's her name, the movie star is Iris. What a beautiful name and it matches her, I thought. I noticed her eyes and those teeth, and my movie star is called a movie star's name, Iris.

"Your daughter," I said. Careful now, Mathew, I thought, "is still in school or something, you know what I mean?"

"Oh no," James said. "She finished her degree in International Business in Dublin City University two years ago." Oh, I thought, my dreaming has just been dashed. There is no use for me. That's the reason she ignored me. These people are high class and educated, while I am a low life, a criminal, a drug user. I've seen the inside of Mountjoy prison. Oh my dreams have been short lived. After a while I tried again.

"Oh, but she can't be that old." I said, "She seems very young, you know what I mean?"

"Oh no, I suppose she looks younger than what she actually is," James said. "But Iris is twenty four now." he continued, "She is a good daughter." I thought I have to try to change direction before he becomes suspicious.

"What about you James." I said, "You're retired or something?"

"Oh no, I am a bank manager in Rathmines." he replied. "Why, do I look that old? Or is it because my daughter is so young?"

"Aah…no……" I was lost for words. "No…I mean…."

"I married late I suppose, and we did not have children right away." James said. "Also, the gap between Bernard and Iris was long, about twelve years, I think." I thought okay, for today, this is enough, don't push it. In the afternoon, it snowed real heavy like, and we sat near the window and watched the snow. It was beautiful to see and admire while sitting in a warm room, but for the people outside there, especially the ones who have to drive around, and for those who have to catch the buses or trains and for those pedestrians, it was tough for them all.

I have been here in the hospital awhile now, and I am losing count of the days. I am inside this prison, and will I count this as one of my stints in prison? I have no idea or no news about my Ma, or Kevin and the lads. It is good in a way, I have to concentrate on my health, no worries about anyone but me, and otherwise maybe I could not cope. Sometimes I sit and try to figure out which uniform of the staff is who and what are their jobs and qualifications. I sit and think it's nice to be educated and be a professional, going to work in the morning and coming back in the evening, instead of the way I am leading my life, waiting for an opportunity to rob, to steal and to burgle a house.

Oh, what I wish for sometimes. I wish my Da was alive, then maybe all my brothers would be alive and all of us his sons would be educated and have good jobs. Maybe we would all be married by now, and have a few grandchildren running around Ma and Da, maybe we could have bought a house somewhere nice and moved from the inner city. Yeah I could have bought a house in the countryside, with a big garden and space for my kids to grow up and get fresh air. Oh dreams, dreams and dreams.

They wheeled James out in the afternoon to be screened and run some tests for his suspected growth, and when he came back he was in low spirits. Later his family rang and spoke with him for long and afterwards he remained quiet. I decided to break the mood.

"Hey James," I said. "What's the story?" I caught him daydreaming.

"Oh, I beg your pardon?" he said.

"Are you alright now?" I said, "You seem lost or something, you know what I mean?"

"Do you like reading Mathew?" he asked me, now he caught me off guard. "I mean books, novels, newspapers, anything, do you enjoy reading?"

"No, I don't read much." I said, "Too busy, you know what I mean?" Myself, I didn't know what I meant but anyway even then, 'busy', busy doing what?

"I asked my wife, if I am going to be staying long in the hospital." James said. "I might as well be reading, to keep abreast with the financial markets and the news of the world, don't you think so?"

"Yeah, yeah, I know what you mean." I replied. "Might as well, you know? Is your daughter coming tomorrow?" I said, and added quickly. "And your wife as well, will they come to visit you? James, you worry a lot." I said. "You'll be alright."

"I know....I know." he said, "We both worry a lot, you and me, don't you think so?"

"Mathew, what would you like to read?" James said, "I will tell Clara, my wife to bring something over for you." And he continued, "What is your interest?" Now, that is something I never thought about. I do not read and I don't like reading. But I am here trying to impress my 'future father in law', I chuckled, how does that sound, 'father in law', ha ha ha, I have to try to say the right things, here.

"Ah, anything is fine, you know, newspapers, sports pages, you know?" I got it, sports pages; at least I can see the pictures only. "I love sports." Now, why I didn't think of that before? When my Da was working in Manchester, he used to bring us the team's jerseys, and we boys and everyone in the family used to and still support Manchester United Football team, and occasionally I do buy the Manchester United jersey and above all, James is from England, yahoo, I got it now. I thought, now we have something to talk about, besides the movie star and her assistant. "James." I said, "Which team do you support?" I continued, now brave and bold. "In the UK, you know?"

"Oh, I just cheer for whichever team wins," James said. "But I suppose I should support Arsenal, as I am from London and Arsenal is a London team." He paused and suddenly. "What about you, Mathew?" James said "Or is it Chelsea?"

"Chelsea? Oh no, but from the English Premier League," I said, correcting myself, "I support Manchester United."

"Is it for any particular reason," James asked me again, "that you should support Manchester United?"

"Me Da used to work in Manchester and so we all support Man U." I said, and continued, "Also seen the team and how they play," I then quickly added, "In the big screen in the pub."

"Have you been in Manchester to watch them play?" James asked and I thought what have I got myself into once again? But before I replied I was saved by the nurse who came into the room.

Chapter Eight

"*H*OW ARE MY FAVOURITE PATIENTS?" She addressed both of us. I felt good for the praise and she asked politely if she could take my blood pressure and glucose reading, as well as from James. Late at night, a doctor on duty came with the night nurse and the doctor told me that the Consultant Oncologist, Dr. Livingstone, had directed that I should be prepared for the operating theatre tomorrow once again.

"Dr. Livingstone needs to check on your leg and the wound before he makes his big decision," said the nurse. So that was the routine which now I already was familiar with, the doctor discussed with me and after a few questions I signed the consent forms. The night duty nurse woke me at six in the morning.

"Can you walk?" she asked me.

"Yeah …..Why?" I replied with a question of my own.

"Then go to the toilet," she said. "And take a minimal wash ready for your surgery." and off she went on her way. I struggled to my feet, pulled myself up and carried the mini vacuum machine with me, took my crutches and walked to the toilets. Even though the toilets were about fifty metres from my room, for me it was like a journey to the moon and back. Every few steps I had to stop and rest and cover myself properly in my one piece cloth.

I managed to go and came back as fresh, as I possibly could and ready for action. No breakfast for me this morning but I was given some tablets, as well as a few sips of water to wash down the tablets. The day nurse was someone I didn't see before; she came and checked the usual, she seemed nice. I read her name tag, Caroline 'the smiling one'.

"Is everything okay?" I asked and quickly added, "The sugar and the pressure?"

"Mhmmm…Yeah." she replied smiling, "Are you nervous?"

"I think so," I replied, "not sure anymore, you know what I mean?"

"You'll be fine." she smiled, "Be brave and you'll be alright." I waited for my destiny. At about nine, the operation theatre attendants arrived, and Caroline the day nurse accompanied me and the green file and we went through the now familiar corridors and lift. When we reached the trolley parking bay they handed me over and Caroline the smiling one.

"Be brave, now," she encouraged me with a smile. "See you later in the ward."

"Thanks Caroline." I said, "I need all the moral support I can get." She smiled and went away. I thought, in every place there are the good ones and the bad ones, that is the way of life, I suppose. A woman doctor came over.

"Hi, Mathew…is it?" She said whilst reading from the green file. "I am the anaesthetic doctor." She then asked me the now routine questions and then she took my arm. "I am going to give you …now….a general anaesthetic……okay?"

"Okay doctor," I agreed, "let's do it." I don't remember anything after that. It was three in the afternoon when I started to come to. I heard voices from the next bed…was it James's bed? Yeah I think so, but the curtains were drawn, so I couldn't see who was there but the voices, yeah it has to be my movie star, it had to be Iris, but I was too weak, and I fell asleep once again.

I became fully awake at five in the afternoon and turned to James. "How's your family?" I said, "Did they visit you today?"

"Oh no, my wife and daughter did not come over." James replied. "The road conditions are very horrible today but we spoke on the phone." And he continued, "How are you feeling Mathew?" and a pause the, "How was your operation?"

"I am okay, now, I suppose." I said. "About the operation, I don't know until the doctor comes, you know what I mean? How's the guy next to your bed?" I asked James. "Is he done yet?"

"Oh, he is already discharged." James replied, "And a new one has come."

"He started talking yet?" I asked.

"No, I think he is still unconscious." James replied.

"Your wife," I started, "did she saw if anything is happening outside, I mean like the snow or anything?" I asked, deciding on the safer bet of mentioning the wife and not the daughter. I have to be careful now, you know? Forgetting I already asked exactly this question just now, but he answered me.

"Oh the snow is still falling." James mentioned while adjusting his glasses. "And the driving conditions have not improved either." One of the nurses came with the phone from their office.

"You have a call, Mathew." She said to me and I was still surprised of who might be calling me here in the hospital, but she gave me the phone.

"Have you heard about Kevin?" the caller asked me and it was a male voice. "Well Kevin has been caught by the Gardai`."

"When, How?" I said worriedly, "What happened?" my heart beating fast as my thoughts kept running.

"Listen Mathew, don't mention my name, you know what I'm saying?" he told me. "Maybe the Gardai are listening to this line."

"What's happening, I don't understand, why shouldn't I mention your name, why would the Gardai listen to the hospital phone line? I'm confused man."

"He was after robbing the post office, you know?" the caller told me. "But the Gardai` were waiting for us, you know what I'm saying?" He went on, "Like someone snitched, you know?"

"When did this happen?" I said my while my heart was racing. "No one told me anything."

"Yeah, yeah, I know." he replied, "You are in the hospital waiting for some big operation, you know." and he went on, "Just the next day after you were admitted in the hospital." Oh that's why, I haven't seen or heard from Kevin but wait, the next day after I was admitted to the hospital? That means Kevin and the lads were planning this job for some time? They didn't tell me about the date, oh maybe to protect me or maybe, ah I don't know what to think anymore, man. But Kevin had mentioned to me about this big job he was after planning.

"So what happened to the other lads?" I asked, "You're free; the Gardai` didn't catch you?" I thought or are you the snitch?

"Kevin and two lads were caught and me and one lad were in another car the Gardai` are looking for us, you know what I mean?"

"So where are you now?" I asked and he replied, "Out of the country, Spain."

"Spain?" I said, amazed, "You are calling me from Spain, now?" I have never been out of Ireland so far in my life. "So what'll happen to them?" I asked him.

"Oh, I don't know." he said, "They were caught with guns, you know what I'm saying? Shots were fired." he said.

"What are you saying man?" I nearly shouted, "Shots fired by who, I don't understand, is Kevin alright?" I was more worried about my hero.

"The Gardai are waiting for us, I tell you." he said, "It's a trap; you know what I'm saying? Someone ratted on us and that's for sure."

"One Garda was shot," he continued, "Not seriously, but in the arm." Oh my God, this is something I was not prepared for.

"And the Gardai fired at us, man, like the movies, I tell ya." he said calmly, as if he was the hero now. "That's when me and the lad we make our escape, you know what I mean?"

"Did any of the lads or Kevin get shot by the Gardai? I asked, fearing the worst and worried for Kevin.

"Yeah, Kevin got hit in the stomach and one lad got hit in the leg, you know what I'm saying?"

"Are they both alright?" I asked, everything going in my head so fast. "Are they okay?"

"Yeah, that's how they got caught, I tell ya, like in the movies."

"What about me Ma." I said changing from Kevin to my Ma, "You know anything about her?"

"No Mathew, I've been hiding since, man I'm on the run." he said, "You want me to check on her, Mathew? I can call someone to check on her."

"Yeah, you'll do that for me?" I asked him, "Tell her I'm asking after her, you know what I mean? But don't ever tell her about Kevin or about the lads, you know what I mean?"

"Ok, Mathew, I've got to go now." he said, "Will call you some other time."

"Bye." I said. "Bye now."

"Bye." he said and the phone got disconnected. I sat there thinking, only the next day after I'm being admitted in the hospital and Kevin and the lads have been caught by the Gardai`, in the act red handed and shots having been exchanged, this is bad, I thought. This is my luck or what? So what will the Gardai` do, maybe they'll want information about the past robberies? I have committed some crimes big and small but I haven't killed anyone, and no rapes either, and that is something we don't do ever.

What about all the members from Kevin's gang? Will Kevin tell about me? I hope he'll keep his mouth shut, or else. I thought or else I'll do what? Mister one leg, I'll hop and hop till I catch him? Now I have something to worry about and it will keep my mind busy enough. Will the Gardai come to arrest me? What will this do to me Ma? Oh God.

A few more days passed with the physiotherapist, and we were going a longer distance every time and now with two crutches. I could now walk slowly with the aid of the two crutches and was painfully and slowly walking to the toilets on my own. Painfully but also reaching my destination somehow and also to the window to watch the snow fall, it was beautiful watching from the inside but one could feel the chill.

I was on my bed resting when Iris, the movie star, no, 'my' movie star, came in the room and this time without her 'assistant', meaning her mom. She was beautiful and she wasn't from this world. She walked into the room, oh no, she didn't walk she floated into the room.

As she entered the room, she did not acknowledge me at all. She just passed a glance at where I was on my bed with my 'one piece'. She looked around and went to her father's bed, she did not see him on the bed, she looked worried and then she was walking out, maybe to go to the nurses and I thought this is my chance, it was now or never to be.

I quickly said. "Hi Iris," she looked shocked, how this did stranger know her name? "You're looking for James, your dad?" Iris looked at me amazed, I thought I have to be brave now, this is going to be tough and I'm not used to seducing the girls, oh my God I'm actually shy with girls, would anyone believe me? "He just went in the toilet," I said, "he'll just be back in a few minutes."

Iris my movie star looked at me. Oh my God, those eyes, so beautiful and full of romance and she just nodded but she was still going to go out of the room. I had to continue and fast.

"You can sit and wait for him," I said, "he won't be long, now." But I knew it would be long he was taken to the operation theatre, but if I tell her the truth, she will go and wait somewhere else and I needed her here to try to interest her, to try to make her notice me and to see me as a normal person with brains, you know? "Iris, you can pull up that chair," I said, "and sit here." I motioned an empty space near my bed.

Thankfully she saw the chair near the window and went to sit there, oh God, she sat far away from me, but still in the same room and she did listen to me on my suggestion, my hopes have been raised. She sat there and was looking outside watching the snow and trees.

And then the new 'window man' said to her, "Hi love, are you alright?" and she was brought back to life. "You seem lost or something, love?" She did not respond. I turned and looked at 'window man' whom I just noticed. Oh yeah, he looked rough and with a heavy voice. I immediately didn't like him, he was pestering my movie star but then it was better him than if it was a young hunk like the rugby player, then my chances would be slim or zero.

"Hey love, give me a glass of water." window man growled. "The jug and glass of water are over there, love." I thought, should I go over and punch him? He is pestering my movie star. She stood up walked outside of the room. I thought you see, she is gone now, you window man fool of a gorilla, you've spoiled my chance. But then I was surprised when Iris walked back in the room and there was a nurse behind her and Iris pointed to the 'gorilla' window man.

"That one over there," she told the nurse, "he's asking for drinking water." Then Iris went back to the chair she was sitting on but her next move was unexpected. She pulled the chair across the room and brought it to the place I had pointed to, and she sat down and more of the unexpected. Iris then smiled at me, I smiled back, she giggled and we understood each other it was because of window man 'gorilla'.

Thank God I said in my heart, actually the 'gorilla' helped me in my mission. Now for the next step, what should I say so as to keep her here and occupied? Not to bore her otherwise she might run away.

"How's your mum?" I said "You didn't come with her today?"

"Oh she is fine." she replied in a voice of the best among singers, she is not only a movie star but a singer as well. "She did not feel like coming over to see dad, today."

Alright I thought, now we have started to converse. I have to continue with my efforts but I have to be careful, she is a graduate and professional while I was a school leaver and a loitering guy, so the talk should be somewhat intelligent.

"She is a fine lady," I said and quickly added. "Your mum, you know."

"Yeah, she is a good mother to me and a good wife to my dad." she said with a faint smile on her lips. "They have been together long and they understand each other," and she continued. "I mean they cannot do without each other."

"How about yourself, Iris," I gathered my courage and asked her. "I understood from your dad that you are working in an office somewhere?" She looked at her watch, a bad sign for me.

"Yeah, I work in real estate, in a company in the city centre." She said, "And actually I am coming from the office now."

"Okay, is the office okay with you being late to go back and all?" I asked her again.

"Oh yeah, I am not going back for the day." she answered, and added. "And most of the time I take prospective clients to houses, apartments and offices, just to show them and make them interested." And she looked at me. "What is your name again? I know Dad told me the other day but I have forgotten. And what do you do yourself" she asked me.

Chapter Nine

"OH COME ON NOW," I said with a look of surprise on my face. "I'm Mathew." As if Iris should have known my name.

"Okay Mathew." she said and then asked me, "What do you do yourself?"

"Oh I'm just doing odd jobs, you know." I replied while trying to find the right words. My face was changing colour as I continued to lie and impress my movie star. "Odd jobs here and there, you know what I mean?" Thank God she did not want to push it or maybe she noticed my face and sensed the lies and the discomfort I was in, but she changed tactic.

"What is wrong with you?" she said, "You have been here quite long in the hospital." I thought, even though I didn't want to discuss about my disease it was far safer a topic than about my life outside the hospital.

"I know. What can I do?" I said, "I have some minor problem in my leg, cancer it is."

"Oh my God." she said while reaching to touch my hand. "I am so sorry Mathew, I did not know." Oh the touch was magic; I thought keep your hand where it is while in my heart I was praying that James wouldn't come back soon.

"Ah, it's alright, you know......." I said, but she interrupted me.

"I am truly sorry for asking you." Iris said. "Maybe you don't like talking about this." In my heart I said Oh no, with you I love to talk about anything but my life outside.

"Oh, it's alright." I replied. "Here the doctors are brilliant you know they are trying their best to save my life and also my leg."

"I know the doctors are fantastic." she said with her 'fantastic' beautifully said with a smile. "They are doing a fine job with my Dad as well." She again looked at her watch and I decided to tell her the truth about her dad. I had better admit early before I spoil everything.

"Iris, I lied to you about your dad." I said, and she looked at me with shock in her eyes. "Actually he's not gone to the toilet but he has been taken for some sort of operation, you know?"

"Oh, I thought so." she said, and added, "And why you had to lie to me if I may ask?" She frowned.

"Oh, I'm sorry," I said, "I just wanted the chance to talk to you." and I continued, "You see, every time you come in here, you just go and talk to your dad and after that you just go out. You don't say anything to me at all."

"Yeah, but there was no need to talk to you, was there?" she asked me in annoyance. "I come and see my dad and go away, I do not have to go and start to speak with every patient in the hospital." She seemed annoyed. I had to save the ship before it sank, I had to think fast.

"Yeah, but still, I am in the same room with your dad and we are friends." I managed to say and added, "Also I'm his hero and protector. You know what I mean?" I smiled.

"Okay, now I understand." she said, "I am sorry; I mean....... it did not click me that way but you are right. You might be his friend but not his protector, right?" And she added, "But coming back to the issue." she said, "You did not have to lie to me." She went on. "Oh and by the way, did you bribe that patient over there to be mean to me so that I move my chair next to you?" She said this while laughing and I saw her beautiful white teeth in that smile.

Oh my God, please dear God, I know I don't pray, but please dear God help me with this beauty here. I think I'm in love, but do I know what love is? And something came out of my mouth unplanned, without my permission.

"Iris, I like you." I blurted out and I waited. Is she going to storm out of the room, is she going to throw a tantrum or will she slap me like in the movies. What you have done now Mathew, I told myself, this is wrong. In the movies first they become friends and then the male asks the lady out for dinner and then in the candlelight and soft music while they dance maybe or while they eat and then only, he asks her to marry him, he brings a diamond ring and he proposes and she accepts but sometimes she slaps him in the face.

And yet look at me, on the hospital bed and unshaven all these days. Smelling of blood and hospital and the first time I talk to her and I tell her 'I like her'. Am I mad or what. I must be the best fool there is, if I tell my Ma or Kevin or the lads they will laugh at me and call me a crazy fool. She stopped laughing.

"What do you mean 'you like me' I do not understand, Mathew." she said in serious tone. "Can you please…. explain to me?"

"Iris, please don't …..Take it….. Wrongly," I pleaded, "I mean…….I like you very much………you know what I mean?"

"No, I do not understand what you mean, please explain. This is becoming interesting." She replied with disappointment in her voice. Okay now Mathew, your death has arrived. If this girl had a gun, she would shoot me now and if her dad comes to hear of this he'll chase me with my one leg through the corridors of the hospital.

"Iris, the first time only when I saw you, I really liked you, you know what I mean?" I said pleading. "You're very beautiful, Iris." Courage man, have courage. "Your eyes, your smile, Iris, I really like you."

"Listen, you do not have a girlfriend out there?" she said, "You know what? I do not have time for this, Mathew. You lied to me and I still sat with you. Of course I know my father has gone for operation today, what do you think I am a fool?" She continued, "And I said to myself, okay this guy is lonely, nobody comes to visit him and maybe he feels like talking, and fine I will pass my time and talk to him. Now it does not mean okay now I love this guy. No mister Romeo, I do not have time for men or boys I love my career and I love my life."

"Iris, please listen to me, I…..I…..I really like and love you. I want to marry you one day, it's not that I just want to have a good time with you but I really want you to marry me. Please Iris believe me, I'm not messing with you please." Iris put both hands up palms facing towards me, her facial features tight and she turned red with anger. I tried to speak but was dumbstruck, looking at her, she was going to cry. "I'm sorry Iris," I said, "I'm such a fool to annoy you."

"Ha ha ha … sorry love, the guy's a loser." the window man 'gorilla' said loudly from his side. "He's not your type, love." I felt like standing up and going to bash the gorilla on the face. And at that moment, my movie star Iris stormed out of the room and that was the end of my Hollywood movie story. I sat there and actually felt the need to cry, for I have lost her forever, I have lost my love even before it started. "Hey lad……" the gorilla man started with me.

"Can you shut your fucking mouth?" I said angrily at him. "You annoy me, you annoyed her and you annoy everybody."

"But I thought I was only……." Gorilla man started to defend himself.

"I don't fucking care what you thought." I shouted back at him. "Just close your fucking mouth!" Oh I hate this man. Please doctors release him before I strangle him in his sleep. Later on, James was brought back, still unconscious. He was left on his bed in the middle. Iris came in and she didn't even look at me I managed to throw a quick glance at her but she didn't notice. She went in and closed the curtain and sat with her Dad.

Then I heard her talking on the phone, maybe with her mother and informing her of the current state of her dad. And when he got to his senses, James started talking and they kept whispering. I was trying to overhear what they were talking about in fear she might report me to her father. I was scared of what he might do, does he own a gun? Oh my God, what have I put myself into? After a long while my movie star Iris left and she didn't even turn to look at me, she didn't even say bye.

"Hey James," I called out just to taste the mood, "you feeling better, now?"

"Yeah, yeah." he replied.

"Your daughter has been here waiting for you long time, you know?" I'm trying to be investigative. "Your wife didn't come, is she alright?"

"Yeah, my wife is okay, I spoke with her and she is fine." James said. "And yourself Mathew, are you okay?" We continued a while then I left him to relax and thank God the gorilla didn't say anything about the episode between me and Iris. Next day I woke up and I was dreading the arrival of my movie star, I didn't fancy looking her in the eyes and seeing the hatred in those beautiful enchanting eyes. I decided that if I hear her coming I will pretend to be asleep so as not to be ashamed.

After breakfast we spoke, me and James for a while and then 'gorilla' was taken to the operating theatre. I then heard the footsteps, two pairs walking like on a catwalk. Models as they are, and when they came in the room the smell of her perfume hit me and it was beautiful. As she and her mother walked in, I closed my eyes pretending to be asleep. If the mother has been told and knows the story, now I'll have more enemies.

They went in and didn't close the curtain and after the hugging and kissing they just sat and were talking about this and that. I felt if I had played my cards right I would have been in that family photo of four, dreams again. I felt like I have to pass water, I should have gone before Iris and her mom came and I have held it for too long now. I cannot hold it any longer and the toilets are far for me fifty meters it is.

So I got out of the bed slowly and stood up, I carried my mini vacuum machine across my shoulders and I put on my slippers, then I took my two crutches. My hands being full, I started to walk out of the room to go to the toilet. Before I reached the door to turn left towards the toilets, I heard a loud giggle and I turned to see what was wrong or what the hilarious thing was.

My eyes met Iris's eyes and she burst out laughing. I was shocked, what have I done to make her laugh like that? She continued laughing and I thought, well everything is good again, my eyes had met hers and she has realized my love and she is happy now and I joined her in laughter, all happy family again. Clara looked at her daughter trying to know what made her laugh so much, and James was not sure either, and then Iris pointed at me and burst out laughing again.

"Mathew, cover yourself behind, your bum is showing." James calmly told me. Oh my God, I felt like melting and disappearing. I felt like flying away like superman. I quickly held my damned one piece hospital gown together from behind and walked briskly away in more pain but what could I do, for I've just performed a 'free view' movie for all to see and I've made a fool of myself again. This fucking one piece hospital gown, I did hate it from the moment I set my eyes on it and today it has performed its worst performance. I hate it a million times.

After I finished my business in the toilet, I did not want to come out and face Iris, no way man I'd rather stay in the toilet and get all the smell but I will not go out to face her, my movie star. I laughed with you and I thought we were laughing together. I didn't realize you were laughing at me. You saw my bum in a 'free view' movie and you laughed at me, what more can I expect? Dear God please save me from this situation and I'm so embarrassed now.

After a long while I had to go back to my bed. I could not sit in the toilet for too long and I couldn't stand in the corridor for too long. The leg was not good, so I had to go back and face the movie star and her assistant. Okay I commanded myself, straight face now, enter the room and I entered the room not looking at anybody and went straight on my bed. I felt the three pairs of eyes looking at me but I struggled and got on my bed, sat with my legs straight, covered myself and pretended to be busy.

I heard the chuckle, I think this was from Iris but I didn't look up. She was forcing herself to keep down her pressure; I could feel the tension, if my eyes meet hers then she will definitely burst out laughing again.

They sat and talked for a while; I covered my face pretending to be asleep. Then it was their time to leave, they hugged and kissed James and they walked slowly out, nobody spoke with me and my movie star just walked, but I was relieved somehow, after I made an idiot of myself un-intentionally.

Chapter Ten

LATER ON JAMES LOOKED AT me. "Mathew my boy." he said, "Are you alright, you do not look too well." How can I feel well when I was a laughing stock a while ago?

"Oh, I'm fine," I said, "Just feeling the pain in my leg." And he looked at me while he adjusted his glasses.

"Mathew, I am sorry......." James started to say. I cut him off.

"James. What for are you sorry?" I asked.

"Oh, it is for my daughter, Iris." James said. "Her behaviour was not pleasant and ...." I cut him off again.

"It was my mistake James," I said "I shouldn't have exposed myself."

"No no, Mathew," now he cut me off. "We are both in the hospital and we have to wear these gowns and the way they made them it leaves us exposed, so it is not your fault at all, Mathew."

"I know, James." I said, "But I feel embarrassed by the situation, you know what I mean?"

"Don't be my son." James 'my friend' said, and I had to turn and look at him. He addressed me as 'his son'? Did I hear correctly? Oh my God, I thought maybe my movie star has spoken to her parents, or just to her father and maybe he knows the story and if he addressed me as 'his son', that might be an acceptance from him. Oh my God, I am so happy; I want to shout to the whole wide world, 'I am so happy'. My movie star has accepted me as I am, and she has told her father and he also accepted me. Wow, come on doctors and release me from this damned hospital, I have to go to my love.

"James." I started, "Did your daughter talk to you?"

"Of course Mathew," James replied, and added. "My daughter spoke to me, why are you asking?" Oh yes, oh YES, he said my movie star has spoken to him about me, about us, wow! I'm so happy, he knows and he said yes, and he accepted me as his son, son-in-law to be precise. Thank God, I love you God, wherever you are, I love you dear God. I was in cloud nine deep in my thoughts when my 'father in law' James said.

"She is my daughter you know, and we speak all the time. What did you have in mind, Mathew?"

"No no, everything is cool, James." I said, "I thought maybe she spoke to you about some particular thing or subject, you know what I mean?"

"I don't get you Mathew." James replied, "Maybe you can tell me about what issue you refer to?"

"Aw no, it's alright James." I said, "No bother." I became quiet. Somehow my dreams have just been shattered. It's not what I had thought; I am just a fantasist, living in la-la land. My movie star has not spoken to her father about us and she has ignored me and pushed me aside from her thoughts, she said her job or career is more important than men, or did she refer to me as nothing, as an idiot. Maybe her parents are looking for somebody well educated and wealthy for their daughter, somebody like a doctor or lawyer or something else, what, maybe an engineer, I don't know.

My dreams are just dreams and there is nothing to it. I should just wait until I know about my cancer and what the doctors are planning to do with my leg. After that when I come home from the hospital, I could go back to my estate and look for me ma, and live the life I had before. I'm no good with these wealthy, educated people. I should just look for somebody from my street and estate only, people who will accept me as I am, no questions asked about my degree or profession or anything.

Oh but I think I love my movie star, I'm twenty six now and throughout my life I had many my girls, but I didn't feel like I feel now for Iris, my movie star. All the girls in my life were just for fun. I had fun and they had fun, no commitments, no love story, nobody telling the other 'I love you', none at all, even 'I like you' was not said often. At the most it was 'you're beautiful' and some small talk.

But the moment I saw Iris, my movie star, I knew it. I knew this was not like the normal ones, I knew it wasn't for sex and I knew she was not a one night stand type. I felt deep in my heart, I knew that I would like to spend the rest of my life with her. I knew she is the one, the only one in my life. I love her eyes, I love her smile with the perfect white teeth, oh my God, just thinking about her I want to cry and shout why am I being denied? Why am I being denied my one true love? For the first time I fall in love, she has taken me as an idiot and she laughed at the 'free view' of my bum.

How can I make her understand that I can change, I can try to be in her social class and I'm ready to change my lifestyle? Please God, I will learn to pray, I will try to come to your church and learn to say prayers and Mass, and I will also be a good citizen. The whole night I couldn't get sleep, I was in deep thoughts and I then remembered my Da, and wondered where is me ma and whatever happened to her? I have to find a way to get in touch with her and maybe she can advise me. But I already know what she might say.

"Forget her, she's not in your class, find your own kind, love." That's what she'll say to me. In the morning after breakfast, the doctors checked James and they came to talk with him, they sat down. Three doctors and two nurses, they closed the curtains and they spoke in low voices, I could not hear anything because I did not want to know, I think I'm learning some manners now, wow I'm changing and that's great. After a while the curtains were opened and the doctors and nurses went away, I looked at my friend James, but he was far away in thoughts so I left him alone till he was ready to talk.

"Mathew." James said all of a sudden calling me, "Are you awake?"

"Hey James," I said, "What's the story?" James looked at me for a while before removing his glasses and wiping them with a piece of cloth. He blew into the glass and he wiped again, then he put the glasses on and adjusted them, squinted and looked at me again.

"Tomorrow the doctors shall take me into the operation theatre, they will check on my hip bone." he said, and continued. "And once the doctors make sure everything is okay with me, I shall be discharged the day after."

"That's great news James." I said, "You're going home." But deep inside I knew it was not great news for me because for now while he is here, at least my movie star comes and visit her father. Even if I'm in her black book, once he's gone, then bye-bye for me and my movie star will be gone forever.

"The doctors told me if they find anything wrong in the results of the tests taken," James said, "Then they will call me to be admitted again." That was why the doctors came to discuss with him and that's the reason he seemed worried.

"Listen James, you're going to be alright, you know what I mean?" I said and continued. "You're young enough, and you look healthy and you'll be fine. You have a nice family and they will take care of you, you know what I mean?" I told him about him, being young and healthy just to please him. I didn't have much to say anyway, he is not going to be my 'father in law' anymore or whatever. I should just be nice to him anyway since he is a good and decent man.

"I beg your pardon young man." he said laughing out loudly, "I am young enough and I look healthy? Ha ha haa! I have to tell this to Clara, my wife. She thinks I am old now, and she keeps pestering me to retire from my work, and here is Mathew, who is not so young himself and praising me, I wonder." James was happy and started to laugh again. I was happy for him, at least I made him laugh and if he is going to tell Clara the wife, definitely Iris the daughter will also be told. So even if she has 'dumped' me but she will remember me, aha, the 'free view' she got of my bum made her laugh.

Okay dear, remember me always. I thought, maybe just maybe, when I come out of the hospital, and they don't chop off my leg, I can dress up nicely, in the best, yeah I can buy me a nice shirt and a tie, then I can pass at her office - 'accidentally' of course - and she'll remember my bum, and I can try for a date or something. That way she will see me in different way than the one piece hospital shit.

Oh yeah, I can buy her flowers. I saw in the movies the hero buys a bunch of flowers and takes them to the lady. Someone also once told me that ladies like flowers so much that even if they are angry, give a girl flowers and everything will be forgiven and forgotten. I have a lot to learn about manners and ways of life of the other class, the wealthy people. Later on only Clara the wife of James and the 'assistant' of my movie star came alone to see James and as usual she didn't even look at my side. She went to James's bed, closed the curtains and I heard the greetings, and they sat talking in whispers and they laughed sometimes and other times I didn't hear anything. I had the urge to ask Clara about Iris, how is she, why she didn't come today? And ask her everything else, but I thought I might rock the boat even more dangerously than it is now, so I kept quiet.

My brain was working: if James is going to go home, then Iris will not set her foot in this hospital ever again, but I can pretend and exchange contact with James, and maybe, by the slimmest of a chance in the world, she might hear from her dad something about me or I might ask about Iris once in awhile pretending to inquire about James's health. Or maybe when I call she might pick up her father's phone... then I can hear her voice. That will be enough for me to keep going. Ah me and my silly dreams, why don't I just forget about her and find my own type? And what is 'my own' type? All human beings are all equal, we are all the same, no discrimination, no class, no difference of colour or skin or religion.

Yeah I demand my rights to be treated equally by you Iris, and your dad and mom. Then I heard Clara saying her goodbyes to James and she opened the curtains, and was walking past my bed. I opened my mouth.

"Excuse me Cl........." I just started saying something. Clara turned and looked at me with very sharp and penetrating eyes. I couldn't complete my sentence which in the first place I did not intend to start with. I quickly turned and pretended like I was looking for something under my bed and talking to myself. Yeah I am a fool and an idiot, I accept, thank you. Later on I spoke.

"Hey James," I said to my 'dear friend' James, "your daughter didn't come today?"

"Oh yeah, she could not come unfortunately." James replied, "She was busy at work, new clients and all."

"And how's your wife?" I said, "She could come alone?"

"Yeah, she has her own car and she drives." James said. "And besides, the roads are much better now. Dublin Corporation are spreading the salt on every road...they are efficient, you know. They have a bunch of hard working people." James was taken early morning the next day to the operating theatre, and he did not come back until nearly one o'clock in the afternoon. His wife came at exactly the time he was being brought back from the operating theatre and she walked with the assistants pushing the trolley, maybe she had been waiting outside the theatre.

Once James was parked in his middle spot, the assistants and nurses left, Clara closed the curtains and she sat with her husband. I heard her talking on the phone, I think it was with Iris; maybe she was giving her updates on James's condition. James slowly awoke at around two thirty, and about four he was fully awake and talking sensible with the wife, they spoke and I heard James talking on the phone, I assumed it was with Iris. Later on Clara left, as usual without a glance at me.

"Hey James," I called to him, "are you fully awake now?"

"Yeah, I am fine," James replied, "I am fully awake."

"What's the story?" I asked, wanting the latest, "Your operation went successfully?"

"Oh yeah, I presume so, unless the doctors says otherwise." James said, "How do you do yourself?"

"I'm fine, was just worried about your operation." I said, "You know what I mean?" and the small talk went on and on. I thought it was good just to establish myself as his friend, so when the time comes to ask for his contacts he will understand the 'friendship' between me and him. Deep, you know.

"So tomorrow you'll be released, eh James?" I said. "That is good for you, to go home."

"Yeah, tomorrow I shall be discharged hopefully." James said. "I just cannot wait till tomorrow."

"You know what time?" I said, and quickly added. "They'll release you from the hospital?" I thought about me and my 'release'. He says 'discharge', I say 'release'.

"Oh, I think sometime in the morning, maybe after breakfast." James said. "The doctor will come later on to talk with me and then I will know for definite."

Chapter Eleven

OKAY NOW OR NEVER TO be had another chance, he might be released early morning or his wife might come then I cannot talk to him, so it has to be tonight, actually now.

"James, you know we stayed quite a long time together in this hospital and…" I started.

"Oh yeah, it was good, was it not so?" He interrupted my flow. I had to change tactics and direction.

"We've been good friends, right?" I said, "You and me, you know?" and quickly added, before he could cut my flow again, "you're going home tomorrow and for me I'll still be here for maybe sometime, you know?" and I continued, "I thought maybe you can give me your contact number and you can take the number of the ward reception, as I don't have any mobile with me and we can keep in touch, you know what I mean?" I completed my sentence and my flow of the plan. Now let's see if it will work or not, the bait has been set let's see about the fish now, Oh God, Oh dear God.

"Yeah, actually that might be a good idea." he said while smiling. "I shall take the number for here from the nurse and I will write mine for you. Yeah, alright, we stayed together for quite a while," James said. "How long was it? A week or maybe it was two weeks? I honestly lost count myself." he was smiling, happy and I thought, does he suspect something or he's just happy I seem to be concerned about him? Well I'll never know. He rang the bell and the night nurse came, it was Caroline the smiling nurse who came in.

"Hello my favourite patients." she said, "How have my patients been all the while?"

"Hi nurse." James said and smiling.

"Hi nurse, Caroline, isn't it?" I also said.

"Wow, you remembered my name." Caroline said smiling. "Now, what can I do for you?" James explained to the nurse, how we've been together in the hospital, and that we formed a bond of friendship and he said nice things about me. It made me proud and I actually felt good.

"Mathew here is a real gentleman." James said to the nurse Caroline. "What I would like from you if you do not mind, that is," and he continued, "please write for me your telephone number for this ward and get me a paper where I can write my contact number to give to Mathew, here." Caroline understood and said she did not mind at all and she replied she'd be happy to do that, and with a smile she went. Then she came back with two pieces of paper and she gave both to James.

"Okay, this one is our ward reception number, just mention you want 'Dolphin's ward' and bed number seventy-seven and the patient's name, if the nurse does not know Mathew, then all this information would definitely be helpful." Caroline said. "And with this other paper you can write your contact for Mathew." James smiled and told her thanks.

"Anything for my patients, and if you need anything else please just call me." Caroline said while smiling and she went back to her work.

"Isn't she wonderful?" James said.

"I know. She sure is." I replied. James wrote for me his contact numbers; the house and mobile then he passed them over to me with his outstretched arm. I looked at the numbers. I thought he'd given me his address as well but of course there wasn't an address, I was expecting too much I thought. Anyway I held the paper as a coveted piece of work not to be lost. "Thanks." I said, "And you have the hospital's one, you can call me and tell me your progress, you know?"

Yeah I thought, I must know your health progress, it is important for me, you know, ha ha ha, I chuckled, so mean of me and my real reason behind this scheme. The doctors passed their rounds as usual and one stopped and after the others went, spoke to James. After a little while the doctor went on his way to join the other doctors. James turned to me, his face gleaming.

"I am going home tomorrow." he announced, "My God, I just cannot wait to get home." I was happy for him but I was going to miss him. Now I thought, even though my initial reason was my movie star Iris, but really I was going to miss him.

"What time will you be released to go home?" I asked.

"Oh, I will be discharged and allowed to go home after breakfast, Mathew." he emphasized the 'discharge' and 'allowed' for me. It is okay, I am going to learn all the words James, all in due time, don't worry.

"Who will come to collect you?" I asked him again, wanting some more information.

"I am not sure, maybe only my wife Clara, or only my daughter Iris or even both of them, you never know with women, Mathew." he said with a wink. "But what I am sure of is that I am going home tomorrow." He was happy and smiling and he raised his two hands up in celebration. "Yippee, isn't that great Mathew?"

"You seem very happy James." I said, "I hope you have somebody to take care of you at home, you know what I mean?" I again started my detective work.

"Yeah, Mathew, you forgot that I have a wife and daughter to take care of me?" James asked in a feigned amazement.

"Yeah, but Ir....your daughter is living on her own, you told me before remember? And she's busy working, you know what I mean?"

"Okay, my daughter is working full time," James said, "but she is still at home and about her flat, she does decide whenever it suits her, so there is no problem on that issue." I decided not to push more for information about my movie star, so I changed the subject.

"You know what James?" I began, "People are going to miss you around here." I said, "You have been a good patient, you know what I mean?" he did not respond on this one.

"Mathew, you are going to be well too." James said, "I will pray for your health and wellbeing when I go to the church." I understood the talk had been going on for too long, so now enough is enough for now and for today.

James woke up very early the next morning. I could hear noises of someone packing or newspapers being crumpled and the like, I opened my eyes and looked at the time; it was already six in the morning. Remembering that today is the day James is going to be released and only after breakfast so maybe my movie star will come to collect him; therefore I want to be presentable when she comes even if I'm in one piece but it has to be clean at least.

So I started to collect myself and my mini vacuum machine, my towel and other stuff and start my slow journey to the toilet and washroom. After I finished my business, I looked at myself in the mirror and realised that I had not shaved since I entered the hospital ages ago.... but I didn't want to shave because standing for long gives me more pain on my leg. I just combed my moustache and beard and put a little bit of cheap after shave which I had.

I looked like an old man, I looked like one of those science professors or those crazy artists, and I even looked like a terrorist, ha ha ha. It was funny, but why should I try to be smart while my movie star already 'dumped' me? And for whom, I should look smart? Ah, it is okay, I thought and I went back to my room and bed, my 'safe haven'. The smiling nurse Caroline came in the room, with her usual smile.

"James, you are leaving us today?" she said, "We will all miss you, right Mathew?"

"Yeah, I know." I said sadly. James looked at me.

"Thank you for looking after me very well, to all of you in the hospital, I appreciate it." He said to Caroline.

"Okay Mathew, you know the routine." Caroline turned to me and she went ahead with the usual tests and checking. After breakfast, which James didn't really eat properly he was anxious and looking at the door every now and then, I wasn't sure if he was expecting his doctor or his family. Once Caroline finished with me, she went to James and touched his shoulder and said in a kind and gentle voice.

"Goodbye James and take care of yourself," Then she turned to me and said, "See you later Mathew; I'll be on duty maybe tomorrow or the day after." Then she strolled out of the room. The doctors walked in and one spoke with James, while at the same time addressing the day nurse, who this time was another Philippine nurse. I read her name tag 'Maritas' she was tall, thin, young, and beautiful.

"James you are now allowed to go home and your discharge papers are being processed. It might take a few minutes and the nurse here will deal with you, okay?"

"Thank you doctor," James said and turned to the nurse. "How long it will take?"

"Not long now." Maritas soft voice replied, "You just go ahead and be ready." and they all went. At about nine in the morning, I heard the shoes clatter and the perfume smell and I knew that walking has to be Iris with or without Clara, and yes, she walked in like a queen, followed by her personal assistant Clara. They walked in, and without even a glance at me walked straight and they went to James, closed the curtain and I heard their normal greetings and kisses and they sat and talked for a while.

Then Clara went out and called the nurse. Maritas walked in with the discharge papers for James and came in to give her last instructions in her soft voice and told them to wait while the porters bring the wheelchair for James. I thought the minutes are ticking by. I was becoming restless, like something was going to happen to me and the feeling was not nice.

The porter came with the wheelchair, and they opened the curtains and they helped James down off the bed and onto the wheelchair. The porter pushed him and James signalled near my bed to stop. He turned and spoke with me.

"Mathew, hang in there. You will be alright and soon you will be out as well." I was dumbstruck, I couldn't utter a word and he was wheeled away followed by the two ladies, first Clara and then Iris. I thought she will at least stop and say something but maybe I was expecting or dreaming.

"Oh Mathew, I am so sorry, but I love you too", but no I was ready for even, "I hate you" just so I can hear her voice, but it was not to be. She walked by, without even a glance at me; I sat there and listened to her footsteps and her beautiful perfume, melting away with my heart. Oh God, you can be so cruel when you want to be.

What was I expecting anyway? Iris running back with outstretched arms to me and crying, "Oh Mathew, don't leave me, I love you sooooo much, I want to spend the rest of my life with you, oh by the way when I am out at work, you can sit at home and watch television all day long, okay love and don't worry I'll work hard for both of us, and we'll go on holidays and have fun together, okay my love Mathew?"

But no .... no .... Mathew, the reality is I am a 'nobody' in this world. Nobody loves me, nobody cares about me. I am Mathew, a thug and a low life criminal. I sat there with the need to cry, the feel of with tears flowing freely down my cheeks. My heart was in pain, my heart was crying, I was in pain, the pain was stronger than even the pain of my leg. Now I understood what love is, when people say 'Love is poison' I used to laugh but now at this moment I understood, yes love is poison. It is killing me deep in my heart. I felt like dying, I felt like the earth should open and swallow me.

I was confused and didn't know what to do. I sat on my bed when the soft voiced Maritas passed and I told her to close the curtains for me. I refused to eat lunch, I did not eat dinner either and when Elvis brought me the food, I told him in an unfriendly manner.

"No, take it away, I'm not hungry." Then Maritas the soft voice even came and kindly asked me.

"Mathew, why are you not eating since morning? Are you not well? Are you in pain? Should I give you your dose of morphine?" I just shook my head and signalled for her to go away and close the curtains and I covered myself from head to toe. I thought, yes 'soft voice' you're right, I'm in pain but your morphine will not heal me, nothing can cure me. I did not want to talk to anyone; I was in a bad mood and sat there sulking. I thought, oh my God, why did you let me see Iris, why did you let me set my eyes on this beauty, my movie star? Why did you let me fall in love? Why did I have to be in the bed next to James?

Why did I have to be in hospital the same time as James? Why, why and why, oh God?

The night nurse also came to me. Maybe she had heard that I have refused to eat. She tried to make small talk but it was in vain so she left me alone. That night, even though I was in a lot of pain from my leg but I did not bother to call the nurse for anything, I felt the pain in my heart is stronger than the pain in my leg. Oh God, just let me die in my sleep, I've no reason to live anymore and I thought about Kevin, I thought about me Ma, if only I could speak to any one of them.

Oh Ma where are you in my time of need? I couldn't get sleep the whole night, I'm not sure because of pain in my leg, pain in my stomach, the 'hunger' or the pain in my heart of 'love'. Did this happen to everyone in the world? Millions and millions of people fall in love and many end up getting married, and many more 'live happily ever after', but do all of them go through this kind of love or is it only me? Maybe God the Almighty is testing me.

Look, I've lived in this world for twenty six good years, and suddenly I get cancer and also suddenly I fall in love. Is it coincidence or what is it? Has it to do with testing me maybe because I don't go to church and I don't believe actually, I'm just a Christian in name only? But I'm sure I'm not alone and there might be thousands or millions more like me. Do all of them get tested the same like me? Ah, there's a lot to be answered.

Chapter Twelve

*I*N THE MORNING, I DID not bother to go to the toilet or to even wash up; I just sat there not even changing my one piece. What for? I thought, for whom? Leave it as it is. I did take my breakfast but just the cup of tea was enough, I couldn't eat the toast and Elvis just looked at me but did not ask and didn't get an answer, so he went away shaking his head. He wasn't much of a talker anyway so that was good for me.

The doctors came and went, the nurses came and went and continued with their daily functions but there wasn't any talk being exchanged between them and me. New patients were brought in, and old were being released but I did not bother anymore.

When I had to go pee then I made an effort only once or twice to go to the toilet. I wasn't myself, a funny guy, a joker, a jolly person, no, not today anyway.

I tried to eat lunch but I couldn't swallow. Dinner was the same, it was just not passing through my throat even if I tried to, even if I was hungry but I had no appetite. The night nurse came and she gave me one look and shook her head. Maybe she understood or just pretended to have understood the mess I was in.

Anyway, the night was another long night and I sat and thought of a lot of things. I thought of the first time I saw my movie star, I thought of that day, the only day I spoke with her, I also thought about the last time I saw her. I thought of what might have been or what should I've said or didn't say and everything was in a haze. I managed to fall asleep and wake up every few hours or maybe minutes, but the night passed and I continued to suffer a slow death.

In the middle of the night or early hours of the morning, during one of my short sleeps, I woke up shouting and the night nurse came quickly and she saw me perspiring heavily and breathing hard. She was worried and wanted to call the doctor on duty but I stopped her: it was just a nightmare, a bad nightmare. I dreamt of my father calling me by name.

"Mathew come to me, it's time to go home now. Your Ma is already here with me and your brothers Donald and Daniel are with us too. Your time is up Mathew, come quickly." He told me, but it was all a dream. The night nurse gave me one look.

"I have to call the doctor on duty to allow me to give you your dose of morphine, Mathew. You're in pain and it will help you sleep." She told me firmly. I then just nodded my head. She smiled and brought the drip thing and gave me the morphine through injection and drip and it took me away slowly, peacefully, until I was gone. I finally woke up at about ten in the morning and I looked around, the activity was already in motion but that kind guy Elvis, had left my tray of breakfast for me on my side table trolley. Poor him, even though he didn't say it but he must have been feeling sorry for me.

I looked around at the new guys in the other beds but I didn't feel like talking to them. I thought that making friendships with patients might hurt me. As the saying goes, 'Once bitten twice shy', so leave it. I took my tray and just had a cup of tea which was enough for me anyway. At eleven thirty in the morning, the nurse came in.

"Mathew, there is a phone call for you." The nurse told me. I jumped and was so excited. Yes it was my movie star, I knew it, and

I just knew it and it had to be her. I took the call with excitement in me.

"Hi, this is Mathew." I said and trying to be polite, "Who is it calling?"

"Hey Mathew, how's it going?" It was a male voice. Oh no, it was not my expected call from my movie star. It was from the lad in Spain, Kevin's gang member. "Are you there Mathew?"

"Yeah, I'm here," I replied. "What's up"

"Don't mention my name, okay Mathew, you know what I mean?" He cut in and added, "Okay, I have news for you Mathew." I thought thank God, it's about me Ma.

"How is she? How's my ma?" I asked, full of excitement, expecting to hear news of me beloved Ma.

"No, not about your Ma, it's about Kevin and the lads." he replied. "About your ma, I still have no news Mathew, but it's all about Kevin, you know?"

"Okay go on," I replied with sadness in my voice. No news about me Ma but there is news about Kevin, so let's hear it.

"Kevin is looking at ten years by the judge, and the two lads each one might get five years, you know?" he said. "It's crazy I tell ya, this is fucking crazy, the judge is…..you know his name…ah I forgot his fucking name…….Mathew, are you there?"

"Listen, but they've not been sentenced, right? And did they get bail?" I asked eager to know what's going on outside.

"No bail but about the sentences, that's for sure. That's what the DPP, the Director of Public Prosecution is demanding you know, and he'll get it, I tell ya," he replied confidently as if he wanted Kevin and lads to be in jail for long. I had to respond.

"Okay I heard you, what about you and the other lad?" I asked as I wanted to hear his defence.

"Me? ………the Gardai are still looking for me, man." he said. "Not planning to come back soon, you know what I mean?" He was defending himself. I knew what he meant but there were still some unanswered questions.

"Listen, do the Gardai know about me?" I asked. "Am I in danger from the Gardai?"

"Ah, now for that I'm not sure Mathew. You know what I mean?" he said. "First they don't have a clue where you are Mathew." he replied confidently. I thought should I be thrilled of this news or what? And then he went on, "also, if they ask you about me, don't tell them a thing you hear me Mathew, nothing at all about me." Was that a threat?

"Don't worry man; you're in Spain, right." I asked him, "I'm here, so I will worry about me and not about you."

"Okay man I have to go now." he answered, satisfied now. "Bye Mathew, bye now."

"Bye." I replied. And that gave me another thing to worry about: he had called me in the hospital number and it's public. He says the Gardai don't know where I am, which cannot be true. The Gardai are an efficient enough force and they are always one step ahead, so the biggest possibility and the fact is they know about me and my activities. About my association with Kevin and right now they know I am at Dublin University Hospital, Dolphin's Ward, room number and bed number seventy-seven.

The Gardai had my record. How many times have I been in and out of jail? How many times have I been arrested on suspicion of this or that matter? Of course the Gardai knew about me and my record. Now I have to be looking at the entrance of the room, not expecting my movie star but the Gardai. Oh my God, when will it end? Will they come and arrest me immediately or will they wait till after my operation?

The day passed with me fearing the worst whenever I heard footsteps or loud voices. I was scared, thinking of what Kevin or any of the lads, who have been arrested, might have said to the Gardai about my involvement in the past or recent events.

Oh, what a life I'm leading. This is not what my parents had planned and dreamed for me. My Da had dreamed and instructed me to be a good and model citizen, not a criminal and not a person who was scared of the Gardai or the authorities or the law. If my Da knew of what has become of his children, I'm sure he'd be turning in his grave with fury and disappointment. Before lunch time came, Elvis passed and looked at me.

"What would you like to have for lunch, Mathew?" he asked with understanding in his eyes. "You have to eat to be well." I looked at him.

What, special meal do you have for me, my friend?" I asked him in reply. He nodded his head.

"Would you like to have pasta or spaghetti Bolognese?" He asked me.

"Okay, can I have the spaghetti Bolognese?" I replied with a shrug. He smiled with a nod and went his way and then I noticed the new window guy. He was in his mid forties, baldy, maybe five feet six as he stood with two crutches and he looked at me and spoke in a loud voice.

"Hey you're lucky, you're the only one who has been asked what you would like for lunch." he smiled and I noticed his accent was Scottish. "Are you special or something?" I turned and looked at the other guy in the middle bed as he responded.

"Guy just passed a brown envelope, you know what I mean?" and he laughed aloud. He was big in body and short in height with a lot of golden hair, aged maybe in his fifties. I thought it was okay; they are just trying to energise the mood and maybe trying to cheer me as well. So I just smiled at both of them.

At lunch time, Elvis came around and brought for me the spaghetti Bolognese. It was piping hot. He gave me my tray and smiled and winked. I understood, that it was special for a friend and he gave the window man his lunch and the middle bed his lunch. But as he was leaving, the window man 'Scottish' spoke.

"Hey my friend, can I have ice cream please?" he said and smiled at the two of us. "The two of you, would you like ice cream as well?" He offered us as well as if he owned the place. I shook my head but the middle bed said.

"Yeah and why not," he asked in reply. Elvis went and later on brought ice cream. He gave one to each of them but 'Scottish' said.

"Can I have another one please?" I thought this guy is bold and he might know his way around here. Elvis didn't object or say anything to him; he just went and brought another one for 'Scottish' and he asked middle bed and me if we wanted another one as well. I declined.

"Okay, I might as well." Middle man replied with a laugh. 'Scottish' man continued licking his ice cream.

"Their ice cream is lovely." he said, licking himself, "Last time I was here I loved their ice cream." I thought this guy is trying to tell us something so I will ask him.

"Have you been in this hospital before?" I asked him. "What was wrong with you then?" He then explained in a long version that he has some sort of bone disease and that every year he has to be in hospital for treatment and usually he would be staying between five to seven days. He also said originally he is from Scotland but he came to Ireland when he was a young man to work in the farms in the west of Ireland.

That while working in one of the farms in Galway, he fell for the daughter of his boss, and that one day he was caught 'red handed' and he was fired. But then he eloped with the boss's daughter and he went to another county as far away as possible to work at another farm. The farm he was working in now belongs to the girl's uncle on the mother's side. And after many years he and his in-laws have now reconciled and they have accepted him somewhat reluctantly.

But he said they don't like him still and he said this with a laugh as if he was boasting about his achievements in life. He said now he has his own little bit of land and a house with grown up children, his wife is still with him and they are happy together and still working for the uncle. His father in law asked him to come back to work for him but he says maybe it's a trap, so he doesn't want to take the chance; he was happy where he was. Okay, now 'Scottish' have told us his entire life history and he was happy.

"If you need anything in this hospital, just ask me as they all know me." He told us in a proud voice. I thought that is good to know; now I shall wait for the middle bed to tell us his story but I vowed they will never hear mine, no way. All this long story and he didn't mention his name so I had to ask him.

"I'm Mathew, what's yours?" to the two of them. 'Scottish' was quick to answer.

"Thomas McDermott is my name but all my friends just call me Tom." And he added while laughing, "Not 'Tom the Cat', and not

'Peeping Tom either', just Tom. He burst out laughing at his own joke. And then the middle bed pronounced proudly.

"I'm Paul Smith." he said, "Good to know each other, you know?"

"Oh yeah, you can wake me up at night any time," Tom the 'Scottish' said, "if you need anything." and Tom went on and on, I think I'll call him 'chatterbox' from now on. In the afternoon, they took Paul to the operating theatre. He was brought back maybe at about five or six and he had a plaster on his arm. Later he explained he fell down in the snow and broke his elbow and tomorrow he'll be released, nothing serious.

Tom, on the other hand was watching the telly until one or two in the morning, maybe even late at night. Then he complained he couldn't get sleep and he asked from the night nurse for a 'Valium' sleeping tablet. The night nurse had to fill a form and called the duty doctor who then came and went straight with the nurse to 'chatterbox' Tom.

The doctor, who was a lady, asked Tom a few questions, and when she was satisfied she signed the form and the nurse got the tablets. I'm not sure if they were from the pharmacy or they had their own medicine cabinet, but Tom was given the tablet and finally he slept.

The next morning I woke up and went to wash myself up but I was feeling depressed in a way, not knowing what was in store for me today. I was already starting to forget, no actually forcing myself to forget about my movie star. She was gone from my life, the issue is not in my hands anymore and there are more urgent matters to tend to and worry about and occupy my thoughts and brain. Like, will the Gardai come to arrest me; will my doctors come to give me any new information about my leg and the operation? Will today be the day I hear some news about me Ma...so I was feeling down first thing in the morning.

Tom the 'chatterbox Scottish' was still asleep when breakfast was brought, and Paul had his breakfast with one hand, he asked for porridge and I got my usual, the toasted bread and boiled egg. At eight the doctors passed through and one of them spoke to me.

"Your doctor, Mr Livingstone will come to see you sometime today and he will give you an update of your reports, okay?" I nodded my head and they told Paul, "You will be discharged at about eleven after the paperwork is done." Then they looked at Tom who was fast asleep and was actually snoring. They smiled and discussed amongst themselves and then one told the day nurse, who today was Maritas, "Let him sleep, his doctor will come later to see him." At eleven Paul was released and he wished me good bye.

"Good luck, Mathew." Then he went on his way. Tom woke at twelve, and looked around and saw me looking at him.

"I couldn't sleep last night, you know?" he said while still sleepy. "Sorry about the telly, was the noise too loud?" I wanted to tell him, no wonder you can't sleep at night if you wake up at twelve noon. And about the noise, of course you disturbed me and not only from the telly but from your snoring also, like a train or yeah, like a frog in the water. I chuckled to myself and smiled.

Chapter Thirteen

*W*HEN LUNCH ARRIVED, TOM ASKED Elvis for two portions and he then explained to me.

"Their portions are very little; one cannot be enough for anybody so I have to ask for two portions."

I thought he was a slim man and he could take two portions while I was actually a little bigger than him and I could not finish even one portion. The man has an appetite and that is good but I was jealous of him. At about three in the afternoon, Dr. Livingstone accompanied by Dr. Browne with the green file in his hands walked slowly in, pulled some chairs and sat down.

"Hello Mathew." Dr. Livingstone said, "You might have thought we have forgotten about you, right?" they both smiled and looked at each other. "You have been very tolerant and a good patient." Dr. Livingstone spoke again, "I know it has been a long time since you were admitted." I kept quiet and not knowing how to react since I didn't know what was coming so I just kept looking into their eyes and remained silent. "We shall take you in tomorrow for surgery, Mathew." Dr. Livingstone again said, "We shall open the wound and take a peek inside your thigh." he looked at me for any reaction. There was none, so after a while he continued. "We shall compare what we see inside your thigh and the scans, X-rays and other reports we have of your leg." Here he paused, "Then it will be easy to decide if we need to amputate your leg or save it."

He looked at me in the eyes and continued, "In other words, we want to see how much of the sarcoma has spread and destroyed your muscles and soft tissues in your leg. Do you understand what I am trying to say here Mathew?" I had to either nod or shake my head, it was a direct question for me, did I understand or not the implications of what lay ahead? I looked at Dr. Livingstone and then I turned my gaze at Dr. Browne. After a while I returned my gaze and fixed my eyes at Dr. Livingstone.

"Doctor, I trust your decision and I believe you'll be able to take the best option there is." I said while I looked at him in the eyes. Trusting him with my life, I then added, "And whatever decision you take I will accept it as the best there is." I could feel his gladness and his appreciation with my acceptance. He looked at Dr. Browne and together they smiled. Dr. Livingstone touched my shoulder.

"I will do the best I can," he said warmly, "that I promise you, Mathew." Dr. Browne nodded his head in approval as well.

"You are in good hands Mathew." Dr. Browne said, "Dr. Livingstone here, is one of the best in his field in the country and so there is nothing for you to worry about, Mathew." he smiled. I thought well, he is looking out for himself, he is praising his boss and it's good for his chances of promotion. And then they were gone. Well now I knew where I stood in connection to my hospital stay: the doctors are trying to save my leg from being cut off and that is good for me. Now I can continue to be patient and stay in the hospital and continue to be in my one piece of dress code. "Hey friend," Tom said addressing me, "sorry I already forgot your name........."

"The name is Mathew," I said, "What's going on?"

"Okay Mathew," Tom said, "what the doctors tell you...is it about your leg?"

"Yeah it's about the leg." I answered. "Tomorrow they'll take me in the operation theatre, you know?" I continued, "They like my thigh and leg that's why every time they want to have a look, you know what I mean?" We both laughed aloud, me and my friend Tommy.

"That doctor who came to see you." Tom said, "I know him, he is very good, he is a professor you know, he teaches other doctors." He said in a serious note to impress me with his knowledge. "And the other one as well, he is a junior doctor, I think a Registrar or something." Tom continued, "But that doctor, what's his name……Professor Livingstone, yeah that's his name…he's good…..he is tops." Tom was very matter of fact person and confident in his information.

Tom told me he smokes and right now he needed to go out to smoke. As he was walking with his crutches, he held one like a machine gun and he put up an act.

"If anyone stops me on the way, I'll become a 'Mafia Don' and shoot them all." and off he went on his way, smiling. I thought that after meeting Tom and seeing his antics, my stay in the hospital might be fun and maybe I shall be able to forget my movie star, who until now I just have been unable to get her out of my mind. Later on Tom came back smiling and he said he smoked two cigarettes and he was happy and yes, nobody stopped him on the way. "They all know me." he said winking, "Don't trouble me and I'll not trouble you. I'm 'Trouble' you see, mate?"

For dinner as usual, Tom asked for two portions and he continued chatting about this and that and about how important he is at the farm where he was working.

"You know I'm an all round man," he said. "I repair all mechanical machineries and other stuff as well." I thought and wondered who is doing your job now while you are in hospital? But I thought better of it not to ask him as I didn't want another lecture from Tom. At ten when the night nurse Maritas was switching off the lights. Tom told her,

"Don't switch off the lights love, we'll switch off later." Tom told her. But she said the rules have to be followed.

"If you need light, you have your bed light for reading, okay Tom?" Maritas replied. Tom just grumbled and then as if it was an afterthought or just to annoy her for refusing on his request about the lights.

"Can I also have two slices of toast bread and a cup of tea, please? I'm a bit hungry." I turned and looked at him, was he for real? The nurse will just tell him off, I mean ten at night, you're asking for food? But the nurse just smiled.

"Okay Tom, I'll make for you." She replied then she turned to me, "Would you also like to have something, Mathew?" I just couldn't believe it. I was here for many days now, maybe two or three weeks. I hadn't seen any nurse making or giving snacks or food at night to patients and yet here is Tom asking for snacks and gladly nurse 'Maritas' is going to make it for him. I then nodded.

"Okay Maritas, I'll have also, why not?" I replied. Then Maritas went and brought two trays and gave one to each of us, I couldn't stop laughing for the whole night whenever I remembered this episode. After we finished she came and took the trays and spoke to Tom, who was watching the telly.

"Please reduce the sound; other patients are sleeping now." Maritas told Tom in a pleading tone. "Why don't you sleep now Tom?" Tom looked at me and then turned to her.

"I cannot get sleep but when I'm ready I'll sleep okay?" He watched the telly while I was in my own world and thinking about tomorrow and the operation. But I wasn't worried much, as Dr. Livingstone had explained, 'that this one is just to have a look only' and I kept thinking of the one day in my life when I was able and failed to talk to my movie star. I was trying to recall every word I said and what she said, and how she looked, her facial expressions, her smile, her eyes, oh what a beauty, she can win 'Miss World' anytime, and she gets my full vote.

I suffered the usual pain in my thigh but I wasn't complaining as my mind was occupied with thoughts, about Kevin, about me Ma, about my movie star, about life. I had a lot of 'what if' situations in my head and mind. At about two or three in the morning, Tom asked the night nurse to get for him valium.

"You know, I cannot sleep." Tom told Maritas, the night nurse. I thought to myself, how can you get sleep, if you're watching the telly till late at night and you wake up at eleven, twelve or one o'clock in the afternoon? But I think they were all used to him so then she filled the forms and called the doctor, who came to talk with Tom and then Tom was given his tablet and he finally slept. At six in the morning Maritas came, woke me up and told me.

"Go freshen yourself up and have a minimal wash, be ready for the theatre, okay?" I woke up, collected myself and my 'tools' and went slowly as if crawling to the toilets, I did my 'business' then washed and wiped myself. After a while I came back and sat on my bed, ready to be taken in the 'slaughter house'. Maritas the nurse came again and checked my blood pressure and blood glucose; she wrote her notes in the green file.

"You'll be fine." she told me. "I'm off now but tomorrow I'm on day time duty and I'll see you, okay?" Maritas then touched my hand in a friendly way. I thought Maritas was nice and caring; she was trying to help me pull through. Another doctor came and talked me through what they are going to do with me in the operation theatre and once he finished, he told me this is a formality the doctors have to perform, so do I have any questions or not understood anything. Once he was sure I understood everything, he gave me the consent form to sign, which I duly did and he went.

Elvis brought breakfast and I didn't have any, as I was fasting and ready for the operation. Tom said he can have my share as well as his two portions, Elvis seemed not sure and he might have thought Tom was only joking but our dear Tom was not joking, he was serious. And he took all the food and put it on one tray, and was enjoying himself. I looked at him in amazement.

"Tom, you are eating a lot....." I said smiling. "And yet you're not fat and your stomach is flat so where's all the food going to?" he tried to laugh, but his mouth was full. He waited a bit and then he flexed his arm muscles.

"Arnold Schwarzenegger's brother." he said laughing. "All the food is going into building my muscles." I looked at him. I was not sure he was joking or in his mind he believed it.

"Only your arm muscles, Tom?" I asked him while laughing, he stopped eating and he pulled up his one piece to show me his biceps.

"Okay Tom....that's enough; I was only messing......" I told him as I was trying to cover my eyes. "Come on Tom cover yourself up and stop stripping in the hospital, somebody will see you." We laughed aloud for a while. When he finished eating, he started to burp out loud.

"Oh I'm full now," Tom said, "and I feel good." I looked at him. He just stuffed himself and now he feels good. Oh my God, we humans sometimes we are funny creatures. At nine thirty in the morning two porters came to take me. Janet was the day nurse and she showed them my bed.

"Are you seventy seven?" one of them asked me in a loud voice. I looked at him.

"No, the name is Mathew zero-zero-seven and licensed to kill." I said just as serious. "And now ready to go with you." The two porters looked at me and they weren't sure am if I was crazy or what. Their faces showed surprise and confusion until Janet burst out laughing and then they understood and got the joke. So we all started laughing and one of them said.

"Whew, that was close and for a moment I thought we have a nutcase here."

"I tell you, they come in all kinds of them." The other one replied.

"Oh my God, that was so…….funny," Janet said. "If only you could see your faces." Then she took the green file and we started our journey through the corridors and lifts until we reached the 'parking zone' and they handed me to the nurses.

"Good luck, James Bond." The porters told me and off they went laughing and talking between the two of them. I'm sure I'll be their topic for the day with their friends and colleagues. Janet held my hand.

"I know you're going through a lot Mathew, but at the end of the day you'll be fine, Good luck." She said and she also left. I thought they're all nice people and caring but sometimes once in a while you meet one or two who are grumpy and not so nice. The anaesthetic doctor came over and she took the green file and did all the formalities again, which by now I was so used to and understood so I didn't mind. Then she injected my arm and slowly I went to la la land.

I came to my senses slowly and from afar I could hear Tom's voice, maybe he got a new audience but he was lecturing. Then when I was fully conscious I looked at the time; it was two in the afternoon. I turned and looked at Tom

"Hey welcome back." he said then added. "And you still have your leg." Of course I would still have my leg, there was no plan for today's operation to cut it but I slowly used my hand to feel my leg, okay it's still there. Then the bombshell from Tom, "While you were away the Gardai were here looking for you, Mathew." I missed a heartbeat and abruptly turned and looked at him. Was this another one of his pranks?

"What do you mean the Gardai?" I asked Tom in complete surprise. "Why should the Gardai look for me? Tom, stop messing with me brain." Tom looked at me.

"To arrest you," he said. "What else will the Gardai want from you?" Tom then saw the fear in my face, I had gone pale and he burst out laughing. "I'm only joking, Mathew." he said and added, "You look scared, have you killed anyone in the operating room?" He burst out laughing. "One of the doctors is missing." I was becoming angry in his senseless laughing at my expense, I was agitated, he took this whole thing as a joke but he didn't know my past life and my present worries.

"Can you please stop messing me brains, Tom?" I shouted at him in anger which caught him by surprise. "Tell me, did the Gardai come in or not? And what do they want from me?" I looked at him in anger now, he saw my face, it was with fear and he recognised it.

"I'm so sorry Mathew," he said, "but the Gardai did come and ask for you." and he continued. "But I told them you were in the operating theatre, being operated upon." Tom then explained to me that two Gardai Officers had come in their uniforms and they had come with the nurse supervisor, and they did ask for me and yes he said I was in the operating room. "They said they'll come back later to see you, Mathew." Tom said. "I'm sorry to ask you Mathew but why you seem very scared of the Gardai?" I turned and faced him.

"Who said I'm scared of the Gardai?" I replied in anger. "I'm just surprised why they should come to look for me."

"Okay. Okay Mathew," Tom said, "Your face says it all, the fear is written all over your face. But it is none of my business anyway."

Chapter Fourteen

I THOUGHT, YEAH IT IS NONE of your business but you will know anyway when they'll come to arrest me. Oh my God, will they handcuff me to the bed, will one of them be guarding me all the time and following me everywhere I go? What have I done? I thought of me Ma. Come and rescue me, where are you Ma at the time I need you most, you're not there to help me. Oh Ma, come to me please.

When I saw my movie star I thought I'd go and live with her but now it seems I'll be going to live in the prison. I was so scared that I was afraid to even open my mouth to speak, the words will either not come out or I'll say the wrong words. Tom made a good decision after that episode, and he remained quiet or when he spoke to the nurses or the new middle bed he spoke with a low voice, and he didn't talk with me but I noticed every now and again he would throw a glance at me. I think what he saw on my face made him keep away from me, which was also good for me as my mind raced with thoughts of a million things.

I was in fear; I was scared for myself, for my life. I thought jail was not a good place to be, I have been inside there twice, even though it was short stints but jail is jail. I would tell anybody who would listen, please don't let yourself go to jail, it is a bad place, it is a mean place. It's a place where you can be drugged, beaten, killed and even raped.

Please dear God, I am in the process of changing my life. Look at me, since I came to the hospital I have changed a lot. Nowadays I'm not even using the 'f' word anymore. I haven't smoked or drank booze since I came to the hospital. Oh dear God, I'm in the process of changing, so please don't send me to jail again. I will die there, jail is a horrible place to be and jail is not at all pleasant. For the rest of the day I remained in fear. Whenever I heard footsteps, I would look at the entrance to our room and expect the Gardai to enter and arrest me. I was fearful. Now I know what it really means when one says 'I was scared to death'; yeah, I really was.

Then I thought but why should I be scared? I was not involved in the latest 'venture', I didn't take part in the attempt to rob the post office, I was here in the hospital and that can be proven. But then, the car that was used was Kevin's car, and I'm always in the car. We share hoodies and jumpers with the lads, we drink and smoke in the car and besides, nowadays they have this DNA thing, so they'll get plenty of my DNA. Besides, I actually knew about this new robbery even though not with full or enough details or about the dates and place.

And besides, the robbery attempt was just a day after I was admitted in the hospital, therefore the planning was done at least a few days before, so yeah the Gardai will think and know I was somehow involved and yeah, I am with Kevin's gang, that is the truth and how can I deny that when everybody knows about that even the local Garda station knows about this.

Oh man, there is no way I can escape now. If I was not sick and in the hospital, I could have escaped to England and stayed there till this blows away, then I could've come back or better still, I could just restart my life there. I think that's what I should do. If I'm not arrested yet, I shall run away to the UK or even to Spain. I heard that a lot of Irish people live in the south of Spain, where's there's sun all year round. Oh man, I cannot wait.

Then I heard heavy footsteps, and my heart stopped beating, Oh my God, I'm dead. I looked at the doorway, fearful of what I could see. Then they entered, but it was the group of doctors on their seven o'clock night rounds. Oooh… God…what I'm going through, only I know….this is self-inflicted suffering.

"Hi Mathew," It was Dr. Browne; I thanked God, "are you well?" I couldn't speak; I just nodded my head in relief. I would have cried but I just looked at him. "Tomorrow, Dr. Livingstone might get the results and he'll talk with you, okay?" he said again as they all moved on to talk with the middle man and then to Tom. But I couldn't listen to anything which was said. I could hear Tom's voice from afar but I couldn't register the meaning, I was in my own cocoon. Elvis came with my dinner.

"Hey Mathew." he asked me, "What about your dinner, can you eat now or should I give it to Tom?" he jokingly said while smiling. I just looked at him and said nothing, but I was hungry so I just signalled him to leave me my tray on the table. And to Tom, "I brought you your two portions." Elvis said. "Is it enough?" Tom looked at me and shaking his head he told Elvis.

"Its okay, Mathew won't be able to have his dinner, I will help him." Tom winked at Elvis and signalled to him not to talk with me anymore, the mood was somewhat gloomy in the room. Elvis understood and left the room to continue his rounds in distributing dinner to all patients in the ward. Later on I just managed to have a cup of tea at ten. "Mathew, you cannot eat, right?" Tom said. "I can help you with your dinner."

"Go ahead Tom." I said, and he came over and sat near me and took the tray and munched his way through.

"Mathew, are you in any trouble with the law?" Tom asked. He had to ask because he needed the information; he is the 'know it all' type of chap, so he has to know. "I can see and sense your fear. It was the same with me when I eloped with my boss's daughter. I lived in fear for a long time." he said and laughing. "Actually, I'm still in fear of my father-in-law, he might decide to shoot me, you know? Maybe he's planning that even until today, you know?"

I looked at him, not knowing to cry or laugh, just the image of him running and his father-in-law with a gun in his hands chasing him and behind them, the daughter and mother running after them, and maybe behind them again the grandchildren or the dogs. That's so funny, I chuckled and it broke the ice and we started laughing as if we saw the scene together. I sensed maybe he was genuine and he was concerned about me. I wasn't sure if I should confide in him about my fears or not.

"Tom, if I decide to tell you." I said, "What will you do, or how will you help me?" Tom looked at me with seriousness in his face.

"I cannot help you in any way, not with the Gardai coming after you." he said. "But you'll feel good if you talk and remove it from your chest." That made perfect sense and yeah, he seemed genuine and he was older than me, maybe he was more experienced in life. So I explained it to him, but only about my fears to do with the criminality of my life and about Kevin, about the law and the visit of the Gardai yesterday.

"And Tom," I said, "yourself told me the Gardai came here to arrest me and........." He shook his head.

"Oh no, I was only joking," he said, "I didn't mean it and I'm sorry..........."

"Aha, I caught you Tom." I said. "Maybe now you know my story, you'll call the Gardai to come to arrest me, right?" He shook his head with eyes wide open.

"No, no ....Mathew." he said. "I cannot do that, I would never, ever"

"It's okay, I'm only messing. Why you are getting jittery now?" I replied. We sat there long for a long time in silence and then after a while, he shook his head.

"Maybe the Gardai wants only to interview you." Tom finally said, the wiser now. "You might have nothing to worry about." He tried to assure me, and told me to get some sleep. As he couldn't get sleep, he asked "Is it okay if I watch the telly?" He explained that there were a few lady TV personalities whom he loved very much and he loved just to sit and watch how they talked and smiled. "At me, they usually smile at me and that's how I feel." Tom explained to me. I looked at him then smiled and told him.

"Go ahead and enjoy the telly. I'm fine and I feel better now after discussing my fears of the law with you." I thought I haven't spoken with him about me Ma, maybe tomorrow I'll discuss with him but not about my movie star, that part is gone forever even though she'll always remain in my soul. I couldn't get proper sleep, I had my fears, I had nightmares about the Gardai arresting me and putting me in prison, the suffering in prison. I dreamt of me Ma, crying for me, I dreamt of my movie star, telling me 'you deserve what you got, I hate you.' I dreamt of Kevin telling me, 'man you're going to join me in prison'.

In my half sleep – half awake state. I heard at a distance Tom, asking and getting his valium and the nurse telling him, 'to switch off the telly and go to sleep, now'. It went on and on, the fear and the nightmares. At one time, I felt tears coming from my eyes. Early morning, as normal practice now a few days after I'm brought from the operation, then I cannot walk and go to the toilets therefore I get to do my 'business' in the can, and the nurses or the assistants help me and they do the cleaning and they bring for me the wash basin filled with warm water and I do my 'minimal wash' on the bed. So the night nurses usually helped.

Nowadays, I've learnt to say "Thanks," and, "Thanks a million." In my previous life I wasn't used to thanking anybody; I just thought it was their duty to do something for me. And sometimes I thought someone who does anything for me it was because that person feared me. I saw myself as a 'tough guy, not to be messed around with' you know what I mean? But now I've realised they were just doing me favours. I was a fool for misunderstanding. Elvis brought us breakfast, and I had mine properly and I also asked for a glass of orange juice which Elvis brought for me, while Tom had his usual two portions and burped aloud, while gently rubbing his stomach.

Chapter Fifteen

LATER ON WHILE I WAS talking to Tom, I heard heavy footsteps and before I realised what or who it was, two Gardai entered. They were in their full uniforms with their black stab vests and stuff around their waists and radio calls, it was intimidating to me and because of my fears I was even more scared. Both were tall, about six feet or taller and one was heavily built and older. I noticed he was a sergeant, while the other one was not thin but not heavy either and younger.

They both entered and removed their caps and then the day nurse Caroline entered and addressed me with her beautiful smile.

"Hey Mathew, how are you feeling this morning?" I couldn't utter a word and then she said very politely. "These two gentlemen want to talk to you in private, is that okay Mathew?" Then she turned to the two Gardai and told them. "This is Mathew, take it easy with him, he is our favourite patient." Caroline smiled at me; it was a reassuring smile and one which at this particular moment I couldn't appreciate. I couldn't even return the smile; I was so frozen with fear.

They pulled up two chairs, one on each side of the bed and they closed the curtains. I thought okay, I'll put both my hands straight and down so it will be easy for each of them to put their handcuffs on me and tie me to the bed frame. The older one smiled.

"I'm Garda Sergeant Liam and this is Garda Frank." They both shook my hands, but I was shaking in fear and I couldn't talk, my tongue was stuck. I thought both of them sensed the fear in me so they were trying to calm me down first, I thought before they arrested me. "How's it going Mathew," The Garda Sergeant Liam said. "I hear you're not well." And then Garda Frank added.

"It's about your leg?" he asked and then, "We're sorry to hear about your cancer." I thought while my mind raced, you're not here to discuss about my cancer, you're not here to inquire about my well being, why don't you just arrest me and let's get it over with? But I managed, nervously.

"I'm doing okay," I replied weakly, "getting well." They looked at each other as if 'should we or not yet' and I was waiting. I thought the time has come. They asked me my address, about my family and about different things which I thought were not relevant.

"We're here about your Ma. Have you any news about your Ma, Mathew?" Frank asked me. I thought they were just buying time with their small talk.

"She's fine I think. Not seen her since I came in the hospital, you know?" I replied with hesitation in my voice. A long silence followed then abruptly.

"Do you know Kevin, Mathew?" Sergeant Liam asked me.

"Yeah I know Kevin, what about him?" I replied with a question. I couldn't hide the fact that I know Kevin because I was in no doubt that they knew about that.

"What's your relationship with him?" Sergeant Liam asked me. I looked at him.

"He's my cousin and also he's my friend. Is something wrong with that?" I replied starting to get irritated.

"You know he's in remand and ...?" Garda Frank said and I cut him short.

"Yeah, I heard about that." I said while anger mixed with fear within me. They both looked at me. I was getting nervous and I wanted to shout at them both. "Come on arrest me instead of playing games with me like cat and mouse." I said angrily instead. Then Liam took my hand and held it. I thought okay now is the time the handcuffs are coming out. I closed my eyes.

"It's about your mother Mathew. Your mother has passed away." Sergeant Liam said and then followed by a long silence. "Mathew your mother is dead." Sergeant Liam repeated again this time with a stronger voice. "Mathew, did you hear what I just said? Do you understand me Mathew?" I looked through him, but I didn't actually see him. Then Garda Frank also held my other hand, both of them were holding my hands on each of my side. Were they going to handcuff me now? What Liam just said, it hadn't really registered yet in my brain at first but then after a long while it sank in.

"What? Are you fucking crazy?" I screamed. "It cannot be, man."

"Mathew, listen to me," Liam said, "your Ma is dead and it's the truth

"No. No. No it cannot be," I cried, "she cannot be dead." And I added, "You're here about Kevin not about me Ma so don't drive me fucking crazy." But after a while I spoke again. "I left me Ma fine and she's alright. You're crazy she can't be dead. You're just messing my fucking head."

"But Mathew that is the truth," Gardai Frank said.

"The Gardai cannot lie about something like this... about your Ma," Sergeant Liam said. "We aren't here to mess with your brain ...... Mathew. Please listen to us."

"No you're messing my brain and I don't believe you ..." I replied while shaking my head. "It cannot be," I said while shouting at them. "You're fucking lying and..."

"Listen Mathew," Sergeant Liam said, "I swear I'm not messing with you. I swear I'm telling you the truth. Mathew you're mother is dead." I couldn't take anymore of this. I pulled my hands from both of them and held my head while shaking my head and sobbing. I didn't ask how she died, what happened or when it happened.

All the questions with no answers that will all come later but for now I didn't accept my poor Ma has died.

"A neighbour found her yesterday, when she took a peek through the windows." Sergeant Liam said. "Your Ma was already dead for some days when the neighbours called the emergency." Sergeant Liam added. "And when the emergency arrived, the ambulance and Gardai had to come too, but they all couldn't do anything else. She was already dead for a good number of days." There was a long silence.

"How did she die?" I asked eventually. I had to know even though it was painful. "Was she alright, I mean?"

"She died of suspected heart attack. Mathew she took overdose of some tablets," Sergeant Liam replied. "The paramedics took her body by ambulance to the hospital morgue and for post-mortem."

"Did someone inform the Gardai`?" I asked absent-minded. "They have to be called; maybe something happened to me Ma. You know what I mean?"

"The Gardai were called. We were there before the door was broken and when we arrived we cordoned off the house for investigation of any foul play. We aren't looking for any suspects Mathew, as it wasn't a foul play." Sergeant Liam said. "So then today after the doctors confirmed it was a drug overdose, the Gardai` left and gave the keys of the house to the Welfare people and the Corporation, who then boarded and locked the house."

"What's going to happen next?" I asked, "Is me Ma okay now?"

"Your Ma's body is at the hospital Morgue. She was only found yesterday but she died a few days ago, maybe three days now. Now as you're the next of kin and the only surviving relative and son you have to be notified first and you'll give the authorities directions on what to be done with your mother's body." Sergeant Liam said while avoiding my eyes. "Mathew, she left a note." Sergeant Liam took a folded note from his pocket and held it for me to take. I looked at the note for a while and then I took it. I held the note close to my heart and then I opened and read it.

She was heartbroken. I, Mathew, her only remaining son was the last straw in her long suffering. First it was the husband, Brian. Then it was the first son Donald. Then her second son Daniel was killed too and now Mathew dying with the cancer. She thought that she couldn't take it anymore. It was enough for her in this life. If and when Mathew dies she will not have anyone else close in this world so why continue to live? There is no reason or excuse for her anymore.

After reading the note I sat there for long time thinking. She gave up on this world, therefore she let the angel of death take her without a struggle; she went peacefully to meet her maker. Maybe when she waited for a few days for Kevin to bring her to the hospital to see me and she didn't hear from Kevin, then she had lost hope. Maybe she thought I was already dead. Maybe this or maybe that, I will just have the maybes.

"Why I was not informed sooner about me Ma? Like yesterday when she was found dead?" I then asked. But they told me they had come yesterday into the main office and after they exchanged information with the doctors. The Gardai were advised not to tell Mathew of the news about his mom as himself was in critical condition in the hospital so as not to make it any worse. Sergeant Liam explained regretfully. Now they wanted to change the subject.

"Mathew, can I ask you something?" Sergeant Liam said, "Why did you think we came to arrest you?" I thought what worse can they do now?

"I don't know," I replied, "maybe after what Kevin did."

"What Kevin did, that we know you were not involved." Sergeant Liam replied. "We already checked you out Mathew. As you know we know a lot about you."

"So what does this mean?" I asked, "I'm free now, you know what I mean?"

"Of course you are free Mathew," Garda Frank said, "you were not under suspicion or anything and you're clean at the moment." He continued with a grin, "Unless you come out of the hospital and you commit a crime, or go back to your old tricks once again then you will be ours again. And this time it will be for a long time. I took a long and deep breath.

"Mathew, about your record as of now, you are clean. Please don't go back to crime; crime doesn't pay as the saying goes. Okay?" Sergeant Liam said. "And as for the death of your old lady, we are very much sorry." I nodded my appreciation. Garda Sergeant Liam and Garda Frank both stood up, their job done, shook my hand firmly and said, "Sorry." And again, "Take care, Mathew." And they were gone while I was left in a daze.

I sat there on my bed, covered my eyes and started to cry again, slowly at first and then sobbing and loudly. I had a deep pain in my chest and knots in my throat. I cried my heart out. My mother, me Ma, me old lady what have I done to you? Why did you go without saying goodbye? I've been a bad son Ma, forgive me Ma, and again please forgive me Ma. I've let you down, I've let Pa down, oh Ma, I love you Ma.

You told me to study but I left studying. You told me to get a job and I did crime as a job instead. You told me to go to church and I went to the bars and pubs to get drunk instead. Ma you told me to have good friends but I kept criminals as my friends. You told me to make good use of my time and I spent the days drinking, smoking, girls, gambling and criminal activity.

Oh Ma, please come back and now I'll listen to you, I'll take care of you; I'll work and use my time in a good way. I'll become like my Pa. Oh Ma, please give me one more chance. I'll be a good son.

Tom came and sat there with me. He hugged me and spoke to me, but I didn't hear when Caroline came in and then actually hugged me. I was ashamed but I couldn't stop crying and lamenting for my mother. At one time I glanced at Caroline and then at Tom and I saw tears in their eyes, I understood they cared for me at this hour of my grief. I cried and sobbed for a long time but Caroline had to leave me and go perform her duties. She kept coming back after every little while. I thought about my poor Ma, she died alone and with deep pain in her heart. The world has been cruel to her. I was angry at God.

"Why you're taking away from me everything that I love?" I cried aloud. "First you took my movie star, now you took my Ma, why God why?" Caroline who was here now looked enquiringly at Tom, but poor Tom also had no clue and he just shrugged.

"Mathew which movies star are you talking about who has just died?" Caroline innocently asked me. I looked at her and knew immediately I had made a blunder so I just shook my head while I sobbed. "Mathew, stop crying." Caroline said, "I'll be your movie star, okay?" And she smiled at me; it was such a genuine smile, it touched my heart especially at this time of my sorrow.

Then Tom was called to see the doctors and Caroline had to go to see her patients. The pain in my leg become unbearable and now I noticed my head was in pain. I had pain in my stomach. I felt pain everywhere including my heart. Later Caroline gave me some tablets plus morphine so I could relax and get some sleep. She felt sorry for me. I relaxed for a while not sure of my surroundings.

I thought about me being brought to the hospital and being admitted. Was it a good thing or a bad thing? It was both and good, but at what cost? By being in the hospital, I wasn't involved in the 'sting' of robbing the post office, so therefore I was saved from going to prison. But at the same time, me Ma died because of my being in the hospital and suffering. So what is right and what is wrong? I can never know the answer to these and many more questions.

Now I realised how much I missed and also loved me Ma but it was too late now to even think about it. If only...if only what Mathew? I asked myself in my thoughts. I refused to eat lunch. Actually, I didn't refuse but I couldn't eat, I didn't know how the day passed I was like a zombie and I wasn't sure what time it was but the day had passed anyhow. Tom was brought back from the operating theatre. When he came back to his senses, I didn't ask him how it was but still he came to sit with me. I just stared blankly at him with my eyes red and tears flowing. I felt sorry for him as well: because of me he was suffering and I could see it in his eyes but I couldn't acknowledge anything.

Chapter Sixteen

$\mathcal{E}$LVIS PASSED SEVERAL TIMES TO see and ask me if he should bring something me eat but I just shook my head. He also felt sorry for me. Caroline kept coming every now and then, to sit with me and hold my hand for support.

"Mathew." Caroline called me sadness in her eyes, "Should I ....try to feed you?" I looked at her, her eyes showed love and kindness and empathy. I thought now Caroline wants to do more than her job requires and why? Because she cares and now she even want to feed me? I haven't been fed since I was a toddler, I think. I know I was very small and it was by me Ma only and nobody else, now this beautiful and caring hospital nurse wants to feed me. Oh God what a situation I'm in! I shook my head at Caroline.

"Thanks, I'm alright." I thought, Caroline I don't need you to feed me but I want me Ma to feed me, I want me Ma to hold me and hug me, but where is she? She is now gone forever, I'll never see her again and I felt that I had no use to be in this world anymore. Maybe if I die then I'll be happier.

In the evening again Elvis tried to bring me dinner and again I couldn't eat and yet again Caroline came and sat with me and she asked, no, actually she tried to feed me. But I wouldn't open my mouth as I didn't want to be fed, by Caroline or anyone else for that matter. Tom tried to talk with me but there was no way. I couldn't stop crying and sobbing, it was heavy in my heart. Caroline looked at me.

"Do you want me to stay here for the night?" Caroline asked me while holding my hand and smiling. "I can be with you of you want me to." But unfortunately I had no feelings for her. I knew now or at least I thought she was or she might be in love with me. Otherwise why would she sacrifice all this for me? But no, I wasn't in love with her. Yeah she was nice, she was beautiful, she was kind hearted, she had all the qualities, but my heart wasn't in love with her, sorry but I couldn't force myself. I knew nobody, no girl or lady would offer her job, her pay, just to stay and look after me? No way man, not possible in my life, no it just doesn't happen. I shook my head at Caroline.

"Thanks Caroline." I replied, "You're so special but now go home and rest, you had a long day." I tried to smile but I'm not sure what showed in my face. She understood and she nodded her head with a smile.

"I'm taking the day duty tomorrow as well...Mathew." Caroline said with a smile, "I mean, just to be with you and to look after you .... okay then?" She was so nice and caring; she was trying to assure me that there are still people in this world who were caring about me. I smiled at her in appreciation but she couldn't take the place in my heart for my movie star. I stayed on my bed, I kept thinking about a lot of things in life and time passed. Tom was tired early today and at about eleven at night he switched off the telly and went to sleep. Maritas was the night nurse again. I think they told her about me and she came in the room, stood near me and held my hand.

"Sorry......Mathew," Maritas spoke to me, "I've heard about your mother.......I'm sorry." I just looked at her. "Did you eat....... since morning?" Maritas asked me again. "I bring for you toast and tea..... Mathew?" They're all nice people, they're trying to take care of me and I felt ashamed. How can I repay these nice people? I just shook my head at Maritas.

"Thanks...I'm fine." I replied as she looked at me with doubt in her eyes.

"If you need anything.....just call me....okay Mathew?" Maritas said as she went out of the room. I couldn't get any sleep so I sat and was thinking about today, what happened, what was said, by whom, at what moment and I still couldn't understand or was I refusing to accept me Ma's death? I don't know what to believe and what not to. At about one at night, when it was quiet and there was no sound, I thought the night duty nurses might also be taking a nap.

I slowly got up from the bed, I tried not to make a sound, and I listened to Tom and the other patient. Tom was already snoring like a tractor on his farm. I went out and took a look along the corridor; I looked on both sides and didn't see anybody in sight. I turned to my right and walked slowly with my two crutches and my mini vacuum machine, in my one piece 'suit' and without a noise, slowly along the corridor.

The TV room was the fourth door on the right and the next room was empty. They were using it as storage for beds, chairs and other items and I had seen this room in one of my many walks. I turned and entered this room. It was dark, and no lights were on and once inside this storage room. I stood for a while so my eyes could get used to the darkness as I didn't want to put the lights on. I didn't want to attract any undue attention to myself.

I didn't want the nurses to wake and see my bed empty and then they would then probably raise the alarm to search for me as what I intended doing required complete secrecy. Once my eyes were used to the darkness, I slowly closed the door and walked in, careful not to accidentally bang into the furniture which in turn would make noise and awaken the nurses and my plan will be ruined. I reached the windows and looked outside and I could see clearly as daytime as the moon was shining; it was the night of full moon. I looked down and I saw the floor I was in was high enough for what I planned to do.

Down there on the ground I could see two cars parked and a few shrubs of green and a pathway with small gravel and sand. I checked the windows and the locks. The locks had a handle which I turned anticlockwise and it opened. I tried to open the window by pulling inside but it didn't budge. Then I tried to push outwards a little bit harder and then it budged a little and then it opened but I stopped midway. Okay that's good. I pulled it back again, closed.

There was a table near the window, I just pulled it a little bit and it was in position. Then I carried a chair slowly without making much noise to the window near the table. I tried to climb onto the chair but it was difficult for me. I thought, now what should do and then I saw several old phone books to the side inside the room. I brought a few and put them down near the chair and I then used the books as steps to climb the chair. At first it was difficult but after a few tries I managed to climb onto the chair. I relaxed to get my breath back and then I slowly again climbed on the table, I felt out of breath and tired. I then slowly put my two crutches on the table without making noise.

Now just to climb up on the window sill and the plan can be carried out smoothly. Eventually the 'D-Day' or for me the 'D-Time' had arrived. I climbed up the window after a bit of difficulty and now I stood on the inside of the window sill. I pushed the window outwards and a gush of cold and fresh air met my face and body. It was cold, it was now December and the winter this year was severe and very cold. Ireland was experiencing minus centigrade temperatures, some nights it was going down to minus fifteen centigrade, though today maybe it was minus five or so.

I stood there and contemplated what I was about to do, I was going to commit suicide I admitted to myself. I started to think and visualize the days since I could remember. I thought about my dead brothers, Donald and Daniel, how we were close and played together and how they fought for me at school and in our street, in the playgrounds and the fields. They both wouldn't let their younger and baby brother be bullied by anybody so sometimes they would get in trouble with a teacher just because of me.

How I missed them so much. I imagined what if they were still alive? We would have been great together, maybe we could have had families and nephews and nieces. What if we had listened to our Pa and went to school properly instead of dropping out? If we really paid attention in school and to the teachers then maybe we could have been people of means and maybe we could have our own company. We could have named our company, 'The Three Brothers', or 'DDM' for our initials.

Oh what if? I cried and sobbed but was careful not to utter a sound... if somebody heard then my plan would go astray. I thought of my Pa. Pa where are you? You were taken when I barely knew you, Pa. The few things I remember about you I knew you would have been a great man and father. Pa, I love you and I miss you. Pa, growing up without a father is the most difficult thing especially when we were boys, Pa. If you were alive today maybe none of your sons would have turned to criminality.

Pa if you were alive, your sons would all be alive now and you would have made sure we studied and become people of importance and good citizens and model workers. Pa, why but why Pa? If only you were alive today. I and my brothers would probably be members of the church and we would have been religious. We would have been responsible people and with wives and families and lovely children. Pa, if you were alive your sons would have given you grandsons and granddaughters for you to play with.

Pa if you were alive, you and Ma, we would make sure you had a good retirement and happy life and maybe we would have bought a farm with a lot of land where all of us could have lived together. Pa, why did you leave your sons to be orphans? And be raised by a one parent family without you Pa? And Ma, why did you decide to leave me without even saying goodbye? Ma, why but why, oh Ma?

I left you and told you I'm going to the hospital, and if you knew you were going to go then Ma you should have told me goodbye Ma. I love you Ma, but you left me alone in this world. Now I'm left alone in this cruel world without my Pa, without my brothers and now without you, Ma.

And then also, Kevin who was my friend, my protector, my cousin and my 'boss' God you also took him away from me. By putting him in prison so he couldn't be near me in my time of need, you took away my best friend who used to listen to me and help me but you took him also. What else do I have left in this world? Now I have this terrible and horrible disease, this cancer. Oh my God, what punishment, dear God, wherever you are, have you chosen for me? You took my parents and you took my brothers, you took my friend and you denied me my movie star.

Now you're going to take my body apart, piece by piece. First my leg will be cut off, maybe now or maybe later but eventually. Then the cancer will spread to the lungs, to the kidneys, to all internal organs and you will make me suffer and suffer, until you dear God are tired of my suffering and then finally you'll take me. Is this fair dear God? Take me now, this I plead and I beg you.

Dear God. Then there came from the skies a creature so beautiful, so charming, and so loving, the moment I saw her I fell deeply in love and I felt affection towards her. Her eyes, her smile, her perfect white teeth...oh those eyes, when they looked at me there was so much love in those eyes that it was melting my heart. Those eyes were intelligent eyes; those eyes knew a lot and those beautiful lips which make that smile. Oh my God, she had painted them red, that's my colour, it excited me then and she did excite me. When she looked and smiled at me I felt I was in heaven. Iris was her name.

But she saw me as an intruder in her life, she saw me as a thug, a hooligan, a gangster, a lowlife, a useless and good for nothing. She saw me as bad luck in her beautiful life. Dear God, that's how you denied me my movie star, you brought her to me and showed me from afar and once you saw that I was smitten by her you then took her away. How cruel you have been to me, dear God.

What you did God is like the famous fable, the cart driver dangling a carrot on a string in front of a mule and holding a stick behind the mule and that's what you did to me God, you were cruel to me. Now I have no reason to live in this cruel world. Why should I live and continue to suffer? God you will take me eventually, right? So why wait? I am coming earlier than you planned, that's all there is to it dear God. I'm coming to join my loved ones.

God, you denied me love and caring from my Pa, you denied me a good education, you denied me my brothers, you denied me my movie star, you denied me my mother and you denied me my life. God you denied me happiness. God! I blame you for all my misfortunes; you are the one big cause. God, but now I'm going to deny you the pleasure of making me suffer with this horrible disease.

Chapter Seventeen

$\mathcal{A}$HA I'M GOING TO HAVE the last laugh, God. And I then stepped out of the window. Now I was standing on the window ledge on my heels while the front of my feet, my toes, were way out and my body was out only my two hands were holding the window sides.

I wiped my tears with my one piece using my shoulder. It was now or never I thought as I closed my eyes then pushed my upper body forward with my arms stretched from behind. I felt the cold and I felt the wind. It was blowing at my one piece and I was more or less naked since I had nothing inside covering me but at this particular moment in time I couldn't have cared less. I didn't know any prayers but I thought I've said everything there is to say to God, so what other prayers are there? Nothing else I thought, and then I spoke to God for the last time.

"God, today I have won. You will never ever get me again. Goodbye." Closing my eyes I started counting from ten backwards. "Ten...nine... eight...seven.... six...five..." Then a strange thing happened to me in front of my eyes. I saw me Ma down far below on the ground. She was shaking her head and telling me something. I couldn't hear so I opened my mouth and asked her to speak up. "I can't hear, Ma could you speak louder?" but no sound came from me.

She spoke again to me but still I couldn't hear what she was trying to tell me. I asked again

'"What?" but no sound from me. I paused my counting maybe at number five so I could try to listen to her because there was a slight cold wind blowing. Then I saw her quite clearly and she spoke to me.

"No Mathew...you cannot do that...God will be angry with you.....you still have your life ahead of you.........you cannot take away your life.......you cannot commit suicide.....Me and Pa won't be happy Mathew.....also Donald and Daniel won't be happy.......don't do it........Mathew. I love you so much......Pa loves you so much.....we all love you so much.......you have to stay and live in this world ...... and you'll achieve your dreams....you'll achieve your Pa's and my dreams..... Mathew.....you have a lot to live for........go back inside. Mathew.....I love you my son..........go back........I will always be with you and guide you...........God loves also you.........Mathew........" And then she just vanished right there in front of me.

I tried to focus my eyes. Again using my shoulder I wiped my eyes but she was gone. I thought was that a dream or I actually saw me Ma's vision? Maybe it was true what she was trying to tell me but then how can it be true? It was just my imagination. She was dead and she cannot come to me now. She said she will always be with me but how that's possible? She's already dead. She said 'God loves me' but I haven't seen that from God...I was just imagining things. So I continued my count from where I left, where was I? Okay I got it now.

"Five...four....three......"

"Mathew.....Mathew" I heard someone calling me. I paused counting and listened. "Mathew...Mathew" Now who's calling me? I wondered. I again tried to focus my eyes trying to look, trying to see. Maybe me Ma came again but nobody was down there. "Mathew...... it is me." The voice seemed to come from behind me this time, like inside the room. I turned my head slowly. Yes it seemed like there was somebody in the room. I tried to see who it was... was it me Ma again?

"Who is it?" I managed to ask, I'm not my sure my voice came out or not.

"Mathew.…..it's me.…..Iris your movie star." Whoever it was said. "Please turn around Mathew." I heard the voice only faintly...was I dreaming? I focused my eyes, yes, it was somebody, a female and she said it was Iris. Which Iris? The only Iris I know is my movie star and it cannot be her...first she 'dumped' me, and second, now at night also in the hospital where did she come from? I continued my counting.

"Two.……..one…."

"Please Mathew…listen to me." The voice was pleading now. "Please stop… Don't do it …….Mathew." The voice was clearly of the only Iris I knew. So I turned again and looked at the figure more carefully. Okay it seemed that she looked like Iris.…oh yeah.……. it was Iris…the Iris I knew.…my movie star.…she smiled and then opened her two hands wide open in a welcoming sign and ready to hug me. "Come to me.….. Mathew." She said, "I love you.…..believe me ….. Mathew ….. I missed you.…please come back to me." I thought this was unbelievable. It couldn't be happening to me, no way man twice in one night? It cannot be, man, but there she was the woman of my life and she was telling me that she loves me and I found that pretty convincing. "Please turn around ….and……get down…Mathew." She said with her outstretched arms wide open and the smile...oh my God……and those eyes.…they had so much love.……I cannot deny her now….I was now confused.

Is it really happening to me? I looked at her for a while and then I accepted defeat. Just then the door of the room opened and Maritas the night duty nurse entered with another nurse and they switched the light on. I turned to look at both of them, their faces were white and pale with shock. But my movie star was gone and I couldn't see her anymore.

"Mathew...what are you doing?" Maritas shouted. "Come down from the window please." She pleaded while both of them were walking slowly towards me.

"No." I heard a croaky voice. "Wait, don't come any closer." Was it me speaking? Was it my voice? They both stopped and covered their mouths with their hands with shock. This was a big thing to happen on their watch and they could be suspended or be sacked or even be taken to court and charged with negligence. Many questions will be raised.

The night nurses were there for a reason. How can a patient go out of the room in the middle of the night and enter another room unnoticed? There will be an inquiry and so many questions. Maritas was there with shock.

"Mathew.........can I come closer? Please Mathew." She said pleading. "Please get down Mathew, Please." I looked at her.

"Where is Iris?" I asked her in my now hoarse voice. "She was here just now in this room." Maritas didn't know what I was talking about.

"Who is Iris...Mathew?" She asked in puzzlement. "We don't have any nurse who is called Iris." While looking at the other nurse as if asking her, 'do you know of any nurse who is called Iris?' The other nurse shook her head.

"No.....there's no nurse called Iris. The Dolphin ward has no Iris." She replied while looking at me and Maritas. "Maybe the other wards or floors they might have an Iris but not ours." I thought they looked shocked and confused or maybe I was the one going mental.

"Iris was here just now." I explained to them. "And she is not working in the hospital." They looked at each other again.

"Okay Mathew...can you please come down so we can talk about this?" Maritas asked and she already had reached near the table. "Who is Iris...? Mathew …...we'll find her for you...just come down please." She stretched her hand towards me her face pleading. The other nurse was still near the door and I thought maybe she was ready to run and call someone if and when I jump from the window towards my chosen destiny.

I then stepped from the window ledge outside to the window sill inside. I then turned my body fully towards the inside of the room. I gave one hand towards Maritas and she smiled at me in encouragement. Then I stepped on to the table and the other nurse as she then saw the situation changing she came forward and smiled at me and also offered her hand. I took both their hands and they helped me step down onto the chair and onto the phone books and I stepped down completely.

They then helped me to sit on the chair and then both of them hugged me. I cried and they cried and hugged me as relief showing in their faces. I thought that they felt they were the heroes and they've just averted a catastrophe from happening. They will think they saved my life which will be their story to their colleagues and friends and maybe the world. I knew it wasn't Maritas and her fellow nurse who stopped me in my 'adventure' but it was me Ma and my movie star. After letting me sob for a long while Maritas turned my face to look at her.

"Mathew....can we take you now to your bed?" Maritas spoke to me, "It's late and you need to get rest and sleep." The other nurse nodded her approval.

"Yes Mathew." she said, "You need to get some rest, now." I gave them my hands; they held me by the elbows and lifted me up slowly to a standing position. They then gave me my two crutches and each held me on one side and we started our journey back. We walked slowly to the door, we walked out and took a left towards my room and when we reached and entered my room, they helped me on to the bed. Maritas started to prepare the painkiller tablets plus morphine and the other nurse brought a glass of water.

"Mathew, take these and you get some sleep." Maritas said, "We'll talk in the morning. Okay?" I just looked at her.

"Maritas," I addressed her by name. "Where is Caroline?" I asked her because I thought yesterday Caroline showed me a lot of caring and love, she offered to spend the night in the hospital, so maybe it was Caroline I saw in my vision and not Iris.

"Mathew, Caroline will be here in the morning." Maritas replied. "You sleep and rest now. Okay?" And then they left me and went to their duty stations. I could hear the two of them walking and now checking the doors, the windows and everything else. I'm sure they'll not sleep or take a nap for the rest of tonight and not only that, I'm sure for every other night now, they're going to be aware of what might have been tonight.

I thought of my intended suicide and kept thinking of the two visions I had had tonight, one of me Ma and one of my movie star. Were the visions real or imaginary? It was four in the morning, when I fell asleep. I opened my eyes and saw the time, it was eight in the morning and then I saw Caroline. She saw I was awake and she came over smiling and she just hugged me and whispered.

"Oh Mathew," Caroline said to me, "you're awake now, thank God." I was surprised and when she again looked at me she had tears in her eyes. I wanted to ask 'What do you know?' but she looked at my eyes. "I couldn't sleep well last night." Caroline said, "I had a feeling something was not right and then today at six in the morning, Maritas called me." She looked at me and had tears in her eyes. "She told me about last night."

After a pause she continued, "And that also you had asked for me, Mathew. I came as soon after and I was here at six thirty." A pause, "I came to see you straight away but you were asleep and I didn't want to wake you up. You were sleeping like a baby. Oh Mathew," She smiled at me. "I'm here now Mathew. You can go and freshen up yourself or do you want me to bring you the washbasin?" She asked me. I told her I would go into the toilet and freshen up myself. She smiled and told me, "Okay, do that and then after we'll talk okay?"

I got down slowly and collected my 'briefcase' or was it the vacuum machine? I thought I shall ask the doctors to remove it now because last night it was a bit difficult to do what I intended, because of it. Otherwise I would have saved time and did what I had to do before they stopped me. I took my two crutches, held my one piece close to me so as not to do a 'free view' and walked slowly to the toilets on the left side of the corridors.

When I reached the toilets I did my business and brushed my teeth. I looked at my moustache and beard and I brushed as well with a comb. The people who knew me won't be able to recognise me now, I thought while smiling. Then I walked back slowly, all freshened up and a 'new' one piece on. Actually I was feeling good but I didn't have a clue why, but I was.

After the night's commotion and yesterday's grief about me Ma's death and all that, I did actually feel good. Was it because of Caroline? Maybe I felt happy because I was still alive? I felt like a newborn or so I thought. I reached my bed; it was already made up and with clean bed sheets. And then before I got up on the bed, Caroline had on her hands another piece of the hospital gown and she gave it to me.

"Mathew, you can put this on." Caroline told me as she me the gown.

"But I already have it on." I replied not knowing what her intention was.

"I know but put this one on as well." Caroline explained, "The other way round." I took it but still I didn't understand but then she helped me. The previous one I wore it to cover my front and behind was still the 'free view'. But then Caroline helped me put this one the normal way like a shirt so that I will be covered from the front and back.

So now with no worries except when sitting or getting up or down the bed. But otherwise, now I even felt better and decent. Caroline smiled.

"Are you better now?" Caroline asked me and I smiled at her.

"I have been here now for how long....maybe four weeks and yet nobody gave me this idea, and I never even thought to ask if it was allowed or not." I said. "But today Caroline, you did your magic. Thanks." She looked very pleased.

"I'm glad, now take your breakfast and relax," she said, "I'll be back." and she went.

Chapter Eighteen

$\mathcal{E}$LVIS BROUGHT ME BREAKFAST AND he looked at me.

"Mathew," he said while shaking his head. "I heard about last night, please don't do that again." Elvis smiled. "Now eat your breakfast and from now on, you should eat well and forget the past. Don't think about the past." Some good advice from Elvis, and he looked at me as if he isn't sure what to say, then. "Forget about that girl, Iris." Elvis advised me. I thought Oh my God, now almost everybody knows about my predicament but I just smiled at Elvis.

"Thanks," I replied and winked at him. Well, I thought my movie star was gone long ago actually but now Caroline is here and Maritas also is showing her interest in me. But the thing is however much Maritas might seem to care about me and maybe she's just doing her duty as a nurse. Not only to care about her patients and showing them empathy but also it could be that she likes me but unfortunately I wasn't interested in her. I'm sure she knows that, that's why she called Caroline to tell her about me and the night's events. Okay, so she withdrew from the challenge or race for Caroline, that's self sacrifice and therefore, hats off to Maritas.

Now about Caroline, yes she does her duty just like Maritas but she has gone a step further...she likes me, no, more like she loves me. She cares and has shown her sadness and empathy when I suffer, when I am in pain and when I despair, Caroline seems to notice and suffers for my sake. I thought I'm one lucky guy. Caroline is very beautiful and it's all a man wishes and dreams for, but, unfortunately try as I might, I don't have the same feelings towards her. I cannot return her love and caring even if I try, my heart only dreams of my movie star, the one and only, Iris. It will be cruel to lie to Caroline or give her false hope when I know I cannot give back what she most deserves.

I wondered about this world and how strange it seems when one desires something then one doesn't get it but the ones which one can get then one refuses it. It's a hopeless world and love is a hopeless thing and it is poison. It destroys people's lives and yet we cannot do without it. It's a funny world and I smiled to myself. I had my breakfast and I asked Elvis for a glass of orange juice to have with my tablets, which he brought to me with a smile. Tom was observing the events without saying a word so far but it looks like he also knew about the previous night's drama.

"Hi Tom," I said eventually. "How's it going?" He looked at me.

"Hi Mathew," Tom replied. "Should I say.......? 'Welcome back'...?" Then he quickly added before he was misunderstood. "I mean you're eating well now." And he came over and stood near me and put his hand on my shoulder. "I've heard what happened last night." he said, "I'm sorry Mathew, if you need to talk anytime just remember that I'm here. Okay?" And he walked out of the room maybe he went to smoke.

At eleven in the morning Maritas came and she touched my arm.

"Mathew, are you alright now?" Maritas said and then added. "I have just now finished completing a lot of forms and have been interviewed by the management about last night." She looked at me. "Don't worry; everything is going to be alright. Okay?" She then smiled at me. "I'll be off for two days but if you need anything, please talk to the nurse on duty. Okay?" She then winked at me. "Also

Caroline is here today for the day duty and she also took today's night duty as well...to be with you."

I smiled as I thought, 'look at how much these two beautiful ladies are competing for my attention and here I am, not even appreciating or return their love'. And it seemed to me that Maritas has already surrendered to Caroline for my attention. Later after lunch which I ate some but not all of and Elvis was glad for me about it, Dr. Browne came with Caroline the nurse. Dr. Browne pulled a chair and sat close to me.

"Hi Mathew," He said with a smile. "How are you feeling today?"

"I'm fine, doctor." I replied and waited. He looked at me.

"I heard about your mother and I'm sorry Mathew, my sympathies are with you." He paused and then continued, "Also I heard you attempted to........commit suicide........but then you didn't go ahead with the attempt." He nodded his head in approval. "That's very good of you.....keep your spirits up." I remained silent. "Okay, I just came to see you and...Dr. Livingstone will also come to see you.......later..... Okay Mathew?" Then he added. "Dr. Livingstone has increased your prescription. You will now take Lyrica 200mg twice a day, Cymbalta 60mg twice a day and Trental 400mg twice a day plus two paracetomol 500mg three times a day. The morphine will be given to you when and as required. Is that okay with you Mathew?" I just sat there looking at him and after a while I nodded. He then left.

At three in the afternoon, two men and one lady all well dressed in suits and they looked like management or something official came in the room brought in by Caroline and the nurses' supervisor. After a brief introduction, Caroline and the nurses' supervisor went out to continue their duties. Then they introduced themselves properly; they were from management and were internal investigator'

"Mathew please do not to worry, this is just an Internal Investigation." They then asked me questions and I responded and explained to them about last night.

"This is not the fault of the night nurses on duty or any failure from the hospital but it was just me myself." I explained to them. They filled paper after paper which I thought was useless and just a waste of time and money, but of course I couldn't tell them that. Then at five in the afternoon they stood up and shook hands with me.

"Thanks for your time Mathew," one of the men said and then added as an afterthought. "By the way, would you like us to contact the 'Samaritans' or arrange for you to get professional counselling?" I thought about it but since the feeling of helplessness has passed. I didn't think I needed any help.

"No thanks I'll be alright." I replied in a low voice.

Yesterday was a very bad day for me and after hearing the news about me Ma, it was a huge shock for me. Then at night everything came together, the mourning, the sorrow, the loneliness, the loss of my love to my movie star, my sickness and my pain. All this became unbearable and I felt I couldn't take it any longer.

But after the events of last night and the outcome and the visions which I saw and spoke to, I now felt I wasn't so distressed any more. I felt much better even though not hundred percent. I still had to get over the loss of my movie star and I have no knowledge of how my disease and my leg will end. Whether my leg will be chopped off? Will I then become a one legged person or what will become of my life? But for now I didn't need counselling. What I have is enough. There's Caroline, Maritas, and good old Tom.

"Thanks, there's no need. I'm alright and well." I said again.

"You have been very helpful Mathew." One of them replied. Then the lady gave me a smile of understanding.

"You are brave Mathew, please keep on fighting and you will be a winner. Okay?" She said and they left with their air of importance. I stayed there on my bed and was recalling what has been said and what if they were trying to implicate the night nurses for negligence. But I had made sure in my statement that the nurses were completely innocent and that it was my fault. Caroline appeared when I was deep in thought and she smiled at me.

"How did it go?" She asked me, "I mean the Internal Investigators who were here with you?" Ah now I understood.

"Yeah, it was okay." I replied but not really interested to discuss it.

"That's alright...do you need anything?" Caroline asked me and I thought okay. What do I need?

"Thanks Caroline." I said, "You're so nice." But in my head I said 'but you cannot give me what I want Caroline. I want my movie star and I cannot ask you because first of all you cannot deliver and second you'll feel bad'. Tom came over and sat down.

"Mathew ….can I ask you something…if you don't mind?" Tom asked and he was hesitating a bit.

"Yeah sure Tom, you can ask. What's it about?" I replied with a question. He thought for a while.

"Girls….Ladies…..Women…..Mathew," He replied. "Is it okay?" I looked at him and knew what was bothering him. He either wanted information for his head of knowledge or he really cared and maybe he was trying to help me.

"No bother Tom, go ahead and shoot." I replied. He became as if he was lost in thought and not sure how to begin.

"Okay there's no doubt Mathew that Caroline likes and loves you. I think that nearly everybody in the ward now knows about it by now." He said this with a smile on his face. "But it seems you're not returning the show of love to her and maybe she's hurting from your behaviour." He continued, "But that aside, I heard rumours that you fell or you like somebody else. Am I right so far?" I looked at him, his face and the seriousness and I then noticed his pencil thin moustache. I wasn't sure he had that from before or if it was new. I put it aside to ask him later on but for now I wanted to burst out laughing since this is my personal problem so why is he taking it as his own? What does he want to become. A matchmaker or what? But I just smiled at him.

"Go on." I said in encouragement and he paused a bit.

"Okay, so who is this other woman…for whom…… you are ready to ignore the love of Caroline……who is so beautiful and…and…and caring?" Tom said and added, "But I was also told or I heard about this other lady who is known as Iris." He paused and continued, "Whose father was with you in the hospital room long before I arrived."

Okay, I thought he knows a lot now let me just listen and see how much more he has in that bald head of his.

"But…..Mathew….my son…my friend…I'm told this lady, Iris…. is not in your class…..and she has no interest in you whatsoever…. that's why……you are like this…" Suddenly he became angry and his face and tone changed. "You tried to commit suicide for somebody who doesn't care about you.....somebody...you'll never...ever.....get? Just a visitor in the ward to see a patient who just happens to be next to your bed and you foolishly thought she was available for you? Was in love with you? And you're ready to throw away the love of somebody like Caroline? In my days I would try to elope with a girl like that. Caroline is such a wonderful person.....and you...she loves for what you are....look at yourself Mathew....just look at yourself. What do you see?"

Tom was furious and was now shouting, he was angry, he was becoming a father figure to me and his face was red with anger.

"Mathew my friend and son," he said. "Face reality.....Iris is just a vision... not real ....a mirage.....a fantasy......while Caroline is real... she's here and now...... you can touch her body........you can hear her voice." He was cooling down. "Be realistic Mathew and make a wise and good decision, a decision which will affect your life.... for now and forever. ....Mathew....the choice is yours." He then walked off with his two crutches. Angry and maybe sad at the same time and he went out of the room into the corridor and wherever he went to smoke.

I was left in deep shock. I have never been talked to so strongly and with such an impassioned plea by somebody in my life. But I felt good and I was teary because I felt that at least someone cared. I know that's why he spoke like that. The evening passed and I had my dinner which I couldn't really finish but I was okay. Caroline was always passing and glancing at me with a smile and maybe she had overheard Tom's impassioned pleas, but I didn't know that.

"Mathew, are you alright?" She kept on asking me, "If you need anything please let me know. Okay?" She tries so hard poor Caroline, I feel sorry for her and I cannot even put an effort to show her that I care for her. At night, Tom was as always watching the telly and admiring the TV announcers and talking to himself, and at ten he felt hungry and asked Caroline for his 'night snack' of tea and toast. And poor Caroline obliged.

"Okay, no problem Tom, just give me a minute or two," Caroline said so sweetly, "and Mathew would you like also a cup of tea and toast?" I felt if I refuse she might feel bad so I smiled at her.

"Thanks Caroline," I replied, "but just one slice please?" She smiled and her face brightened up. I think she felt good that I accepted her offer. I knew that I was in a dilemma still but what could I do?

Chapter Nineteen

ALREADY TOM HAS STRONGLY EXPRESSED his views and I have nobody else to talk with. I kept remembering me Ma. If she was still alive today, I know I could have talked to her and maybe she would have been judgemental on the class divide issue but I know she would have given me some good reasoning.

If Kevin was around then he definitely would have been forthright. Maybe when I came out of the hospital I should visit him in prison and talk to him. I thought that I do have to visit him whatever the case may be. I had difficulty getting to sleep you know, it was not even twenty four hours since my attempted suicide and it was not long since I knew of me Ma's death. I made up my mind once I came out of the hospital; I shall visit the neighbourhood of where I grew up and where me Ma died.

Even though the house has been locked up and is out of bounds, this was because she was the only one named in the Corporation Housing contract. My name was not mentioned in the contract. But then, my clothing and my family's items were still in the house. I have to collect everything after I come out of the hospital. Okay so now I was homeless. I made a note in my mind to talk with the Community or Social Nurse of the hospital to put on a request for emergency accommodation for me after I came out of the hospital if the Corporation refuses to let me live in me Ma's house. While I was deep in thought, Caroline came quietly and she opened the curtains just a little to peek inside.

"Hey Mathew, are you still awake?" She asked nicely. "Are you in pain? Should I get you something to ease your pain?" I thought 'Oh Caroline, yes I was in pain and more than pain, I'm in a dilemma and you're offering to ease my pain. Caroline, but how can you help me out?' But instead I just smiled at her.

"Just thinking about the past few hours' events and sorrow you know?" I replied. She walked inside and closed the curtains, I then added. "You know Caroline ......you've been very good to me....I just don't know how I can say thanks to you." She looked at me with her gorgeous eyes and she was lovely.

"You're thinking a lot about Iris, right Mathew?" She said with sadness in her voice. I thought oh my God, she has finally accepted defeat and she knows she cannot compete with my movie star; it's just not fair to her. I've been so cruel to everybody but myself, yeah I've been selfish, very selfish.

"Caroline...I .....I....." I was struggling to speak but she just smiled her radiant smile.

"Do you have her number.....maybe I'll try to contact her... for you?" She said.

"Caroline...I'm sorry.....I cannot....I don't have her personal number." I said while feeling ashamed at the same time and I was looking down. "I have her........father's contacts." I completed my sentence, but I couldn't look at her. She only smiled.

"Okay then...give me her father's contacts and I'll call him tomorrow....and I'll leave a message for her." She said so nicely. "Is that......what you...really want Mathew?" Caroline asked me. Oh God, I thought it was like a knife slicing through the heart, it's just not fair.

"No Caroline." I said abruptly looking at her in the eye. "Don't call her...... I'm sorry Caroline.....I'm putting you through too much pain and sadness….it is not fair to you Caroline…..” I protested but she cut me off and said softly while touching my hand.

“But Mathew…It’s alright…..one cannot always get what one wants….so if it’s meant not to be…then that’s it….but I do like and love you Mathew…if only you give me a chance……” She said and added softly. “I know I cannot compete with Iris ………..” Caroline said but couldn’t go on.

“No. Caroline…please don’t say that……I do like you but…. but…….” I tried to protest but she patted my hand.

“That’s what I’m saying…….if only you give me a chance…… we could now be talking…and discussing our future together…..Oh Mathew……I really care about you.” She suddenly burst into tears; I felt a knot in my stomach. What am I doing to this beautiful lady? I’m punishing her for my self-interest and it seems like I’m using her and I felt so down. I had that gutter feeling of myself as a useless and sham individual coming into the hospital and playing with real people’s feelings. I took Caroline into my arms and hugged her as she was sobbing.

“I’m sorry my dear Caroline. I’m confused….. And I’m sorry for hurting your feelings…..I don’t know what to say……..I’m a useless bastard…” I said while also sobbing slowly and quietly shaking my head. “Caroline….I’ve an idea……..will you listen to me please?” I said raising her head to look at me. “Let’s leave this subject alone…for the next twenty four hours……..we shall not contact Iris………if she appears ……. meaning, if she gets in touch or visits me in person…. as I saw in my vision….then I’ll listen to what she has to say……about my love and my feelings towards her….if she rejects my love…Caroline… if Iris rejects me…..then It’s all over…..once and for all…..” I paused looking into her eyes, “between Iris and me.”

She smiled but I knew she was in deep pain. Here is somebody she loves and he is negotiating her love.

“Then……please if you forgive me…..Caroline……I shall ask…..I will declare my love and affection for you…..I know that this is not fair to you in any way…….I’m being selfish here….and very cruel…..I’m using you as a ‘spare tyre’…I’m sorry Caroline…but I can have it no other way…If you don't mind…my dear and sweet Caroline." She hugged me so tightly as if she didn't feel secure to let me go.

I then held her face between my two hands and I felt and wanted to kiss her lips but I was scared it might send the wrong message too early for now anyway. I then kissed her forehead instead.

"Mathew……I can live with that…that phrase you just used………'Spare tyre'…..I agree. Let's wait and see if Iris, the woman of your dreams comes into the picture… then that's what God has written." She said and added, "But if she does not come… Mathew…in twenty four hours…as you promised…then you are mine…. forever…… and ever." She continued, "I want to promise you so much now…but it is okay….. I shall wait…..it is going to be very hard and nail biting the next twenty four hours ……..but you know that. I'll also try to be selfish…..I'll pray this Iris woman ……does not materialize."

She got up and wiped her eyes with a clean tissue, she blew her nose and she smiled.

"Now if you'll excuse me…I am going to the chapel…to pray….see you later…or in the morning." She said. "Try to sleep now…we have a long twenty four hours ahead of us…..I shall take the day off tomorrow to give you space but I shall be here for the night duty tomorrow…you know what I mean?"

And she went out of the curtains and the room. She left her beautiful smell of perfume and presence inside the room with me. Yes, I was a hopeless bastard and also a selfish and cruel person. I'm playing with people's feelings and testing their love. But I felt better, I had told Caroline the truth and I explained to her how I felt and my true feelings. So I've been honest with her, which is a plus for me. It shows the changes I'm going through. Previously I wouldn't care a bit if I lied or not, as long as I got what I wanted but now the changes shows.

At least now Caroline knows where she stands regarding me, instead of me lying to her and playing with her feelings and love. Then I fell asleep. In the morning at six I woke and sat on the bed and wondered what plans the day ahead has for me. While I was getting down from the bed, Caroline appeared with a smile.

"Morning Mathew," she said and asked, "already awake?" I smiled back at her.

"Morning Caroline," I replied. She then got for me my two pieces of the hospital gowns.

"Do you need anything else?" She asked me, "Okay go freshen up and then I have to check your pressure and blood glucose. Okay?" I nodded. I walked slowly to my 'destination' the toilets. After doing all I had to do I then walked back, feeling fresh and good and thinking today is the day either I get my movie star or I get Caroline to be mine and close the chapter of Iris forever. I wondered to myself.

What were the chances of Iris of even just passing in the hospital to see me or just for her to call and say hi? The chances were very slim or non-existent. So today is the day to erase her from my mind and brain forever and so today is the 'D-day' of my love life in Dublin University Hospital.

Wow, I thought what an adventure I got myself into. I got to my bed and usually it's about nine in the morning when the room attendants or student nurses who come to change the bed sheets and clean the room. But for me Caroline had already changed the bed sheets and my bed is clean and fresh. I got on the bed and Caroline came into the room.

"Are you feeling okay Mathew?" She asked me with her ever ready smile, and then she checked the blood pressure and blood glucose with much care and tenderness. "I'll talk to you later….before I go…okay?" She said. And then there was my ever ready adviser and friend himself, Tom, who appeared with his two crutches and he then held one like a machine gun pointing at me.

"This is 'Scarface'…….you giving me trouble…boy….you hiding something from me……eh….Mathew….come on….?" Tom said with a smile while pretending and acting to be serious. I laughed with him and then he came over.

"Hey Tom, how's it going?" I asked him.

"Hi Mathew," he said, "did you sleep well……last night?" I looked at him trying to read his face.

"Yeah…..okay," I said, "what about you?" I replied him and he reduced his voice.

"I heard some commotion last night." Tom said with a wink. "Anyway…..talk to you later." He went back to his bed. Caroline came and she closed the curtains and came standing near me.

"Hey Mathew," she said while looking at her watch. "Soon I have to leave." She smiled and added, "I'm going to miss you Mathew........ for the day.....the whole day...it's going to be a long day.... for me, Mathew."

"I know." I said sadly. "But I'll see you in the evening, right?" She held my hand and kissed it and I felt good but sad at the same time. Caroline was tender and loving but the problem was with me, I couldn't love her back. I had such a dilemma in front of me. But soon it's going to be over; it was less than twelve hours to go now.

"Mathew......I am going to go now...but I'll see you in the evening." Caroline said. "I'm going to miss you Mathew.........and I shall be praying to God for Iris not to appear or be heard from...for......ever..... Mathew." Her eyes were red and teary as she held my hand tight and I squeezed it.

"I have nothing to say Caroline." I said, "I.....I.....I.....I couldn't bring myself to finish the sentence, what was it...'I love you' or 'I care about you' or what should I tell Caroline? It was a difficult situation. I wouldn't like to wish it on anyone in my present circumstances. Caroline understood and she kissed me softly on my lips.

"It is okay Mathew....I understand...what I can say...." She said. "What has to be will be...I have no power to stop it.....or speed it up...or change it....but if I had the power then I would definitely stop Iris coming near you...and you will be mine forever...and ever....oh Mathew...how much I wish..."

"Please Caroline," I said. "Stop it.....you will make me.....oh I don't know..."She stood up straight opened the curtains and went out of the room. I sat there for a long time thinking and wishing if only this and if only that. Elvis brought breakfast and I had mine in silence and in deep thoughts. Maybe Elvis said something but I didn't hear and then Tom said something either to me or to himself but I did not hear that either.

At ten in the morning, the doctors passed again and this time Dr. Livingstone was with them and he stopped at my bed and stood near me. He looked at me for a while which made me scared.

"Is something the matter?" I asked him. He smiled.

"Mathew, how have you been lately?" He said and before I answered he continued, "I got the report and I sent Dr. Browne to see you. I am being kept in touch with all your progress and I have increased your prescriptions, right?" I just nodded my head and he continued, "How do you feel generally...about your leg and your health?"

"Okay, the pain is there in the leg." I replied, "Sometimes the pain is unbearable and I have to get some painkiller but sometimes it is better... just up and down, you know what I mean?" Dr. Livingstone nodded.

"What about your mental health?" He asked while looking me in the eyes with a faint smile. "How do you feel now?"

Yeah, I know doctor....what I wanted to attempt.....I mean ....commit.....was a dumb idea....you know what I mean?" I replied, feeling ashamed at the same time. "It's over doctor...I'm alright now... I'm good." He smiled and patted me on the shoulder.

"Okay, good to hear that Mathew.......if there's anything...please try and talk to someone, anyone from the nurses, doctors or other staff." He said, "You can even ask to see me and we will talk things over, okay Mathew?"

"Yeah I'm grand." I replied and then he left with the other doctors.

Chapter Twenty

$\mathcal{W}$HEN THE GROUP OF DOCTORS had gone, then Tom came over and he pulled up a chair and sat down near me. He stayed silent for a little while. Then touching his lower back and neck he complained of the pain he had in his back and he said they were treating him now with 'epidural' injections.

These were very painful injections and they go directly into the spine or the lower back. And he started to massage himself on his lower back, his neck, his arms and thighs. Tom said but now he felt much better and maybe within a day or two he will be out and on his way back to the West of Ireland to continue his adventures with his father-in-law.

"Tom, tell me honestly." I said abruptly to Tom. "What would you do if you were in my position?" He looked at me for a long time.

"What position are you now talking about, Mathew?" Tom asked in a feigned pretence. "You've a lot of issues so which one are you talking about? Is it about your leg, about the doctors, about the hospital, about the death of your mom or about your complicated love life?" Tom continued.

"Aw come now Tom, you know what I'm talking about." I said to him while smiling, "It is about as you said it correctly, my 'complicated love life', you know what I mean?"

"To be honest with you," Tom said, "I would forget about the other one. What's her name? I haven't even seen her but I tell you Mathew, Caroline is the best any man would wish and dream for, honestly." And Tom went on. "She is everything a woman can be. Besides, she loves and adores you." Tom said. "And besides, I am jealous of you and if I were younger, then maybe I would try to elope with her." He started laughing. "It has become my specialty you know, the eloping part."

I nodded my head in understanding, and thinking yes Tom was right but he was not in my position. I've fallen in love with a woman whom I cannot imagine to be without. I couldn't accept that today is the day I have to erase Iris, my movie star, from my heart, from my mind, from my brain, from my imagination and from my life forever. Because once I accept and say yes to Caroline, then that's it, whatever the case I've to commit myself to her and not even think or mention Iris again.

I knew that whoever I get today, be it Caroline or Iris, then I've to change my life and be committed and not look at other women. I needed the motivation to change my life and I knew whoever it is, either Caroline or Iris, I have got myself the right one to love to remove me from the despair I was in. While I was daydreaming, Elvis came in the room.

"Hey Mathew," he said to me. "What would you like for lunch today?" He usually comes between ten and eleven in the morning to take lunch orders, the menu varies and usually you have a choice of about three meals.

"What special you have for today?" I asked Elvis and he responded.

"Rice with chicken curry, pasta Bolognese and salad," Elvis said and he added, "Take the pasta Bolognese." I nodded my head.

"Okay then, I'll have the pasta and don't forget the ice cream as well please." I then heard Tom's voice.

"Hi my friend Elvis," Tom said. "I will have same like Mathew's but please for me add two ice creams and two jellies. Okay?" I admired Tom's appetite. For his body and flat stomach he ate quite well. After a while I heard Tom talking on his mobile and he was sort of agitated and was speaking in a loud angry voice. Later he came over but I didn't want to ask him about his phone call, although he seemed like he wanted to talk it over with me. He sat down fuming and angry.

"Tom," I said to him, "are you alright? You don't seem to be good, is something the matter?" Tom looked at me shaking his head.

"It's the wife." Tom replied and then he kept quiet but continued shaking his head and I waited, a few minutes passed before Tom came back to life once again. "I'm here at the hospital for many days now," Tom said, "and the wife she rings, you know what she wants? She wants money, for what, food, for medicine? No, she wants money for Christmas shopping. She also wants to buy gifts for her parents. Can you imagine this silliness?" Tom looked at me with anger in his face... or was it disappointment?

"I'm sorry I have to unload this on you," Tom said, "but I left her with enough money and also she has access to my bank account but she still needs more. Should I now go and rob a bank to satisfy her shopping?" I didn't say anything as I didn't want to add 'oil to the fire' as it was, but keeping silent was the best in this kind of situation. I wanted Tom to cool down, as otherwise he might get a heart attack. Once he had cooled down, I then pointed to his crutches and said in a low voice.

"What about Al Pacino and Scarface?" Tom looked at me and it seemed that what I said didn't register in his brain. So I reminded him about the play acting he did a few days before and then he remembered and he lifted one crutch and did the machine gun on his hip.

"Everybody raise your hands," Tom said and added, "give me all your money because my wife needs the money for buying Christmas presents for her parents and the whole damn village." He made the sound of a machine gun, tat tat tat... "Give me your money or I'll shoot you all." I raised my hands up in the air and in a shaky voice.

"I don't have any money with me sir," I said, "but you can take whatever you see around and also my lunch when Elvis brings it for me." Tom smiled and together we started laughing and play acting and thank God, Tom was normal again. Lunch time, Elvis with his trolleys and trays delivered our much awaited lunch, which we ate and later after Tom finished his portion and added more he burped aloud a few times. "Manners, Tom. Manners, Tom." I said across the room, Tom laughed.

"Sorry mate that was lovely lunch." Tom replied.

"Did you manage to finish all?" I asked Tom.

"Oh yeah, you have any left-over for me?" Tom replied with a request. I looked at him in amazement.

"Are you serious? Do you want more or are you just messing?" I asked him, "I think it's enough, Tom." Tom laughed and he said he was full but just was messing with me, and I knew now he was okay and had cooled down fully. Then he went for a walk which I knew meant he was going to smoke and think. I sat on my bed and relaxed. I was always trying to catch a glimpse whenever someone passed in the corridor, and expecting someone would enter my room to see me.

No visitors for me at all. But I was still expecting a miracle, I still had a window of hope which I left open expecting or rather wishing, Iris, my movie star, would just walk in with a smile and a hug and will come to see me. Tom came back and we just exchanged small talk to pass the time having nothing to do. For me, I was trying to hide the fact that I was tense and was anxious at the same time.

I had a feeling and I knew that today was not an ordinary day for me; today my life will change forever. At five in the evening as it was already dark since now we are in December and it is winter, one of the nurses came and told me with a smile.

"Mathew, someone is here to see you," she said. "Is it okay if she comes in?" My mind started racing, I had a visitor, someone is here to see me, can she come in…she….my heart was beating fast.

"It's okay; whoever it is can come to see me." I said. "I don't mind." And I then heard the click clack of the shoes then I smelled the perfume. I then knew immediately who it was but I couldn't believe it and she walked in with a smile on her face. I noticed she was tanned. Oh my God, she was beautiful.

"Hi Mathew," she said, but I wasn't in this world. It wasn't real;

somebody must be playing tricks on me. I just remained dumbfounded, my mouth wide open but no words coming out, my eyes fixed on her but not seeing. No it cannot be true and I was dreaming. She walked in and then she hugged me and gave me a kiss on each cheek. "Are you not glad to see me Mathew?" She asked me, "You look like you have seen a ghost." Yes I have seen a ghost. Are you real? I wanted to ask her and then the nurse with a smile on her face came near me and touched my shoulder.

"Mathew it is Iris, do you remember her?" She asked and added, "She was here before when her dad was next to your bed, you must remember her, right?" I nodded my head and collected my thoughts and I turned and looked hard at Iris, my movie star, yes she was real and she came to see me, I knew it, I just knew she would come. I smiled at Iris, my movie star.

"Of course I remember Iris! She is my movie star," I said while looking at Iris in the eyes. "How can I forget? I was just in a shock to see you, my dear; it's been a long time." The nurse understood and she smiled.

"I'll leave the two of you together for a while," the nurse said. Then she went and closed the curtains behind her to give us privacy and yes privacy we needed. We had a lot to talk about and a lot of catching up. Iris sat on the bed with me, and we looked at each other in the eyes, each waiting for the other to say something. Then Iris hugged me.

"Oh Mathew, I missed you so much." She said, "I have been thinking a lot about you these past days." We continued hugging and my eyes started to water. I wanted to cry with happiness but I felt crying is not for men, men are not supposed to show emotion so I held myself back. I felt wetness in my arm and then I heard a sobbing sound. Oh my God, Iris was crying. I released her from the hugging and I took her face in my hands.

I looked at her in those beautiful eyes and oh yes, she was very beautiful. I couldn't believe Iris was right now in my arms.

"Mathew, I missed you sooooo much." Iris said and she kissed me on my lips. "I was on holiday in the Canaries and while I was on the beach and reading a book, I realised that I am in love with you, Mathew. I do really love you but I don't know how or why." She sat there and started to explain to me. After her father was discharged from the hospital, they took him home and everyday he was asking Iris either to visit me or call me in the hospital in order to know about my health and wellbeing.

But her mother knew that James, her husband was pushing Iris to me and she was against this. She saw me as a low life maybe a criminal or drug user or whatever, and I was not worthy of her only daughter. So Iris was caught in between. But still, her parent's wishes were not her main concern as she was a strong willed and self minded individual. But she knew she had a soft spot somewhere in her heart for me and she was also confused about the social status and class and about my past even though she didn't know a lot about me.

So she had gone on holidays with her work colleagues. Iris insisted they were all women and no men were among them. And while in the Canaries on her holiday, she had nobody there to influence her and she thought and planned and tried to see herself after ten years, twenty years and so forth, where she would be and with whom and how? She thought about people she knew, how they coped in their careers and their personal lives, how they coped in their marriages, she took these as examples and case points to learn about.

She made graphs, drawings and diagrams to help her learn about life and the future, to help her predict and forecast the future, to help her decide on what is right and what is wrong. Iris wanted a commitment from a man whom she was going to spend her life with; she didn't want to change a man after every few years. She wanted stability, she wanted what her own mother and father had, a long happy marriage where there was mutual respect and love and harmony in the house.

She made a long list and she decided and made her choice. Mathew was the man but only if he managed to tick all the boxes of Iris' long 'Questionnaire'.

"Yesterday I came back from the Canaries and I could not wait for today so I could come to see you." Iris said and added, "I had to go to the office in the morning and I called the hospital to check and see if you were still in the hospital." She paused and continued, "I was just hoping and I crossed my fingers that you were still in the hospital, otherwise where would I find you?" And yes, they told her I was in the hospital, which she was delighted about and at half past four she couldn't wait any longer.

"I drove over as fast as I could to come to see you, Mathew," she smiled and said. "I knew you have been in the hospital all these days and weeks and you didn't have any visitors. But still for my sake, tell me are you still single and available?" She laughed at her own joke. Oh that smile of hers, that laughter, those lips, oh she was so beautiful. But her joke made me come awake. She knew that as long as I was in the hospital, I was free but she didn't know of the competition. She didn't know about Caroline, my Caroline, and now I'm in a true dilemma.

Chapter Twenty-One

*T*WO OF THE MOST BEAUTIFUL women and one which I was sure of as being caring and loving me, me of all the people, me as I saw myself as being a worthless and not lovable material. But I'm being sought after by the two most beautiful women in the world. I felt I had to tell Iris about Caroline and if she decides that I'm not worth her love then that's it, but no lying from me to any of them. So I told Iris.

"First we see your list and then I'll tell you about myself." I told Iris and said, "Let's see if we're compatible with each other or that I meet your requirements. Okay my love?" She brought out a paper and opened it to reveal the list, which was neatly written in her beautiful small handwriting. She took out a pen.

"Mathew, this is my list and after we finish my list then you can ask me any questions or state your requirements." Iris said and added, "As I explained before, I don't do boyfriends and I don't do children first and then after many years comes marriage. No, I don't do 'trial and error' type of relationships." She explained what she wanted was a stable relationship which will eventually lead to marriage and soon, not years, not months, but soon, she didn't like '*hanky-panky*' type of relationships for fun. "Are you ready for my type of relationship, Mathew?" Iris asked me and quickly added, "But first you have to tell me everything about yourself, no lies please, as I wouldn't want surprises later on. Can you do that please Mathew?"

I then explained my short life story to this strange woman whom I met just a few weeks ago but who has taken my life by storm. It is as if I have known her for a very long time. I was explaining to her, no, I was actually confessing about my criminal past, about my intimate life, about my worst fears and about almost everything. I was like a lamb to my Iris and she held me by a chain tied to my heart. I told her about the love of my mother and my dead father and brothers and also about Kevin and the gang.

Everything and leaving nothing out, it was hard but I did it. I sobbed when I spoke about me Ma and her death

"She was dead for maybe three days, alone." I told Iris of how my mother's dead body was rotten and she had to be buried quickly. "Within a few days of her being removed from the house, the Corporation buried her. I couldn't attend her removal or burial neither was Kevin, but her sister, my aunt and a few relatives were there. I had given the go ahead to the Corporation to bury her. She was buried in Glasnevin cemetery and after I come out of the hospital I will go to visit her."

Iris felt for me, she sobbed listening to my story and she hugged me tighter to protect me. Then she spoke to me tenderly. "Despair not, my love and do come with me and I will help you to forget your sorrows and your pain." She expected me to move from the inner city of which I didn't have a place to stay anyway and she wanted me to cut off all relationships with my former friends as they were a bad influence on me.

She wanted me to go back to getting an education and the target should be getting a bachelors degree from the University or College, which was fine with me and that being my dream and my parent's wishes anyway. No more heavy drinking of alcohol, no more smoking and no more obscene language, the 'f's'.

There must be no secrets between us, which was what I wanted anyway. And Iris said she would help me achieve all these things if we work together and we were in agreement. Okay, I thought for me all these I had no problems with and actually I would love the challenge but of course I had my reservations as well.

"As I don't have a current job, I won't be able to have a flat or house of my own and if I go back to getting an education, how can I survive and how can I be able to take care of myself and my 'family'? You know what I mean?" Iris smiled.

"Okay, about the house, you can stay in my flat while I stay at my parents. And when you go back to getting an education, besides having a free education the government will give you an allowance to support you, and about taking care of your 'family' that will come afterwards." Iris went on further to explain that she would be studying as well; she would be doing her master's degree. She said that after being discharged from the hospital I could go to her parent's house to recover and after that I can move into her flat and start studying part time in the VTOS programme as a mature adult student.

I should start with the Leaving Cert and go from there. She would help and support me financially if I needed to but with my government's allowance I should be able to manage that. She said she will not move in with me unless and until we get married.

"If there's no marriage then there's no living together at all, for that I'm sorry." Iris strongly insisted when she said this. "As I told you a few minutes ago I don't do boyfriends." Iris said, "As soon as you are comfortable with the arrangements and you see yourself that you can manage and be able to change and then we shall talk about the future. Is that okay with you?" Iris paused and went on, "you see Mathew," Iris added, "I was hard on you the other day but now I am comfortable with you so now I can tell you without a doubt or fear," she continued. "I do now love you Mathew, but do you still love me? Are you willing for the transition of your life?" Iris looked at me with such beautiful and pleading eyes.

I had no idea where this change of heart came from. Was it her holiday in the Canaries Islands? Or was it from her father? Or was it from my prayers? Or she just felt sorry for me and of my attempted suicide?

"Oh Iris, my movie star," I said, "I love you so much, I really do, you just cannot imagine how much I love you or how many times I've dreamed of this very moment." I took her face and brought her near my face, our noses touching and looking at each other's eyes then I kissed her lips, so tender so nice, I then held her for sometime before I told her. "I have a confession to make, my love."

Iris pulled herself back and looked at me with shock. I explained to her about Caroline. I explained to her about my apparent suicide attempt and about the visions I had and the aftermath of that and that it was Caroline who gave me the strength when I needed. It was Caroline who gave me courage and it was Caroline who showed and gave me love when I mostly needed it. It was Caroline, who was with me and took care of me far beyond and above her duties and I told Iris about yesterday's talk with Caroline and that today was the 'D-day' for our love.

"I was afraid of this, I had a feeling something might not be right." Iris said. "I ignored you for too long and left you without any apology and now this. I deserve this, oh Mathew I am so sorry. What shall I do now?" She started crying and sobbing. I heard Tom's footsteps walking around and I was sure he was listening to the unfolding drama and everything. Maybe Tom wanted to come in and join in our love conversations and when Caroline comes in, there shall be a 'round table' of four in the meeting.

"I'm sorry Iris my love," I said, "but I had to tell you the truth." Then I heard Elvis bringing in dinner.

"Mathew, are you alright in there?" Elvis asked aloud.

"I'm okay Elvis. Can you just leave my dinner tray on the table please? And thanks Elvis." I responded and to Tom who continued to walk around the room. "Hey Tom, I'm alright no bother." I said aloud and added for his information, "I'm with Iris, my movie star. Do you remember I told you about her? She came to see me Tom. Isn't that great?"

"Can I come in for just a second to see this Iris whom I have heard so much about?" Tom asked.

"Come in and be quick Tom, we're busy here you know." I then replied. Tom stepped in through the curtains and he held his hand on his open mouth while he looked at Iris.

"Yes you are right Mathew," Tom said with awe in his eyes and voice, "she is stunning and you are a very lucky bastard if you excuse my language, Miss." Tom turned to Iris. "Mathew here has been killing himself about you and I was thinking, who is this Iris who's killing my friend? But now I've seen you I understand." Then he turned back to me. "Mathew my friend, you are a very lucky man and I do envy you but now, soon you have to make a decision and my advice if you ask me is.......I don't know...you're on your own here...good luck." Tom turned to Iris, "Nice meeting you and if you win him, then please take care of Mathew. He is a good lad and funny too." Iris was looking at me and I was wondering if this was really happening to me.

Today, now, two very pretty and beautiful women who are both educated and with careers, from good families and they have good jobs and all, and yet they want to spend the rest of their lives with me? They're ready to share all they have with me? Me? Good for nothing Mathew? I just cannot believe this is really happening to me. I came in the hospital only a few weeks ago and now this? How can I possibly explain to anyone of how fortunate I have become in these few weeks?

I now have a say with these two caring women and they will listen. I now have the power to choose only one and to tell the other one 'I'm sorry'. How this world works? I'll never know the answer to that. In these past few weeks a lot has happened in my life that can usually happen in a longer time frame and also in a different place but not in a hospital.

I sat there on my hospital bed in my two piece hospital gown thanks to Caroline. And thinking in the next hour or so I have to make a decision that will affect three lives and I myself was not sure. In my outside life and before the hospital, I was the hunter when it comes to women but now it seemed like I was the hunted and I was supposed to choose which of the two hunters will shoot me and become the winner.

I wished someone could help me to make the right choice. We

were silent, me and Iris, each with our inner thoughts and I wanted to break the silence.

"Iris, how's your dad? .....and how's your mom?" I asked her and she shook her head as if coming back to life, from her deep thoughts.

"Mhh...what did you say?" Iris said in a voice that seemed like a whisper and I repeated the question to her. "My dad is doing well and is walking now, he is fine," Iris said, "and mom also is well, no complaints there." I looked at her.

"Iris, you said after I come out of the hospital you wanted me to come to stay in your parents' house." I said. "How will your parents take it...especially your mom whom you already said doesn't like me?" Iris looked at me then smiled.

"First, to make clear to you it's not that my mom does not like you, it is just that she was not happy of this relationship," Iris explained. "And besides that, she now has accepted whatever my decision will be. Yesterday we sat down, the three of us and had a discussion which I can tell you now, made my father happy and he approved of my decision, therefore my mother has also now accepted the inevitable."

She looked at me while holding my hand. "Furthermore, after you are discharged from the hospital you will come in our house where you will stay in the guest room and as my father's guest and friend. Don't mind the age gap between you and my dad, he considers you as a friend. You can take it as a period of evaluation if you know what I mean." Iris laughed and continued, "You will be evaluated in everything you do so be careful, no alcohol, no smoking, no obscenities, no bad groups or influences.

It's going to be tough especially as it is going to be my mother and not my father who will be doing the observations and evaluating you, my love." She looked at me with those pleading, soft eyes. "Mathew, do you mind?" Caroline looked at me as she asked me, "Giving all those that you enjoy, just for me? Are you ready to sacrifice?" I looked at Iris, my movie star.

"I am ready to sacrifice and give up all those things and not only for you, but even if it was for Caroline, I would have done it. But especially for me, because while I have been in the hospital I have had time to think a lot and it was my decision, my decision alone to change and try to be a different man. I wanted to get an education for my father and my mother. I wanted to move from what I was to what I want to be." I explained to Iris that I wanted just as much, a commitment as hers and that I was ready for a new life. I added either with her or with Caroline. And she started sobbing again.

"Oh Mathew, I am being selfish. Please choose me and I love you deeply Mathew." Iris pleaded between sobs. "I also am ready to sacrifice, I want us to be happy, I want us to build a future together Mathew, please honey. Don't let me down." I held her tightly.

"My love, I'm in a dilemma and I cannot decide and make a choice between you and Caroline." I confessed and told her, "You see Iris from the moment I saw you I knew you would be the one that's why I gathered my courage to tell you my feelings the other day and you must remember your answers and attitude that day but still I had my hopes and dreams for you." I looked at her and continued, "And then came Caroline, and she is so caring and she has all the qualities and she is ready to sacrifice everything for me and for my love. She loves me dearly Iris, believe me. Just wait till you see her and you'll like her too."

I heard her say something from her throat like, 'Oh yeah I'll surely like her, she is my main opposition and you are telling me I'll like her, are you crazy or what?'

"It's better we wait for Caroline, don't you think so too?" I told Iris. I was dreading the moment when Caroline would come and meets Iris but it had to be, there was no avoiding that moment and it was coming nearer and soon. Though I wanted Iris to stay with me as long as possible I still had to think about her feelings, "Iris, are you okay and comfortable or do you want to go?" I asked her and quickly added in case she misunderstood me, "Maybe you have to go for a meeting or be somewhere?"

"No I am fine really, I am in no hurry and I can stay and wait to meet this so called Caroline of yours." She replied as she shook her head, "Or do you want me to leave?"

"I don't want you to leave, I'm just nervous myself Iris," I replied and added, "I was just worried about you, are you going to be comfortable meeting with Caroline?" She nodded her head and in play acting she flexed her arm muscles.

"Let Caroline or anyone else come," Iris said, "I am ready to fight them all for my man, my Mathew, my love, my super hero. Come on bring it on." Iris laughed but was as nervous as I was and we laughed together or at least we pretended to laugh, but the nervousness and anxiety showed.

Chapter Twenty-Two

$\mathcal{W}$HEN IT WAS AT ABOUT half six in the evening, I heard talking and laughing in the corridor and a sixth sense told me it might be that Caroline has arrived at the 'field of war', and the combatants were armed and ready. I heard Tom's voice also in the corridor. I was not sure if Tom was 'arming' Caroline for battle or what. I think Tom would have voted for Caroline and all the hospital's staff in the ward would vote for Caroline of course she was their colleague.

It seemed Iris was on her own, as there was no support for her and she has to fight her battles alone. And yes, it was Caroline in the corridor she had come earlier than necessary, maybe because of our agreement or because she wanted 'closure' to her torment and of her love for me. She entered the room and she said aloud.

"Hi everyone….Hi Tom…..Hi Mathew….are you there Mathew…. can I open the curtains….can I come in?" My heart was beating heavily.

"Hey Caroline, please come in." I replied and Caroline opened and passed through the curtains and she closed it back. She stood there with a forced smile and looked around, she looked at Iris and she looked at me. I looked at Caroline.

"Caroline, this is Iris, I think you know her." I said and added, "I was explaining to Iris all about you, I mean... us, and our agreement of yesterday. Iris now knows everything." And I then turned to Iris. "Iris, this is Caroline." I said, "I was explaining to you about me and Caroline and how helpful she has been to me." Caroline was composed as she walked towards Iris.

I could sense the tension which was in the room. I could hear or rather feel the throbbing of all our hearts. Iris saw that Caroline was walking towards her and she stood up ready for whatever was going to happen. In my heart I was praying. 'Please dear God, please avert this situation and let nothing serious happen. Please dear God, let this situation be reached by mutual agreement and peacefully.' I was so scared of what was going to happen and I could see it in front of my eyes.

I have seen it before, I have witnessed similar situations when two or more women go to fight. It was always ugly and difficult to separate them and it was usually followed by all obscenities known to man. Everything was all in slow motion. It was like a part from the movie 'The Good, The Bad, and The Ugly'. I could also hear the music of the same movie in my head.

As Caroline slowly walked towards Iris while I was just sitting on the bed and being unable to do anything but watch the unfolding drama and pray. Caroline reached Iris and they were eye to eye and the most surprising thing happened in front of my eyes. Caroline offered her hand to Iris with a smile.

"Hi Iris, I'm Caroline." Caroline spoke ever so sweetly, "I remember you from the time you were visiting your dad? How's he doing now?" I now thought, okay, Caroline have been a true lady and what will Iris do now? Will she refuse the handshake; will she start a fight or what's going to be Iris's reaction? But Iris returned the offer and they shook hands. That was a peaceful gesture offered by Caroline and returned by Iris.

A gesture which caught Iris and me included by surprise, and then

Iris did one better, she kissed Caroline on both cheeks and then together they hugged. I felt like joining them on the hugging part but I was unable to move, I was frozen. They were sobbing and hugging and then Caroline slowly detached herself while still holding Iris.

"Iris, you look soooo pretty." Caroline had a tear or two and was smiling. "I cannot compete with you for Mathew's heart and love." Caroline said and added, "You are the winner, and I was just hoping all along you won't come at the last minute and grab my Mathew's heart, but you did, Iris, but you did." Caroline added while wiping a tear from her eye, "Why you had to come today, Iris?" Iris was just as shocked and wasn't able to answer the questions. Instead, she could only look at Caroline.

"Caroline, you are so beautiful yourself and I mean it." Iris replied, "I'm so sorry myself Caroline. I did not mean to put you in this position, honest to God." And then she added, "Actually you deserve him more than me, Caroline. Mathew told me a lot about you and you are an angel, truly you are Caroline." I now felt I was left out, now there was peace and tranquillity. I breathed again with life and looked at both of them, as they were truly two of the most beautiful women and they were both composed, both loving, both caring and both with good manners.

I envied myself and thanked God for my luck but still I was in a dilemma. I still had to choose one and only one I must choose. The decision was difficult and painful, gaining one love will make me lose another.

"Hey ladies, did you forget I still exist?" I said aloud. "I know you've now bonded but I still exist you know." They both laughed their beautiful laughter and came my way and they both hugged me. I was taken by surprise; it was like a 'koala hug' in a threesome. We hugged for a few minutes and Caroline and Iris were either sobbing or whispering, I didn't know. I felt like the '*King of Zamunda*' in that faraway land where the king had plenty of wives and every year he got married again and again. Then Iris took and held Caroline's hand and looked at me.

"Mathew," Iris said, "It's now time....for you to make your decision, pick one of us and the other will go quietly. It is what you call the

'D-Day of love' the choice is yours to make so please tell us. Is it Caroline or me?" I thought is this a punishment or what, now they have banded together and they wanted to punish me. I wouldn't be surprised if the two of them together dumped me and walked away leaving me the loser and a complete fool.

I knew Tom would laugh till he died. That bastard Tom and why is he still walking around and listening to our 'three party conference'? Then I said to myself, what has poor Tom done now? Nothing, I'm just angry at him for nothing, he didn't contribute anything to this dilemma of mine and this is of my own making. I wanted to shout out aloud 'somebody help me, I need your help, please make a decision for me' but I couldn't just shout and also there wasn't anyone out there who could help me. 'God, can you send me an angel to be my mediator or something? Who will make the right choice on my behalf? Come on God please don't let me down, you know that I love you dear God, right?' but no angel was sent by God. It seems God chose to let me alone face my problem in this situation.

"Hi Mathew, Hi Iris," it was Caroline who brought me back to reality. "I know the solution to our problem." Oh my God, she was a Godsend. "Iris, please can you go near Mathew?" Caroline said, "Just stand next to him." And Iris obediently did as she was told, she came and stood next to me and then Caroline turned to me, "Mathew, can you please hold Iris's hand?" I held Iris's hand and my heart started pounding again.

I had a thought that maybe tomorrow when the doctors come for their daily visits I should tell them to check my heart as it got quite a beating today, up and down, thump …thump …thump …and so on.

"Okay, Mathew, Iris," Caroline said, "you two are perfect for each other, please be assured of my full support whenever you need me." Tears were flowing down her cheeks as Caroline smiled and continued, "Iris, I as a nurse will continue doing my job whenever I am on duty so please fear not about me and lastly don't forget to invite me to your wedding." And with that she cried aloud and she opened the curtains and she went out running.

Maybe she went to hide and cry her heart out, poor Caroline. I couldn't do better than that; she was a very brave woman. So I and Iris were left holding hands and I was still in shock of losing Caroline but Iris was thrilled and she shouted and jumped in the air.

"Yippee" Iris screamed, "Mathew can you believe it? You are all mine now, oh my God, Mathew….I am soooooooo happy." She started crying with happiness and I felt a lump of something stuck in my throat. Was I happy to have Iris or was I sad to lose Caroline? I wasn't sure myself, either being happy or to be sad. I was confused, I wanted Iris so much but now that I got her I felt unsure. Was it the right choice or not? Only time will tell but for now, I'd better get in the happy mood otherwise Iris also will walk away from me.

So I hugged Iris and for the first time in my life I kissed a woman with real love and affection. I felt my limbs melting, I felt my head light-headed, I felt I was in heaven, I felt so good.

"Oh Mathew, I love you so much." Iris was saying, "I nearly lost you my love." I held her tightly as I told her.

"Iris, I love you just as much." I told her, "I knew you were the one from the moment I saw you, my Iris, my movie star, you are so beautiful my love." We held each other for eternity.

"Please Mathew," Iris said and continued, "promise me you will never love or look at another woman ever again." I on my part felt the same.

"Iris my love," I said, "you are the only one for me for now, for today, for tomorrow and forever. I'll love and cherish you always. I promise I'll not let you down," I paused and added, "I'll work hard towards our mutual goals and we'll make it together, we can do it, Iris my love, the one and only." I heard Tom's footsteps and his grunts, like a wounded or hungry lion. I told Iris, "Should I call Tom in and tell him the good news?" Tom had become like my elder brother, besides as my advisor. Iris nodded her head.

"It's okay, you can tell him but I think he already knows, he's been walking up and down for hours now and it is just the curtains that separate us." I called Tom in and he entered with a smile.

"Mathew, my friend," Tom said, "As I told you before, you are one lucky bastard."

"Tom, should I tell you the good news or do you already know everything which took place here today?" I said and continued, "The good news and the not so good news as well?" Tom looked ashamed or annoyed to be accused of eavesdropping but he didn't mind the accusations, as he was just as excited as I was.

"Mathew my friend, you can accuse me all you want," Tom said while laughing, "but it doesn't affect me, you know why? Because I have witnessed a true love story today, it is just like the Hollywood movies." Tom went on, "You only watch on the telly or read the 'Mills and Boon' love books that my wife reads." Tom paused here and burst laughing, "I can claim that I, Tom, have been a part of this true life love story. Wow." Tom shook my hand and gave me a bear hug which I thought, felt like he would squeeze me to death and he went ahead and shook Iris's hand.

Before he decided to hug Iris, who was not skinny but petite I would say, and I saw her as tender and soft, not to be hurt anyway by Tom.

"Hey Tom be careful with Iris, don't squeeze her to death, I still need her. You know?" That stopped him midway from hugging her, but Iris being ever so playful and rising to the situation also to save Tom's face, she hugged him lightly and Tom was delighted and we all laughed together.

"Don't be jealous Mathew," Tom said, "Iris is all yours, forever, eh?" He winked at me. I thought yes, the bastard was really listening to what was said and to what was going on behind the curtains. Tom looked at his watch and I understood it was late but I didn't realize how late. Looking at my own watch I saw it was nine fifteen already. Iris looked at her watch.

"Oh, my God, time is really going fast," she said, "I have been here since five, I'd better be going before the nurses' chase me away." I looked at Tom, expecting him now to leave us alone but he was firmly in the room and he was cherishing the moment. He didn't seem like going anywhere and I needed to say goodnight to my love. So I had to tell him.

"Tom, can you leave us alone now if you don't mind, please." I said as I winked at him. He responded politely and with understanding.

"Oh yeah, we'll talk later, see you around lovely lady." Tom said as he bowed and left. Iris was giggling.

"Mathew, you were mean to the man," and she continued to giggle. I smiled as I shrugged and I decided to change the subject.

"Iris, my love," I said, "how will your parents take the news?" I knew we already discussed about this issue but I just wanted the reassurance. She held my hand tightly.

"Mathew, my darling," Iris said, "at this very moment, my father and mother are aware that I am here at the hospital with you. Also they know as I am not yet home, it means everything is well and successful otherwise I would have been home by now, crying and sulking." Iris continued, "Also, they must be awake waiting for me in person to give them the good news. My parents are very much concerned with my happiness and my future so when I am happy, they are happy for me. Mathew, please do not worry about my parents, they are fine with you," she then continued, "as a matter of fact my love, my father who was joined recently even though reluctantly, by my mother, they have been pushing me to accept your love and proposition. So now they will be over the moon, my love."

Chapter Twenty-Three

*I*RIS THEN LOOKED AT ME, squinting. "What else worries you?" Iris asked. "Come on, let us open your head and look at your brain and then your heart." She was giggling and I must admit she was lovely. I deserve praise for my choice and my luck, and if only my mom was alive she today, she would've been proud of me.

"Iris, my movie star and the love of my life," I said, "when I come out of the hospital and........." Iris interrupted me.

"Discharged, when you are discharged," I looked at her; she interrupted me to correct my English? Should I be annoyed with her? Should I show her that I'm angry at being corrected? I think she read me and understood. "Mathew, I am sorry my love," Iris said. "I thought I was just trying to help you improve your usage of English and grammar, but I can see you are upset. Sorry my love, please don't be angry with me as I meant well." She pleaded and I melted and so she was right. I agreed previously to change my language and learn and to be honest. I have changed a lot since I was....aha got it....since I was 'admitted'...... yeah

I have been listening to the telly and everyone around me. How they speak and how they were speaking. I was also reading the newspapers whenever I could get a chance, so I shouldn't be annoyed at all with my movie star.

"I'm sorry, Iris." I said. "It will take time for me to adjust and improve but I'll keep on trying and learn," I smiled at her and added, "and it's okay you can interrupt me and correct me, but on one condition," Iris smiled back at me and she was relaxed,

"Okay, boss." Iris said with an imitative authoritative voice. "What's the condition boss?" I smiled again to show her I've accepted the funny side of her.

"Please don't correct me in front of other people; you'll embarrass me, if you know what I mean. Please?" I completed. She nodded and crossed her hands across her chest.

"Cross my heart, I promise you and for me also, you can correct me on anything but only when we are alone, okay love?" We both started to laugh and made peace with each other and we shook hands in agreement.

"It's a deal." I said and after a while I tried again. "As I was saying, when I am......discharged....from the hospital, I would like to go on one knee and I would ask for your hand officially and I would buy you a nice ring....which by the way... what I can only afford........." She started to giggle and then tears came from her eyes.

"Please Mathew; ask me now," Iris was actually pleading, "I cannot wait that long, even if it's tomorrow.........please remove me from my torment........please my love, ask me.....now...please." I decided to go ahead, it was important for her but just as well, it was for me too.

"I Mathew," I started as I giggled, "hereby ask you Iris, while I'm on one knee of course, for your hand in marriage." I was only acting as if I was on one knee. Of course I had to because of my physical disability. I looked at her and before she said anything I added, "I promise that I Mathew, will love you, will cherish you and will take care of you for as long as I live. Please say yes, my darling, for I love you genuinely, humbly and truthfully, my darling the one and only Iris." I looked at Iris and she was crying and laughing at the same time and tears flowing.

"Yes, yes and again yes." Iris said amid her tears. "I accept sincerely and from the bottom of my heart, my beloved Mathew.....I will also love you dearly and without reservation. I promise I will take care of you in my whole life, my love, and beyond.....oh Mathew...I am so happy...my darling.....I love you sooooooo much." I hugged her and I let her cry and my own tears were flowing down my cheeks.

It was eleven at night when Iris went home, even then, because the nurses kept on coming and they wanted to switch off the lights, which they eventually they did but I switched on the bed light and the nurses had no other way to force her out. But I thought it's late for her to be driving alone at night so I told her to go home and I'll see her the next day. Iris gave me her mobile number and she said she will pop up in the morning before she went in the office, if it was okay with me, to which I replied of course it was okay and we kissed goodnight.

By then Tom was now ready to come to sit with me and he wanted me to update him about everything but I felt tired and sleepy.

"Goodnight Tom, I'm tired now; I shall talk to you tomorrow." I told Tom and he was disappointed but could not help it, it was true and it was after eleven at night. I then remembered that I had not had my dinner but had let it pass, because while Iris was there a nurse brought for me my night medications so that was okay. I lay on the bed and started to go through the day's events. It was a very eventful day and truly one which one might call historical. The night nurse passed.

"Excuse me nurse." I called aloud, "Is Caroline around, I cannot see her, she is the night nurse, isn't she?" The nurse smiled, because they all knew and she politely answered.

"Sorry Mathew." She then added, "Caroline took the night off plus a few days as well." I was not sure of this or was I just acting naïve?

"Why did she take a few days off? Is she alright?" I asked while acting as if nothing had happened that evening but the nurse shook her head.

"Well she went out crying and didn't talk to anyone." The nurse said, "Why? You don't know the reason?" She asked me and she continued after seeing my face was blank. "Mathew, she was jilted," the nurse said. "She was rejected by someone whom she loved so much and whom she was ready to give up her life for .... come on Mathew....you want to tell me you don't know why she had to go home .... how can she stay and face the fact that you're in here with another woman ....while she also loved you so much? It wasn't fair for her you know?" She was angry as she said all this.

I didn't have anything to say, this nurse said it all and it seemed she was expressing the feelings of all the hospital staff. It was one of their own who 'lost the battle' so as to speak. I felt bad especially when this nurse used the words 'jilted and rejected' it wasn't true. Caroline understood the reality and she understood that I couldn't return her love.

She understood that she couldn't compete with Iris. Caroline knew this. I know she was hurt, but she was a truly remarkable woman and she had taken it in her stride. But she couldn't be here, that is true but I wished I could see and talk to her but I couldn't, especially at this time of night. I was reminded once again, the saying of the loss of one you win another. Or in order to gain X you must lose Y, you cannot get both.

But with this nurse I let the thought pass, I didn't say anything. I wasn't ready for a lecture about love and commitment at this time of night. I went to sleep and soon after I could hear Tom snoring away. I slept soundly and had nice dreams, about my Ma, and Da and my brothers, they all seemed happy. It was as if a message was coming to me that my family especially my Ma, was happy and approved of my love with Iris. I felt I was either smiling or laughing in my sleep when it was time to wake up for another unknown day.

The night nurse woke me up at seven in the morning and telling me to be ready, that the doctors were making their rounds. I managed to sit up as they arrived and spoke to me briefly. They were smiling at me, maybe they already got the 'hot press' news from last night. Anyway, they spoke to Tom and they now ignored middle bed patient, who kept changing after every day or two. After they left, I got up and went slowly with my two crutches to the wash room and did my business. I looked at myself in the mirror, and thought, 'yes, I've changed.

I looked at my moustache and beard and remembered that Iris didn't even comment, she didn't say that I should remove or keep it, nor did Caroline for that matter. They left me with my own freedom and whatever I wanted. I put on my now familiar and useful two fresh gowns and went back to my bed where Elvis was ready with a hot cup of tea and my two slices of toast. I then requested from Elvis.

"Can you please give me one more slice?" I asked Elvis, "last night I didn't have my dinner, you know?" he smiled and gave me two extra slices.

"I know all about yesterday night, news travel fast in here so be careful on what you say or do in here, Mathew." Elvis replied and with that he went to Tom, who as usual now, got himself two portions, the other patient in the middle bed was fasting for an operation and as Elvis went out, "see you later." he told me. Tom was in the meantime, munching and had his mouth full.

"I am being discharged today, Mathew," he said suddenly, "I don't know how I'll travel. Look outside, the snow is heavy. I don't know if I can get a bus or train." I looked at him, he didn't seem happy to be going home after a long stay in the hospital.

"Tom, my friend and brother," I said, "aren't you happy to be going home?" I wasn't sure what seemed to bother him, the loss of more drama from 'Mathew's Love Triangle', or the transportation to the West of Ireland, or his wife's demand for money, or maybe the parents in law interference in his life. Tom grunted and continued munching.

"The difficulty to travel is one and also the nagging of my wife and her children is another," I knew he had three children all over eighteen, and he was the father but I let it pass.

"What time will you be going?" I asked again, "I'll miss having you around, you know? And the nurses will all miss you Tom." That seemed to cheer him up, about the nurses missing him. "You've been a good advisor and a friend Tom." I told him with genuineness in my heart. "My stay in the hospital won't be the same without you around to cheer me up and advise me on love matters, which you are an expert with. And especially your singing will be greatly missed Tom." Tom looked at me and tried to read my face. He wasn't sure if I was just messing with him or I was serious, but then he burst out laughing.

"Yeah, it was good fun," Tom said, "but the doctor told me to come again next week, so maybe they will give me a bed or I'll be here just as a day patient. So if you are still here, I'll come to say hi to you Mathew." I looked at him; I thought will he come to see me or to get the news which he's going to miss? But I just looked at him. I thought, look at Tom, he's being discharged, and he's not happy to go home, while me, even now if they tell me I can go, then I'll run as fast as I could to get away from the hospital. I've been here for a very long time. I've lost count on how many weeks I've been in the hospital. After a while Tom looked at me.

"Oh poor Caroline, I feel sorry for her," Tom said, "If only I could help her." I thought 'here we go again'.

"Tom, will you please stop mentioning Caroline?" I said in anger, "you're hurting me when you mention her. I feel for her Tom and what has been, has been. Now please stop mentioning her name and let's talk about Iris now, please. …Okay?" I pleaded with Tom and he was taken aback by my anger. I saw his face with disappointment at my reaction so I turned to him. "Or you'll not be invited for our wedding, Tom." I teased and he laughed.

"Wow, that part I must have missed." Tom said, and added, "Already you're fast you bastard, wow, only one day and you already proposed and the wedding is on the way?" He started to laugh, "next week when I come to see you, you'll tell me 'a baby is on the way' too, you bastard Mathew." Tom burst out laughing. Then he continued, "Will you really invite me to the wedding? I would love to attend. Please Mathew talk to Iris not to forget me. Okay?"

"You'll tell her yourself, she said she'll come in the morning while on her way to the office," I added, "also on one condition…at the wedding, please don't mention anything about Caroline, or about the events which have been happening in the hospital. Okay Tom?" He nodded and then he burst again with laughter. "All this time up to now, I thought of myself as a very smart man, after I eloped with my boss's daughter but today I believe I have met a smarter man than me. You Mathew are the real deal."

Tom was saying amid his laughter. "I shall never forget you Mathew, in the hospital, with a patient's daughter, and a nurse, all willing and ready to die for you. And what do you, Mathew, have to offer, nothing, man, you are just on your hospital bed with a hospital gown on you, that is like half naked and yet you managed to fall in love. Yes, today I have met a legend." With that Tom went on his way, out of the room to his smoking place.

Chapter Twenty-Four

$\mathcal{A}$FTER A WHILE IRIS WALKED in and kissed me lightly on the lips, then both cheeks and then hugged me.

"Hi love," Iris said, "good morning…..sorry I am late. I was stuck in traffic." She looked radiant and beautiful, in her grey skirt, white blouse, grey coat, and a red scarf around her neck and grey high heeled shoes. She smelled beautiful with her perfume. She had a black handbag, and a black overcoat.

"Hi my movie star and beloved Iris," I replied overwhelmed by love. Maybe I had thought this up, maybe it was all a dream and maybe Iris, my movie star wasn't here just yesterday. I'll wake up and see it as a dream or trick that was played on me. But here she was in person so I didn't pinch myself because I believed it was now real.

"I won't stay as I have to rush to the office, I'm already late as it is," Iris said, "but I will surely be here in the evening. Is it okay my love?" I nodded and smiled. She didn't need to explain and apologise and I wasn't used to this but I took it on board.

"Did you reach home safely last night, my love?" I said, "And was your parents' worried? …………..how did they take the news about you….and me?" I asked Iris and she looked up as if she was thinking.

"Mmmmm, let's see, yes I reached home safely. No my parents were a bit worried as it was late," Iris said, "and yes, last night I told my parents the news about you and me. My father was delighted and he was over the moon, he said it was a good decision and that I won't regret it. My father assured me on your behalf. Can you imagine that, Mathew?" And she continued, "My mother, let's see now………yes, she was happy for me……..reluctantly of course at first, but………..she said as long as I am happy, then she too is thrilled." Iris looked at me again, "So there goes your worries, my love. We'll discuss more when I come in the evening. Okay darling?"

Then she removed from her handbag a mobile phone and handed over to me. "You keep this phone, honey. My number is already there; if you need me any time, please just call me. Okay?" I took the phone and kept it on the side table and I thought, I've no need for a mobile phone, I am already here in the hospital for several weeks, and bigger events have come and gone. My mother died…and was buried…while I had no contact….so now….I don't really need a phone…..but if I refuse the phone, Iris would be annoyed so I accepted it without a word.

She asked me if I have seen the doctors today and if they said anything about me or my medical procedures and why there was nothing going on. She was worried for me. Then Tom appeared as if on cue.

"Hi Iris, remember me? I'm Tom." Tom said while smiling, "My friend, Mathew here, told me everything………." Iris looked at me with questioning eyes, like 'Mathew, you told Tom everything?' I just shook my head and shrugged, Tom seemed like he got the message as he continued, "I mean he told me the good news about you two. I'm delighted and very happy for both of you, but do not forget to invite me for the big day, alright?" And he winked at Iris, and she burst out laughing with happiness as she hugged Tom.

"Of course, of course Tom, we will definitely invite you and your family…. right Mathew my love?" I nodded and laughed.

"He wants to be invited by force, Iris." I said, while looking at Iris and then Tom. "He also wants his in-laws to be invited, and his bosses, past and present…right Tom?" Tom became annoyed and turned to Iris.

"Don't mind him, Iris," Tom said, "he's already drunk……with your love." Tom laughed. We all laughed, and then Iris went away to the office, but she left her presence through her beautiful perfume smell. By ten Tom had already dressed, and we said our goodbye's and exchanged contact information. At eleven the hospital attendant came with a wheelchair, and Tom was seated and taken down, to begin his way home to the west of Ireland. I was sad for Tom to leave, as I was already so used to him. He made jokes and he made me laugh, besides him being a bit nosey, but it was okay with me since he was my advisor as well.

I inquired again about Caroline when I saw that Maritas was on day duty, but she was in another room, not mine.

"Hey Maritas," I called her out, "is Caroline on duty today?" Maritas, who like everyone else in the ward, knew all the details.

"No she's not in today. What do you need her for?" She replied angrily and then added, "How is Iris, your true love Mathew? I saw her earlier here in the ward, she is pretty, yeah?" Was she being sarcastic or what? But I let it pass.

"Can you send her a message, please," I said to Maritas. "I need to see and talk to her. It's important, you know what I mean? Please?" I pleaded with Maritas. She smiled.

"Okay I'll send Caroline a text message, and if she replies then okay. And maybe Caroline doesn't want to see or talk to you anymore, okay Mathew?" Elvis came to take orders for lunch and he was looking for Tom for his two portions. Elvis looked confused as he didn't find Tom in his bed.

"Elvis," I said, "Tom has been discharged and gone…..sorry, maybe he was too excited he forgot to tell you during breakfast." Elvis then smiled.

"Aha, that is alright then," he said and added, "I thought he jumped from the window……" Elvis burst out laughing. He was laughing at his own joke when abruptly he stopped. I had not joined in laughing at his joke and my face was blank and Elvis realised his mistake. "Oh my God, I am so sorry Mathew." He apologised, "Oh my God, I had forgotten Mathew, sorry, I was only joking, I didn't mean to……" He was pleading with me. I felt sorry for the poor guy, as he had made the joke innocently.

"Ah Elvis, you're fine," I said to assure him, "no offence taken don't bother, you're cool Elvis, no worries." I smiled at him and he was feeling sorry and shaking his head. Later Maritas passed and came to my bed.

"Mathew, I sent the text to Caroline," she said, "so if she replies I will tell you, okay?" I nodded my head.

"Thanks a million, Maritas." I thanked her and I had hoped Caroline would reply and manage to see me, if not at least be able to talk to me. I thought about Iris: will she mind that I want to talk with Caroline? But she has to understand, even though I love Iris and she is the one I truly fell in love from day one. But Caroline came in between during the empty space, and she had filled the empty space quite well, and that meant a lot to me. I cannot just ignore the fact that Caroline was my saviour the other night and she cared for me too.

So I had a right to be worried about her too and to explain to her about me and Iris. I felt that she has a right to know that I didn't dump her or reject her, but it was just circumstances and my love for Iris. I hoped she would understand, poor Caroline. I had my lunch when Elvis brought it and he didn't say anything. He didn't even meet my eyes. I thought maybe he still felt bad about his joke. I had finished having my lunch and was resting when I heard a phone ringing.

I looked at the middle bed, the guy had gone for his operation, and then at the window bed. Someone new had been brought in but he was fast asleep, so where was the sound coming from? It was silent and then it began ringing again. Then I remembered the phone Iris had brought for me. I started to look for it and I found it under the pillow. Quickly I took it and pressed the green button.

"Hello." I said, "Whom do you want?" I thought maybe someone was calling for Iris, or it was a wrong number or whatever. Then I heard a giggling sound.

"Hello darling." A soft voice came on the phone, I was now definitely sure it was a wrong number.

"Who is it?" I barked, "You've got the wrong number."

"Hi darling, it is me Iris," a female voice said. "You have already forgotten me so soon, Mathew?" Oh my God, I didn't recognise her voice on the phone. I felt embarrassed.

"Hi beautiful," I said. "I'm very sorry. I'm not used to your voice on the phone….sorry about that." Iris said it was alright.

"I am on my break and I thought of you, so I called to see how you are, darling. I miss you Mathew, already. I can't wait to see you." I was debating should I tell her now, that I'm looking for Caroline, just to talk with her and nothing more, that it's just nothing to threaten our love and commitment. But I then decided I shall tell her when she comes in the evening. I shall tell her in person, not on the phone, not while she's in the office.

I thought it's nothing really, but Iris might think I'm going behind her back with Caroline, and she might also hate poor Caroline. I personally didn't want hatred between the two of them. I wanted Caroline to remain a friend for both of us, myself and Iris.

"Iris, my darling," I said, "I too am missing you. Try to finish early from the office and come over, there's a lot to talk about, you know what I mean, my love?" I heard she was giggling as well as a few other voices behind her, probably her colleagues.

"Alright my love," Iris said, "the girls send their regards to you Mathew, my love." Okay, the giggling was from her friends.

"Thank them for me, Iris," I said. "See you later, then, okay darling?"

"Okay then. Bye."

"Bye, now."

"Bye. Bye," we disconnected. I'm not used to talking very long on the phone, I cannot find words and I didn't much like the phones, especially these new ones. The so-called 'smart phones, android' and the like, I thought of myself as an 'old fashioned guy' who is not used to the very fast moving technology. The tablets, kindle, black berry, face book, twitter, and a lot of other stuff. I wished we were back in the times when you have a mobile phone which is just that, the function is to talk with the other person and that's it, no cameras, no internet, no videos, no face book, and social media, all these things, I thought they are just confusing.

Anyway, the new generation are now so used to and so dependent on these gadgets, which, without them they cannot function anymore. Go to a shop now and with a very simple maths they cannot do without the assistance of a calculator. What a pity and I couldn't imagine what the future generations will have to play with next. I was in deep thoughts thinking about gadgets when Maritas came over to me.

"Good news Mathew," she said with a smile and a low voice. "I spoke with Caroline. First she refused, but after I explained to her nicely that it's okay, no harm will come then she agreed to talk to you." I was delighted. At least I'll get a chance to explain to Caroline about my love for Iris, and what she means to me but that Caroline will remain in my heart. I'll not forget her easily.

"Thanks a million Maritas," I said to her, "you're an angel." I asked Maritas when Caroline will be talking to me. Should I call her now? I now have a mobile phone, or she can call me. But Maritas, with a smile on her face, she gave me a pat on my shoulder.

"Relax Mathew. Caroline already said she'll talk to you, so you wait, maybe today, maybe tomorrow but you have to relax, okay?" I said okay with a disappointed look on my face and accepted that Caroline agreed to talk to me. So when she'll talk to me it doesn't matter and I just nodded my head in agreement. I was supposed to be a happy man. I was being treated at the hospital, I was in love with a very beautiful woman and I was turning my life around, looking for a better future ahead of me.

Chapter Twenty-Five

*A*T FOUR IN THE AFTERNOON Iris appeared, smiling as she approached me with outstretched arms wide open.

"Here I am my love, my handsome Mathew," she said as she came in, kissing me on the lips and the cheeks and then hugged me. "I missed you sooo much my darling." I looked at her and I realized that every time I see her she was more and more beautiful. Those eyes were always killing me. What were they, I wondered, are they hazel or brown? That, I didn't know.

The only thing which I knew was that Iris was beautiful and she belonged to me. Me, Mathew from the inner city, and …ah stop it Mathew, you're degrading yourself every time….come on…cherish the moment and look towards the present and the future', I told myself.

"Darling Iris," I said, "won't the company you're working for fire you, my love? Like today, you went late in the morning and look at the time now, you're already out." I looked worried and it showed in my face, but Iris smiled at me and then she pinched my cheeks and brought her face closer to mine.

"Let them fire me, Mathew," Iris said, "for you my love, it is okay but stop worrying anyway. My supervisor already knows about you and our love and she understands, okay my love? Now tell me about your day." So first I asked Iris about her brother, who was in the states.

"Iris dear, have you spoken to your elder brother, what's his name?" I said, "About us, I mean." She nodded her head and said last night she spoke to him. He was like a father to her, being older and all so she gave him full respect and usually even before her parents, Iris consults with her brother first.

"His name is Bernard, but we call him Ben." Iris said, "And yes, he is excited and happy for me. He would like to talk with you sometime and so are my father and mother." Then Iris removed two small red boxes, and she smiled as she gave one to me.

"What's inside the box?" I looked surprised as I asked.

"Open it," Iris said with a smile. I then opened the box, which I already had a feeling of what it might be. Inside the box was a beautiful ring. I asked Iris to explain. "I bought these two simple rings, one for you and one for me." Iris said, "They are not exactly engagement rings. That we will do after you are out of the hospital, okay dear? But for now, I want to see a ring on my finger so I can believe that I am engaged to you my dear Mathew. I am in love Mathew, so please do it for my sake." She begged me. I then put the ring on her finger and she put one on my finger, she was so happy and she kissed and hugged me tightly.

"Oh Mathew, I love you so much," Iris said. "I feel like I have known you my entire life Mathew, and yet I feel like I have missed your entire life. Where was I, all this time? Oh my love, I love you so much." She was looking at her finger with pride and affection and she hugged me and kissed me again and again. I didn't want to spoil her happiness by bringing up the subject of Caroline, as I wasn't sure how she would react. So we continued our love story for a while.

Then Maritas passed and I introduced them, and they shook hands and Iris kissed Maritas on both cheeks, I thought Iris was friendly, and took it in her stride. She was not a snob or a show off and even Maritas was taken aback by the friendliness she received from Iris. I thought even Maritas didn't expect the show of natural affection and courtesy from Iris and maybe she expected hostile feelings. I then asked Iris about the cost of the phone and now for the rings. She smiled and asked me how much I thought it cost. I said I didn't have any idea.

"Okay Mathew," Iris said and she went on, "the phone is not new, it is mine, and you can have it, and the ring, you can pay me back after you come out of the hospital and you are healthy enough to go to the bank." She smiled and added, "Meanwhile I shall keep all the accounts until later, is that agreed? And for the proper engagement rings and all other things, we shall discuss after you are out and also when and if we need. Is that fine with you my darling?" I knew I couldn't afford this ring or the engagement ring, but I felt I couldn't just sit and receive things from a woman whom I'm going to marry.

I hadn't thought about finances. When I proposed or fell in love with Iris or Caroline for that matter I thought, oh yeah I love this woman and I want to marry her, that's it? There's a lot of money needed to help change my life, and what do I have in my bank account, the weekly amount I'm given by the government for being unemployed, shame on me.

But then I've been here a lot of weeks, so there'll be a large enough amount in the bank, and I can buy for Iris, something nice in return. Oh yeah we'll see. I think Iris saw in my face or maybe she already could read my face and my feelings, because she looked at me again touching my cheeks.

"Mathew, I understand your financial situation," Iris said with love in her voice and pleading, "but for now, can you remove the thoughts of money from your head? And please let me deal with all that. You should only think and worry about your health for now." Iris said then added, "Please my darling, I don't mind. What I need from you is only your love and affection, my love. Please don't be ashamed if I give you anything. And another thing, just promise me once you complete and get your degree and when you get a good job, you'll pay me back for everything, every ………single …………cent." She emphasised as she giggled and looked in my eyes.

I just nodded, I had no words. She was right, I couldn't compete with her for money and she was doing this out of love. She was not buying me off or something like that, no, it was love, and I truly loved Iris. It wasn't that I was demanding money in exchange for my love, not at all. It was just two people who loved each other and one happened to be better off financially than the other, so it was only natural to give each other what one can afford.

We sat and talked about our love, about the future and I expressed this to Iris.

"Iris, my love, I don't want to be a burden to you, you know what I mean and......?" I protested. She took her index finger straight to my lips to silence me.

"Shhhhhh...... do not say another word, my darling." Iris said, "Burden? What burden are you talking about, Mathew?" She then added and maybe she was annoyed, "You aren't a burden on me or my family. I already told you....the plans ...and if you think you have better plans, ...then let's hear them." I tried to speak but it was true, I had no plans. I had nothing to offer her.

Even if I wanted to take her back to the inner city where I live, no, where I used to live, there's no house or place for me. My mother's house was boarded by the Housing Corporation, soon after she died, so where I'll take Iris? Or maybe.......to Kevin's house, no he was in jail and his wife will not take me in. One night once in a while with Kevin was different but now without Kevin, no way will Kevin's wife agree.

And besides, I agreed to change my life around and starting with my language, then accommodation, then education, then work and in-between, marriage. And being hard on myself, I won't be able to do all those things so I needed a push and help and fortunately so for me. I got myself a pretty and caring movie star, and she is able to support me, I mean us, in the beginning until I'm ready to take on the responsibility of running the family.

I want my children in a different environment from what I grew up with, so I need help from Iris to transform myself from what I was and to what I want to be.

"Iris my love, I didn't mean in a bad way," I said sort of pleading, "your mom, your dad, and your brother, what will they think of me, if they see me as a free loader, you know what I mean, my love?" I protested but she shook her head.

"They all understand. I have explained to them the entire circumstances of our love and future plans," Iris said, "and they know it is what I want and they all support me, so remove these worries from this head of yours, my darling." She shook my head as she said it. "Now, let us change the subject. What time are the doctors coming on their rounds? I need to speak with them," Iris said with seriousness in her voice. "It has been a long time now since you have been admitted, so I want to know what is happening." It seemed like Iris was going to take charge now and I felt sorry for the doctors.

She went out to the corridor, where there were the nurses' offices or desks, and I could hear her talking with the nurses' supervisor and after a while she came back. I didn't ask her what it was about but she told me herself.

"I told the nurses' supervisor, that I wanted to talk with your doctor and if he is not in, then any other doctor who knows your case." Iris explained to me. "I complained that you have been too long in here. I remember you have been here even before my dad was admitted, and he stayed and was discharged and till today you are still here."

"Iris, my love, maybe they love me around here, that's why they're keeping me here. They don't want to discharge me." I said with a smile. "You should tell them to give me my own room then we can be free, just you and me, you know, you can even move in with me, you know what I mean?" I burst out laughing at my own joke, Iris at first looked upset and then she joined me in laughter.

"I am serious Mathew," Iris said, "and you're making fun of me." After a while, the nurses' supervisor came and politely addressed Iris, glancing at me from time to time.

"I sent your complaint to the doctor on duty," she said. "He'll try to get your doctor if he is around, okay?" I just nodded my head while Iris seemed serious.

"Thanks, and please update me when you get any news." It was all business-like. At six in the evening, Elvis brought our dinner, and at half past six, Dr. Brown walked in with the nurses' supervisor and the nurse on duty, Dr. Brown tried to force a smile and it seemed he had to leave an important place or something to come quickly to attend a genuine complaint from one angry lady. He looked at me then at Iris, as if confused, who is she who is making a lot of noises?

And there he is, used to the silent Mathew, who has no one fighting for him. Maybe he wasn't on the ward's list of people who were updated with news of the on-goings in the wards and the love stories, especially from the Dolphin's Ward bed number seventy-seven.

"Hello Mathew." Dr. Browne looked at me, then turned and looked at Iris. "You must be the lady who is asking to see me?" Before Iris responded, I quickly took over.

"Dr. Browne, please meet Iris, my fiancée, and Iris this is Dr. Browne, he works with Dr. Livingstone, who is my doctor." I spoke with the introductions so fast and I thought the battle was averted for the moment. They shook hands.

"You see, I was in a meeting, when Dr. Livingstone instructed me to attend to this complaint." Dr. Browne said, with his hands turned up as if pleading. "What seems the problem...that I can help you with, Mathew?" He was talking softly and before I answered, Iris took over as my official spokesperson.

"Doctor........ I was just worried that Mathew has been here for a long time, is it five, six weeks, or maybe even more." Iris said with authority. "So I just need you to explain to me, when is he going to be operated on, or if not, then when will he be discharged?" Dr. Browne smiled. "You see, I am sorry we haven't been in touch much but right now we were in a meeting discussing your case." Dr. Browne said and added while looking at me. "As soon as we are done with the meeting then Dr. Livingstone himself will come to talk to you, is that alright with you Mathew?" Again, before Iris said anything, I quickly spoke so as to calm the situation.

"You know doctor, since Iris started to know me, she's seen me only in these hospital gowns and sometimes she was looking at my butt, you know what I mean?" I said with a giggle, "I mean, she hasn't seen me dressed in anything else, and she would like to see me in a suit and maybe dancing with her. That's why Iris is worried, you know what I mean, eh.....Doctor?" I finished and Dr. Browne got the message and he laughed so everybody laughed with us for a little bit longer. Then he had to go and excused himself, and he went out with both the nurses following him.

For Iris it was a victory, and she felt good and she said so. I knew that maybe Dr. Browne was telling the truth, that they were meeting and then planning to come to see me. But also I thought the stronger point was because of Iris and her strong words of complaint. So maybe now they knew someone is with me, the circle will go quicker for me and also the treatment, maybe, just maybe, I thought.

Chapter Twenty-Six

So we waited and Iris went near the window to use her mobile phone to call home.

She spoke with her mom then her dad and then brought the phone to me.

"My father would like to talk to you, dear." I thought oh God, what can I say to him? Before, it was easy because he was just a patient beside my bed and he wasn't there to judge me, but now as my future father-in-law, it was different. Before I was addressing him as 'James', but now, what should I call him? I wondered.

"Hello Mathew." James came on the line, "Are you there...can you hear me? I hesitated and then answered.

"Hello James," I felt no, it didn't seem right. "Hello sir," I said again. "How have you been, sir?" I heard him chuckle.

"Mathew. Son, you don't have to call me sir," James replied, "you can just call me James." We then spoke for a few minutes and I was praying for him not to give me his wife, not now I thought, not yet anyway. "Now Mathew, my son," I heard James again, "my daughter Iris, whom I know you fell in love with from the moment you saw her in the hospital," a chuckle again, "has explained to me everything. I am happy for both of you and you two have our family's full support. Therefore don't let it worry you a bit, is that clear, son?" James added after a moment of silence. "I believe you two love each other and you have already exchanged rings. I wouldn't be surprised if you two decide to do the wedding while you are still at the hospital."

He laughed to himself and I waited. Let the man express himself.

"But I don't think so, because for the wedding, we have a few family and friends, so we would need to organise it the right way." James paused a bit and then continued, "Mhhh……Now you take care of yourself and your health. I cannot visit you but when you come over I shall see you and we will discuss some more. And Mathew, Iris's mother cannot talk to you now, she is a bit busy cooking dinner, ha ha ha. It was nice talking to you Mathew. You be good, okay son?" James ended the conversation and disconnected.

I breathed in a sense of relaxation. It was like I had just run the Dublin Marathon. I was perspiring and Iris was looking at me and was giggling and then she took a towel and wiped my face and then kissed me on the lips.

"It was tough, eh?" She asked me. "My father is your friend; maybe you also shared dirty jokes together when he was here with you and now look at you, sweating all over. Wait until you speak with my mom and then I will really look at your face!" She burst out laughing at me while I just shook my head and smiled at her. She was beautiful, my movie star. I thought if talking to her father made me like this so how it'll be when I speak with her mother? I thought her mother might as well be from another planet altogether. But when the time will come, I'll face her. If she's too much; I can run and hide from her and I laughed within myself.

I pictured Iris's mother with a dirty apron, holding a wooden spoon in her hand, wearing high heels, and of course in full make up, chasing me around the kitchen and around the house and me just running and trying to hide under the dining table, somewhere in the kitchen, behind the sofas in the living room and at the same time calling Iris's name to come to save me from her vicious mother. I was chuckling about this.

"What's so funny, are you laughing at me, love?" Iris asked me. I shook my head as I continued to smile.

"I'm just remembering old stories, my darling." I couldn't bring myself to tell her the truth, how can I tell her, what I'm imagining about her beloved mother? No way, man, I cannot, she'll strangle me herself before I reach her mom. At seven fifteen, I heard voices coming from the corridor and I could recognise that it was the doctors, and they appeared and entered the room. They walked in slowly, their faces grim and I sensed it was as if the devil has just entered bringing bad news.

The Consultant Oncologist, Dr. Livingstone came in with Dr. Browne, and followed by the day nurse and the night nurse. I think the Supervisor was gone already. I sensed there was tension in their approach and it was not good news. They both looked tired.

"Hello Mathew." Dr. Livingstone addressed me and then he turned to Iris. "Hello young lady, you must be Iris, Mathew's fiancée." He shook my hand and he shook Iris's hand also as he acknowledged her and I was pleased for that. I was sitting on the bed as usual with my legs stretched straight in front of me. Iris was standing near me. Dr. Browne looked at both of us.

"Please be seated," Dr. Browne told Iris. It brought my thoughts to Judge Judy and we were in the court and the Judge had just entered, and the bailiff shouts 'please be seated', I wanted to giggle but I stopped myself. The nurses brought two chairs for the two doctors who then sat down while the nurses were left standing with their files ready to take notes. I felt that they were going to pass my death sentence. I had a feeling that this wasn't going to be a pleasant meeting, if we can call it a meeting.

"Mathew, I heard the good news about you and the young lady here, Iris." Dr. Livingstone said as he forced a smile. I was watching him carefully, for his body language and Dr. Browne's were not comfortable, I had a feeling he was trying to get around to it first with small talk and then hit me with the bombshell. "I pray you'll be very happy together. We wish you both the best from me and all the staff in the ward and the hospital." Dr. Livingstone said. Then he turned to the nurses. I noticed that he and Dr. Browne were avoiding my eyes. "It's not every day we get a love story in the hospital or a patient falling in love with a nurse or a visitor." Dr. Livingstone said and he then looked at Dr. Browne. "But it's a good story; we are all delighted for you Mathew."

I smiled faintly, and Iris was holding my hand. I think she also felt the tension and the approaching bad news. Then Dr. Livingstone couldn't hold it any longer, he blurted out.

"I am sorry to be the one to tell you this, Mathew, but your leg has…..to be ………. amputated ……below the hip bone." He said this while looking down. He couldn't meet my eyes. There was a long silence, nobody could utter a word. "Mathew," Dr. Livingstone said. "Your histopathology report has come back." He then looked at me and I returned the stare. "I am sorry; there hasn't been any good news for you." Dr. Livingstone said again and continued, "We have to amputate your right leg just below the hip joint." He said and quickly continued, "Otherwise the cancer will spread to your lungs and other organs in your body and that can be fatal."

They waited for my reaction. None, I was too shocked to react.

"I am sorry Mathew, Dr. Browne will explain to you the procedures and timetable for the surgery." Dr. Livingstone said as he stood up and touched my shoulder for a little while. He was gone before I could react. Dr. Browne just sat there not knowing what to say, while my eyes become red and tears started to roll down my cheeks. He looked at me while I started to sob. I didn't have the strength to fight this. I had no more 'F' words; I was becoming a gentleman now, and now this? I was deeply in love and I was planning to get married and to change my life.

I had spoken to God and explained to Him that I was going to become a gentleman, a good citizen, a good husband and a provider for my Iris and my many future children, which I always dreamt about, but now this? I turned to look at Iris, who had become my strength now and she was also sobbing. She held my shoulders from behind and she was massaging me slowly but she didn't have words to show her sympathy. I continued to sob slowly at first and then loudly. Iris held me tightly, tears rolling down her cheeks.

Her hand then was stroking my hair and I thought I couldn't take it anymore. I thought, 'Why me, oh dear God? Why me of all the people? After a while I looked first at Dr. Browne and then the nurses, they all had teary eyes. After they went I continued to sob. I thought I am finished now, kaput. I should start planning my funeral instead of my wedding. It's over for me. I cannot live with one leg. How will I look, how will I go on with my life. I will be called, 'Mathew the one legged fella' by all my friends and strangers alike. I was used to living dangerously and on the edge, stealing and drugs and all but with one leg, the gang will not accept me anymore. I'll be a risk to them all.

Then I remembered no, the gang and living dangerously was gone for me, I had promised myself to be a new man and I was going to get married. But now I started to imagine myself with one leg and two crutches hopping in and around the city and oh no, it wasn't a pretty sight. I told Iris that it was over, she can go on home now and that I'll be alright. She refused.

"No Mathew, I am here and I'll stay here with you." Iris replied, but I just looked at her. I didn't have the strength anymore.

"Iris my movie star, my love, it's over now, there isn't going to be any wedding between you and me, it's over Iris." She held my face tightly.

"What are you talking about now, Mathew?" Iris said. "Please explain to me I don't understand." Iris was pleading now. I told her now I'm dying and even if I'm not, what with one leg? I was shaking my head with disappointment, with failure.

"You don't need a cripple as a husband, Iris." I explained, "You don't need a cripple to feed, to take care of, to drive around and to do everything for him, and yet he wasn't any good or help at all. No Iris, it's over, instead of a wedding let me plan my funeral now." Iris held me tightly and was swaying me like a baby. It was like 'hush a bye baby'.

"No Mathew," Iris said. "You are going to be fine, even with one leg, you are going to do, and be able to achieve everything we planned to achieve. Please believe in yourself Mathew, please do my beloved, together we can do it." And then she added, "Besides, you cannot play with my life, one minute you love me so much you want to get married and then the next minute you want to cancel the love and everything. No my friend, I didn't hear any doctor talking about you dying, no sir.

Also if you have to lose a leg for you to stay alive, then so be it. You can lose both legs and I will still love you the same.

I have pledged my love to you and now I won't renege just for a minor defect. No, I loved you while you've been in the hospital and suffering with the same killer disease, but I still loved you. And one more thing, my friend, there's no guarantee in life. I can just go out and be involved in an accident and die, while you will be alive for the next hundred years. Also, the more reason you should have to be brave and get out quickly and we can get married fast so we can enjoy in the company of each other and be together even for short while of our lives." Iris spoke with passion and anger in her voice. It scared me but she was absolutely right.

What she was saying was one hundred percent correct and I was frozen and had forgotten about my amputation scheduled for tomorrow. Later on Dr. Browne came to talk with me and explained about the procedures.

"Tomorrow is the big day, Mathew." Dr. Browne said. "Your surgery will be performed tomorrow morning." I just kept quiet, I had nothing to say. "We're planning it for early morning," he said, "but you never know, if an emergency comes, we have to postpone yours, but definitely it is planned for tomorrow." Dr. Browne attempted to smile, as if this was the greatest news for me. I still didn't say anything. "Do you understand what I am telling you Mathew?" he said, "Or do you want to ask me anything?" I just shook my head, there was nothing to ask.

Dr. Browne removed and opened the file and after all the normal questions and answers.

"Who is your next of kin?" He asked me. In the beginning I had put my mother as next of kin but now she wasn't there anymore so I replied after a long pause.

"Iris, she is my fiancée." Dr. Browne noted it with a nod and he explained to me the procedure they were planning to perform in the theatre tomorrow. The cancer had spread as they believed on to the femur bone and area of my right leg, the tissue or muscles around and the femur bone, that's why they need to cut it off, or as Dr. Browne said to 'amputate', and then he gave me the form to sign, which I did.

"You have to fast from midnight," Dr. Browne said, "the night duty nurse will be with you if you need anything at night, Okay?" I thought, okay, but what should I need? My leg is being cut off and what will I possibly need? I'll need nothing but my funeral arrangements as soon as possible. Iris just sat and held my hand. She had nothing to say, I had nothing to say either and I just saw my dreams being shattered in front of my very eyes. I have been brought down with a bang.

I've been in the hospital for too long that sometimes I forget what and why I was here for. But the reality hits hard sometimes. I am suffering from cancer or I had cancer, and it was within my thigh, it was a sarcoma, and it was eating my soft muscles and tissues away. That is the reality. Why then, was I shocked when I already knew all about this, because I was too busy? I was busy planning and scheming about my love life, with on one side Iris and on the other side Caroline. I hadn't time to think about my cancer and the treatment.

Maybe I had taken everything for granted. Maybe I thought I'll just walk away tomorrow and everything will be fine and I'll be as healthy as I was previously. That's a fairy tale, man, and this is reality. I sat there for a long time with my movie star, with nothing to say, but inside our hearts we were saying a lot to each other. Then at half ten, Iris said she would go home and change and come back to spend the night and be with me. But when she asked the nurse, Iris was told that nobody was allowed to be with a patient at night, it wasn't permitted.

"Not to worry we will keep an eye on Mathew all the time so he'll not attempt suicide again." The nurse explained to Iris. But it seemed Iris hadn't known about the suicide attempt, she had no idea of that night's events and so she was shocked. I also had thought I had told her about that night.

"About what, did you just say?" Iris screamed, "What suicide attempt? Mathew had made an attempted suicide? When was this?" Iris became hysterical. The nurse became apologetic.

"Oh I'm sorry," she pleaded, "I'm deeply sorry, I shouldn't have said that. Please forgive me. Oh my God, what have I done?" I heard the commotion and asked Iris.

"What is it honey?" I asked not knowing what was said, "Is

something wrong?" She started sobbing and I had no idea what it was all about, but then the nurse came to me.

"I'm sorry Mathew," the nurse said. "I thought she knew about your....your ...." she couldn't bring herself to say the words 'suicide' again. "It just came from my mouth. I didn't mean to, I'm sorry Mathew." Then I understood what it was all about, I now understood why Iris was hysterical. I then explained to Iris, briefly at least of what went on that night. And that's why I was close to Caroline and other stuff. Iris shook her head, the fear showing in her eyes, the knowledge that she was the one of the main reasons I wanted to take my life, and that if I had succeeded, I wouldn't be here today, and that she wouldn't even know. After one hour, she cooled down and I told Iris, it was okay.

"You can go and come tomorrow in the evening, when you finish work." Iris refused flatly this. "Nope, I will call the office in the morning and take a few days off to be with you, Mathew," Iris said. "I will go now but I shall be here first thing in the morning, my darling." But she also was told that the doors open at about seven thirty in the morning, and the operation probably would take place at around ten in the morning. After we said our goodbyes and goodnights, she left with a heavy heart, and I was left alone to think about the day's events.

I thought one can never know what'll happen in a day, and that; in fact, a lot can happen and change somebody's life in one way or another. Well, we'll see what lay ahead for tomorrow. After all, the night's long and the day's are even longer in terms of events.

Chapter Twenty-Seven

I WOKE UP THE NEXT MORNING and thought, 'let me walk to the bathroom to wash up, since it's my last day and last hour to use my leg'. Then using the two crutches I walked to the toilets and freshened up and came back with a smile on my face. Okay let it come, what can be worse, losing a leg or losing my life? Let them take my leg, at least I'll still be alive. I can talk and eat and do a lot of other things. The night nurse did the routine check up for me.

"You're fit and okay to proceed with the operation, Mathew." The night nurse told me after the health checks and she also told me the day duty nurse will do the rest for me and prepare me as well, and she apologised again. "I'm really sorry Mathew."

"No bother for that, and thanks for being around last night," I assured her. Later on at seven thirty, somebody appeared whom I wasn't really expecting. It was the day nurse, who came with a smile when she looked at me.

"Hi Mathew," Caroline said, "How are you feeling today?" I

thought oh my God, look who's here and she's just glowing. "I am your duty nurse for the day; if you need anything just give me a shout, okay?" I couldn't utter a word. I was both surprised and happy to see her at the same time. Caroline had come to say hi to me, and without any hint of bad feelings towards me. How wonderful she is, I thought.

She could've gone away or done something to avoid seeing me ever again; she simply could've chosen to be on duty in another ward. In fact, she had several other choices she could've made, and yet she didn't choose any of them.

"Hi Caroline," I said. "I'm so glad to see you." I was trying to put on a brave face for the current situation. "You got my message that I wanted to talk to you?" I asked her, and she just nodded with a faint smile. "I wanted to explain and apologise to you personally, Caroline, I'm so sorry for what happened." Caroline came near me and then put her finger on my lips.

"Shhhhhhhh," Caroline said, "you don't need to explain anything or apologise for anything to me, my dear." I just looked at her, and her eyes became watery.

"I'm really sorry Caroline, believe me," I said. "You're such a wonderful and caring person, one of the very best I've ever known, and I've been so cruel to you...." She hushed me again.

"Not another word Mathew," she said in a strong voice, "or I'll walk away, I mean it." I couldn't let her go away like this, so I didn't say another word, I just looked at her. "How is Iris?" Caroline spoke again after a brief silence. "Will she take it well when she sees me around?" I nodded my agreement.

"She'll be okay to see you." I said hesitantly, myself not really knowing what Iris's reaction would be when she finds out and actually sees Caroline on duty today.

"Look Mathew," Caroline said again. "If Iris will not be happy to see me, then I can ask my supervisor for me to change my duty to another ward, okay?" I nodded again. "And one more thing, Mathew," Caroline said. "I'll always care about you." I nodded again.

"Caroline, if I may say so," I said, "you've opened my eyes and broadened my world. I'll never forget about you. You've changed my awareness of people and the world, and for that I thank you, my dear Caroline." Caroline smiled and nodded her acceptance and understanding.

"Look Mathew, whatever happened between us and everything else, happened for a reason and for that, we all, I mean you, me and Iris, we should be able to understand and accept it. And once we accept this reasoning and what it means, then we are all winners and we will remain friends." I smiled and said to her.

"You've now become a poet, or a philosopher of some kind?" Caroline chuckled.

"Ah stop it Mathew, you are making me embarrassed." Caroline came over and gave me a friendly hug, I then thought. What if Iris walks in now? What will she think? She will definitely think I'm a two timing bastard, but she also might be an understanding person and she might not suspect anything wrong, but just a friendly hug. "Just remember, if and when Iris dumps you for any reason, I will be always waiting for you. You will have a place in my heart always." And she held her hand to her heart.

"Thanks Caroline." I managed to reply. But Caroline started to laugh and giggle.

"I'm only messing with you," Caroline said, "come on now; Iris is a very caring and loving woman. I have met and spoken with her and I can judge, I can tell she will not let you down. And you, I know, you will not let her down, either. You're both matched for each other....... be happy together always and.........." And just then Iris entered. She had heard the words of Caroline and she was quite impressed.

"Now, now, Caroline," Iris said, and me and Caroline, were caught by surprise, but both of us were innocent, ha ha ha lucky us, I thought. "How are you dear?" I thought she was talking to me and I replied that I was fine but Iris laughed and told me. "I was not talking to you Mathew, I was talking to Caroline." We all laughed and it broke the ice, or I might say the 'frozen moment' when Caroline wasn't sure of Iris's reaction.

Iris went forward and kissed Caroline on both cheeks, and then came to me she also kissed me on both cheeks, and one on the lips.

"Now I am talking to Mathew....How are you my darling?" Iris said, "Did you sleep well?" I replied that I slept well and I'm alright.

Again Iris turned to Caroline. "Caroline dear, you will tell me the truth," Iris said with a smile. "Did he sleep well or was he up to something last night?" Caroline didn't know the answer and she wasn't sure Iris was being sarcastic or was genuine. Maybe she was fishing for information about me and Caroline?

"I came on duty this morning only, I wasn't here last night." Caroline said. Iris smiled at her.

"I know dear," Iris said, "don't worry; I was just trying to cheer Mathew up." Iris then added, "Caroline, do you know what time Mathew will be taken to the operating theatre?" Caroline replied, explaining that she wasn't sure but it might be soon, because Dr. Livingstone liked to perform his operations early in the morning. Therefore for me, it was scheduled for ten in the morning but it might be pushed forward if there was an emergency. Iris asked if she might be allowed to go with me. Caroline shook her head.

"I am sorry Iris but the hospital's regulations do not allow visitors near or around the operating theatre." Caroline answered. "But you can wait here in this room, or the TV room. You see Iris, even us ward nurses are not allowed to stay around the operating theatre." Caroline added, "We only take the patient's file with the patient and we hand it over to the operating theatre nurses, that's all." Caroline then asked if I or Iris needed anything for now, otherwise she would be out on the floor where she has to take care of other patients as well. "Just call me, if you need me, please." Caroline said and with that, she went on her way.

I admired her for her composure. I thought whoever marries her will be a real lucky guy, and I hoped a good and deserving person should marry her, not just any 'Tom, Dick or Harry' type of person. Now I could pay notice to Iris. She wore a light green blouse, a dark green skirt and jacket and scarf, and the colours matched perfectly with her eyes. And I thought whatever colour she chose, it matches her eyes. She was a pretty woman, and she knew how to dress up and select the colours to suit her. My movie star was one beautiful woman.

"How's your Ma and Da?" I asked Iris, and she looked at me while thinking for some time.

"Mathew darling, if you don't mind," Iris said, "can you repeat please." I knew what she was trying to do, so again I asked her.

"Iris my love, how's your Mother and Father?" She then smiled.

"That's better, my love. They are both fine and they are praying for you, Mathew." Iris then added, "They wanted to come with me to be with you, but I stopped them both. I told them they can come after the operation. Is that alright dear?" I smiled and nodded. So my future in-laws were worried about me, and my movie star's secretary wanted to come to see me. Oh! What a turn of events! "Mathew, my dear sweetheart," Iris said. "You are going for the operation this morning, and please, I beg you, please do not think about it. Stop worrying, everything will turn out to be okay. Just pray in your heart and remember that I love you very much and I am waiting for you here. Is that fine, my darling?" I nodded, and I thought about love. Love is something else.

I didn't know what love was previously, but now I have realised what love is, and what love can do to a person. As we sat there each with deep thoughts in our heads, I tried to bring humour to the moment.

"Darling Iris," I said, "after the doctors chop off my leg............." She turned abruptly and looked at me and wasn't sure where I was going with the 'chopping' business. "Will you then marry a one-legged cripple and................" Iris became annoyed.

"Stop it, stop this nonsense Mathew," Iris said with annoyance showing in her face. "Why are you being so...........so........." I finished for her.

"Funny." I said and started to laugh. She started beating me playfully with her small fists.

"You, Mathew," Iris was annoyed and I continued to laugh.

"Beloved Iris," I said, "you cannot take a joke? I'm only messing with you, just to lighten up the moment, honey, you know what I mean?" She glared at me.

"No jokes about you being cripple or one legged." Iris said angrily, "I can takes jokes, but when you talk about the person I love most, I will not take it, Mathew, got it?" She showed me her fist, and playfully pretended to punch me in the face. "Do you see this fist?" Iris asked. "If you insult my beloved fiancé again, then you'll get a black eye! Nobody is allowed to joke or as you say, mess with my Mathew, understood?" I nodded my head playfully showing fear in my face, and we laughed together and hugged.

The time came when Caroline arrived with the green file in her hands, followed by two attendants who came in to take me from the ward. Iris kissed me, and sobbing with tears flowing down, Caroline held Iris, and took her to one side and spoke with her slowly like a mother to her daughter, and I saw Iris nodding her head. Caroline held Iris and they hugged.

Then Caroline came to me and we were on our way. I didn't know what Caroline said to Iris, and I didn't have the desire to ask Caroline at this time. So I just lay on the bed and enjoyed my ride. At the same time under the duvet, I was touching and feeling my right leg. I was talking and saying goodbye to my leg, as if it could hear and understand me. My eyes were watery but I was carefully wiping them without Caroline seeing me. I had a lot in my head to think about but the time was not enough, everything was happening at a kind of super speed, and it made me remember some ads on TV about super fast Internet Broadband speeds, and I smiled at the thought.

We reached our destination and they parked me in an empty trolley space, waiting for my turn. There were about five trolleys ahead of me, but I now knew that there were a few operating theatres, so multiple operations can go ahead with different consultants. As each had their own patients and each consultant was a specialist in a different part of the human body. And so I waited for my turn. My file was handed over to the other nurse and Caroline came over to me.

"Mathew dear," Caroline said. "God will be with you, do not worry, everything will be alright." She smiled and held my hand. "I will be with Iris, and together we will pray for you, okay? Good Luck." She kissed me on the cheek and she went, walking away quickly before I could say anything else. The nurse from the operating theatre came over and opened the file, then the questions were once again asked and the answers given. She paused at 'next of kin'.

"Who is your next of kin?" She asked and eagerly was waiting for a reply.

"Iris," I replied, she looked at me and asked me again.

"Is Iris your mother? Here it was Margaret as the name of your mother who was next of kin, and then changed to Iris. Who is this Iris?" I smiled.

"Iris is my fiancée and she is my next of kin." I said with a smile. The nurse was even more confused.

"You mean, you decided to leave out your own mother and then changed to your fiancée?" She asked in a surprised tone and I shook my head, as I was trying to make her understand. It seemed to me that my answers were confusing her even more.

"My mother died while I was here in the hospital," I said as I was trying to explain, "and Iris is my new fiancée whom I got while I was in the hospital." I saw her face, she was still confused, and so I continued. "You see I've been in this hospital for a long time now, five or six weeks or maybe even more. My mother died and then she was buried, but I then got a new girlfriend and she became my fiancée while still in here. And no, before you ask me, nothing has happened between me and my fiancée, we just fell in love and we decided that we wanted to get married, so we got engaged. Are you still confused and do not understand me, nurse?" I explained to her about my short but fast adventure in my stay, but with a tone of annoyance in my voice.

She decided to leave it there, but I was sure she's now got a story to tell her colleagues at break time. She completed the forms and she checked my leg and hand name tags, and she walked away while shaking her head. After some time, a female doctor came and asked me again a few questions from the file, and checked me.

She was satisfied, and she and the nurse were pushing my trolley inside the operating theatre. I was trying to look around; when we stopped I could see from the wide windows the sea in the distance, beautiful and blue, warm and peaceful.

"I am now going to give you a general anaesthetic to make you feel relaxed, alright Mathew?" The doctor explained to me and she injected in my IV already on my arm, and within a few minutes I was gone. I was in another world.

Chapter Twenty-Eight

I STARTED TO OPEN MY EYES slowly and looking around trying to remember where I was and then the anaesthetic doctor came to me.

"Hi Mathew," She said. "You are now in the recovery room now." I could barely hear, I was in and out, my eyes asleep and the doctor's voice was far away in the distance. After a while I could open my eyes for a few seconds, and I noticed there were a lot of recovery beds in small partitions, and the nurses and doctors were busy going to this patient and that one and so forth. Myself, I wasn't sure where I am or what is happening with me, but I was regaining awareness slowly.

After a while, maybe an hour or more in the recovery room, I felt my trolley bed was being pushed around again, and I could sense my journey through the corridors and on the lift. Then I think I was brought back to my ward and then my room and parked in my space. I could hear voices in the distance, but I couldn't figure out who it was. I wasn't here yet, I was still in another world.

As I was returning to consciousness, I started to remember where

I was, and what it was all about. I felt someone holding my hand and trying to call my name and I could hear other voices as well. It took a while to open my eyes slightly and look who it was who was holding my hand. I could feel the hand which was holding me was feminine and I could see faces looking at me, but was unsure who they were.

"Mathew, Mathew……." someone was calling my name, I wasn't sure who it was but the voice sounded familiar. I tried to focus but I wasn't able to see, so I closed my eyes again. "Mathew……Can you hear me…………." I nodded my head weakly without opening my eyes and the hand which was holding me squeezed my hand and I softly squeezed back. It went on for some time and then I slowly opened my eyes again. I looked around and tried to focus. I saw one or two persons around me and they were looking down at me.

I tried to recognise one and I saw it was Iris. She was the one holding my hand and she smiled at me. I then turned to see who the other person was and I recognised it was Caroline and she smiled at me as well. My hand went in search of her hand and she pulled it away but I noticed Iris nodding her head at Caroline, and she gave me her hand and I held it as well. We stayed like this for a long time maybe, then eventually Caroline slowly pulled her hand and with both her hands she patted me and sort of pulled the duvet to cover me nicely. I looked at her face and she was smiling and tears were flowing down her cheeks and I then turned again to Iris. She also was smiling and sobbing. I didn't understand what was going on.

I just couldn't remember. Then it came back to me. I was supposed to have undergone an operation, but what was it for? I didn't have the rush to know things or speak. I wasn't fully aware and awake, it seemed that I wasn't in any hurry but it was coming back slowly as if frame by frame, in slow motion. Then I realised that the operation was to cut off my leg, which was cancerous, and the cancer had 'eaten' my thigh muscles and soft tissues and was now spreading to the bone and upwards in my body.

Now knowing and being sure that the operation was to cut off my leg. I wanted to feel the empty space that was once my leg, but still my body movements were not strong and so I couldn't 'send' my hand to feel for it. I wanted ask Iris or Caroline.

"I.......I......" nothing was coming out of my opened mouth, I waited, but tears started to roll down my cheeks and to the pillow. Iris was wiping my tears and stroking my head at the same time.

"Mathew...you are going to be fine." Iris spoke to me. I nodded my head and turned to see Caroline nodding while also smiling even though she was teary eyed herself. Iris then kissed my forehead. "I love you Mathew," Iris said and then realised Caroline was also there. "We all love you Mathew darling." I managed to nod my head and then words came out.

"The .... operation............" Iris and Caroline looked at each other, and Iris nodded at me.

"The operation went well, Mathew." Iris said, "You're going to be okay, darling." I still felt I didn't get an answer to my question.

"My....my....leg......" I asked again as they both looked at each other.

"Mathew.....I......we....do not know......" Iris said and when she got stuck Caroline took over.

"The doctor will be with you shortly," Caroline said, "please just sit and relax." Caroline then spoke to Iris, "I'll go and fetch the doctor, you stay with Mathew." And she went. Iris just sat there with me and we waited for the doctor to come. I couldn't feel my right leg and I knew of course that an empty space cannot be felt or touched. Then Caroline came back after a while with Dr. Browne. They entered and closed the curtain behind them. Dr. Browne smiled and in his soft and polite voice.

"Hello Mathew, how are you feeling, now?" Dr. Browne asked me.

"Doctor, how's the operation........and...has my leg.........my leg has been chopped off?" I managed to ask but Dr. Browne looked at me and smiled and looked at Iris as well.

"The good news is that your leg has not been...... amputated..... Mathew." Dr. Browne said and patting me on my hand while smiling. "It was a complicated surgery and the team.....led by the Consultant Dr. Livingstone himself......were in favour of not amputating your leg..... after we had opened to check your thigh again ....we examined the tissues and bone at the affected tumour site," he paused, then continued,

"Dr. Livingstone himself will come to see you later and explain to you all about the procedures, and on his decision not to....amputate your leg...but for now, we want you to rest and........" I cut him off.

"But doctor, I cannot feel my leg." I spoke as I was worried and went on, "are you telling me the truth.....or just messing my head?" Dr. Browne smiled at me and then asked Caroline to help me raise my head a little bit, but not sit fully. Caroline and Iris helped me and then Dr. Browne, slowly opened my duvet cover to reveal the bloodied clothes and bed sheets, but there it was....my leg..........! My thigh was covered with bandages from the hip to the knee, but my leg was there, all of it. I touched it with my hands where I could reach the bandaged part and I saw my foot and I wriggled my toes. With tears in my eyes I asked Dr. Browne.

"Can you.....can you ...please ......pinch my lower leg ....so I can feel........if it's truly my leg?" Dr. Browne chuckled and pinched me. Yes, oh yes, I could feel the pinch and his hand on my leg, even though faintly, but yes, the feeling was of my body, yes my leg. Oh my God, I still had my leg; I wondered what miracle had happened this time. I thought God is full of surprises. Dr. Browne then covered me back and slowly Iris and Caroline put me back in a reclining position. "Are you satisfied now, Mathew?" Dr. Browne asked me. "I was not lying to you, you know?"

I nodded my head. "Thanks Doctor...thanks." I answered then Iris called the doctor to one side and spoke with Dr. Browne in private and she came back smiling. Then Dr. Browne gave instructions to Caroline on what medications were to be given to me and he wrote or scribbled on the green file, which by now was becoming thicker and thicker every day.

After he left and Caroline went to see her other patients, Iris stayed with me and we just talked but nothing serious or nothing in particular. We were both happy for the outcome so far and I was excited my leg was not.....amputated......yet. We both agreed that we had to wait for Dr. Livingstone to know for sure what was happening and what the plan for the future plan would be. Are they going to leave and try to treat my leg as it was or maybe they will decide to ......amputate .... in the future, or what was the story? We just sat there and speculated.

"What time is it now?" I asked Iris and she replied that it was six in the evening. I realised then that the operation had taken a long time and also it took a long time for me to recover. "Darling, have you had lunch?" I asked, "I'm thirsty myself." I knew that I wouldn't be able to actually eat anything yet, otherwise I would vomit.

"Honey, I have not eaten anything since breakfast either," Iris replied and went on, "I was just drinking water all this time….I have been worried about you….I could not bring myself to eat anything." I told her that she could have gone to the hospital cafeteria downstairs in the lobby and grabbed a sandwich or something. Iris looked at me with soft and loving eyes. "I was in the hospital chapel praying for you, my darling." Iris said. "I was not thinking about lunch…only about you… my love." I nodded with understanding.

"Okay, now I'm okay, so will you please go and grab something to eat?" I said. "I don't want you to starve to death, and then who'll take care of me……love?" I said, messing with Iris, and smiling.

"You know what Mathew," Iris said, "even Caroline was with me in the chapel and she was praying for you, too. She was crying. Mathew, Caroline loves you; you know that, don't you?" I nodded my head, because I knew that but then I felt a tinge of jealousy in Iris's voice. These are women, and they need assurances all the time. I felt I had to say something.

"Iris, Caroline's love is different from yours. She is not a threat to you my love; do you know what I mean?" I explained. "Caroline understands our love between you and me Iris, and she has accepted it whole heartedly so there's nothing for you to worry about, my love." Iris nodded her head in agreement.

"I know that Mathew, I have seen the love in her eyes. I should be jealous, Mathew, but I am not," Iris said and went on, "sometimes I feel like I have snatched you from her Mathew, I really do." I understood and I wanted to tell her, yes, you did snatch me from Caroline, but I had a feeling it might come out wrong or in bad taste, and it might offend my movie star. Already each has accepted the other, so I shouldn't do or say anything to make them enemies or otherwise I'll hurt and feel I've wronged the one who lost the battle, or gave up, and that is Caroline.

No, it wasn't fair to either one. They were both wonderful and loving and caring women who deserve nothing but the best in the world. The two most brilliant ladies in my life at the moment, they were a billion in one or let me say in two, and I, Mathew, was the one lucky guy in the whole world who not only managed to be loved by one but by both of them. Me, Mathew, would you believe it? If three months ago, I had told anyone about what is happening now, then I would have been taken to the mental institution, for they might have thought I had lost the plot. But now in the present time it was a reality. I was one lucky man, or rather the luckiest man in the whole world.

At quarter to eight, Caroline came to ask me and Iris permission, would you believe it? She wanted to know if it was okay for her to leave, now that her shift was over and to go home and rest, or we would like her to stay with us. I looked at her.

"Caroline you don't need to ask our permission to go off-duty," I answered. "It's your right, you know?" and Iris smiled.

"Caroline, dear," Iris said, "you have been so good and loving, my dear." Iris went on, "you have been so concerned about Mathew and your prayers have been answered, you know?" Caroline blushed. Maybe she didn't want me to know about her concerns and about her being in the chapel and praying. I smiled at her.

"Caroline," I said, "thanks, I appreciate all you've done for me." Caroline looked at me lovingly and I encouraged Iris to add her comments as I didn't want to be the only one talking with Caroline. I wanted to avoid problems.

"Caroline my dear," Iris said as she stood up and went to Caroline, and holding Caroline's hands, "go home and rest, make sure you eat something, dear. Mathew will be fine now. You have done a lot today already and thank you very much, dear." Iris kissed Caroline on both her cheeks, or they exchanged kisses on both cheeks, Caroline said she will be coming tomorrow that she had taken the day duty. She bade us goodbye and goodnight and then she left. I felt so proud of her, for all her dignity and composure.

After Caroline was gone, Iris told me that her parents were calling constantly to check and ask about my condition. Iris kept them up-to-date with my health and operation and they were thrilled to learn about my leg being saved and all. Iris told them that I could not speak with them yet but maybe tomorrow and they both understood.

"Iris," I began, and looking at her, "you don't want to share me with your parents, now do you?" I said jokingly and added "You're afraid your mom will fall for me?" Iris looked at me and pretended she was shocked.

"Mathew," Iris said, "I am shocked. How can you think like that at a time like this, and with my mother, of all people? You have a dirty mind Mathew, I am really shocked." Iris then boxed me on the cheek with her tiny fist jokingly.

"Iris, my darling," I said. "I'm only messing with you my love; don't take it seriously, dear." We went on like this, just messing around with small talk.

Chapter Twenty-Nine

*A*T EIGHT FIFTEEN. IN WALKED Dr. Livingstone followed swiftly by Dr. Browne and Maritas, the night nurse. They came in and just stood there observing me and Dr. Livingstone and his ever constant smile on his intelligent and experienced face.

"Hello Mathew." Dr. Livingstone began. "How are you feeling?" Before I could answer, he continued, "You must be feeling anxious to know what is happening, right?" and he went on, "But at the same time you must be very pleased indeed that your leg has not been amputated." I waited, he paused and then he continued looking at me. "I believe Dr. Browne has already explained to you what we did and the reasons behind it, right?" Dr. Livingstone said again. "You must be wondering, what will happen to your leg next."

He then went ahead and explained to me what Dr. Browne had already said that afternoon, and he went on.

"We scraped the cancerous tumour that had reached your femur, which is the bone on your thigh, as much as possible and we also removed a large amount of tissue. So instead of amputating your entire leg, we tried this method. And I believe there will be no need for further surgery to amputate your leg. But if and when the need arises in the future then we will take that route and go ahead and amputate."

Dr. Livingstone paused and seemed to think that he should either explain more or this will be enough for now.

"You will remain in the hospital for a few more days," he started again. "Your next surgery will be by the plastic surgeons to try to cover your wound, which is deep to your femur bone and long and wide." A pause, "They will take skin from another part of your body, maybe the other thigh or your backside and do a skin graft. After that, and all the while we will continue to monitor your development. If the skin is accepted and covers your wound and the plastic surgeons are happy then we will be able to discharge you."

Dr. Livingstone paused again, and looked at all the faces around him as if reading each one of his audience for an effect.

"Once you are discharged and you go home, you have to have someone looking after you and also your local public health nurse will come every day to clean your wound and change the dressings. In the beginning you will be required to rest a lot so the skin graft is accepted at the sight of your wound. You will have to reduce your movements. After about three months you will get an appointment to go to Saint Luke's hospital, where you will be seen by a Radiology Consultant, who will then plan with you your next treatments and after care. You will have chemotherapy and might as well get radiotherapy, though the Consultant might decide not to."

Dr. Livingstone then looked at his watch and realised that he had been talking for too long, and it was just like a lecture.

"Mathew, do you have any questions?" I thought for a while and had listened and tried to take in whatever I could.

"You didn't amputate my leg now and whatever you did, as you say will be okay for now, but for how long? How long before you know if it's successful or not?" Dr. Browne decided to come in and answer this one.

"Mathew, by the time you are discharged, we shall have a fairly good idea about that, so we'll know by then." And he looked at me for more questions. But then I just shook my head, I had nothing more to ask. What they had already said was a lot for me to absorb for now, so I felt I couldn't take in any more in my head, my memory's Gigabyte wasn't large enough, I though with a silent chuckle.

"Excuse me Doctor." Iris spoke with authority. "You have explained a lot, but as you said Mathew will be looked after in Saint Luke's hospital. What about yourself, you won't be seeing Mathew any longer? I thought you were his main doctor." Dr. Livingstone laughed a hearty laughter and it was like he was caught out.

"While Mathew is still in the hospital, he is my patient," Dr. Livingstone explained, "and even after that, when his main hospital will be Saint Luke's, and he will have a Radiology Consultant looking after him, all his report copies will be coming to me. I will be seeing him every three months at the beginning and then after every six months, and so on and so forth. Mathew is my patient, and will continue to be my patient. I and the Radiology Consultant in St. Luke's will be working as a team." Dr. Livingstone smiled. "The two of you shouldn't be worried, Mathew will be in good hands and will receive good treatment and after care. As we all have already seen, Mathew is well loved and liked by everybody he meets." Dr. Livingstone said this with a look of understanding and smiling at Iris. Iris blushed and nodded her head.

When Dr. Livingstone didn't get more questions, he glanced at his watch again. He had stayed nearly forty minutes and it was time for him to move on, so he said his goodbyes and he walked out with Dr. Browne in tow. Iris sat down near me and she held my hand in her hand and with her other hand she was stroking my head. After a while she rested her head on my chest and we stayed silent for a long time. There was nothing to talk about but each one of us was deep in our own thoughts.

Time passed, and there was nothing to say between us. Our love was deep and under no threat from anyone. Caroline could be seen as part of our love triangle but on the outside part of the triangle. I felt sorry about it being that way, but it was beyond my power. It was as it is with a reason; I thought everything happens with a reason. I liked Caroline a lot but it was Iris whom I loved most, and that was the truth from the very beginning, I didn't lie to Caroline and she knew this and accepted the truth. Then the night nurse, Maritas came over with two cups of tea.

"Mathew, try to drink this, but slowly, and later I'll give you something to eat, okay." Maritas said to me, and she turned to Iris. "Iris you too, have a cup of tea now then if you want I can bring for you some toast as well, okay?" Iris thanked her and nodded. We drank our tea, which felt so good and refreshing after the long hours of fasting, and I didn't vomit. Then I turned and spoke to Iris.

"Iris darling," I said, "it's getting late, don't you think you should now go home and rest?" Iris looked at her watch. Yes, it was late. "You've been here the whole day and also your parents must be worried," I added to give it more strength. She understood and she hugged me and kissed me softly on the lips and even though she didn't want to leave me, it was late and she needed to go home to rest.

"Mathew, sleep well." Iris said lovingly. "I'll see you in the morning. Do you need me to bring for you anything from home or the shops, my love?" I shook my head.

"Thanks but no, my love, you just go and rest," I replied. "I'll see you tomorrow and send my love to your parents, honey." Iris went home though reluctantly. At eleven at night Maritas brought me a cup of tea with two slices of toast which I ate, and my stomach was happy too. I thanked Maritas and I told her.

"You're so kind Maritas." I said with a smile, and she smiled too.

"You're a good patient Mathew, everybody likes you and you talk nicely to everyone." Maritas explained. "As you can see, even women are fighting for you, so you are very lucky Mathew. I'll pray for you to be healthy and happy. You see everybody likes a good person." With that she went on her way. I lay in my bed, touching and feeling my leg every now and then. I thought God is great and please dear God forgive me, sometimes I challenge you, but actually you can perform miracles, for example like you did today. So please dear God, make me healthy and happy. I also realised that we humans take a lot of everyday things for granted but when we lose it one day then we realise how important it was.

I again was thinking about today's events, oh yeah, it was a long day and full of drama. I had gone in the operating theatre knowing they're going to ……….… ampu…..tate …….my leg. I had said goodbye to my leg, then after many hours, I then realised I still have my leg, they had not ……... amputated …….my leg, what a day it was! With the events since I was…admitted…. in the hospital and up until now….I could've written a book about my adventures and misadventures in this great hospital and my great love stories.

And then I remembered and thought how many times have I been in the operating theatre? I've even forgotten the count. I'll name my book …… 'My Adventures at the Great Dublin University Hospital, by Mathew the Great' I laughed within myself and continued to dream and visualize the events. I remembered me Ma, and me Da, and me brothers. I thought about Kevin, who was now history in my life and the lads also were all history for me. I'm going to come out of the hospital, and I'm going to walk. Eventually I'll get an education; I'll get work, and get married and raise a family.

Oh, it was so nice to dream and plan and hope, because without hope there is no desire or will to live, and I wanted to live and to be with Iris, always and forever. Maritas passed and saw me still half awake. She came over and covered me properly with the duvet.

"Tomorrow morning I myself and the attendants will change the bed sheets and your gowns and you'll get fresh ones." Maritas told me as she gave me some pain killers after I told her about my pains and she then told me. "If the pain persists, I'll give you a tablet of morphine." I also had the urinal, a portable special plastic or metal bottle or can, which I'm given whenever I get the operation done and for a day or two afterwards. When I can't move and walk to the toilets for passing urine, these portable urinals help me to pass urine while lying on the bed. And the nurses and attendants or student nurses remove them whenever the urinals are full and empty them in the toilets and bring me fresh ones.

Maritas switched off the lights in the room and silently she went out and I could hear her footsteps in the corridor as she continued on in her work. While in these thoughts I fell asleep. I didn't sleep well as the pain was on the extreme point of painfulness. I felt the pain inside my bones and inside the marrow of either my right leg or sometimes both and I had no explanation on why the other leg should have pain as well. Maritas was coming to check on me frequently throughout the night.

At six in the morning, Maritas the night nurse came again to see me and she gave me two tablets of painkillers and a glass of water which I then thanked her for. Maritas took the portable urinal and went to empty it and brought another one for me, I felt embarrassed but what could I do? She was doing all these chores with a smile. I felt that she was so nice and caring.

"I'm sorry Maritas." I apologised to her but she just smiled,

"Why are you sorry, Mathew?" Maritas asked, "It's my duty to all my patients and you are no exception, Mathew."

"Who's going to be the day nurse for today?" I then asked Maritas. Maritas understood the hidden meaning of the question.

"I think maybe Caroline will come to be on duty but I don't know for sure. It's up to the supervisor; she's the one who's planning the duty roster." Maritas replied. At seven in the morning, the doctors passed through on their rounds and Dr. Browne stopped and asked about my sleep, the thigh and the pain. Then at seven thirty, another nurse came to be the day duty nurse and I was sort of disappointed it wasn't Caroline, but life has to go on. She must have been real tired and therefore took a day off but she will come, of that I was sure. I will see her again. Elvis brought me my tray of toast and tea, we spoke a few words and he said he would see me later.

At nine Iris came. I could hear her footsteps and before she entered the room, I smelled the sweet smell of her perfume and then she entered. She looked beautiful as ever and with her smile with her soft red lipstick, her eyes were smiling as well, she looked radiant and glowing. And then to my surprise behind her walked her personal assistant, her mother, and she also looked beautiful and she smiled at me for the first time ever, I thought.

"Hi my love, look who's here to see you." Iris said with a big smile as she led her mom forward. Iris kissed me on both cheeks and a soft kiss on the lips. "How did you sleep, honey, with all the pain?" Iris said again. "Did the night nurse treat you well, my love?" Before I could reply, her mom came forward and she kissed me on both cheeks.

"How are you Mathew," she asked me, "I am sorry for what you are going through. I and James are always asking about you and your health. Isn't that right, my darling?" She turned to her daughter Iris for confirmation that she was always asking about me. I wanted to laugh, but it would have been rude on my part to my future in-law. Also, I was supposed to do everything in my power to impress Iris's parents, especially her mother, and here I was, nearly bursting out with laughter. Iris pulled a chair over for her mother, and made her sit down. Then she herself wanted to sit on the bed and I stopped her.

"Honey, don't sit on the bed, they still have to come and change the bed sheets." I told her, while I tried to cover myself and the bed which had a lot of blood, with the duvet. Iris understood and went out and spoke with the nurse or the supervisor and then she came back with a frown.

"I told them to clean you up and change the bed and all." Iris said, "I told them that my patient feels uncomfortable and the room is smelling of blood, and the supervisor told me that someone will be coming in a short while to freshen you up, Mathew dear." I then whispered to Iris, so her mother wouldn't hear.

"Iris, why did you bring your mother so early? You see now, she sees me as bloodied and dirty and my bed as well, and the smell." I whispered in her ear, "You could've brought her later on or in the afternoon, now she'll reject me, darling." Iris nodded and whispered back but loud enough for her mother to hear.

"But Mathew dear, my mother insisted she had to come to see you," Iris whispered again, "maybe she wanted to talk with you in a private conversation, my love." Iris winked at me.

Chapter Thirty

I FELT OH MY GOD, THE lady insisted on coming to see me this early in the morning and she didn't want to wait. She surely must've something important to discuss with me. Maybe she's here to tell me to leave her daughter alone, and for me to get lost. Maybe she found out about my previous life and she's here to threaten me with the Gardai. Maybe, just maybe, there were a lot of maybes for me.

But we kept on talking about the weather and about the traffic and making small talk. Two male attendants came and asked for Iris and her mother to excuse them, they wanted to change the sheets on my bed. Iris and her mother went out to the TV room and the two attendants closed the curtains. As it so happens whenever I had an operation, afterwards I cannot move much and now the attendants helped me to change my two hospital gowns.

They changed the bed sheets as well while I was still on the bed, turning me to this side and then turning me to the other side. They had brought a wash basin with warm water, which I then used to clean myself.

They were professionals who knew their jobs and went on smoothly trying as much as possible not to hurt me while at the same time talking to me. And once the bed was clean, they opened the curtains and the nurse called Iris and her mother back in the room. I felt clean and fresh. Iris and her mom came back in the room and Iris sat near me on the bed while her mom sat on the chair.

"Thanks to you, I now feel better and fresh." I told Iris. She nodded.

"Oh yeah, I do not like complaining but once in a while, you need to, Mathew." Iris said, trying to explain herself to me. "It is not in me, but I like to fight for my rights." I understood and I nodded my approval. The nurse entered the room.

"Someone will come to change the dressing of your wound, but there's no need to worry," she said. "You'll only be given a local anaesthetic so you'll not feel pain. Don't worry Mathew, the guy knows his job, he's very professional." With that she went on her way. I didn't know that they would need to clean or change the dressing today. I had only understood that maybe after a day or two they will take me for skin grafting. But all was well, whatever the doctors had planned for me, I believed it was for the best and it was good for my health.

I had put my full trust in Dr. Livingstone, and he with his team of doctors, nurses and other staff, so I shall be ready whenever they need me. To break the silence and unease between myself and Iris's mother, we had to find a topic to talk about, so I thought, well, why not be the one to start, anyway.

"Sorry, Iris's mom, I forgot your name," I said, as if she had given me her name in the first place.

"Oh I am sorry! My name is Clara, and yours is Mathew of course," Clara replied, feeling a bit embarrassed. And I pushed ahead.

"Thanks for your prayers, and how's James doing?" James being Iris's father, so I was now going on a first name basis, and I thought why not, at least for now.

"James is doing great, he wanted to come as well, but we thought he should rest at home, isn't that so darling?" Clara had turned to Iris once again for approval.

"Yeah, I will bring Dad when he is better." Iris replied. I then continued.

"Clara, even though you're Iris's mother but the first time I saw you, even now, you look like her elder sister. You don't look like her mother at all, you know what I mean?" Poor Clara blushed and her hand went to her face, maybe to feel her skin, but I did get to her and it pleased her. She started giggling and feeling shy, while Iris knew I was just trying to impress her mom, but it made her giggle and she hugged her mother.

"Oh mom, I am jealous now. Mathew has fallen for you." Iris said to her mom, and Clara buried her face in her hands and she continued to giggle. I thought Clara didn't expect this, but I think my comments might change her image of me and she might decide to accept me willingly after all. Even if she had come for war, my 'softening approach' might win me over.

"No, really, I mean it Iris." I said, "Your mom is very pretty and young looking. I had thought she was your sister when you first came, when I saw you both the first time. You remember when you came to visit James in the hospital and it was snowing outside and freezing, back in November, right?" I smiled. "I am not messing with you Iris, your mom is beautiful, and I'm sure you got your beauty from her." Clara continued to blush and giggle and bury her face in her hands and Iris was giggling as well. She must be delighted that I managed to break her mom and was able to connect. "But you, my love, Iris, it is you whom I love," I said, "So don't think your mom is a threat, no way, my darling." We all burst out laughing.

"Mathew, is that how you managed to win my daughter?" Clara asked amid the laughter, "With your sweet tongue?" I thought Iris knew that was actually the truth, but could she have admitted that to her mom?

"Yeah, mom, in fact that is the reality," Iris said while giggling, "I fell for Mathew's words and his charms." I then asked Clara,

"Did Iris tell you and James about us?" I asked but I didn't want to give more details, as Iris had told me she already spoke to her parents and about the full plan, but I just wanted to hear from Clara's mouth. I wanted to hear her reaction and acceptance or refusal of Iris's plan. I thought it was altogether different between laughing together and to accept me as her future son-in-law. Maybe what she had in mind was more like 'The Beauty and the Beast'. Clara stopped laughing, and her face changed slightly, and I thought, here goes.

"Iris explained to me and James everything about you, and about your love towards each other, Mathew." Clara said. "There are no secrets between us three, myself, James and Iris." I thought, wow, she insisted on the words 'us three'; well let's see where this goes to. Clara continued, "Also Iris told us about your impromptu engagement here in hospital room." Now Clara lost me with the word 'impromptu' even though I did get the meaning of the complete sentence. I thought I shall ask Iris later, on the meaning of the word. Clara then added. "James and I were disappointed that you had your engagement in here, but still we were very excited about the news. It was such wonderful news. Mathew, James and I are very happy for both of you."

I had worried when the word 'disappointed' was mentioned, but now I felt relief and inhaled with ease, and Clara continued.

"Mathew dear ….please remove all your worries from your head. Iris has told us about your plans……. about you wanting to get a better education ….about you getting a better job and……about your plans for marriage. Today I came here on behalf of both myself and James … to convey to you that you are welcome in our home. We want to see our only daughter happy, and we want to get involved in your wedding." Clara paused and then continued. "Iris has spoken highly of you Mathew; please do not disappoint either Iris or us. Please don't let Iris down in any way. Just remember her happiness will always come first for us, her parents and family."

All this while, Iris had remained silent while holding my hand and occasionally patting my head, and sometimes touching her mother. I now saw how close the mother and daughter were and how much Iris meant to her parents. I felt like asking Clara, that if in the beginning or until now she was against me, what made her change her attitude towards me. But I thought, first she'll know that Iris tells me everything and second, after the long lecture, I didn't feel I needed another one from my future mother--in-law. I nodded my head.

"Clara, I promise you and James," I said, "I shall love and treasure Iris all my life. I promise I'll not be a burden on Iris and I will work hard to take care of my family." I went on, "You'll have put your trust in me and I promise I'll not let you down, Clara." Iris hugged me tightly.

"Okay, enough, both of you. Long lectures and promises from both of you! Also, my mother has to go home now to rest and my darling Mathew has also to rest now." Iris said as she chuckled, "Okay mom, I'll take you home now before you melt again from Mathew's words." We all laughed together, a sign of a happy family. "Darling, don't take lunch today, I shall bring you something from home. Is it okay with you, or would you like to have the hospital lunch? Maybe it's already your favourite." Iris said to me while smiling.

Iris took her mother home and she promised she would be back soon. That was okay with me. In fact, I had enough of fear from my future mother-in-law, Clara, but the meeting, if you can call that a meeting or 'The Interview' went very well. I think I made an impression on Clara. I'll wait until Iris comes back and she'll tell me how I did with her mother, and whether it was okay, or if I said something wrong. Oh, and about the word, what does 'impromptu' mean? And I hope Iris won't think that I was trying to make a pass at her mother. Oh God forbid, I wouldn't do a thing like that.

But of course she was still beautiful despite her age, but to make a pass at her? That would have been in my other world, my previous life, maybe, just maybe. But for now, I'm the new me, decent, well mannered, polite, and trying to use good grammar and proper English. I will also change the way I dress. I have to look different as well, and walk different, but then I remembered about my leg. Oh well, now I still have my leg and I pray I will be able to keep my leg during all my time I'm alive.

Time passed while I was daydreaming and eventually it was the nurse who brought me back to the present when she announced.

"Mathew, it's time to change your wound dressing." She came in followed by a male nurse with his bag and equipment, and my green file. He set everything down on the table neatly, while I was trying to look and identify the items. Some I could understand what they might be used for, but others I couldn't understand. But I suppose the doctor or nurse knew what he was doing. I just watched as he went to work.

"Hello Mathew, I am Jowinski." He announced. "First I'm going to give you a local anaesthetic and that we will clean your wound and dress you up nice and neat, alright Mathew?" I nodded anxiously with butterflies in my stomach. Jowinski noticed my fears and smiled. "Don't worry Mathew, it won't hurt, and I've done this many times. I'm an experienced person with this, and also I'm a qualified nurse, so just relax and you will feel nothing." He assured me with a smile.

Jowinski then closed the curtains, brought a stool which he sat on, removed my duvet covering and started to remove the bandages from my thigh. The doctors had put on the 'vacuum pump' after each operation, so there was one now also and which Jowinski used to inject the anaesthetic. After about five minutes he switched off the pump and removed all the plasters and the dressings. I tried to look, I caught a glimpse of my thigh and the wound, it was very red and deep and I could see the bone. I calculated roughly the size of the wound, it was about twelve inches long from the top of the knee going upwards to my hip, and maybe four inches wide and the deepest part which was towards the hip, was about two inches deep. This was my rough estimate.

Jowinski went about his work slowly, and every now and then he glimpsed at my face to check on the pain. Whenever I flinched, he would slow down and wait a few seconds and then continue. Once he had cleaned the wound, he started to dress it with new and clean dressings; he went about his work slowly and with great care. Once he was done he switched on the pump, and 'brrrrrrrrrrr' it started, and he wiped the blood off my thigh, wiped clean every place and removed the sterilized plastic mat which he had put below my leg and thigh.

It was over; he wrote his report in the green file, which was still growing thicker by the day. Jowinski was very professional and he thanked me. Before I had time to thank him, he opened the curtains, but still I managed.

"Thanks, my friend you're very professional and efficient." Jowinski smiled, nodded and off he went. Then the nurse came and checked everything was clean. She was satisfied.

"Well Mathew, how was it?" She asked me and I smiled back at her.

"Yeah, he was very good, I was sort of scared at first but it was okay. There wasn't much pain, thanks." She then took the green file and wrote some notes as well.

Chapter Thirty-One

ELVIS PASSED TO SEE WHAT I wanted for lunch. "Elvis, is it okay today if you don't bring anything for me?" I said to Elvis. "Iris will bring me lunch, is it okay with you, do you mind?"

"Yeah Mathew," Elvis replied as he said smiled. "It's okay with me and if you're not full or maybe you don't like. Let me know, I'll bring for you your tray of lunch, okay?" I nodded; Elvis was a good man and very gentle and polite. I liked him.

"Thanks a lot Elvis, you're grand." And he went. It wasn't long before Iris came back and she was carrying a plastic bag filled with very nice-smelling food.

"Hi honey." Iris said, "Am I late? I brought you something to eat, something delicious and tasty, yummy, yummy." She giggled and licked her lips. I smiled at her, chuckled and I thought, 'you're not late honey, but what were you referring to as being late, my darling?' I thought in my silly head, 'is it about Caroline and me you're referring to as being late?' I giggled and just put my palms together and rubbed them with delight, she was pleased.

"Bring the food on," I said with glee, "I'm starving baby, yum, yum." Iris then set up everything and we started eating together when the nurse just passed.

"Welcome nurse, you can join us for lunch." Iris told her while she was munching and mouth full. The nurse just smiled.

"It's okay you go ahead. I knew I smelled something nice and also it looks delicious but I just had my lunch, so thanks anyway." She went on her way. We ate our way through the plates and sure the food was delicious and well cooked. It was steak, baked beans, chips and egg chops and orange juice.

"Honey, this food is delicious." I was munching and eating with my two hands holding the fork and knife. "When did you have time to make this tasty lunch?" Iris giggled and wiped her mouth with a towel.

"My mom made the food last night." Iris replied. "Do you like it? Are you enjoying?" I nodded my head as I didn't want to waste my time, talking. I didn't have this tasty a lunch for a long time. I had actually forgotten the taste of home cooked meals. Nowadays I was just so used to Elvis' 'Meals-on-Wheels' so we continued on eating and enjoying the meal. When I was full and I thought I had overeaten beyond my stomach's capacity, I then had my orange juice. I wiped my mouth and hands, and Iris removed and packed everything nicely to bring back home.

"Iris, my beloved, the one and only, my saviour, my movie star," I said in appreciative mood. Iris giggled, knowing the flattering words coming from my mouth were the result of the good meal I just had. "If you and your mom are planning to feed me like this, I shall soon grow this big." I opened my hands wide in a show of being big. Iris burst out laughing and she hugged me.

"Oh Mathew my love," Iris said, "I was worried maybe you wouldn't like our food, as you were used to the hospital food by now and you would refuse. So I would end up eating all alone." She made her face like she was lonely and funny and we laughed together. I then told Iris about my wound being cleaned and the change of dressing and all. Iris blamed herself. "Oh I should have been here with you my love," Iris was pleading. "I completely had forgotten about that. I am so sorry Mathew my love, please forgive me, honey." She was ready to cry. I thought it really was nothing to worry about.

"It's alright honey, no bother at all," I said. "It was just touch and go, I didn't feel a thing." I tried to assure Iris. "And besides maybe Jow.... Jowisnk .....Jowinski, the guy who came to clean my wound, wouldn't let you in." Iris looked at me and tried to read my face if I was just messing or being serious. She didn't get anything from my face.

"Oh darling, are you in pain now?" Iris said lovingly. I then decided to change the subject.

"Darling, tell me about your mother." I said while my face was serious. "Did I pass the interview or not, was she pleased with me?" Iris looked at me and she pinched my cheeks.

"You cheeky devil, you," she said. "You made my mother so happy and that's why she sent you lunch. Come on, did you not realise that by now?" I frowned and said.

"What?" I had missed the point.

"You told my mother she was young looking and beautiful, you praised her beauty. That is why she gave me lunch to bring to you! You pleased her, you naughty boy, you made her blush." Iris replied then paused. She then added. "And that is the first thing she told my father, that she had a new suitor, can you imagine? My mother threatening my father! 'You'd better treat me well, otherwise there's a new bachelor in town!' My father was astonished and surprised! Who is this man who wants to take his wife away from him?"

Iris chuckled and continued, "But I had to tell my father not to worry, there is a very old man in the hospital that was all full of white hair and is just like 'Shakespeare' reciting poetry to all the ladies."

Iris paused to get her breath back and she went on, "So we all laughed once my dad got the joke. Mathew dear, my mother came this morning to the hospital, not knowing what lay ahead. She was also reluctant to come, but when she went from here after meeting you, she fell for your charms. Mathew my love, you impressed my mother so much so, that she has changed her attitude towards you. In short she now likes you." Iris then went on. "Wow, Mathew you passed the test. Yippee, I am so happy my love; both my parents now like you my darling."

And that was the result. And so I passed, and I felt good now that I was accepted by both of Iris's parents. I now felt I was on my way towards my new goals, and the future seemed bright and beautiful. I wanted to get down from the bed and go for a walk, or if I could, run. It was that much that I was happy. But I couldn't move from my bed and even the short walks cannot be for at least a day or two more. I asked Iris if she wanted to go home and rest, because she could not stay the whole day with me in the hospital.

She could become bored just being in the hospital room the whole day. I was also thinking about myself. I would need to relax or take a nap. But she refused.

"Darling as long I am with you, I am happy, and if whenever you feel like resting or sleeping, please you should just go ahead, and not to worry about me, I'll be fine." Iris replied and I couldn't force her, I just felt sorry for her. Maybe she was used to being in the office and talking on the phone, seeing people, talking to people, have meetings, and doing different things, but here she is stuck in the hospital room like a caged bird.

She then removed from her handbag, a book and she showed me.

"Look Mathew, whenever I am bored or get stuck somewhere, I have my book for reading and passing the time." Iris said smiling. "So you don't worry about me, I am happy just to be with you and that's all I want for now, my darling." The nurse passed by and she brought me some tablets, which I took without a question. She gave me a glass of water and then she went out the door. Iris looked at me swallowing the medicine.

"What are those tablets for?" Iris asked me, "You just took them." I looked at her and just shrugged and smiled.

"Honey, I don't know what these tablets are for and I don't need to know either," I replied, a bit annoyed, "whenever the nurses give me any tablets I just take them, no questions, no bother my darling." She looked at me in amazement.

"Mathew my darling," Iris said, "are you for real?" And she went on, "You should ask them before you take any medicine, honey."I shook my head and I shrugged again.

"I trust them, they cannot give me poison. You know what I mean, my love." I replied with irritation in my voice. Iris didn't pursue the issue. I knew it bothered her. Maybe she would inquire from the nurses at a later time. After a while, I couldn't keep my eyes open so I went ahead and took a nap. When I opened my eyes I saw Iris sitting on the chair near me, reading her novel. It was a 'Mills & Boon' romance story. I looked at her, and she noticed I had opened my eyes.

"Hi stranger, welcome back," Iris greeted me with a smile, "you were snoring. Did you have nice dreams?" I smiled back at Iris.

"I was dreaming about you, my love," I replied, "how beautiful you were and how much love you had for me. I could see it in your eyes."

"Liar," she said as she giggled. "Come on love it is okay, you can tell me if you had dreamt of someone else." Iris winked at me and I smiled back at her.

"I dreamt you were an angel sent by God himself to save me," and I went on, "and you were a very beautiful angel. With long flowing hair, hazel eyes a beautiful smile and white perfect teeth and that, my beautiful movie star, is the truth, nothing but the truth of my dream. You can believe me, or you can choose not to believe me my darling, but that is the whole truth and you can cross my heart." Iris burst out laughing, and she held her hands to cover her mouth. She bent over and laughed so much, even the nurse and another one came and saw the way Iris was laughing, and they just shook their heads and laughed along with us and went on their way.

"Mathew...Mathew........." Iris was saying amid her laughter. "That's the same way you won my mother, Oh my God." She continued, "You are such a poet, Mathew, you really know how to melt a girl's heart, don't you, my love?" We laughed some more for some time. Iris's mobile phone rang and she took it and spoke for a while then brought it to me.

"Mathew my darling," Iris said, "my father wants to talk to you." I took the phone from Iris.

"Hello, is that Mathew?" I heard James' thick voice.

"Hello James, yeah it's me Mathew on the line." I replied back,

"How's it going James?" There was silence and then I heard James's voice. "Oh yeah Mathew, I am doing well myself and what about you, son?" I thought, wow, he's calling me son, that's definitely an acceptance term. It felt good. Soon I'll start addressing him 'yes father', but not yet anyway. Better to play it safe.

"I'm doing great, no bother," I decided to continue just to test the waters; "your daughter Iris is taking very good care of me, James. She is wonderful, and I'm so glad and happy James, really." I waited. What I shall get now? Would it be bombardment or encouragement? Of course I knew I had the support of James, long ago but still, feelings do tend to change every now and then and so I waited. I heard the old man chuckle.

"Ha ha ha Mathew, I'm so glad for both of you, I am happy Iris is looking after you. I would say Mathew, you are one lucky man. Indeed, you are, Mathew." I knew that I was a very lucky man, that is true, to be loved by Iris, it was like a dream. Even now I wouldn't believe it. Iris, my movie star, loves me Mathew. James and I spoke about the weather and I asked about his health, to which he replied that he was doing well and he added. "We shall talk again Mathew. You take care of yourself and get well soon." James said, very slowly, and politely, "I'm waiting to see you here, Mathew, at my home. You will be my guest, do you understand, son?"

"I do understand James and thanks a million for everything and all your support, I do appreciate and God bless you sir." James chuckled again.

"Clara, my wife, spoke highly of you Mathew." James said. "You are a very polite boy and you do have good manners, Mathew. We are both glad for Iris and you, you are good together and please look after each other well, do you understand Mathew?" James continued and I replied, trying not to push hard, for myself to be in their family.

"Yes sir, I consider myself very lucky to get to know such a good family as yours. And I promise sir, I will love and cherish your daughter all my life. Believe me sir; you'll not be disappointed with me, James." I spoke to re-assure my future father-in-law. I was glad for myself with the language I was using nowadays, I felt and understood that every day I was getting better and better. It was important for me to speak politely and with respect, not only to Iris, or my future in laws, but to everybody, and I felt good.

I was becoming a changed man. I was working hard towards that goal, and Iris was my tutor and teacher and all, Iris deserves the praise. We said our goodbyes on the phone, me and James. It was good talking to James, my future, soon to be father-in-law. I felt thrilled and happy. I thought it showed in my face because all the time Iris was looking at me and smiling.

"I am so happy Mathew, my love," Iris said. "My father seems to love you as a son. Did you know that, my love?" I nodded, because yeah, I knew that. "Your father is a great man," I replied and added, "he speaks well and he respected me even before I knew you Iris. Your father has manners. He didn't treat me like the low life I was, but he spoke nicely to everyone and that made me like him from the beginning when I met him as a fellow patient." That was the truth, but I thought there were lies as well. I remember in the beginning I had seen him as a disturbance to me and he was annoying me.

But with time and once Iris entered the picture, then I started liking him or at first I was using him to get to my movie star, so there was a bit of a lie but it won't hurt anybody, and Iris doesn't have to know. Let her believe my version of the story and yes her father was a good man and he seemed and it was obvious, that he liked and respected me and also he was ready to accept me as his son-in-law. I also knew that James and Clara loved their daughter a lot. Iris was not interested in men and relationships but now surprisingly she fell in love with a person like me, a self confessed 'low life', so the parents had a case in their hands of 'Better the Devil you know', and so they took a decision to accept me.

That's the reason of why James was pushing and supporting me to be their future son-in-law. Wow, I thought, I'm so good at reasoning and solving the unknown hard cases. Ha ha! I smiled and chuckled at my intelligent and brilliant mind.

Chapter Thirty-Two

NOTHING MUCH HAPPENED THAT AFTERNOON and evening and when Elvis brought me the afternoon tea. I took it even though my stomach was still full from the heavy lunch I had taken. Later when Elvis again brought dinner, I politely refused.

"Elvis my friend," I told him, "I'm really full. I cannot have anything else right now. Maybe later I can have a glass of milk or a cup of tea, you don't mind now. Do you my friend?" Elvis, the gentleman he was, smiled.

"You're not trying to refuse my meals now, Mathew," he said, "now that your beautiful lady is cooking and bringing nice meals for you. But you'll still need my meals, Mathew." Elvis laughed, I knew he was just messing with me and it was a good banter between friends. "Elvis my friend, you're not jealous of my Iris, eh?" I asked him with a smile. "She's a black belt in Tae Kwan Do, you know what I mean? She can chop you up like salami." I did with my hand the 'chop chop' action. Iris decided to interrupt.

"Oh stop it now the two of you, I am here myself in front of you and you're talking about me." Iris said with a giggle.

"I am only messing." Elvis worriedly defended himself, and I winked at Iris.

"Don't worry Elvis no bother, you're alright, see you later." Elvis smiled and we all laughed and he went on his way. I knew Elvis cared about my well being and he'll miss me when I'm gone, of that I was sure. He was a good guy.

Later on, Dr. Browne passed by and came to see me but didn't sit down, he asked about the dressing change which was done earlier in the day.

"How was it Mathew, was it painful for you? We do use local anaesthetic for dress change like yours. But how do you feel now?" Dr. Browne asked me. I answered him.

"It wasn't as painful as I thought it would be. The guy was a professional; he did the dressing with care. But now there is more pain so I'm getting the paracetomol and when the pain is too much; the nurses give me morphine tablets and so I'm doing well." I explained and Dr. Browne was happy to hear that.

"The plastic surgeons will take you for the surgery the day after tomorrow, that's when they have scheduled you for your skin graft surgery. So tomorrow you can have a day of rest. Is that fine with you Mathew?" Dr. Browne asked as he put his hand on my shoulder. This time Iris didn't utter a word, she seemed satisfied with the schedule. Then Dr. Browne went and I heard him talking to the nurses, maybe explaining to them about my schedule and all.

The nurses changed shifts and at about nine at night, Iris asked if she could now go home to rest and that she would come again tomorrow. I asked her, because tomorrow there is no plan of me having any type of surgery, why then she doesn't go to work and she can come in the evening instead of having to come for the whole day and do nothing? She thought about it for a while.

"That is fine if you don't mind being on your own my darling." Iris then asked me and I replied that it was okay with me, and in fact she can save her days of leave and use them later, and so we agreed. But she put down her conditions.

"If only you promise, that at any time if and when you need me, just give me a call and I shall come quickly." Iris said with a plea.

"That's okay with me." I responded with a grin on my face. We then kissed goodnight and she went home. The night nurse came to ask me, if I wanted anything to eat, because Elvis had left instructions about me and that I didn't have my dinner but that I might have it if and when I'm hungry. It was very thoughtful of Elvis.

"Can I have a glass of milk if it's not a bother?" The nurse smiled and she then brought me a glass of cold milk and a few biscuits and she asked if I wanted toast or anything. I replied, "Thanks a million nurse, you're so kind. God Bless you." She smiled. I thought these people are so nice and kind, they have hard work, they deal with all kinds of patients, some of us are so demanding and some patients might be abusive. But these hospital staff, they just smile as much as they can and they go on doing their jobs and most of the time they go and perform beyond their duty.

They were amazing people; they were kind and caring people. I wasn't sure if it's like this in all the wards, all the hospitals or if it was only in my ward. No it cannot be so, I thought, it has to be in all the hospitals, they have to be the same standard, maybe it was according to their training. Time passed and I tried to sleep but the pain started to increase. Then I was struggling to get to sleep and struggling on my bed, trying to sleep this way and turning the other way but whatever position I took, the pain was just unbearable.

The nurse came in and she saw me and went to get a morphine tablet. It was nearly two am and then I fell asleep. I think I had nice dreams. I dreamt I was in the clouds with my happiness and contentment.

"Mathew, hello Mathew....can you hear me........wake up now Mathew." I could hear the voice of someone and it was a female voice. But I couldn't open my eyes and then someone was shaking me lightly. "Mathew.......the Doctors will be here soon....can you please wake up?" I managed to open my eyes and the night nurse was smiling at me. I pulled myself together and sat up when I realised it was already morning. How the morning came quickly, I never knew. The nurse put the pillows nicely against my back.

Then the doctors came in the room and they were talking amongst themselves and then they went on their way with none of them speaking to me. I wondered why the nurse would wake me up from my beautiful dreams just so the doctors can pass with a glance of me only. Then the attendant came with a basin of warm water. I washed myself and brushed my teeth there on the bed. The nurse then brought me my two gowns now, ever since Caroline had saved my modesty and she helped me change into the clean ones. The attendants changed the bed sheets. I was now clean and fresh and I felt good.

I thought the attendants seemed to have cleaned and changed the bed sheets early today so maybe they wanted to avoid Iris's wrath before she arrives. They've done their jobs and I'm good for Iris's approval or maybe it was just that they were free and they started with me and my bed, that's all. Elvis brought me breakfast and I enjoyed it and we spoke.

About nine in the morning Iris came but she was dressed for the office and she didn't sit. She just kissed me good morning, inspected the bed sheets and my gown, she checked the dressing of my wound and she asked me if I had breakfast, how did I sleep, did I miss her. I replied with all the right answers, and she was satisfied all around. She seemed businesslike.

"I am off to the office now but please call me if there's anything at all," Iris told me and added, "I will see you in the evening. Is that okay, my darling? Do you need anything else?" I admired her business-look.

"No darling, everything is fine with me and today there's no plan for anything to be done for me. So I'll see you in the evening." We kissed and she rushed off.

Chapter Thirty-Three

*A*T ABOUT ELEVEN IN THE morning, two men walked in behind the day nurse, who, for today, was Janet.

"Mathew, you've got visitors. These two gentlemen were looking for you." Janet said and turned to the two men. "Is he the right patient you're looking for?" Janet spoke to the two guys and then she turned to me. "Mathew your friends are here to see you," Janet turned and went on her way. I was dumbfounded, I didn't know these two and they were complete strangers to me. I didn't recognise either of them and they looked mean.

They looked like people from my recent past-life that much I could tell. They came inside the room and came near the bed, when one of them closed the curtains and then each one came on each side of the bed. I had a bad feeling about these two and I felt sourness on my tongue. Both were dressed in hoodies, joggers, and trainers and they had peak caps down to their eyes as if to hide their faces, which wasn't a good sign. One had blond hair protruding behind his ears; he had earrings and a lot of tattoos around his neck and arms. He was a tough looking fellow, maybe six feet two with bluish eyes. The other one was shorter; maybe about five feet ten, he was heftier with dark hair and dark eyes. He had lot of tattoos as well, a cap on his head and earrings.

They were both tough and mean looking and they were not smiling. I thought that I wasn't comfortable being around these two fellas right now but this was exactly what I looked like previously to other people. I was comfortable being that way and being around the lads at that time but now, things have changed. See how time and circumstances change? I'm sure when I used to be dressed up like these two, other people were not comfortable with me either but it was only now that I realised it.

I wasn't sure these two scumbags were actually looking for me or they were looking for someone else. Maybe it was just a case of mistaken identity. Anyway, I'll see how it goes.

"Hey lads, do I know you?" I asked them in a way of getting introductions. Both of them sniggered at me.

"You're Mathew, right?" the tall one asked me.

"You know Kevin?" the shorter one now. I thought, okay. These two are good people and if they know Kevin then definitely they were 'friends', and as the saying goes 'a friend of a friend is my friend'. Maybe they brought me a message from 'bro' Kevin, so it was alright. I relaxed.

"Yeah, I'm Mathew, and yeah I know Kevin, he's my cousin, you know," I said with a bit of excitement. "How's Kevin doing, is he okay, is he out now?" They both looked at each other and their eyes turned red and they became mean.

"Kevin's still remanded in prison. I was with him and I was released two days ago." The taller one said in an angry tone. I wasn't sure now, where was this going.

"How's Kevin doing? I can't visit him you know, but when I come out of the hospital I'll go see him, you know what I mean?" I said this while smiling to try to show them my friendliness and how close I was with Kevin. "You can pull up some chairs and sit down lads." But they didn't budge. "Lads, can you tell me if Kevin's alright, you're making me worried now, you know what I mean?" I spoke again. "And what about the other lads, are they okay also?" I continued while trying to find the connection with them, but it seemed in vain, I was just blubbering.

Then, without a warning, the shorter one punched me hard on the shoulder and then both of them held me down by my shoulders with my hospital gown tightening and pulling me upwards and towards them, each on the side. I was thinking should I shout for help or should I try to reach for the switch to ring and call the nurse. While I was in these thoughts, the taller one removed a pistol from his waist and shoved it at my head, while the shorter one gave me a punch in the face.

I smelled and tasted blood in my mouth but I used my tongue to check on my teeth and they all seemed fine and not broken. I realised now that these two weren't friends at all, so what can they be then and what do they want? Okay, maybe they're enemies, and so 'an enemy of my friend is my enemy'. Now I was their prisoner and hostage. I wasn't sure what they wanted, but now I already knew they weren't friends, and they weren't here for fun or family reunion.

They were two evil men, and they came here to look for me with bad intentions. I knew they could easily shoot me dead without it being a bother to them, so I had to play along with them for my own safety as well as for the safety of the other patients and the staff. These people usually don't think first and they might regret things later when it was already too late.

"Hold on now, lads," I tried to plead with them. "What's going on?" The shorter one brought his face to mine.

"You're the fucking one who ratted on Kevin and the lads and now they're all in the joint because of you, bastard." He punched me again in the face. I felt the punch, hit directly on my eye and I thought, here goes my handsome face and now a black eye but I also thought, what did he mention about Kevin and the lads?

"You're fucking dead Mathew," the taller one said. "Kevin wants you dead." No, I couldn't believe what he said, it's not possible. Kevin wants me dead? And he thinks I'm the one who ratted on them? I didn't even know about the exact date and time of the 'gig' they were going to do, I was shut out from much information as it were. I later thought maybe Kevin was trying to protect me because I wasn't well. But now he's given a contract for my head? My own cousin and friend, who was like my own big brother, no, it couldn't possibly be so. I had to think fast for my own life so I thought I had to play for time with these goons.

"Look, you guys are mistaken. Kevin's' my cousin and I don't know anything about that gig which Kevin and the lads were caught for by the Gardai. Believe me; I was here on this very bed." I pleaded with them. "I promise I wasn't the one who ratted on Kevin and the lads, I only came to know about this whole thing later, much later, believe me lads." But it was in vain.

These people had a contract and they had to do it, time was running out for them, anybody could walk in now and raise the alarm. The shorter one took a pillow and covered my face, while the taller one took another pillow and put it on my head and then he pointed the gun tightly with the pillow on my head. And then he pulled the trigger...'click'.

I closed my eyes, I was gone and now I was dead. I could see the clouds, I was in the clouds. I was walking towards my mother but she was signalling me to go back and then I opened my eyes. I'm still alive and there was no sign of blood or brain matter from my head. I didn't feel a thing, just only the pressure of the gun and the hand holding the pillow on my face. I then realised that the gun had jammed and I was still alive at least for a few more seconds before he fired again.

With both my hands, I pulled the hand holding the pillow on my face and it caught him by surprise. I looked at the shorter one with anger showing in my face but I was actually in fear, in my heart. I prayed that Iris or any nurse or anyone shouldn't appear now. These scumbags are crazy and they won't hesitate to shoot anyone.

"Please lads, understand me and let me talk to Kevin, he'll understand." I pleaded with both of them. "I'm not the one who ratted on Kevin and the lads. Kevin is my bro, you guys are wrong." My voice was high pitched and then I heard footsteps. Quickly, the tall one hid the gun and the shorter one was still confused. Janet the nurse appeared and opened the curtains a bit, she took a peek inside to see if I was okay and she saw these two 'friends' of mine were putting the pillows nicely behind my back. Janet smiled.

"Mathew, your two friends care about you," she said innocently, "I can see they're taking care of you." The two scumbags smiled and pretended they really liked me and were acting nice and friendly. They were grunting and then they smiled at Janet. Janet being satisfied she closed the curtains and left. I heaved a sigh of relief for Janet's safety.

"Okay lads, look," I said quickly trying to sound serious, "let me talk to Kevin, you don't understand, I promise you, I'm cool." The taller one looked at me, his face very close to mine.

"Kevin knows the Gardai visited you here in the hospital and you ratted on Kevin and the lads." The taller one said. "What did you tell the Gardai?" and then the shorter one brought his fist to my face and pushed my face without actually hitting me but it hurt anyway. "Why should the Gardai visit you in the hospital, what business did you have with the Gardai?" I thought, okay, now I understand.

Kevin somehow got the information that the Gardai visited me in the hospital, and this is what rattled him and him in his anger thought it might be me who ratted on him and the lads. How can I convince these two scumbags that I need to speak to and convince Kevin that it wasn't me who ratted on them?

"Lads, the Gardai visited me to tell me that me Ma died, you know what I mean?" I said again pleading for my life because the taller one had removed his gun again and both of them were getting agitated and wanted to complete the contract as quickly as possible and get away. "Me Ma had died and nobody told me. Kevin was supposed to take care of me Ma, you know what I mean? And the Gardai just came to see me and brought me the news that me Ma died. And later they came to inform me that she already got buried and had Mass and all while I'm still in hospital. I never been out, you understand? But nobody was after telling me, lads, I tell you this is the truth, I promise you. You can check after the Gardai, if you don't believe me, know what I mean?" I continued to plead.

I knew my life was at stake here. If these scumbags fire again, I'm gone, dead. It will be the end of Mathew and his beautiful dreams and the bright future with his beautiful wife Iris and the good in-laws and everything else. Oh God, I think I need you at all times of my life because I get into a lot of complications and difficulties in my life. My life is full of adventures and mishaps. Then I noticed that these two scumbags seemed to hesitate for a while. I thought this might be my chance, and maybe I'm getting inside their small brains, so I tried again.

"Believe me lads," I said in a low pleading voice, "you can check with Kevin himself, you can also check with the Gardai. If I'm after lying to you, lads, you can come back to finish me." I thought, and I'll be waiting for you to come to kill me, ha ha, but they had to go to verify my case with Kevin. These two scumbags must believe me, because otherwise I'm dead meat. They looked at each other and the shorter one slapped me hard on the face.

"Wait, we need to talk. Don't you try anything funny, do you hear me?" The shorter one ordered me. I nodded, and they went near the window. They discussed between themselves, they argued a bit, shaking their heads and nodding at each other. Then the taller one removed his mobile, called someone and spoke for a few seconds, and nodded and he smiled. I wasn't sure if this meant it was in my favour or not, because the shorter one frowned after the phone call.

They talked between themselves some more. Then they came back to me each one took his previous position and they looked serious. I thought, okay God, whatever my fate is, let it be, I cannot change my destiny, but you, God, can, so I trust you and whatever you have written for me. The shorter one punched me again hard on my mouth. I again tasted and smelled blood and the blood trickled from my lips and mouth, down my chin.

I just managed, "Uhh." I didn't want to raise my voice but not for my sake. Me, I thought, I'm gone now but I was worried for the others, and especially Iris. Iris shouldn't appear now, please God, and I thanked God that Caroline was not on duty today. I then felt the cold metal of the gun on my temple.

"Mathew, you shit, you'd better say your prayers now, because you're a dead man." The taller one said with a threatening voice and the shorter one added for a better effect.

"Yeah, man, tell us the truth or you're dead." I had to plead all over again.

"Lads, I beg you, please let me talk to Kevin, he'll understand," I said. "Me Ma, is his aunt you know, and she's after dying, man, I tell you the truth. You can check my story with Kevin. The Gardai came because of me Ma and not because of Kevin or the lads, I tell you this is the truth, you can believe me lads, I promise you on me Ma's grave. I tell you the truth; you know what I mean, lads, right?"

I turned to look at each of their faces, I got the feeling they believed me or they were just confused and they didn't know what to do, either to complete the contract or to call it off. Maybe they were afraid of Kevin's rage if they aborted the contract. But then it seemed I got to them both. They each loosened their grip on the way they were holding me and the taller one looked at my face again. I was thinking how bad it had become, and swollen.

"What's wrong with you, why are you in hospital?" The taller one asked me in a threatening manner. I thought this sounds good to me. So before the shorter one spoke or this taller one changed his mind, I had to think fast.

"Ah, just cancer, you know, they want to cut off my leg. You know what I mean?" I looked at the taller one who had asked me the question, and he seemed shocked.

"Jaysus," the shorter one said, "oh shit." He turned around and held his head with one hand.

"Are you serious? Are you fucking saying the truth or you're just messing our brain." The taller one asked and the shorter turned to hear the answer.

"I mean it lads, no one is messing about these things, you've got to believe me," I continued to plead and went on, "I got this terrible disease in my leg, on the thigh and they might chop my leg off, you know what I mean, lads?" I then opened my duvet cover and showed them my leg which was bandaged, bloodied and had the pump going 'brrrrrrrrrr'. I thought what if they take their gun and hit me with it on the wound? It would be like I invited them to do just that. "See lads, what I mean? Also you see this pump, it is removing the excess fluid from the wound; see I'm not lying to you lads." I continued to plead with them in a soft voice. They nodded in unison, the taller one took his gun and put inside his hoodie pocket and he said to me with a smirk on his face.

"Sorry man, it's just business, nothing personal, you know what I mean?" I nodded my 'thanks' and 'understanding' and the shorter one looked at me.

"Sorry about your leg……and your face…..got it?" The shorter one said with a nod. I nodded my head again.

"No bother." I said. And they turned and slowly walked out through the curtains and walked away silently as they had come. I breathed hard with a sigh of relief and tears started to flow down my cheeks. I Thanked God Almighty, the one who was high above, for saving me once again, and I thought I wasn't one who appreciated God.

About my face, I can deal with. I couldn't see how much I was hurt or how my face looked but I felt around my head and felt a few lumps. I had a feeling I had one or two black eyes. I checked myself for broken teeth, didn't feel any but the lips were swollen.

Chapter Thirty-Four

I TOOK MY TIME AND SOBBED, and said thanks to God that Iris was not here today and now. Otherwise, as I knew her, she wouldn't take it with these scumbags, and there might have been fatalities and death in the ward. I had kept my cool and I played it safe, I thought I was brave today. Maybe, I wasn't sure now. Maybe I was just a coward to let those two scumbags beat me around and threaten me.

I thought of calling Iris, as she said if there's 'anything' I should call her but then if I call her she might panic and drive fast and something might happen to her while on the road. I didn't want to scare her, so I decided not to call her first. I then pulled the string for the ringer to call the nurse, I rang 'ringgggggg' two times and I lay myself down, half sitting, half lying. I heard footsteps coming my way and then Janet peeked through the room.

"Someone called the nurse?" The other two patients were fast asleep not knowing what was happening in the 'World of Mathew'. I thanked God also that Tom was gone or he wouldn't have let this happen. Janet opened my curtains to peek inside and she seemed like she wasn't sure. "Mathew, did you press the ringer? Your two friends are gone?" I nodded but I couldn't talk.

There was a lot of emotion in my chest and then she noticed something was not right so she pulled the curtains apart and opened it fully, then she saw my bloodied face and the duvet had blood and my face was swollen. She then shouted in a shrill voice to call her supervisor but at the same time, not loud enough to cause panic to other patients. I think her training took over. The supervisor came quickly, and they both looked at me while covering their mouths with their hands in shock.

"What happened here? Who did….who did this…...to you Mathew?" The supervisor was asking me in a panic. I couldn't answer. Tears were flowing down my cheeks. Janet continued to cover her mouth while the reality struck her.

"Those two people who came to visit Mathew must be the ones. Oh my God. It must be them." Janet said with shock in her voice. The nurses' Supervisor looked at Janet.

"What two people, when, Janet, tell me, quickly" The supervisor asked and then told Janet to look after me but not to touch anything. She closed the curtains and she went in the corridor where they had their reception and offices and I could hear her talking in quick succession. I later came to understand she called Iris, and she called the doctor on duty and Dr. Browne and the hospital security who in turn contacted the Gardai. In no time the room was full the attendants were called to remove the other two patients to another room for a while and my room was closed and out of bound for other staff.

When the Gardai came they started to take photographs of my face from different angles, and my bed and the room and the blood stained duvet cover, also my hospital gown. They drew the room plan and started questioning Janet. Iris came and was shaking and she came straight to me. The Gardai tried to stop her but they couldn't hold her. She hugged me tightly and started to cry.

"Oh my Mathew, oh my Mathew, what happened to you, my darling." A female Garda took her aside and spoke with her and she calmed down but remained in the room. My eyes were both swollen and I couldn't see clearly. I had two lovely black eyes. Dr. Browne and a few other doctors came to see me and each one checked me and gave instructions to another nurse who came to be on behalf of Janet who was now shaking and in shock. She felt responsible and knew that I might have lost my life while in her care. She was sobbing and was comforted by her supervisor and another female Garda.

I was checked for my 'new' wounds, and received a few stitches right there on the bed. A doctor and nurse were called from the A&E and they wanted to take me for a head X-ray, but I said no, I think there's no need. They stitched my lips from outside, my left eyebrow, my chin, the right side of my temple where I was cut. On my other injuries they applied some cream, like around the eyes and inside the mouth and other places. Then the nurses and Iris helped me change the hospital gowns and bed sheets and duvet cover. All these were taken by the Gardai as evidence.

The Gardai questioned me and I had to describe as much as I could about the two scumbags. I managed to give the Gardai a good description and the type of gun, and the talk, how it went and so on. I told the Gardai Inspector who came later that he should talk to the two Gardai who had come a few weeks back to tell me about my Ma, and also they had the case about Kevin and the lads. The Gardai Inspector said he would follow that up, that he thought he remembered the case and he knew the Gardai I spoke to earlier, no bother. The Gardai Inspector then spoke to me.

"Mathew, you're a very brave young man," He said. "In such situations, people tend to shout for help but you, Mathew, kept quite while you were being terrorised and taking a beating. Why? Because, you did not want to endanger others, now that's bravery in my book, what do you guys think?" he asked the other Gardai, and they all nodded and gave their approval.

"Mathew, consider yourself very lucky, the gun got jammed and you managed to keep calm and you negotiated yourself out of your situation. Mathew, you're the man." The Gardai Sergeant said with a smile and got nods from his colleagues and the Inspector.

"Would you like to be moved to another ward or maybe another hospital, Mathew?" Dr. Browne asked me, feeling sorry for me. "Maybe you will feel safer that way?" Iris was now near me and was holding my hand and stroking my head slowly, careful not to hurt me.

"Doctor, I think I'll stay here in the same hospital, same ward, same room, and same bed, if it's alright with you." I replied with confidence, the fear being gone now. The Gardai Inspector nodded his approval as well. "I shall post one Gardai on twenty four hour watch here for a while, if you allow me Mathew and Dr. Browne." The Gardai Inspector whose name I didn't catch spoke to both me and Dr. Browne. I shrugged. For me it was okay, and I'll feel safer anyway.

"I wouldn't mind myself." I said and looked at Dr. Browne.

"That is fine with me, and the hospital has no problem with that and Mathew will definitely feel safer." Dr. Browne responded and turned to look at the security people of the hospital, who also nodded their approval.

"No objection on our part," one person from the security service said. "After what happened today, we'll all feel safer if we can get a Gardai round the clock. It will feel safe for our patients and our staff and especially to Mathew." The nurses' supervisor said she was in full agreement. Iris, who was very concerned about me and she nodded her agreement and then looked at me with her soft eyes.

"Oh my poor Mathew, I am so sorry my darling," Iris said. "What could I have done without you, my darling Mathew? This is very bad. How can two criminals just enter a hospital ward and threaten or rather attempt to kill a patient? This is so wrong. It is unbelievable." Then Iris regained her nerve and addressed the Gardai Inspector. "Inspector, why would these people target Mathew," Iris asked in an authoritative voice, "and if it is what you think, is there any way you guys from the Gardai, I mean, can send a message to Kevin that Mathew has nothing to do with this……this…….. whatever it is they are worried about?" she concluded.

There was silence in the room. Iris decided to continue her queries.

"Now, how can Mathew and me included, together, live a normal life without fear that someone somewhere is after Mathew, and will kill him and maybe kill his family as well?" and Iris looked straight at the Gardai Inspector for an answer.

"We in the Gardai have our ways and I assure you Miss.....I didn't get your name....and how you fit into this....." The Gardai Inspector started to explain and then abruptly asked Iris. She changed colour but I managed to squeeze her hand to calm her down.

"My name is Iris and I am Mathew's fiancée, we are planning to get married as soon as possible if he comes out from here alive… and…….." Poor Iris, she burst out crying, her emotions got the best of her and she couldn't control herself. "I am sorry," she was crying, "I am so sorry." The Inspector signalled to one of the female Garda, who then went to comfort Iris and softly talked to her. There was a long silence while everybody was gathering their thoughts.

"I am really sorry, Miss," the Gardai Inspector said politely, "It's my mistake and please accept my apology." Iris looked at him and nodded and she nodded at the female Garda as well and she then turned back to me and held my head to her chest. Then one of the Gardai plainclothes moved closer and introduced himself as Gardai Sergeant 'something'.

"Mathew, and Iris, as the Inspector was saying, we in the Gardai have our ways of doing things. Therefore we assure you, we shall do everything in our power, to stop these people and this Kevin from ever threatening you again. Please have faith and trust in us and we promise you these people will not bother you again." I decided to ask the one question which was bothering me.

"Inspector …Sergeant…Kevin …was…..is……my cousin…... he was my brothers' best friend………..we grew up together ………..in the same housing estate." I paused a while and then continued, "Kevin was like an elder brother to me, he was close to me, he was my friend and also he was what you might call…. confidante….so why would he give out a contract, for my death? Why did he want me dead? I'd like to know this…please." They couldn't give me an answer, they all seemed quiet for some time and then the Inspector volunteered to try to give me a satisfactory reply.

"Mathew, as you well might know yourself," the Gardai Inspector started and went on, "these people are ruthless, and they deal in drugs, weapons, robberies, burglaries, you name it, they do it. Therefore, they will not hesitate, even for a second, to kill. They'll kill anyone who they feel is a threat to their illegal activities. Be it their friend, cousin, brother, or their own father."

He then stopped, took a deep breath, and continued.

"Mathew, son, you are lucky in two ways. First you were lucky today, very lucky indeed, it might be someone up there who loves you so much and is looking out for you, believe me young man. And the second point is that you might consider yourself lucky because you came out of this game of gangs and illegal activities before it was too late."

That speech got the approval of everyone in the room. Everyone was nodding their heads. It was like a 'well done' or like applause. I also knew the Inspector had said it well, but now everyone in the room would know about my past. Luckily I had already confessed it to Iris or otherwise it would have been 'Goodbye Gangster Mathew'. So we all agreed that the Gardai will keep one Garda on duty till further notice and also, they'll come again to interview me whenever they needed. And they promised to keep me and Iris informed and updated on the proceedings of solving the issue with Kevin, because after all, it was my life that was at stake.

The Gardai thanked us all and then they went out followed by the hospital security people. The doctors stayed a while and then they went as well, promising to come later to check on me. Janet was asked if she wanted to go home and get some rest but she refused. She was in shock but she said she would complete her shift. The nurses' supervisor remained on duty as well and the other patients were kept in another room. For me, it was to become my room alone till the day I was discharged.

For those involved with today's events, they were all affected somehow and they'll all get counselling in due time. Iris stayed with me and hugged me and I had to repeat to her the whole story once again but this time it was for her ears only. Every now and then a nurse would come and say sorry about the events and went their way. The news started to flow and spread through the hospital grapevine. I couldn't speak properly but I managed somehow, and Elvis was to be instructed to change my menu to liquid only for a while, and with a straw, that is.

Chapter Thirty-Five

 $\mathcal{A}$ ND AS SOON AS HE got the news, Elvis came and stood by me for a while and spoke softly and expressed his sadness at my 'continuous misfortunes' as he put it but he said he'll pray for me.

"Pray for both of us, Elvis, not Mathew alone." Iris joked with him. Elvis got the joke and he replied.

"Yeah, I'll pray for both of you and for your happiness and future lives but now you're with Mathew, you'll need a bodyguard. So whenever you need me I'm available for hire." With that we all laughed, but it hurt when I laughed, so I just smiled. Iris then called her parents and told them what happened to me and they got hysterical and scared for me, especially her mom, Clara. She wanted to drive over immediately. She became worried about me but Iris spoke to her mom and calmed her down, and then Iris gave me the phone.

"Hello.....is that Mathew...dear?" I heard Clara on the phone.

"Hi Clara, this is Mathew. How's it going?" I replied and asked her. Then I realised that because of those two scumbags I had forgotten some basic manners of talking, so I said again. "How are you Clara, and how's James?" It wasn't easy but I had to talk with my concerned parents-in-laws. I heard James' voice from afar, but then Clara spoke again.

"Oh Mathew dear, I am sooo sorry... for whatever happened to you today," Clara said and she went on, pleading, "can I please drive over to see you dear.....I am so worried about you but my daughter is telling me not to come over...please Mathew talk to her." Iris signalled to me and wasn't sure what to say.

"Okay Clara, I'll talk to Iris, but there's no need for you to come now. It's already getting late and the traffic is heavy now anyway." While I was talking to Clara, Iris was telling me what to say to her mother. "Iris will bring you over tomorrow. Yeah, no problem I'll talk to Iris, no bother." I replied and tried to reason with her, while at the same time Iris was giving and showing me in signs on what to say. I was getting confused, it was like to talking to several people at the same time but eventually I gave the phone back to Iris, after I had spoken with James.

Iris took the phone, she spoke some more with her parents and they calmed down. Iris came back to sit with me.

"Ooooh." She sighed. I looked at her.

"Iris my love, don't be angry with your parents," I said, "they're just worried after you told them about me. Also Clara, being a mother, it was only natural for her to be worried for me, Iris my love." I looked at her, we held hands and I went on. "She likes me now, so she's just worried and she'll keep worrying until she sees me. Then her heart will accept that I'm alright and not harmed, you know what I mean, Iris, my sweetheart." Iris was nodding her head and the she took my head on her chest and stroked my hair with love and affection.

I felt so good, on one side I had my Iris full of love and affection and on the other side was her mother, who was more worried about me. It felt like she was my own mother. What a wonderful feeling I had right now and it seemed like I was on cloud nine. Later on, three men in suits came into the room after being allowed by the uniformed Garda who sat just outside the door of my room. They came in and introduced themselves. They were from the Dublin University Hospital's top management and they spoke politely and expressed their apologies.

The one, who looked like he was more senior than the other two, spoke first.

"The hospital is sending our deepest apologies for what happened today, Mathew," he paused and looked at his two colleagues. They nodded their approval and he went on, "And we assure you, we have already formed a team to investigate this matter internally and also the Department of Health together with the Health Service Executive, the 'HSE' will form a joint team to make an external investigation." He paused again and waited.

Once he got the nods from junior colleagues, he then continued.

"The Hospital together with the Gardai cooperation, once we pinpoint the main loopholes we shall try to close them. I know it's going to be a difficult task, taking into consideration that hundreds of people visit the hospitals every day, but we shall see the outcome of the inquiries and investigations and their recommendations." He paused again and because he was big and tall, he seemed out of breath.

Then one of the other two, maybe he was number two in rank out of these three suits, saw his opportunity to speak now.

"The main thing Mathew...is....steps have been taken to protect you. Because you're a patient in our hospital, you're a guest of Dublin University Hospital and therefore, we are deemed to take upon ourselves to take necessary steps in order to protect you." He let it sink and he went on. "Together with the Garda Siochana, we shall try our level best at that." Then he kept quiet and looked at number three, as if to say 'now it's your turn to lecture this boy', so suit number three opened his mouth.

"Mathew, if you need anything and at any time then please let us know, send a message through any staff at the hospital and we will try to be at your service, if and when possible." With that it seemed he had finished and so the senior one took over once again.

"Mathew, we shall leave you now to be with your beautiful friend and once again, we are very sorry." He paused and then added. "Goodnight Mathew." With that, he shook my hand and then Iris and the other two followed their boss to shake our hands and they all went out. I thought, wow, next is the Taoiseach with the full cabinet and then the president of Ireland. It seemed today I've become a very important person, to be visited by all these important people and being guarded 24 hours a day by the Garda Siochana.

I chuckled to myself, when I thought about being guarded and protected by the Garda now at present outside the door. While in my previous life I would be either running away from the Garda, or I would be guarded by the Garda while I'm inside the prison, but today it's quite the opposite. I thought about life and the wonders of life.

A while later Elvis brought me a glass of a strawberry flavoured milk shake with a straw and he told me if I wanted some more or needed anything else just to inform him or the nurses at anytime. It was 'special instructions' from the hospital management.

"Mathew, you're the first patient to be served this way, with special instructions since I started work in this hospital five years ago." Elvis explained with a smile. "You're one special patient, since you were admitted here. Everyday there is an adventure featuring you as a hero Mathew." Elvis then laughed, Iris joined him and I smiled. Then Elvis continued. "Sorry Mathew, I'm not usually like this but I take you as a friend and that's why I mess with you." Elvis became apologetic.

"No bother, Elvis." I nodded as I told Elvis and he chuckled as he went on his rounds. The night duty nurse came and I heard a lot of whispers. I thought she was shocked to see a Garda and learning from her colleagues the events of the day. She had to come to see the 'important person' of the day.

"Hi Mathew," the nurse said as her hands were shaking with either excitement or fear. "I'm so sorry, I heard what happened today. I'm here for night duty and if you need anything please let me know, alright?" I nodded and then she said, "Hi," to Iris, and smiling she went on outside the room. Then two Gardai entered the room, after saying hi to me and Iris, they introduced themselves to me and Iris. They told me that one was leaving now and the other one will be on duty.

"Just outside the door, you just need to cough. I'll hear you and come over." One of them said and then they went out of the room together. After a while Dr. Browne and a plastic surgeon team member, Dr. Keane, came and sat down with me. With them was the night nurse and we talked for a while and then Dr. Keane asked me.

"Mathew, after all of today's events, do you feel you can go ahead with tomorrow's scheduled skin graft surgery or ……..," he paused and added, "Would you like the surgery to be postponed to a later date, or maybe a day or two?" But before I answered, Dr. Browne added.

"How do feel yourself, Mathew, physically and mentally, after a rough and eventful day?" I looked at Iris and smiled at her and then I turned to Dr. Keane.

"I would like the surgery to be done as quickly as possible. Also I'm already exhausted being in the hospital for so long," I said and then added, "besides, the longer I stay the more adventures you guys are gonna face. I think I've done enough damage for now, you know what I mean?" I laughed at my own joke and Iris joined me but the others seemed not sure how to take it.

"Oh yeah, what adventures and misadventures, oh my God," Iris added while laughing. Then Dr. Browne joined and laughed as well.

"What a day!" Dr. Browne said with a bit of a laugh.

"I know what you mean Mathew, so tomorrow it is then," Dr. Keane replied in understanding and he continued. "Now we have to go through a series of questions which I am sure you're familiar with by now. But it is normal procedure as you already know, Mathew. So don't mind please." Dr. Keane explained. I nodded my understanding.

"It is okay Doctor, you can go ahead and I'll sign. No bother." I replied. So he started the questions and when he reached 'next of kin' he smiled when I replied. "It's Iris, who's not only my love and heart but also my fiancée." We held hands and Iris with a show of love and deep affection, kissed me on the cheek and we all had a good laugh. Before I signed the papers, I noticed the address that was written was the same one of me Ma, because it used to be my address but since that time, things have changed. I told Dr. Keane to cancel that address.

"So which address shall I put down, now?" He asked me and I told him to put the hospital address but before he said anything else, Iris interrupted.

"Excuse me Doctor; I was not paying attention, what is happening about the address?" Iris asked and Dr. Keane explained to her about the change in address, and with a smile she told the doctor. "Please Doctor; you can put down Mathew's new address as I will give you just now."

And she gave her parent's address and Dr. Keane looked at me in a questioning manner to see if I had any objections. I just shrugged.

"She's the boss! You can put down her address as I shall be moving in with her soon." I explained to Dr. Keane as I laughed aloud and Iris punched me on the shoulder in playing mood with her small fist. I then signed the papers in the green file. Then both the doctors left and the nurse stayed for a while longer wanting to know if I needed anything, and that I should let her know if I'm in pain and that I'm supposed to fast from midnight for my scheduled surgery tomorrow. We both thanked her.

At about eleven at night, Iris had to go as it was already late and her mother had called twice already. I think Clara wanted to hear firsthand from Iris the story about my day. I told Iris to give my love to both her parents but not to bring them early in the morning as I will be taken to the operating theatre in the morning. Therefore it wouldn't be fair for her parents just to come and sit and wait.

But actually I was thinking about myself, having visitors early in the morning and not yet having washed up or changed to clean clothes was not pleasant. Iris kissed me on the lips lightly and the cheeks and then she was gone. I sat on my own and after a while the nurse entered the room.

"Can I have a glass of milk and two tablets of painkillers please?" I asked her.

"Yes. Would you like a milk shake instead of plain milk?" She replied with a smile.

"That'd be great, thanks, you're very kind." I then replied with an even bigger smile. The nurse brought me a tall glass of large milk shake and two tablets with a glass of plain water. Once I finished drinking she came to take the empty glasses and she switched off the light. I stayed awake for a long time as it was now becoming my habit; it was time to reflect on the day's events, the good things that happened and the misfortunes of the day. I thought about the two scumbags and how I got involved in Kevin's devious scheme.

I had trusted him with my life, he was everything to me and I would have given up my life for him, yet he went so far as to order my assassination? Without even getting a clarification from me or proof that it was me who ratted on him and the lads, how can one be like this, so cold and cruel, without feelings and any humanity? But as the Gardai Inspector had said, these people, these criminals, have no humanity in them, it was so correct. How did I let myself get involved in criminality all my life? The answer to that, I didn't know but still, I considered myself as I was one of the lucky ones, and at just twenty six to realise and come out of that life.

I happened to come out of it and ended up on the other side of the wall. How many of both young and old people are out there who don't have the opportunity to leave a life of criminal activities, and they end up on drugs, they live rough, unhappy, and die young. Even if they don't die young, they end up in jails or on the run, and they have no happiness or contentment in life whatsoever. I then remembered my beloved mom, and I cried for her.

What a day like this would have done to her, I couldn't imagine. I dreamt of my Da, the good, proud and gentle man he was, ever against the criminals and their activities, he had a natural dislike of them. He would always sneer when he saw them or passed them on the street or when they attempted to walk through his back garden. I gave myself a promise to me Da & Ma. 'I promise you I shall achieve your dreams, I shall get a good education, I shall work in an honest and legal job, I shall live honestly, I shall always tell the truth, I shall be a good and model citizen, I shall help others who are less fortunate. Da and Ma just give me your blessings and talk to God on my behalf, and I promise you, I'll fulfil your and my dreams. I'll make you proud of me, your son, Mathew'. And as the Americans would say, 'So help me God'. And with that I fell asleep, but it was only after I got my morphine tablet and a sip of water.

Chapter Thirty-Six

I WOKE UP FILLED WITH ANXIETY about what lay ahead of me for the day. It seemed everyday something new would happen to me and contribute to some major change in my life and future. I managed to get down from the bed and slowly use the walker, I walked outside the room, saw the Garda walking about the corridor and I said hi to him and he nodded back. I continued and walked slowly to the washroom. It was painful but I managed to do my business and brush my teeth and wash up.

I changed the two gowns, put on the fresh ones I had taken from the trolley along the corridor, with clean towels. When I came out of the washroom, I saw the Garda officer, walking about outside the toilets. I think he had followed me but I didn't ask him, and he just went by as if he was just walking. With great pain, I walked back to my room and bed and on the way; I left the used towels and gowns in the laundry basket in the corridor. The nurse was happy, as I had managed to take myself to the washroom and toilet, and well, it was less work for her anyway.

The nurse came and took check-ups for blood pressure and blood glucose, and whatever else and she wrote it all down in the green file. She then gave me my usual prescription tablets.

"Mathew dear, now you are ready to go for your surgery." The nurse said and smiled. "Are you feeling nervous?" I smiled back at her.

"Ah…I think so." I replied. She looked at me and added.

"Don't be, you've gone through a lot already but this is just the finishing touch. So don't worry, you're going to pull through." I smiled and thought okay that helps a lot. As the time passed and with me having nothing to do but wait for the attendants to come to take me, I kept listening out for the footsteps and perfume of my movie star. The time went by….nine….nine thirty……ten…..ten thirty……ten forty-five……..ten fifty-five in the morning and still no sign of my beloved one. Bad thoughts started to come in my head and mind.

Aha, footsteps, okay maybe it's her footsteps finally, but male voices were talking to the Garda outside and then the day nurse and two attendants followed by a new Garda Officer came in. No sign of my Iris. They checked the green file and then the two attendants took me with my trolley, and followed by the nurse holding the file. I didn't notice how we were going but my mind was with Iris. She's abandoned me, maybe yesterday's events got into her, and the fear of criminals hunting me down, even following to her parent's house and therefore endangering herself and her parents.

It's not possible that Iris, my beloved, hasn't come by now. It was already eleven in the morning, and she knows I have an operation today and yet she doesn't come to be with me? That's not possible. It doesn't seem to be her behaviour or attitude, or maybe she wasn't happy for me to tell her not to bring her mom early in the morning. Maybe she was offended by that. I now know she has dumped me. It was too good to last, anyway.

Maybe previously, she had only listened to me about my past, and she either felt sorry for me or she just wanted to please her dad, but now, eventually, reality has become obvious and she has finally realised that it was all a mistake, it was all a fantasy. Maybe she has now realised she was in la la land, but what really was a certainty for her? It is that 'Mathew is a criminal and has criminal friends, and therefore is not only a danger to him, but to me and my parents as well'. And that realisation made her decision easier and with all these facts now she might have decided, 'I don't need this criminal in my life'.

I had a fear about having Iris loving me, and especially as she didn't even know me properly. She didn't know my past or even my present besides seeing my butt the other day, it was just too good to continue and it was too good to be true. I had nothing to offer to the woman, while she had everything and yet she fell for me? It didn't make sense. I was deep in my thoughts of insecurity that I didn't notice at all how I had already been taken through various pre-surgery preparation stages, and now I was already in the operating theatre, having been given the general anaesthetic, and was on my way to reaching full unconsciousness.

I came back slowly, first in the recovery room and then was off again, and then I was in the ward. I could hear voices but I couldn't match the voices. I was in and out of consciousness. Then I remembered what my thoughts had been before I lost consciousness, it was about Iris dumping me, so my brain refused to come to full awareness. I had no reason to become aware that there would be no Iris, and it will only hurt me more so I blocked my mind. I couldn't hear voices anymore. I just lost it and stayed in my deep sleep.

Later, much later I finally opened my eyes, I think it was the feeling of hunger that made me open my eyes and I became aware, I looked at the time it was one in the morning. I thought what I should do now. I rang the ringer 'rrrrrrr' and the nurse appeared with the Garda officer who was on duty. The officer looked at me with worry in his eyes but the nurse assured him.

"It's alright, nothing is wrong; he just needs some assistance, Officer." She explained. Then the nurse turned to me. "Hi Mathew, welcome back," she said with a smile, "everybody was worried about you, Mathew, are you feeling better now?" I nodded and smiled.

"Sorry Nurse but I'm just a bit hungry," I said, pleading. "Can you manage anything even a glass of milk please?" She smiled, and went away and after a while she came back with a tray. There was a cup of tea, a glass of milk shake and two slices of bread.

"This was kept for you. Try to eat and be strong Mathew." I thought, to eat, I shall eat just so I can live but not to be strong, to be strong for whom? My movie star has dumped me so I have nobody now, Caroline has also disappeared for many days now and also if she hears about the events, she will also dump me and run as far away as possible. No woman will ever come near me again, which decent woman will want a criminal as a husband? Oh, my life is over. I had given myself false high hopes and dreams, but now it was all over and 'kaput', 'finito', the end.

When I finished having the late meal, the nurse brought for me my prescribed tablets, including a tablet of morphine; I took these with a glass of water. She then asked if I needed anything else.

"Thanks nurse. You're so good and thanks a million nurse, you're an angel." She smiled and then told me, if I require anything just to call her. I continued to make myself suffer with my thoughts and my disappointment in life. How much of a loser I was and how useless I am, how my past life will always haunt me. And how we define 'decency' in someone, everybody is decent in their own way, it's just us who expect too much from other people, and we categorise who are decent people and who are not decent people. What gives us the right to look down on others?

Is it the upbringing, is it the area you live in, is it the surname or family name you carry, is it the colour of your skin, is it the language one speaks, is it the accent one has, is it the education one has, is it the country one comes from? What exactly defines and put humans into groups and classes and the like? I think with time, all of us humans; we've lost the real meaning of this world, and the earth. I thought, okay, Iris has dumped me and my poor 'spare tyre' Caroline now's gone. So what am I left with? I just have my own 'class' of people and so I have to be content in that regard. That's my destiny, that's my fate and that's my luck. I finally fell asleep.

Another day another time, I woke up at six thirty in the morning, but today and for the next few days no movement from me, according to what Dr. Keane had earlier explained to me. So I stayed in my bed and using the portable bottle I did my 'small business' and waited for someone to bring me, the wash basin, which as soon as the nurse heard I was awake she came and brought it for me, filled with warm water. I brushed and washed my face. I thanked her politely.

"You were talking and sobbing in your sleep, was it the pain, or were you having bad dreams, nightmares, Mathew?" I shrugged in reply, not wanting to go into details.

"I don't have a clue." I replied. Later after the nurses changed shifts, Dr. Browne came with Dr. Keane.

"Hello Mathew," Dr. Browne said, and Dr. Keane added.

"Hello Mathew, what happened to you yesterday? It seemed you were angry with us, you didn't want to wake up." I just smiled as Dr. Browne looked at me.

"How are you feeling now Mathew?" Dr. Browne asked me and went on, "Dr. Keane will talk to you now and Dr. Livingstone might pass at a later time to see you, is that alright?" I just nodded. Dr. Keane started to explain.

"Mathew, what we did yesterday was that we removed some skin from another part of you, from your thigh. We grafted the skin and 'implanted' it on to your wound, so it is a skin graft surgery which we performed." Dr. Keane paused and went on. "The surgery was successful, now what we need is for you not to move a lot, so the 'donor' skin can be accepted by the 'host' and that way you will recover fast and be better sooner." Dr. Keane paused again to let it sink in my head. "And the good news is, if we see that there is faster acceptance, and then you are good to be discharged. But we will give you conditions to be observed at home, of course, but you will be discharged to celebrate Christmas at home with your loved ones. Isn't that good news Mathew?" Dr. Keane was proud of himself and he wrung his hands together. He saw himself as the messenger of good news.

But unfortunately, he didn't realise I now had nowhere to go and I had no 'loved ones' either, I was a lost sheep waiting to be rescued by Jesus or God himself. I understood from the hospital's grapevine that if a patient has nowhere to go, then he or she is either sent to the old peoples' homes or to the homeless shelters, so maybe I was in that category now. I saw myself as homeless, loveless, parentless, childless, and friendless, a worthless and useless individual. A good for nothing, unwanted and rejected by society. Dr. Browne also was happy for me, and he and Dr. Keane then went and they gave some instructions to the nurse and it all was now written in my famous green file.

Chapter Thirty-Seven

Elvis came with my breakfast, and when he saw me, he just burst out laughing, he seemed happy this morning and soon I learned the reasons.

"Mathew. Oh Mathew, you made us all worried yesterday," Elvis said while still laughing with happiness, "Iris was red eyed and her mother was also red eyed with worry and fear." I looked at him. Was this guy okay in his mind or did he miss something? Is he confused or what?

"Elvis, are you out of your mind?" I asked him and he saw that I was annoyed with his laughter.

"Why, Mathew. What did I say wrong?" Elvis asked, defending himself.

"Elvis, you're talking about yesterday, right?" I asked in a serious tone. "Yesterday Iris didn't come to the hospital, so what are you talking about, my friend?" Elvis laughed again.

"No Mathew, you were asleep, and you refused to wake up." He explained. "Iris came in the morning and stayed till evening; she went and came back with her mother. Today I heard that they had stayed very late last night, waiting for you to open your eyes. Mathew, you can believe me, my friend." He paused and then added, "That woman loves you, Mathew and you're one lucky guy. Just like Tom was saying. And Iris' mother also seems to like you, too, Mathew. Be happy my friend"

Then the nurse appeared. She was the same day nurse as yesterday, and she heard my conversation with Elvis and she also confirmed what Elvis was saying. So I was the one who seemed to have lost it, my movie star actually had come and was here the whole day until very late at night, plus her mom also came. They came for me, and here I was sulking like a spoiled brat. Wow, I'm glad I got to know the news before Iris came and saw me sulking and angry and what else. I came to my senses.

Elvis had gone on with his job, the nurse had also gone. And who was in front of me but my movie star and her assistant, Iris herself in the flesh, with her mom standing there looking at me. Then Iris kissed me on both cheeks and a bit hard on the lips.

"You …you…. made us so fearful yesterday, my darling Mathew." Iris said as tears were flowing on her pink cheeks. She was sobbing with happiness to see me; she hugged me and didn't want to leave me. And then her mom also hugged me and I saw she also was sobbing. I couldn't believe it, and look at me, underestimating and unappreciative of their love.

"Mathew, my son….how are you today? Iris couldn't sleep last night. We were all worried about you even James wanted to come too, but we told him he can come later." Clara said this to me, and I felt overjoyed. I still had the love of my movie star and her family; she didn't dump me as I had feared. Iris explained and apologised for yesterday being late. Her car had been clamped when she went into town to buy something for me and by the time she came to the hospital, I had gone to the operating theatre.

She had begged the nurse to be taken to me, just to see me even for a minute, but she was told the hospital's regulations just don't allow it and that there are health and safety issues. So eventually she decided to just wait in the room, and then in the afternoon Iris went home to bring her mother and they came back together and stayed in the room. Then I was brought in after the operation and they waited and tried to talk to me, but to no avail, I just wasn't coming to my senses. I was in a deep sleep, they waited until very late. Iris didn't want to leave me but she was told she couldn't spend the night in the hospital, so eventually at about eleven thirty at night, she had to leave. So all was forgiven and forgotten, so as to speak. I was just insecure.

"How's your dad, Iris?" I eventually asked. Iris frowned and replied.

"Dad, oh, dad is really worried about you, Mathew. He wants to come to see you so much, but I am the one who is stopping him. So he's just waiting for when you are coming back home, my love." At about twelve thirty, Clara had to go home and Iris excused herself to take her mom home and told me, "I will be back soon, my love." Then her mom looked at me.

"Mathew, stay well and healthy, okay dear?" Clara spoke to me and I smiled at her, and then Iris went with her mom. Elvis brought my lunch and we chatted a bit.

"Try to eat well, Mathew my friend," Elvis said to me. "You need the strength." I then thanked him and he continued on his 'runs'. At about three, Iris came back and she brought me some snacks and sat and chatted about the traffic, about the weather, and life. And then at five in the afternoon, Dr. Livingstone himself came accompanied with Dr. Browne and the nurse.

"Hello Mathew," Dr. Livingstone said with a smile on his face. "You have been through a lot for your young age. I am sorry about the turn of events in your young life." I just shrugged and he went on. "The hospital management have been in constant touch with the Garda Siochana and they are aware of your past life and present life, so in that matter you do not have to worry. All these events will not interfere with your treatment either here in the Dublin University Hospital or any other hospital." He paused and then looked at me. "Other than that, regarding your treatment, the plastic surgeons are so far happy with the skin graft surgery and if everything goes well, and they are happy with your recovery, then I can discharge you to go and celebrate

Christmas at home. We will not keep you any longer than necessary." Dr. Livingstone said.

Dr. Livingstone smiled again as he added. "You have been a very good patient, besides being a brave young man and you are well liked by all the staff." He asked if that is fine with me, which of course it was what I wanted, to go home and the sooner the better.

"Yeah Doctor, it is very fine with me." I said smiling. Dr. Browne just nodded his agreement with his 'boss' and they left, the nurse following them with my green file. Elvis brought my dinner and I sat with Iris holding hands and discussing our future plans. I spoke with James and Clara on Iris's mobile and she also spoke with her parents. Then at ten, we kissed each other goodnight and she went to relax at home. The night nurse brought me my medicine and she said if and when I need anything just to call her. I said thank you.

I then stayed with my own thoughts, but today I was on the positive note, unlike yesterday when I was in a more negative mind. Now it was up to me to stay in bed and not move a lot, to get well and wait for the skin to stick to the flesh in order for me to be able to be discharged. Everything was going smoothly at last, the fear had gone, the loneliness had gone and I felt good and hopeful of the future. I slept and enjoyed a lot of good and very nice dreams.

On the twenty second of December, it was cold and cloudy. After Elvis gave me my tray of breakfast he stayed a bit and we talked.

"Elvis my friend, I might be released this morning. No, actually I'm being discharged this morning." I told Elvis and he looked at me with sadness in his eyes.

"I'm going to miss you Mathew. If you're going to be discharged today and then it might be after lunch as the paperwork takes some time," Elvis explained. "But still, whatever time you'll go, I'm going to miss you Mathew. You've been a good patient and you've had a lot of news Mathew." He then gave me a hug and a hearty laugh, but I could see tears in his eyes and he then walked quickly away. At half past eight, Caroline appeared, and she was so glad to see me, and so was I.

"Hi Mathew, how have you been dear?" Caroline asked with a cool voice.

"Hi Caroline," I said, nearly wanting to add love, honey, or darling, but I stopped myself, it wasn't going to be fair to her. "You were lost, Caroline, what happened, did you go for a short holiday?" I smiled at her. My poor and beautiful Caroline nodded.

"Yeah, after all the events, Mathew, I needed a holiday where I could go and try to remove someone very dear from my mind." I knew that was a reference to me, and I felt bad, but what could I possibly do? "I heard the events that happened while I was away, Mathew, I'm so sorry, I wish I was here, and I could have fought them." I looked at her, she was lovely.

"Caroline thanks for all and everything, and today I'm going to be discharged," I said. I paused and then added. "You've been a great friend, Caroline. Please can you give your contact information to Iris, and we can keep in touch and also invite you to our wedding, you know what I mean?" I noticed when I had mentioned Iris's name, she flinched. Poor Caroline, she was still in pain.

I then realised it wouldn't even be fair to invite her to my wedding. It will be too painful for Caroline, seeing Iris in front of the hall or Church, with the veil on her head, instead of herself, poor Caroline, how can I help you my dear? She just nodded and then quickly went out of the room, I knew she was going to hide and cry her heart out somewhere.

Chapter Thirty-Eight

I NOTICED THAT IRIS HADN'T COME till now, but she'll come because she knows I'm going to be released or discharged this morning. After a while, one woman and a man came in and they were followed by Caroline. The man wore a pair of jeans, black shoes and shirt, was tall, and the woman was short and a bit plump. Both had briefcases and files and a lot of papers. Each introduced themselves to me and pulled up the chairs and sat down near each other. Then Caroline said before she left.

"I'll be out in the ward. If you need me, just call me, please." Caroline spoke to me. They said they were from the Social Services, and they were here to see me, and that they knew of my circumstances.

"Sorry, but what circumstances are you talking about?" I asked them with fear in my voice. They looked at each other, and it seemed the lady was the boss or senior to the other. She was the one who spoke.

"We understand you were living with your mother in a Dublin

Corporation dwelling. And that the residence was only in your mother's name alone and you were not a named tenant of the said dwelling," she paused. "Is that correct information, Mathew?" I looked at her and nodded.

"Yeah, that's right, the house was in me Ma's name." I replied, waiting to see where this was going.

"While you were admitted and have been in the hospital, your mother died... I am sure you have this........ Information ...." she was saying. But I cut her off, mid sentence.

"I've the information that me Ma's dead, alright, so what all this is about anyway?" I was visibly shaken, having been reminded of me Ma's death, and I wasn't there to bury her and all that. They both looked at me and then each other.

"We are very sorry to bring this up Mathew," the man said and continued. "But we need to establish the correctness of this information before we can tell you the next plan of action. Is that alright with you Mathew?" Then he looked at the lady, to continue.

"Alright, to make it short Mathew, the Dublin Corporation has taken over and re-possessed that dwelling and has boarded it up. There were a few important belongings of your mom's and possibly yours as well, which we could keep for you to collect once you're well, but the other stuff had to be burned for health & safety reasons," the lady said and went on. "We have all the belongings, Mathew and you can collect them from our offices whenever you are ready, okay?" I nodded, and quickly she added. "Now that you have been set to be discharged from your long stay in the hospital, and that you are homeless now, we will take full responsibility from now on, from the hospital. That means the hospital, will now hand you over to us in the Social Services." She paused and it hit me, 'homeless' now that I'm homeless, I have nowhere to go, no place to sleep, I was a homeless person. I have now been categorised as 'a homeless man'.

My thoughts went back years before. After my father had died, first my brothers and later me, as soon as we turned eighteen, in spite of our mother's objection and advice, we chose to remove our names from the Corporation's list of residents in my mother's house. That way we were avoiding the rent increase and therefore, we could stay without working or paying rent, but also nobody could follow our movements and we had no 'fixed address', so we were able to cover our criminal activities. We had thought at that time we were smart, but now I realise, it was just the opposite.

And I have just lost our Corporation house, which we had lived in for a long time. A house I grew up in, my family home, it's gone now. I have become a 'homeless' person, and now the state will take on the responsibility of putting me in a shelter for homeless people.

"So we are here to take you first to a nursing home, and once you get fully recovered then we'll send you to a homeless shelter for a while." I tried to protest but my voice didn't come out, I tried to tell them about me moving to Iris's parents' house, and that I'll be their guest, but my words fell on deaf ears. They said they had no such information in their files, and their superiors had instructed them to carry out this exercise.

They were calling me being sent to a homeless shelter an 'exercise'. I raised my voice in anger, but they told me if I didn't go with them quietly they could call security and I'll be carried anyway, as I cannot walk. I was looking around to see where Iris was, to save me and protect me from these evil people. I thought quickly to buy more time for myself and also to try to scare them.

"There is a Garda Officer outside who will help me." I threatened, but they just laughed in my face. Then the woman replied.

"The Garda Officer and the Hospital security will listen to us and not to you. We, the Social Services are the Government's officers, while you are just a …….. just a………." Then she stopped abruptly, but I knew what she wanted to say, 'criminal'. The commotion caused the Garda Officer to look inside the room.

"Is everything in order here?" he asked. The man replied.

"Yes officer, for now, everything is in order. Thanks." Then Caroline came in, and she saw what was going on. She saw my face, red, already full of bruises and stitches and two black eyes, but Caroline couldn't take my side, not in front of these two 'Government's officers'.

"Can I help in any way, guys?" Caroline asked politely.

"Thanks nurse, but we can handle this." The man replied in a rude tone. Caroline nodded to me and then did something I didn't expect.

"Sorry guys, my patient's blood pressure is high and it's not good. Can you wait outside while I check with my patient, please?" The man and the woman both became confused and they didn't expect this from a nurse, but Caroline became authoritative. She went and brought the trolley of equipment and she told the nurses' supervisor to come quickly and Caroline ordered the two officers out.

"Excuse me, quickly guys, will you both wait outside?" and she literally removed them and closed the door behind them. Then Caroline told her supervisor, "Can you please check Mathew's heart and pressure while I call the doctor?" and the supervisor did as she was told, and Caroline got Iris's mobile number from somewhere in the file and called her. "Iris dear, this is Caroline, the nurse in the hospital. Please don't ask me anything now ...... just come quickly in the hospital ...... No Mathew is alright. But I need you urgently .... yes .... Iris please hurry ......bye......bye now." Caroline then hung up the phone, and took over from her supervisor. "Let me handle the patient. Please, can you go and put in a call for Dr. Browne, urgently, and please don't let those people in here for a while." Caroline asked her supervisor.

The nurses' supervisor again, did as she was asked. Caroline relaxed a little bit. She was in charge and in control of the situation but she was only buying time and she knew it. We were now alone, just myself and Caroline. She breathed a great sigh.

"Thank God." Caroline said. I smiled at her, and thought how she completely took control of the situation and she was very brave. She might get fired for this but she was one smart lady.

"Thanks a million Caroline, you just saved me from those two savages." I told her with a smile and relief in my face. Caroline looked at me with her soft, caring and loving eyes.

"I didn't know what they wanted and if I had known, Mathew, I wouldn't have let them in, believe me." Caroline said again. I did believe her, and she then told me, "I've called Iris, she'll be here very soon. Until then we will keep them out. Also I've asked for Dr. Browne to come and I will deal with him. Don't you worry my dear Mathew," Caroline said bravely and without fear.

"Caroline dear, for that brave action you've just done, all in order just to protect me, can't it get you into trouble with your bosses?" I asked her in concern. "I wouldn't want anything bad to happen to you, especially because of me. You're very dear to me Caroline, you know what I mean?" She nodded, happiness showing in her face, seeing and listening to my appreciation.

"Mathew, for you, I will do anything. You just don't know how much you are dearer to me than you can imagine, Mathew." Caroline explained in her soft voice.

"Caroline, you called Iris…….." I said. But she interrupted me.

"You belong to Iris, Mathew. I have accepted this fact, and I cannot change it. And if I didn't call her, I would then have taken responsibility for you myself. But because I am a nurse here in the same hospital, and attending you as my patient, they wouldn't take me seriously and they could have brought charges against me, as 'conflict of interest'. But don't worry, Mathew dear." Caroline said. She paused, and then added, "If I have to lose my job for you, then I will do it, Mathew. But I won't let them take you to a shelter, no way, my dear." Caroline said this with full confidence and sincerity. I knew now, as I knew then, that if Iris had not come back for me, then I would have taken Caroline, or Caroline would have taken me, and I would never have regretted it in my life. She has such full confidence, and calm.

Dr. Browne came and Caroline explained the situation as it was at the moment and also explained to him what she had to do 'for our patient, who was already hyperventilating and was becoming sick'. Dr. Browne then assured Caroline.

"You did the right thing, nurse. We will keep them waiting till Iris comes and we shall then see how to deal with the situation. Is that fine with you, nurse?" Dr. Browne was addressing Caroline as 'nurse' but he actually knew the full story behind Caroline and me and Iris, and about 'The Love Triangle' so Dr. Browne gave his full support to Caroline and all was well so far.

But I was worried, I have seen the bravery and commitment Caroline had, but will Iris be able to stand up to those 'savages' for me? Will Iris have the conviction and authority to stop those 'savages' from bringing me to the homeless shelter? Just then Iris my movie star entered the 'scene' followed by none other than Clara, the 'personal assistant'. They walked in, their faces looked worried and straight away Iris came to hug me and she started to check and 'examine' me, where was I hurt or what pain do I have?

"What's going on here?" Iris asked to no one in particular, and with great anxiety, and then she noticed Caroline.

"Caroline, what's wrong with Mathew, I came as quickly as I could, please tell me." Caroline took Iris by the hand, made her sit down, and then Caroline knelt in front of Iris. Like a mother to a worried child.

"Iris, Mathew is fine, and as we know, today he will be discharged, alright dear?" Caroline said and went on. "But there is another ugly development which has risen, so relax and let me explain to you and then let us discuss how we can solve it, alright Iris, my dear?" Iris nodded and held her hand on her heart, the other hand holding Caroline's hand. I was forgotten at the moment.

This moment of planning was only between my two lovely ladies, the two most important women in my life. It looked and it actually was that my future was in these two ladies' hands. Caroline explained the situation as it was and until what it is at the moment. Then Caroline stood up and went to the door and called Dr. Browne in. It seemed that he was an unwilling part of the 'conspiracy' now, and the nurses' supervisor was an 'only when needed' situation.

Dr. Browne came in and spoke in a low voice to Iris and guided her on what to say and all. But then luckily for all of us, Dr. Keane of the plastic surgery team came along, and therefore the two 'savages' will have to wait longer in which ever room or 'prison' they were kept. Dr. Keane acknowledged Iris and just glanced at Clara, who until now, even though she was in the room, but she had kept out of everybody's way.

Chapter Thirty-Nine

DR. KEANE THEN ASKED ME. "How are you today Mathew, are you feeling alright?"

"Hi Doctor, I'm well and ready to go home, whichever home that is." I replied with a knowing smile. Dr. Keane laughed while he looked around in a questioning manner.

"Who told you that you are going home? Did anyone here tell Mathew, he is going to be discharged today?" he then said with a serious face. "I have to see the wound first, how is it progressing and all, then I can decide. Do you understand me Mathew? Do not keep your hopes high, please." Dr. Keane added. I breathed with a knot in my stomach. Oh no, this doesn't seem good. I looked at Iris and she shrugged, with sadness in her eyes. James wanted to come to see me today, but Iris told her dad, that she's going to bring me home today. But now this was the news.

I thought okay, I've managed stay in the hospital, for how long now? I cannot stay a few more days? Even if it's going to be Christmas, so what's the difference? I can still manage somehow as my health's more important than, celebrating Christmas with a new family. Ah, it's not in my hands anyway. And, I thought then there are those two 'savages' outside.

Dr. Keane was observing me and my reaction. Then he turned to Caroline and with an understanding look.

"Nurse, bring all the tools of the trade." He told Caroline, but Caroline first was confused by this term but then she understood and she brought a pair of scissors and a mat with dressings. Caroline took the mat and my leg was raised by Dr. Keane, Caroline then put the mat below my leg and she laid the dressings on the bed. Dr. Keane took the scissors and started to cut the dressing from my thigh. He started from the knee side going upwards to my hip, and then removed all the bandages and dressings.

I managed to take a peek. The wound was deep, long, wide and ugly. I imagined the way if I lay myself down and sideways, I can fill the wound with water and put a few tiny fishes and '*voila*' it was a fish pond. I stopped making fun of myself and I looked at Dr. Keane's facial expression. I was trying to read from his face if it was good or bad news but he was only concentrating with the job at hand, and that was my wound. Then he took some liquid with a cotton wool or sponge and was slowly wiping the wound, he continued for some time. When it seemed like he finished, he frowned, and looked at Caroline.

"Nurse," Dr. Keane spoke loudly to Caroline, who was actually standing next to him and it really scared me, and I then knew I was not going anywhere today, a disappointment to Iris, and it will be a disappointment to those two 'savages' as well. "Nurse," he repeated again and continued with a harsh voice. "This patient is going to be discharged today, please do all the paperwork and give me the file I will sign now, but Dr. Livingstone will sign for his patient's discharge. And now can you do the dressing please, is that alright, nurse?" and he burst out laughing and looked at Caroline. "I am so sorry nurse I scared you, please forgive me. I just felt like having a laugh. After all this patient has given us a lot to talk about, really."

Dr. Keane continued to laugh and then he turned to me and said.

"Mathew, you are going home today, can you believe it?" I thought there was some good craic with Dr. Keane after all. Anyway I'm going home today, but then I remembered about the battle ahead, I became sad as I didn't know what my fate would be with those two 'savages' waiting for me outside. Dr. Browne was just smiling and enjoying the craic. Iris came over and hugged me and Clara came to hug me.

"Mathew dear, don't worry." Iris assured me, amid the hugging. I looked at Caroline, maybe she wanted to hug me also but Iris was here, and she felt she was only a nurse and nothing else to me. But I felt for her and said something loud enough for everybody to hear.

"Caroline, aren't you glad, I'm going home? Come and give me a hug as well." Poor Caroline was caught off-guard and she was confused. She looked at Iris, then at Clara, and again back at Iris. She didn't know what to do.

"Come on Caroline; give the poor man a hug." Iris told her with a smile and then Caroline was relieved and she came forward and hugged me.

"I am glad you are being discharged at last, Mathew," Caroline said and then she turned to Iris.

"Iris, now we have a battle to attend to," Caroline told Iris, and added. "I have to go and deal with these papers, Iris you deal with those Social Services officers and if you need me please call me, but also Dr. Browne will be with you throughout to give you moral support, alright everybody? Now let's do it." Caroline volunteered for Dr. Browne.

I admired her for her organisational skills. She was in charge of the situation. Caroline went out to her supervisor and gave her the file, and the supervisor would know what has to be done. Then Caroline came back. She did the fresh dressing for my thigh, nicely and carefully not to hurt me. There was so much love as she did the dressing.

"Iris before those people come again, can you help Mathew to change into his normal clothes, and to pack his belongings, please?" Caroline told Iris. So Iris closed the curtains and with the exception of Clara, all three helped me to change and once I was ready, they opened the curtains, and only then Caroline went to fetch the officers.

Caroline came back with them. They walked in slowly, the man and the woman. The two 'savages' had by now calmed down somehow but seemed annoyed or angry they were kept waiting for very long, but they also knew that they had no authority in here. Caroline spoke first.

"This is Iris, she is the patient's fiancée," She introduced them with a smile of victory on her face. "Iris, these two are from the Social Services and they are here to see if the patient is going to be taken care of." Caroline said as she winked at Iris. I thought the two 'savages' realised the implications of the statement just made by this nurse.

"So please can you explain to me what you are here for? And what is your plan?" Iris asked with authority in her voice.

"We already explained to the patient, Mathew, all about the situation that he's in," the lady said and went on, angrily, "now we're going to take him to the nursing home where he'll stay for a few days to recover, and after that he'll then be brought to a homeless shelter."

"Wait a minute, why would you take him, to whatever you are saying, a homeless shelter? Is that what I just heard?" Iris was angry but didn't want to show, or lose her composure. "What authority do you have, to take someone who obviously has a choice and free will, to a nursing home and then to homeless shelter as you just said?" Iris continued her voice on high, but with full authority. She then stood up and came over to me, she sat and took my head on her chest and patted my head, throwing a kiss here and a kiss there, showing them the love and affection she had for me. "Do the Social Services think they just picked up Mathew from the street, from a dumpster, full of drugs and no food, nowhere to sleep, nowhere to go? That you are going to provide for him food and shelter?" Iris continued with her barrage, now she seemed annoyed and angry.

The woman stood angrily and the man also stood, I thought they were going away, but the lady opened the file and removed a paper to show to Iris.

"Here read this, we have authority over this patient and he has nobody to look after him. He has no residence, so it is the Government's duty to look after him, for his well-being." Iris did not take the paper she just chose to ignore it. Then the nurses' supervisor came back with the green file and an envelope and some papers. She gave everything to Dr. Browne.

"Excuse me everybody," Dr. Browne spoke in a tone of getting attention and with an air of authority, but smiling. "All the discharge documents are ready and Mathew is ready to go home now." He paused and went on while looking at the two savages. "Frances and Dwayne from the Social Services demand, it seems, to take the patient to the homeless shelter, and the patient himself is here and is fully aware of what is going on. But at the same time, the patient has a name. And Mathew is an adult who is well capable of taking his own decisions without being forced to do something against his wishes," Dr. Browne said, and then looked directly in the face of the man from Social Services. "Mathew is neither a child, nor a mental patient. Let the man express his wishes, and all of us should respect those wishes, alright everybody?"

Everybody became quiet for a while, then Dr. Browne came to me, he winked at Iris who was already with me, and Caroline moved closer to me with the file.

"In this envelope, Mathew, there is a prescription for your medication for one month, and also some reports for yourself to keep for your records. We will write and fax to your local health centre and give them your address, which we have in your file. The Public Health Nurse will be coming to do the dressing for your wound, once every day and thereafter they will decide on the best course of action to take," he again paused with a quick glance at the two 'savages' and continued. "We will notify your General Practitioner, and whenever you have an emergency or anything then your GP will be your first point of contact. We have given you an appointment to see the plastic surgeon consultant after three weeks here in this hospital, and also Dr. Livingstone will see you after four weeks, in the Royal Hospital in Cabra, in his clinic. All the appointments letters and your prescriptions are in the envelope." He again paused. "Do you have any questions, either of you?"

Dr. Browne looked at me, then Iris and then Caroline, but evidently it was a message to the observers.

"Mathew, on behalf of Dr. Livingstone, and the hospital staff, I wish to thank you for being a good patient, polite, with good manners, and also....for your bravery and your ...... adventures," he then smiled. "We also wish you a happy life and a good future to you both." He praised me and I was happy to hear that.

Dr. Browne then shook my hand, and then to Iris, he smiled and winked at her and shook her hand too.

"You take good care of our patient, alright?" I looked at those two 'savages' and I thought, aren't they getting the message, these people? Dr. Browne then signalled to the nurses' supervisor, who then opened the door, and one attendant with a wheelchair came in the room. The attendant, together with Caroline helped me to sit on the wheelchair, and ready to go. The Garda Officer came in and addressed Dr. Browne.

"As soon as the patient leaves, I am going back to the station, our job is then finished," He then looked at me and added. "The hospital will also provide the Gardai with Mathew's forwarding address, where we'll keep in contact with him. If there's anything we need to get in touch with him, is that alright? I nodded and he shook hands with Dr. Browne and stood at the door waiting for me to pass and go from the room.

Everybody became tense in the room, waiting to see the reaction of everybody else. The two 'savages' saw that they were outnumbered and 'outflanked' and meanwhile I was waiting to be pushed in the wheelchair to my destiny. I smiled at Caroline and spread my two hands wide. She understood, and came over to me and I hugged her and kissed her on both cheeks.

"Caroline dear, I thank you from the bottom of my heart, you've been very good with me and understanding, caring and loving ….nurse … Thanks a million, dear." I shook hands with Dr. Browne and the nurses' supervisor, and then I addressed those two, and for the first time I called them by their names which I had heard when Dr. Browne spoke to them.

"Frances …..Dwayne ……I think you should make up your mind…. and avoid unnecessary confrontation," I spoke with confidence. "You see now, there's no need here to get hyper. It's not like you've lost the Lotto. We can all be friendly with each other and we can resolve this issue peacefully and everybody becomes a winner. You know what I mean?" Nobody laughed, but I saw Caroline giggle and I was proud myself, for the speech.

But deep in my heart, I wasn't sure, did they really have the authority to forcibly take me to the homeless shelter and nursing home, or not, but I didn't want to take a chance. Iris was busy talking to her colleagues in the office, and when she finished her calls, she went forward to Frances and looked at her and Dwayne.

"Frances, I know you guys have an obligation to look after Mathew according to the information which you have. But the circumstances have changed somewhat, and you as officials of your department have the powers to take decisions on the spot fitting the situation on the ground." Iris paused for effect, and I thought, maybe when she was on the phone, she was informed of the powers these people had, so that's why she's decided to change tactics. "Now, Mathew and I are engaged, and my parents have offered to take Mathew as our guest. We can give you our address and you will be free to come and visit and see for yourself that Mathew is taken care of, and not abused as you might have been worried."

The two 'savages' by now made me feel like changing this term to a nicer one, but I couldn't find anything suitable for them so far. Then Iris turned to Dwayne.

"Can I now, please take my fiancé and patient home, as he is tired and need to rest, if you don't mind?" Iris spoke directly at Dwayne and then he signalled Frances. They went in a corner to confer. It only took them a few minutes then both of them turned to face me and nodded.

"Mathew, you can go with them if they really can take care of you and not abuse you. We'll definitely come and check on you soon." Frances spoke, finally accepting defeat and facing reality of the situation at hand.

"Mathew, what we wanted to do was for your own good, the Social Services have a responsibility, and we tried to protect you. We're not the bad guys as you all might have thought. We're just doing our job the best we can. Believe me." Dwayne explained their situation and I did believe the poor guy, even though they only accepted the facts once they knew that they were 'heavily' defeated. Everyone in the room clapped.

Quickly before the two officers changed their minds, I heard Iris.

"Mathew, my darling, my sweetheart and my beloved, can we go home now?" Iris said with a singing voice. Teary eyed as she was, she put her hand in mine and held me tight.

"Let's go, my darling. Bye bye, everybody. Thanks to you all for everything and I really do appreciate it." I said aloud. Caroline and everybody came to the corridor as I was being pushed by the attendant and holding hands with Iris, I caught a glimpse of Caroline. She was crying, the poor girl, as she was standing with the others and waving to me.

"Bye Mathew. Iris, please take care of our special patient ...... please." Caroline said in a soft singing voice, as we waved back. Finally Iris was taking me home, our home together. I felt like I was dreaming. Was this all a fantasy? No, it was real and it was true love from our sides, mine and my beloved Iris. She's the one who had earlier told me not to despair, even with all my sorrows. She had said, "Despair Not, my darling."

Acknowledgments

To all my sons

You gave me encouragement, left me alone when I needed to be alone, and for your love, support and affection;

To Nabeel Murad, for reviewing my manuscript and for being a bit too critical;

To Junaid Murad, for your relentless support and inquisitiveness and of course 'the blurb';

To Sameer Murad, who designed my book cover and set up my Website;

To Aileen Convery, for reading my manuscript and for giving me, a frank feedback;

To Moire Sionnach, for editing and proofreading the final manuscript;

To my dear friends John Brogan, Michael Brogan, and Catherine Boyhan:

To all the above & others, I say thank you for all your support and encouragement!

The author Murad Karim

Contact: info@muradkarim.com

www.muradkarim.com